NO ANGEL

Ashna Graves

Lychgate Press 2012

Lychgate Press

Copyright © 2012 by Ashna Graves
First U.S. Edition

ISBN-13: 978-0988288706
ISBN-10: 0988288702

All rights reserved.

Lychgate Press
Corvallis, Oregon
editor@lychgatepress.com

Cover design by W. Lee Gilroy

Chapter One

The killing of Angel de Silva stunned the good people of Willamette, Oregon. Forever smiling despite his rags, Angel wouldn't hurt a fly. If you looked sad or troubled when you passed his chosen bench by the post office steps, he would shake his head at the dollar you tried to tuck into the bedroll on his shopping cart and hand you one of his trademark stars folded from gum wrapper silver.

"You have a real fine day now," he would say, and that was one of the things you really appreciated about Angel. He never said, "Hey, have a good one." It was always, "You have a real fine day now," with a smile that showed dimples under the thin black beard.

Rain or shine, summer and winter for more years than anyone had counted, Angel had slept in a downtown doorway, and when a fine spring drizzle fell on the morning of his outdoor memorial service, the crowd ignored it, sitting quietly in front of the park gazebo on folding chairs, few bothering to cover their heads. The move to indoors was not announced. Somehow, word spread with little talk, and one by one or in small groups the mourners left their seats and crossed the sodden lawn to the First Church of Christ on the corner. In silence they entered through the open double doors, and as the pews filled, the air thickened with the damp animal smell of wool, intimate and earthy.

A priest carried the large photograph of a dark and gentle face into the church and stood it on a table in front of the pulpit. He did not wipe the water-streaked glass. A half-grown girl walked up the aisle behind him, her sleeveless shirt exposing thin, wet arms. She placed a single rose in front of the picture and left the church walking fast with her head down.

The priest tapped a microphone, creating a hush, but it was not the man of God who spoke into the sudden silence. A bearded, bear-like man lurched from a front pew and turned to face the crowd, his husky voice carrying without electronic help. "When the flowers came out in color, Willamette lost its little brother."

He shook his big head, steadied himself with a hand on the end of the pew, and began again, chanting the words with tribal rhythm.

When the flowers came out in color,
Willamette lost its little brother.

I wish I could have been there on that terrible night.
Angel was a gentleman, he wouldn't start a fight.
Angel was his own man, he never punched a clock.
He always did what he wanted, he liked to laugh and talk.

With no place to call home, he was a friend to young and old,
He gave everything he had, he never bought and sold.
Angel was a brother to everyone in this town.
Why weren't we there when evil struck him down?

Some come into this world to take and not to give.
Angel gave everything, even his right to live.
Wherever you are, we know you already forgave,
We're not angels like you, but we're tryin' not to hate.

Weeping and blinded, the speaker fell back into his pew, into arms that reached to catch and hold him. A woman in a long dress stepped up to the microphone and sent "Amazing Grace" into the high, arched ceiling. When the song was done, the priest hugged the singer before taking her place.

"Did you see Jesus in Angel?" he asked, looking from person to person as though for an answer. Then, with a sad smile, "Did any of us see Jesus in Angel? What we saw there was not the Jesus we looked for but the Jesus we got."

A tiny Asian woman spoke in a soft, clear voice. "Six years ago I came here homeless and I met Angel. He introduced himself and said he was Willamette's Welcome Wagon. He taught me the techniques of Dumpster diving. After I got a job as a nurse's aide at the hospital, they brought him in one time. He needed blood. I felt I was giving back some of the life he gave me so freely."

A round-headed man looked at the floor and talked fast. "Angel was the full embodiment of what I call a true Christian. To this day I give to shelters, churches, soup kitchens, because there might be more people out there like Angel. Now there's no Angel but I will keep on giving as long as I have anything to give."

A gaunt blonde in a half-buttoned black sweater was pushed forward, hugging her thin shoulders. "My name is Lisette. I just got out of jail that time and couldn't find my friend. Angel asked me had I ate dinner and I said no and he gave me two dollars. I won't never forget that as long as I live."

A woman in braids sang a wailing Cheyenne lament. A man with a gray ponytail played a bamboo flute, the plain song curling among the mourners, gathering them close and releasing them again with a single long note that thinned to silence.

A boy called Sandy spoke into the hush, his young voice steady and earnest. "I met Angel when I was six and my mother and I were homeless, and sometimes he gave me a ride in his chrome Cadillac—that was his shopping cart. He used to tell me stories out in front of Stone Soup. Angel would say bad things happen but that doesn't mean we have to believe in bad things. I'm trying, Angel, I'm trying not to believe in bad things, but you aren't here to help me anymore."

An old woman in a raincoat stood up last. "When I went into the post office he was always on his bench there by the door, and he said, 'Watch your step now, Missus, it's a little wet.' He had a strong hug and I don't think he ever gave up trying to make the world a little bit better than it was yesterday. Now he's gone to where all the restrooms are open around the clock and the police don't make him move on in the night. But you know what? I bet he still sleeps outside."

Jeneva Leopold sat at the end of a pew toward the back of the church. She did not cry or bow her head, though the hand that held her pen lay motionless in her lap. She was not taking notes. After the first few words describing the scene she had stopped writing and now studied the crowd, puzzled and uneasy in a way that had nothing to do with murder. How could this have happened? How could a homeless man have commanded such love? And not just from fellow street people but solid citizens with haircuts and umbrellas, townspeople who had turned out by the score to grieve together.

How could this have happened—and she had missed it?

She, Jeneva Leopold, the official town know-it-all, had missed it.

Angel de Silva had sat on a bench day after day outside the old stone post office on Second Street and managed to win a following worthy of a celebrity, *yet she had never exchanged a single word with him.* There was simply no accounting for it. She knew everyone in Willamette worth knowing. As the *Willamette Current*'s only local columnist she had to know the town inside out. The community was her subject, even her passion.

She was the eyes and ears of the town but sitting here surrounded by grief she felt blind and deaf. No one here had come as a gesture, to show concern and outrage at a vicious murder on the clean, well-planted streets. They had not come to make a statement, to express outrage or fear at a random act of violence, to protest a killing that had shaken the town to its collective bones.

They had come to mourn a beloved friend—a friend who was not her friend.

The woman in the raincoat sat down. The priest bowed his head in silence, and in silence the many friends of Angel de Silva left the church. Neva sat on, waiting for the church to empty, looking down to avoid catching anyone's eye and being drawn into conversation. She needed to think, not talk.

Naturally, she had seen Angel on the post office bench. He could not be missed. Day after day, month after month, on sunny days or soggy, he was there smiling, nodding, or simply gazing into the distance. But nothing about him had struck her in particular, had made him stand out from the handful of other homeless regulars around the small downtown. He had never addressed her directly, never asked for a handout, never said *Jesus loves you, sister*.

And yet, he must have stood out. He must have been obviously special. A dozen passionate mourners had just said so.

She looked up. Angel's picture gazed back at her over the empty pews. Shoving the notebook into her jacket pocket, she went up the aisle to the table that had become a shrine, with two daffodils and a branch of daphne now lying with the single red rose. The portrait was a photocopied enlargement, the tones more gray than black and white, the lines fuzzy. Water had leaked in behind the glass and as she watched, a damp streak spread down across Angel's forehead and through his right eye.

"Wretched day," said a voice she recognized as the priest's rumble. "Wretched day."

"But extraordinary, really extraordinary. Did you expect this?"

"I can't say I did. Certainly not the variety, of his following. What's your angle going to be, or is it fair to ask?"

"Perfectly fair, but no angle at all, I'm sorry to say. I didn't know him."

The priest's look of surprise seemed to echo her own puzzlement. "Strange, isn't it?" she said before he could speak. "How could I miss him? But I did, and I have nothing special to say so it's better to say nothing. Frankie's story will be on the front page with plenty of pictures and that will be enough."

"Well, I'm sorry to hear it. I always appreciate your perspective on things."

"Thank you. Thank you very much. And I appreciated your comments about Angel. We haven't met properly, I believe."

"Father Arnold, from St. Anne's. We expected to be in the park but fortunately they let us move in here."

"Did you know him well?"

"Only through the soup kitchen, though he hadn't been coming much lately. A terrible business, really terrible. What a nightmare for the family, black sheep or not. I was particularly struck by his mother, what she said about her son being called homeless. 'He wasn't homeless. He always had a home with his family.'"

They nodded somberly in unison. It had been the only moving line in the news accounts following the murder. Neva had thought, naturally, of Ethan, her own beloved source of midnight anguish, especially during his daredevil teens. Though now safely in graduate school, he still could haunt her nights by popping up in a memory frame along with a fragile kayak in rushing water, or a sheer rock face with a dangling climbing rope. On reading the quote, she had felt a wrenching urge to call Angel's mother, but what could she have said? *I'm so sorry about your son, we're all so sorry. I share your anguish . . .* She knew nothing of real anguish—her child was alive and well. And she had not known Angel de Silva.

"Hostages to fortune," murmured the priest. "A cliché, but who could say it better."

The rain had stopped. Standing on the deserted church porch, Neva drew a long breath of spring air as she scanned the scene for Frankie and *Current* photographer Kelly Redpath. They were not to be seen, and most of the mourners had gone already as well, with only a few hurrying away across the park and down the sidewalks, hunched against sorrow and damp. A patrol car sat at the curb next to the small plaza that separated the church from the park. An officer leaned against the hood, his arms crossed and his air casual, though he had clearly been watching the crowd as it left the church, just as he now scrutinized Neva for an instant before recognizing her. He nodded, drew a pad from his pocket, made a note, and got into the car.

Since the morning last week when Angel's body had been discovered near the downtown doorway where he slept, there had been rumors of an arrest, but no arrest had been made, no warrant issued, no suspect named. If the police knew anything more than the basic facts of the death as reported in the first news story, they were doing a good job keeping it to themselves.

Hitching her bag firmly onto her shoulder, Neva set off on foot for the

Current building three blocks south of the park, walking briskly at first but soon slowing down to watch the clouds. They were massed overhead in mottled confusion, moving like a restless crowd looking for a way out. It was the time of year when they could break suddenly, could let the sun shine through onto cherry blossoms or tender green leaves that would glow for a heart-stopping moment and then fade as the sky closed once more and the light was again wet and brooding.

But the clouds did not open today. And as she arrived at the staff door on the east side of the *Current* building the rain returned. Cold drops struck her lifted face as she looked up, took a breath, then heaved open the heavy metal door. The transition as she stepped inside was even more striking than usual, the air heavy with the smell of ink and burned coffee, plus a musty reek from the wet jackets crowded onto hooks along the coatroom wall. Someone must have heated a breakfast burrito in the lunch room microwave. And J.D. had been smoking in the newsroom again, no doubt working late last night and mad at the world. The city editor didn't even pretend to follow the smoking ban. *Any more idiotic rules and I'm out of here*, she'd snarled when the ban was posted. *Next thing you know, they'll be telling us to crap strawberries to keep from stinking up the toilets.*

The city editor's chaotic desk, like all the desks in the newsroom, was deserted. The night owls were still passed out in their beds, while the day crew were out on their beats or, more likely, at the Beanery fueling up. She had expected to find Frankie hammering away at the keyboard, but he must have found some thread to follow. The only live body in sight belonged to Todd Ambrose, editor-in-chief, whose office looked out on the newsroom through a glass wall. He sat in classic Ambrose position, cowboy boots on the desk, phone to his ear, a smile on his long face. Neva had never discovered who was at the other end of his lengthy chats. When teased about it, he chuckled and made a sly reference to fans, though he was not one of that vanishing breed of editors who write columns and editorials. He did, however, take deep interest in every word his staff wrote, including Neva's column, which he described as the "pet tiger of the *Current*, a nice kitty that everybody loves until they wake up one morning and discover it ate the baby."

"I don't eat babies," Neva insisted. "I like rich old power-brokers, well smoked."

Ambrose wiggled two fingers in her direction, a greeting rather than a summons, mercifully. She nodded and looked away in case he suddenly recalled that she had come from the memorial gathering and asked for a rundown. Let him get it from Frankie. She had a column to write and no subject to write about.

Safely in her office with the door closed, she dropped her bag into the desk drawer that was kept empty for the purpose and sat down on the dark blue swivel chair. The office was small but she never returned to it without a sense of privilege. It was the only private office on the news side of the building apart from Ambrose's, and a good deal less exposed. The rest of the news team—every single reporter and editor—claimed nothing more than a desk and every desk was within coughing distance of the others in the long, dim newsroom. Though Neva's office was no more than a large closet with a single narrow window looking onto the parking lot, it had absorbed a surprising number of improvements over the years, even a small armchair. Compared with the noisy, cluttered world on the other side of the door, it was a haven of warm color and comfort.

But, apart from the momentary satisfaction of closing a door behind her, she found little comfort here today. She was not used to being at a loss for subject matter. Her next column was due in twenty-four hours, which was plenty of time, but still she felt uneasy. Two hours ago she had expected to write about Angel and be done by mid-afternoon, early enough to go home and begin cleaning up the leavings of winter from the garden. Now she was lost, adrift, without inspiration. It was too late to write about the memorial gathering even if she wanted to, for the subject demanded exact quotes and precise details that could come only from good notes. Already the particulars were fading—had the burly poet said *Willamette lost its little brother when the flowers came out in color* or *When the flowers came out in color, Willamette lost its little brother*? The girl with the rose, had her cropped hair been blond or brown? And what had the woman in the raincoat said? *He's in heaven now but I bet he still sleeps outdoors?* Or had she said *outside*?

If Frankie had taken careful notes and managed to make proper use of them in the writing, it would be a great story. It could have been a great column. Letting her gaze travel over the cluttered desk, she found the folder in which she tucked away column ideas. It was discouragingly flat.

Still, she reached for it. The telephone rang and her hand smoothly changed direction, though she did not pick up the vintage black handset with its curly cord. She let her hand hover as she considered the possibility of rescue.

Some of her best columns had begun with an unexpected call, with a stranger's voice pouring out a story or a tip: *You may not believe this, but I just got a letter from my sister who died fifteen years ago . . . Sorry, I can't give you my name, but I guarantee that you'll be interested in the third page of the proposed school budget. Look carefully at item seven . .*

. Just in case you don't know, there's a notice on that walnut tree by the library that they're going to cut it down to expand the parking. It's the oldest tree in Willamette . . .

On the other hand, it could be a reader with some long-winded personal story that she would know within seconds was not column material, but she would have to listen nonetheless, would have to encourage or commiserate, as needed. Or it could be an appointment reminder for a tooth cleaning or her yearly breast exam—quite a joke, that, having to go for "breast" exams when all she had left were two thin scars stretched over her ribcage. The ultimate bad joke would be to get "breast" cancer in the quarter-inch of flesh the surgeon had left behind.

The phone rang twice more. She picked it up.

"This message is being forwarded to Jeneva Leopold," said the metallic voice of the *Current's* centralized switchboard. "It was left at 11:05 a.m. today. Fifty-eight seconds. To listen, press 2."

Neva pressed 2. The voice was that of a man, not one she knew. *"Ms. Leopold, you don't know me but I'm a faithful reader, well, not all the time as I can't afford the paper every day, but I look out for your pieces when I can. I have some interesting information I thought you might like to hear, bearing on a subject of recent news, but not on the phone. It's kind of sensitive, if you know what I mean. I'd leave you my number because I trust you but I threw out my phone a while back for reasons you'll see when I tell you my story. Could you meet me today? I'm thinking two o'clock or thereabouts. For the same reasons mentioned already I'm keeping out of sight, so here's what to do. You know the old brick warehouse at the north end of First Street, where they had that fire last year? It didn't but burn the wall a little. Anyway, there's a door with a padlock. It won't be locked even if it looks like it. I'll be waiting in there. Believe me, you'll be interested in my story. And if you don't show up I'll be there again tomorrow at two just in case you don't get this message right away."*

Four times through and she had it down verbatim. The caller sounded confident that she would respond, and his delivery was fast and obsessive, as though once started on a pet subject he would be difficult to stop. This was just fine; she would be spared the difficult work of having to draw the story out of him. Trying to picture the caller based on his voice she drew a blank, but there was no puzzle about the "subject of recent news" he wanted to sound off about. He would be waiting in a warehouse on First Street directly across from the river, which could mean only one thing—his "interesting information" was about the riverfront park battle. This was a subject she'd written about already but a new angle imparted by clandestine assignation was just the thing for a day that had appeared to be fizzling out and leaving her stranded without a subject. If nothing else, she could make a little mystery of it, a tale about the weird ways journalists get information.

You didn't actually meet a stranger in a warehouse? Alone?

It would make a good opening line.

Chapter Two

Once upon a time, the riverfront had been the bustling heart of Willamette. The bank had been crowded with flour and shingle mills, machine shops, an ice plant, a creamery, shipping offices, bars, a church—the usual waterfront enterprises in a young western town. But it was all long gone. The business district had shifted west away from the river, and now cottonwoods, alders, and willows covered the bank as though the Willamette did not flow through a town at all. The narrow strip of ground at the top of the bank that once boomed with commerce was now a meandering, casual park with a bike path and motley benches.

Walking along the path, Neva savored the scent of cottonwood buds and considered whether she could make a column out of the ironic fact that this park existed only because a plan pushed through by downtown business boosters had failed. Forty years ago, they had persuaded the community that heavy traffic, especially logging trucks, should be routed away from downtown and the best place to send it was along the mostly abandoned waterfront. Every single building on the water side of the street had been torn down or moved, but once the buildings were gone, nothing more had happened—no waterfront bypass.

She wasn't certain what had stopped the project, whether it was lack of money or maybe a case of wiser heads prevailing, but townspeople had taken the newly empty strip of riverbank for their own. They had planted trees and built memorial benches and, at length, officialdom had paved the bike path, the whole ending up a rustic riverfront park. As a consequence, Willamette was in a curious position; the pendulum had now swung back to an appreciation for the old and picturesque, for refurbishing rather than demolition, but there was nothing left on the riverbank to renovate, no old shingle mills to turn into shops and restaurants overlooking the water.

The few old buildings that remained on the opposite side of First Street were no great shakes architecturally, quite apart from not overlooking the water. Built in the early 1900s of local lumber and brick, they had begun as small shops, a brewery, various warehouses, and a lone garage for the earliest cars. These days they were mostly boarded up, though some were used for storage and a few had been reclaimed, one as a restaurant, another as a bar.

And now voters had approved bond money for a proper park. The proposed design had called for an improved path, several plazas for community gatherings and maybe a farmers market, some sculpture and a fountain for children to play in. Two months ago, the detailed plans were publicized and oh, what a hue and cry had followed. Cut down the native trees! Double the width of the current bike path! Install a street light every twenty feet!

The most vocal opponents had banded into a group dubbed SORE—Save Our Riverfront Environment—and demanded new hearings on the design. Defenders of the proposal said no new hearings were needed as the voters had already spoken by approving the bond measure.

Her anonymous caller would no doubt be against the design. She'd been in this business long enough to recognize the urgency of paranoia; she wouldn't be surprised if he not only opposed the design but saw a conspiracy in it somewhere.

Before crossing First Street to the warehouse, Neva stood for a moment studying it from the bike path. It looked no different from others up and down the street. Two stories, built of red brick, it was nearly as featureless as a wall. There were no windows and the flat roof had no overhang. Only a lone door broke the surface, a door so dark it appeared black though as she picked her way through the potholes that littered this end of the street she saw that the color came from weathering rather than paint.

The door was slightly inset in a frame of solid old wood. A heavy padlock secured it, or appeared to, but when she grasped the cold metal and twisted, the lock opened easily just as the caller had said. She lifted the hasp, hooked the lock back through the staple, and pushed open the door.

The rush of warm air—fruity, fragrant air—was so unexpected she stepped back. The next moment she was inside the warehouse, blinking as her eyes adjusted to the dimness. The space was vast and empty apart from square-hewn pillars that marched away in lines. Between the pillars was empty floor, the planks worn smooth and shiny.

Three steps took her to the nearest pillar. With a quick, impulsive movement she put her arms around it and pressed her cheek to the wood. Solid as earth, it felt alive, like the tree it had come from so long ago, most likely Douglas fir from the ancient forests of Oregon.

Looking past the pillar she could just make out wide wood steps at the rear of the warehouse. The bottom steps were in darkness while the upper steps rose into pale green light that had no business being inside a windowless warehouse.

"Shut the door!" boomed a male voice. A heavy shoe thumped onto the top step.

Neva had taken several steps into the warehouse but now retreated to the door. With one foot outside, she turned to look back and discovered a lean figure bearing down on her with both hands outstretched in welcome.

"You're a Pisces," he said, grasping her left hand between both of his and rubbing briskly, his calloused palms scouring her skin. "They have cold hands." Letting go with his right hand, he pulled her inside and shut the door.

Again taking her hand in both of his he moved toward the stairs, tugging her along while murmuring encouraging words as she resisted. "It's okay," he said. "I saw you at the church this morning. You wouldn't have seen me, but I was there. Lyle. Lyle McRae. We have to go up."

Maybe it was the fruity air, or the mild green light, or the dry warmth of the little man's hands—whatever the reason she stopped resisting and let herself be towed toward the stairs.

"Trust your feet," he said. "There's nothing in the way."

They climbed into the light, McRae going first, now leading with only one hand. The stairs ended at a square opening in the ceiling like a trapdoor with no cover. He cleared the opening, dropped her hand, and turned to watch her reaction as her head rose above the floor level.

"My God," she said, and stopped with her feet still four steps down.

"They're my babies." Lyle reached down again for her hand. "Come up, come up."

"It's fantastic," she said, standing beside him and gazing around in disbelief. "I had no idea."

They were surrounded by leaves, blossoms, vines, trunks—a lush jungle that rose to a high glass ceiling. From the thin chill of a Willamette spring, they had stepped into tropical summer.

"They're my babies," he said again.

"What is that incredible vine with the white flowers?"

"Vanilla," he said. "It's an orchid. Here, this way."

She followed him down a leafy aisle toward the back of the warehouse where a wall of windows rose to the glass ceiling. Before they reached the windows he turned into an open space just large enough to enclose a wicker chair and a short bench set close together. He settled her in the chair with the fussiness of an elderly hostess, then sat on the bench facing her with his knees together and his hands between them like a child.

"I'm having trouble believing this," she said. "I walk along the river all the time, right past here. I had no idea. I mean there's no way to tell from outside, nothing shows." Already she was describing the hidden greenhouse for readers... *No more than a hundred feet from the riverfront, it is always summer, always the season of fruits and flowers, where vanilla orchids scent the heavy air* . . . "I must have passed this warehouse a thousand times. How do you keep it so secret?"

"Nobody bothers me here," he said. "Where's your notebook? You need to write down my story."

"Of course." Neva's hand went to the shoulder bag she had lowered to the floor beside the chair. Since most subjects freeze at the sight of a reporter's notebook, she had developed a habit of keeping it out of sight while settling into an interview, but Lyle watched with the impatience of a retriever as she drew the narrow pad from her bag. Once upon a time, his overalls must have been white but now they were dark with earth stains, the pockets bulging with tools and twine. The sleeves of his work shirt were rolled above stringy, freckled forearms. What she had taken at first glance for baldness turned out to be colorless hair that lay flat against his scalp as though wet.

"Angel was the first to die but he won't be the last," he said with sudden fury, aiming his words at her hand that held the pen. "Write that down."

"Angel?" *But we're here to talk about the riverfront* . . .

"That's what I said. He was the first but he won't be the last. You have to write it down."

"Yes, yes of course," she said, scrawling "Angel first" on the page while looking hard at the gardener. What did this wiry character in ancient overalls have to do with Angel de Silva?

"Okay. Here's the thing," he said. "I'm next on their list. I tried to tell the police but they think I'm a nutcase anyway, a nutcase gardener that doesn't know anything about anything except roots and bulbs. Sure I do my own thing, but I've got eyes and ears, and I'm out there on my knees. I'm in the park. I can see and hear. I'm out there from March to October, in Azalea Park and around the courthouse, and the thing is, I work at night most of the time. Nobody to bother me. I do my work, I mind my own business, but like I said, I'm not blind either. I see things, I know things."

"You're going pretty fast, Lyle. Let's get the basics down first and then you can explain more clearly what you mean about Angel. You say you work for city parks?"

"I don't exactly work for the city. Let's just say I have an arrangement, a very mutually satisfactory arrangement. They offered me a job as a gardener, but I'm not a gardener, I'm a landscape architect. I don't have the license because of a stupid disagreement, but I took all the courses, courses up the wazoo. If the city wants me they have to pay landscape architect wages, not gardener, you see what I mean? The thing is, I went to school. I know my business, and if they can't see any farther than a license, a piece of paper, if they can't pay a man what he's worth and give him his right title, they can just shove it, as the song says. I mean, I do the work, I've been doing it for years, but I don't get paid so I'm not really a city employee. This way I'm my own man. Nobody tells me what to do. I grow plants for the city and the city leaves me alone. And when I'm not out there in the flowerbeds, I'm in here, growing what I want right in my own private front yard."

Without taking his eyes from Neva's scribbling hand, he gestured toward the far end of the greenhouse where a few feet of end wall showed above the treetops.

"You live here, in the warehouse?"

"I have to keep watch on things, keep good care of my babies. Did you get all that?"

She nodded, though she was finding it difficult to focus on his words, not because of the jerky delivery but because her mind was resisting. The lush life around them commanded attention. McRae's tumbling words were a confused mess driven by personal grievance, and she could not see how any of it related to Angel and at the moment she didn't care. She didn't want to hear it. She wanted to know about the greenhouse. Had he created it single-handed? How? When? How did he manage climate control, water, drainage?

"You'd be surprised what you see under God's blue sky, and right here in River City, too," he insisted as though in argument. "Some people have their heads in the sand but I'm out there at night, like I said. Two of them did it. Ernold Quick and Vance Fowler, but Quickie's the leader. 'Just a quickie, between friends.' That's what he says and then you know you're in for it."

The gardener pulled his hands out from between his knees and thrust them in flat under his thighs so he could tilt forward to look down at her notebook. Directing his voice at the notebook as though it were a microphone, he said, "They're the leaders, Quickie and Vance. Have you got that? They have a gang, kids mostly, boys but some girls too. Whoever's on the streets. They ride around on old dirt bikes with handlebars that stick way up. They're Quickie's eyes, you could say, his early warning system. They all have phones, to tell him where the cops are. That way, whatever's going on at the park, Azalea Park, buying and selling or whatever, he doesn't have to worry about sudden trouble."

"Do you mean drug deals?" Neva's hand kept moving across the page though she was looking at the top of the gardener's pale head and not at her notebook. Really, this was too wild, too crazy, and extremely disappointing. The man was plain nuts. This was sweet little Willamette he was talking about, not Portland or Seattle, or even Eugene, where the smell of dope was as familiar on the streets as smoke from the lumber mill teepee burners used to be.

"And then there's the blackmail," Lyle said with even greater intensity. "The kids are bait, what they call entrapment, you know what I mean? You know Win Niagra? He manages the craft center in the basement of that church at the park, where they had the so-called memorial service. You can't miss him, big and tall, with a braid. Niagra was really stupid and fell for their jailbait and now he's being blackmailed. They tried it out on me, boys, girls, but I've been around the block more than once and, unlike some people, I remember where I've been. Am I going too fast?"

Youth gang, drug deals, and now blackmail for attempted pedophilia in Azalea Park! She crossed the park almost every day, sometimes two or three times coming and going from the *Current* building. She had never noticed any signs of a gang, no youth cruising on old dirt bikes with high handlebars, no shady characters engaged in surreptitious dealings, not even a trace of graffiti. There was nowhere in the small park to hide, nowhere to be clandestine. Of course there was drug dealing in town—dealers are in every community—but the park was a sunny, open place full of young mothers and downtown workers and shoppers taking the air on a bench or the grass when it was dry. There was a cluster of benches at the southeast corner by the church where a few homeless men sometimes congregated, but they passed around bottles in brown paper bags, and were too feeble to carry out any sort of plot or action of any kind apart from whistles and catcalls.

The meeting had been a mistake. She had been lured into some kind of personal fantasy world, and now she had to get herself out of it. She would have to humor the gardener while making it clear that she could not write about such things, not without facts to back up the tale. "You're doing fine, Lyle, just fine, very clear. It's all extremely interesting, and certainly surprising, but this is not material—"

"I'm not done. I haven't told you about Angel yet. You need to hear about Angel." His eyes shifted to hers at last, and he put out a hand as though to stop her though she had made no move to stand up. "This goes back a ways. That's important. The thing is, Quickie had it in for Angel ever since Angel turned him in last year for stealing his disability money. You don't do that, not on the streets. Angel was passed out drunk and

Quickie didn't have to do anything but take the money out of his pocket. Angel knew who did it. Everybody knew who did it. Still, you don't tell the cops, not on another street person, but Angel was really pissed off because it wasn't the first time they'd robbed him, so he told the police and Quickie was arrested. It was really bad because Quickie was already on probation that time. He had to do six months in the state pen. After that Angel was a dead man. It was just a matter of time, we all knew it."

"You're saying that Ernold Quick killed Angel because Angel had informed on him and he had to go to jail? Six months doesn't seem long enough to want to beat someone to death."

"It's enough for Quickie. He's an animal. I saw him rip off a kitten's head because it threw up on him, just a little bit of milk. You have to see his temper. And he had six months in jail thinking about it."

"This is all extremely interesting, Lyle, but it's also very strange, and not like anything I've ever heard of in this town before."

"You don't know the streets. You don't believe me."

"I'm too surprised to know what to think. Maybe I'm naïve, and you're probably right that I don't know the streets, not the way some people do, but I am observant. I'm in Azalea Park on most days and this is not what I see. I just see normal park activities. It's a small park. There's nowhere to get out of sight."

"You're not there at night. You have to be there at night. But you're not asking the right questions. You didn't ask why Angel was carrying all that money the night he died."

"Five hundred dollars, wasn't it? I believe the news story said he had just cashed his disability check."

"He never carried that much, not since Quickie rolled him. He never carried more than about ten dollars on him. He gave his whole disability to Debo over there at Happ's Hardware to keep for him, and every day she gave him just enough for his forty-ouncer and a little food. She never let him have any more than that, not even if he got mad. That was their deal. So why was he carrying five hundred dollars?"

"I couldn't begin to guess. Do you know?"

"Sure I know. He told me. He knew Quick and Vance would take it off his body and get caught with it. I bet if you had that money you'd see his name written on it."

"Are you saying he carried it as a sort of prior evidence of his own murder? Why not just leave town or get protection? It wouldn't be any use once he was dead."

"Angel was an idiot. All that stuff they said today was bullshit, just bullshit, just plain stupid. He wasn't any angel, no way. What are you doing? I'm not done."

Neva had closed her notebook without conscious decision, but flipped it open again with a businesslike snap. Eventually he would talk himself out and then maybe he would listen to her explanations about libel and the limits on what can be said in print about private citizens—Niagra, Quick, Fowler—who have not been arrested or been the subject of news stories for any other reason. If she managed to let him down gently he might cooperate on a greenhouse column, though not today, not when he was overwrought and even, it appeared, deluded.

"You don't know the main thing yet," he said. "Here it is. I was as dumb as Angel. That's the truth. I testified at the trial the same as him. It's not like it was a secret. Like I said, everybody knew it was Quickie and Vance that robbed Angel but Angel asked me to be a witness. I should have said no. I should have said no way, I'm not saying anything. But I was an idiot and now I'm next. That's the thing. I'm next on his list. Now you know."

McRae slumped, shook his head, wiped his hands on his stained pant legs. She waited but he was silent, his words gone as suddenly as his animation. Looking with regret at the healthy greenery behind him, Neva tried to think of what to say, of how to close the conversation amicably while not entirely letting him down. At length she managed, "Where are they now, do you know? The two men."

"Anywhere. Gone. I don't know."

"If you're in danger—"

"I am. I said so."

"I mean, given that you are in danger, what precautions are you taking? Surely they know where to find you, or could discover it soon enough."

"I don't go out much. Nobody comes here. Anyway, there's nobody to take care of my babies. And I keep that lock on."

"Wouldn't it be better to have one that actually locks?"

"Oh, it locks good. I can't be bothered with keys. They get lost anyway."

"Lyle, why have you told me all this? It's extremely interesting, but you must know I can't write it without an arrest or something. I'd be accusing two people of murder on the strength of one other person's word. Even if I didn't name them it would be considered libelous. And the editors would never let it into the paper."

"I never said I wanted you to write anything. I just wanted you to know. You've got it all there in your notebook. They'll believe you."

The law enforcement building was an architectural blot that had been the direct product of Sixties paranoia. Willamette State University was anything but a hotbed of student unrest—only about fifty demonstrators had turned out at the height of the Vietnam War protests, according to an old news story—but still the county sheriff and city police chief had prepared for the worst. They had joined forces to build a new joint law enforcement headquarters intended to be impregnable. Even by the innocent and legal, as it turned out. The three-story concrete box covered half a city block but there was no getting into the building directly from the sidewalk. The entry doors were as far from the street as possible, and could be reached only by navigating drab concrete stairs and walkways where a cold wind always blew. It was especially cold after the tropical heat of the greenhouse. Pushing her hands into the pockets of her cotton jacket, Neva sent up a word of thanks that she was not arriving at this mausoleum in handcuffs.

Before pushing through the heavy glass door of the city police section of the building, she considered whether to ask for the officer in charge of juvenile crime or for her old friend Chief Kitty Fiori. In several recent columns, she had done her best to shoot down the city/county proposal for an expensive new jail, but still she and the chief would remain on their usual good terms, she was certain. The jail issue was a professional matter and had no bearing on their personal relationship. On the other hand, it would be easier to manipulate an officer into giving her information than to tackle Kitty, a master at appearing to be 100 percent cooperative while giving away nothing of significance. In the early days, before she had caught on, Neva would leave an interview thinking she'd got the best of it, only to realize that she had given Fiori far more information than she'd managed to extract from the chief, a rare reversal of roles.

Not that she expected to get much information today—laughter was more likely. The gardener's tale was absurd, but, unfortunately, it had now become hers and she could not simply ignore it. If there was a shred of truth in it, and if she did nothing, and if something actually happened to Lyle McRae, well, she owed him at least the courtesy of making a few inquiries. He trusted her and trust conferred is responsibility accepted, even if unwillingly. "It's not a nice world," he had said at the warehouse door as though imparting a heavy secret. "I'll be watching out for you."

Angel had been killed a week ago, and if it really was common knowledge on the streets that Ernold Quick and Vance Fowler had done the hideous deed the police would know about it. The men would have been questioned, at least. Five minutes with the right officer was all she needed to settle the question.

As she opened the right half of the heavy double doors, she thought of the assistant police chief, Gale Marcum. She had not warmed to the man in their few encounters since he was hired some years back but he would be far easier to play for information than the wily Fiori, and seconds in command often had that chip on the shoulder that made them want to show off. *I should be the boss here.* Just to show he was in the loop, Marcum might dredge up every fact and rumor on the subject of the murder—but there was an equal risk that he'd do the opposite, that he would be officious and rule-bound in a way that actual top dogs don't have to bother with. On reflection, this seemed more like the Marcum she'd glimpsed, tight-fisted rather than a show-off, playing the game close, if not with the finesse of his chief. In fact, if Marcum happened to be the only officer available today she'd leave and try again tomorrow.

The young woman clerk said the officer in charge of juvenile crime was Captain Oleander, and if Jeneva would take a seat she'd let him know he had a visitor. Before Neva could decide whether to thumb through glossy pages about dogs, motorcycles, or fine homes of the west, the door to the building's inner recesses opened and a tall man with the weathered look of a logger or fisherman appeared, his hand extended.

"Lars Oleander. Come on in."

Oleander led the way down a windowless, thinly carpeted corridor to a cramped office where he settled at a desk that would have been right for a man half his size. Fit and at ease, he was military neat, though his manner had a touch of school-boy diffidence as he observed, "My wife's one of your fans. Your column on Habitat for Humanity's on the fridge. She helped found the local effort. She also likes it when you write about animals."

"It's always nice to hear what readers enjoy," Neva said, hiding her puzzlement. The Habitat for Humanity column had been a reasonably good one, but when had she ever written about animals? "I guess you could say I'm here today to talk about a certain kind of animal, smallish human animals."

"Adolescent animals that tend to get into trouble when they herd?"

"Ah, there's the voice of experience. I've just been told quite a story and I'm hoping you can help me sift truth from fiction."

"I'll do my best, ma'am." The captain settled back in the chair with a listening look on his broad face.

Neva sketched the scenario in far fewer words than her informant had used, her tone light and intended to convey skepticism. At the mention of McRae's name Oleander dropped his air of a tolerant uncle, and by the end of her account, his face bore the set look of an immigration official at the end of a long day. "Well," he said. "I see. Did you go to the warehouse alone?"

"I always work alone. I expected him to talk about the riverfront park controversy."

"Have you told me everything he said?"

"The gist of it. He rambled on for quite a while."

"He's a nutcase."

"So there's no truth in the story? Actually, that's what I expected but I have to check it out anyway, which I'm sure you can understand."

Oleander's reply was slow to form but Neva sat in patient silence, studying a photograph on the wall behind him. A family portrait, it showed a hearty young Oleander with his arm around a kind-looking woman—the animal lover—whose head just reached his shoulder. In front of Oleander stood a sandy-haired boy about twelve. In front of Mrs. Oleander was a girl half that age, her curly hair held away from her face with twin koala bear clips. All four appeared ready to burst into laughter.

"Like anyplace today we've got our gang issues, our homeless issues, and our drug issues," Oleander said, speaking now with formal gravity. "But compared to just about anywhere you want to name it's no big deal. We do our job. There's been an increase in graffiti, as the paper reported not too long ago, and more people are on the streets because of the economy. There was a minor gang episode some time back. The kids messed around with drug dealing, but they weren't very good at it. We took the needed action. No more story. I'm not saying there aren't drugs being bought, sold and used, but not by any organized gang of kids in the park or downtown, not anymore."

"Did they ride around on mountain bikes with high handle bars?"

"It doesn't matter how they got around as long as it stopped. Which it did."

"And the child prostitution and blackmail?"

"Pure fantasy. The man's deluded. He spends too much time on his knees with nobody but the daffodils and posies for company. You don't want to believe a word he says."

"What about Ernold Quick and Vance Fowler? Were they involved?"

"Fowler was taken into custody an hour ago. I don't know how Mr. McRae could know about that."

"I don't believe he does or he wouldn't be so afraid. What about Quick?"

"Quick appears to have left town."

"Do you mean he ran away?"

"I don't mean anything except that he's a person of concern who appears to have left town. That's all I've been told."

"So it appears McRae was on the right track about the murder at least."

"As I said, Fowler and Quick are persons of interest, that's all for the moment. And now I have to ask, what is your business in all this? It's hardly a subject for your sort of column."

"My sort of column . . . I'm not sure what that means. I write about anything, any subject having to do with this town or life in general. In fact, I'd like to write a column about you."

"I thought you were here about McRae. I don't, I mean I'm not very interesting."

"I don't believe that for a second."

"Well, Jean would love it. Maybe another time."

"That's the oldest put-off going," Neva teased. "I think readers would be very interested so I'm taking your 'later' seriously, don't think I'll forget. As for 'my sort of column,' the only surprising thing is that I haven't written about Angel yet. I didn't see you there but you must have heard about his memorial gathering this morning. He had friends all through the community. Naturally that interests me. I didn't know him, and I haven't had anything new to say, to add to the story."

"Angel was something else, all right, but you have folks making him into a saint because of what happened. That's not the Angel de Silva we know down here. You'd have a hard job counting the hours of law enforcement time he's used up. Normal folks don't end up on the streets. Just remember that. As for Fowler's arrest, the media will get a press release this afternoon."

"Will it say anything about Quick?"

"Definitely not. And I'd advise you to keep it to yourself for the time being. Sorry, I didn't mean that to sound like a threat. Let's just say publicity would make our job harder. And now, Ms. Leopold — "

"Neva, please."

"Neva. One thing you should know. Quick was on parole after he got out of prison. Three weeks ago he was slapped in jail for parole violations but they had to let him go after fifteen days. No room in the jail. That night, the night he got out, Angel died. A little food for thought."

Neva regarded the officer steadily. What he really was talking about, of course, was the proposed bond to pay for the new jail, the jail she had condemned as too costly, too large, wrong location—everything, in fact, was wrong with it. Now Oleander was saying that Angel had died indirectly because the current jail was so small they had to let offenders go before their time was up. In other words, by opposing construction of the new jail, she was making the community an easier place for killers like Quickie to operate. It was surprising to hear this kind of nonsense from a sensible man like Oleander.

"Maybe you didn't hear the news this morning," she said. "One of the big insurance companies, I don't remember which one, did a study on small cities around the country. They compared crime statistics, natural disasters, traffic deaths, and so on and they concluded that Willamette is the safest town in the country. The *safest*—number one in the whole nation. The people arguing for a new jail say we're in the middle of a crime wave because the old jail's so small they have a revolving door. How can we be the safest place in the country and facing a crime wave at the same time?"

Without having to think, Oleander said, "Last night on the way home I heard on the radio that they've got a captive alien in jail in Ireland somewhere. And they don't mean an illegal immigrant. Just because it's on the radio or TV doesn't mean it's true."

It was impossible not to laugh or to help liking the man. "I can't dispute that, Captain. I've made some spectacular mistakes myself, as you most likely know given that I make them in public. But it's also true that most of us get most of our information through the daily news and without it we'd know a lot less about the world, Internet or no Internet."

"Well, I'm an old-fashioned newspaper reader myself. I don't go for this reading online. And now I have to say again, there are a lot better and more useful things you could be writing about, Ms. Leopold. These aren't nice people, not worth your time, that's for certain. They're all the dregs of society. Street people don't act like you and me, and if you go expecting them to, you'll be disappointed. That's one thing I learned in this business for twenty-seven years. Don't go expecting logical behavior from folks that don't live logical lives."

"Lyle McRae isn't a street person. And maybe he really is in danger. He seems to have been right about who killed Angel so he may be right that they were out to get him too. Shouldn't he be protected in some way until Quick is arrested?"

The slow shake of Oleander's head continued through a lengthy silence that ended when he stood up and said with finality, "A nutcase, like I said. A teller of tall tales. Anyway, Quick's most likely in Canada by now."

Chapter Three

On her way back to the *Current*, Neva detoured to the warehouse. Lyle would be relieved to know that Fowler was behind bars and Quick had fled. It was one small favor she could do, and most likely the only one.

But the lock was clicked shut this time despite the gardener's comment about keys, and pounding on the door brought no response. There was no crack to slip a note through, and to leave it in sight would not do. He would find out about the arrest from the morning paper, and this would have to be soon enough.

Relieved to have been spared another meeting with the intense gardener so soon, she chose a route back to the office that took her through Azalea Park. The park filled a city block west of downtown. It was a green gem, a graceful oasis of shapely elms, maples, magnolias and evergreens with two circles of lawn inside a figure-eight walkway. Across the street to the north was the city library. To the south were the crafts center and the First Church of Christ. The paved path that bounded the two lawns was drifted with papery elm seeds and overhead a flock of noisy grosbeaks feasted on the seeds that had not yet fallen, shaking the branches and knocking down more seeds in a delicate rain. Strolling through the seed shower, Neva considered the day's failures. Despite two interesting interviews and a memorial service beyond anything she could have imagined, she still had no ready column subject.

This was simply a quirk of the business. Sometimes the most promising events turned out to be a bust while some of her best columns had come from nothing much at all. In fact, it was a nothing sort of subject that had got her started writing columns in the first place. She had been in her second year as a reporter for the *Seattle Times* and was crossing a park one sunny afternoon when she felt an urge to sit down on the grass. Soon, a large, awkward young woman had sat down near her and said in the open manner of a child, "There's a bee on your toe."

Sure enough, there had been a fat bee crawling across Neva's bare toes in the sandal. The two of them watched it for a while in silence, and then she had tried to find out about the young woman but had managed to learn only two facts: it was the girl's birthday, and she was about to get on a bus to leave town. Her sole interest was in the bee, and she could not be diverted until, at last, Neva had lifted the slow creature off with a blade of grass.

Back in the newsroom a short while later, it had struck Neva that they had been a long way from a bus station, and that the young woman was so child-like that she must have wandered away from where she belonged—got away from her keepers, to put it plainly—and might be in danger out on her own. Ten telephone calls later, she had finally located the right group home. Yes, they most certainly were missing a mentally handicapped young woman. Jancy had disappeared hours ago, where could they find her?

They did not find her, not that day. Neva had written a spontaneous column about the encounter, not so much on the chance that it would help locate the girl but because she had been moved. The editors liked the piece, ran it the next day, and a reader had called to report that Jancy had been found sleeping in his garage. Soon Neva was writing a monthly column, then one a week, and within the year had accepted the job of full-time columnist at the *Current*. The move down to a small daily had been made as an experiment but she had known almost from the start that she could not do better than sane little Willamette for bringing up her son. For two decades she had turned out three columns per week—and during all those years she had found herself at a loss for a subject so rarely that each time felt like a novel dilemma.

The world offered up subjects like runaway violets in a garden. Generally, all you had to do was pick them.

Stopping near a bench, she put aside her thoughts and concentrated on what she could see. Over in the play area two mothers pushed toddlers on swings. A girl sat on the steps of the gazebo strumming an acoustic guitar to an audience of a single robin. Defense attorney Tolbert White pedaled his recumbent bicycle along the south side of the park as he did several times every day, riding to the courthouse from his office, pipe smoke trailing behind.

Tolb waved, one of the mothers called out, "Loved your piece on the jail," and the girl set down her guitar to eat a sandwich.

No subject leaped out but even so her step was lighter as she walked on. Spring in Willamette was a very fine season indeed—and Azalea Park remained as sweet as a park could be.

Back at the paper, Neva went straight to the editor's office.

Ambrose swung his boots off the desk, sat up straight and slapped the arms of his chair. "They made an arrest? Why haven't we heard about it?"

"You just did," Neva said, savoring in advance the growl she knew was coming.

"You know what I mean, dammit. Where are my reporters, asleep at the wheel?" He stood up to scan the newsroom through the glass wall, focusing particularly on the empty desk of police reporter Charlie Frank. "You say there's a press release? What do you know about all this? What have you been digging into?"

Gratified by his look of aggrieved suspicion, part of a game they had played for years, Neva said, "I've uncovered a drug, sex and blackmail gang working out of Azalea Park on bicycles."

"With AK-47s no doubt," he said, delighted, and left the office to find the city editor.

Neva checked for messages, was relieved to find nothing that needed following up, and headed for the staff door, bound for home. The special City Council meeting on the riverfront plan was at seven and it was not quite five now. She could work in the garden for an hour and still have time to eat and shower before the meeting if she could get out of here without being cornered for more information.

She was halfway through the coatroom when the staff door burst open and Charlie Frank rushed in waving a sheet of paper. "They got him. They arrested the killer. It was a street people thing, a drunk killing another drunk for money."

Neva put out a hand for the press release. True to what Oleander had said, there was no mention of a second suspect, but she had not expected them to say that the motive was theft. The $500 Angel was known to have been carrying must have been found on Vance Fowler, hence the conclusion that the money was the object. Oleander had scorned Lyle's claim that the object was revenge, but you don't have to kill a man—especially a drunk—to take a measly five hundred bucks.

"What's the matter?" Frankie demanded.

Neva smiled at the young reporter's quick perception. He was not only fast but ambitious, and within weeks of joining the news staff with a new journalism degree in hand he had taken to watching her closely. "To catch crumbs," he'd said after being scooped on his beat for the second time. Her reminder that she'd been working the town for nearly twenty years had soothed his feelings, and since then they'd cooperated on several stories. Already, after just six months, he was one of the best writers on the paper, though he had yet to learn discretion and could not help blurting when he was excited, which was most of the time.

NO ANGEL

"The motive may have been revenge rather than theft," she said. "And you, at least, should know that there is a possibility of a second suspect."

"Says who?"

"Captain Oleander. Well, a 'person of interest' is the way he put it."

"It's not even his case. He's a juvenile guy. What were you talking to him for? Are you digging into the Angel thing?"

"Not if I can possibly help it. The memorial should have been good column material but it didn't click for me in that way, maybe because I seem to be the only person in town who didn't know him."

"Ditto here. Does Ambrose know about the arrest?"

"Afraid so."

"Well, hell. I thought I had some news for a change."

"That's all he knows, no details. I said you'd be bringing a press release." It was not exactly what she'd said but near enough.

"Thanks. And now, be fair, what have you dug up? What do you mean the motive was revenge? And who's the other suspect?"

Neva returned the press release and smiled up at the lean, eager young face. "You need a shave, kiddo. As for details, the bits I've been told are mostly unsubstantiated and probably crazy in any case. I really don't plan to write about it. Tell you what, if I find out anything that looks like a fact I'll let you know. How about that?"

"What *are* you working on?"

"The riverfront park again, believe it or not. Big meeting tonight, yippee."

"Well, it's your fault."

"How so?"

"If you hadn't written about that geotextile stuff it would have slipped right by everybody and the city would have had the whole thing bulldozed before breakfast."

"I'd be happy to take the credit or the blame, but I just happened to get the plan a day early, if you remember. They thought I was a cheerleader at that point."

"Nothing's simple in this town, is it? You'd think if we could do one thing without controversy it would be building a park. It's really a wonder we don't have more murders. Folks around here get mad enough over parks—and even parking—to shoot on sight."

"It's all a matter of protecting our quality of life, Frankie. If you have to sacrifice a virgin or two, well, there's certainly some historic precedent."

"You sound cynical today. I thought Willamette was your idea of heaven on earth."

"Will-AM-ette, DAMN it!" Neva said as she did every time someone from Chicago, New York or other foreign locale—Missouri in Frankie's case—said WILL-a-mette.

"At least I've stopped saying Or-i-GONE. Let me know when they sacrifice the next virgin. Murder is my beat, remember."

At home, Neva went indoors only long enough to drop her bag and exchange her jacket for a sweatshirt. A light rain had begun to fall again, the sort of spring mist that feels beneficent rather than cold or even truly wet. The flowering quince was in full bloom and red camellias covered the tall shrub by the door, but the rest of the back yard was a scene of rampant plant chaos. The ivy had nearly swallowed the fence, every one of the half dozen clematis vines was an overgrown tangle, the grape had eaten the potting shed and run up into the hawthorn tree, the honeysuckle made a hedge where an eight-foot trellis used to be, even the decorous wisteria had leaped from her proper archway to a rain gutter.

Just when had the vines taken over? Surely it wasn't just because she'd abandoned home and garden last summer for the high desert country of Eastern Oregon. The green tide must have been rising in her yard for years and she simply hadn't noticed.

She brushed wet leaves from a bench and sat down on the damp wood. This was a gloomy yard. It had not struck her so forcibly before, but now the crowding branches heavy with rain, the choking vines, and the grass that was already too long for the push mower felt heavy and even sad. A sudden longing swept through her to strip it all down to bare earth, to peel the matted green and brown coat off and put rock in its place, warm yellow rock that would feel sunny even in gray January.

Well, why not? If she could not move east of the mountains to her beloved desert, she would bring the desert home. The grass that drenched her shoes and pant legs would be carted away down to the last blade. The fences, trellises and shed would stand out clean again, free of smothering green. Maybe she would paint the side of the weathered gray shed a rich yellow-ochre or earth red. The rotting chips on what remained of the paths would be shoveled away and replaced with yellow gravel that would send warmth up through her feet on a June afternoon and into her heart in December.

And taking up the whole middle of the yard, ah, this would be the crowning marvel—a big flagstone patio in shades of yellow and gold like the quartz over in Oregon's mining country.

The vision of an entirely different garden was so clear in Neva's mind that she began at once to cut swathes in the ivy with a pruning saw, a trick she'd learned from a tree trimmer during a column interview—the same way she'd learned so many useful tidbits over the years. Pulling back the vines with her left hand as though pulling back long hair, she slashed at the tough runners close to the ground, chopping rather than sawing. The ivy peeled away in a tangled roll, exposing an ancient flowerbed and behind it a cedar fence she had not seen in years.

Dinner was toast, cheese and wine consumed at the kitchen counter where she could look out at the wonderful devastation she had wrought in just one scant hour.

If not for the meeting she would have worked until dark, but at 6:40 she had to get back into reporter mode. Hurrying through the front hall with the riverfront plan under her arm, she discovered the telephone message light blinking. The number on the Caller I.D. had a city government prefix, which was odd—official calls generally went to her office.

"Jeneva?" said the voice of a woman who didn't give her name and didn't need to. Neva would have recognized city engineer Anya Alexandrova's clipped voice in a howling gale or under water. "How are you? Just wanted to remind you about the special session of the City Council tonight. You know it was moved to the fire hall. We expect quite a crowd. Sorry to bother you at home but I didn't get around to calling the paper earlier."

Now why would the engineer bother to remind her of the special session? Alexandrova was in charge of the project, and naturally had loved Neva's first column before the levy election. The column had praised the plan and said the town was right to restore its best asset after years of neglect. But her second column, following the release of detailed plans, had incensed the engineer, particularly her description of the design as "sterile and too geometric for a natural shoreline." The column had helped fuel a protest that in turn triggered further hearings that city staff considered a colossal nuisance. The engineer had made it clear in a chance conversation at the Old World Deli a week ago that all she wanted was to be left alone to get on with the job. And why "the Birkenstock crowd" had to get involved at this late date she didn't know.

"Where were they two years ago when we held those community focus groups to get started on the design? I don't know why Johnny-come-latelies think they should have any say." Her normally rosy face had flushed dark red. Physically trim and layered in earth-toned garments with visible Patagonia and Marmot labels, she looked more like an Outward Bound leader than a city department head. "I believe in public process, but give me a break, Neva. Why are you siding with them? You really fell for the old baloney on this one."

Baloney... Was it baloney to wonder how the $6.5 million contract had gone to a local firm when bids had come in from all over the Northwest? Was it baloney to wonder, as opponents were doing loudly, whether the design was being driven by the greed of downtown property owners rather than community preference for a greener, more graceful plan? How could the city call it a "park" when the design featured extensive pavement, including a two-way street, parking on both sides, a ten-foot-wide "multi-modal corridor" known in its more modest form as a bike path, three plazas with uninspired concrete and wood seating in place of the memorial benches . . . and to do this required removing every tree and shrub, to be replaced by "selected native species in keeping with the riparian locale." What could be more native than the existing alder, maple, cottonwood, ash and willows, many planted and hand-watered by community members when the strip first became a park?

And then there was that god-awful geotextile. She had got hold of a sample of the ersatz material, a thick, rubbery mat that was to cover the bank as a stabilizer. It would be punctured with holes for planting the new trees and shrubs. Just the thought of it smothering the ground made her shudder.

The real problem, Neva had argued in her latest column, was that large projects nearly always look like large projects, that is, over-engineered and sterile rather than having been allowed to grow piece by individual piece. What made European riverfronts and downtowns appealing was their development over centuries, on a human scale, with quirky features no engineer would be likely to suggest but that appealed to the inner-Hobbit most of us harbor, especially Americans, hungry as we are for history and character. Granted, Willamette's few old riverfront warehouses, commercial buildings, and barn-like former bus station didn't add up to a huge amount of character and history, she had written, but a little history is better than none.

The group opposing the city plan—the self-designated SORE—had come up with an alternative scheme that eliminated the geotextile, limited vehicle traffic, and saved most of the trees and at least some of the benches, but it still would result in a designed rather than evolved environment. The question now was which design really was better, the City's or SORE's? It was unlikely that yet another public hearing would answer the question, but with tempers running high the meeting would not be dull and it might yield a third column on the subject, an easy out for meeting her tomorrow afternoon's deadline.

Rather than go straight to the fire station she detoured south three blocks to Azalea Park. She would be late for the hearing but no official group had ever been known to get started on the interesting subject without first indulging in approving minutes, revising the agenda, hearing committee reports . . . If she could live out her remaining years without ever attending another meeting it would be worth giving up a whole year of life in a devil's bargain.

Only three sides of the park were accessible by car, the fourth having been closed to create a plaza between the church and arts center and the small playground at the south edge of the lawn. Not a living soul stirred in the park, neither a solid citizen out for a stroll nor a skulking youth out for mischief. The City Hall parking lot across Sixth Street to the east was empty. She pulled into it, got out of the car, listened briefly to the distant whoosh of traffic in the busy part of downtown two blocks distant, then crossed the gravel lot and entered the park at the corner by the church.

A light wind stirred the branches of the elms overhead as she strolled in and out of dark patches where the streetlights failed to reach. She saw, heard and felt nothing alarming, and met no one. Once around the double loop, she cut over to the steps of the church, climbed to the porch and waited. The only activity was an occasional car arriving on the far side of the park for some library event. The lack of action was just as she had expected but still she felt oddly let down, as though some part of her had hoped to find that Lyle McRae was right about the gang and the captain wrong. McRae had been right that Quick and Fowler were up to some kind of no good, sufficient to get Vance arrested and Quick wanted. The gardener had said the gang members slept during the day in two apartments that Quick rented on Ninth Street, and came out at night to be his eyes and ears. If Quick really had left town, the kids—if they were anything more than McRae's invention—might have disbanded or been spooked into keeping out of sight for a while.

Nothing happened for five long minutes, which she timed by checking the luminous clock on the county courthouse tower that rose above the trees. The meeting had begun fifteen minutes ago. She started down the steps but was stopped by a scraping sound. It came from around the corner of the church and suggested small animal activity rather than human, maybe a raccoon or possum. Easing from step to step, she leaned to look into the flower border that ran along the church's west wall. A dark figure dashed from the shrubbery, but even as her heart leaped, the rushing form passed under a streetlamp, spotlighting a pale head and overalls.

"Lyle!"

The figure did not stop.

"Lyle, wait. It's me, Jeneva. I'll step into the light. It's all right, I'm alone."

The gardener returned slowly, peering left and right as he crossed the open stretch of paving stones, and demanded in a harsh whisper, "What are you doing here?"

"Just looking to see what I might see. Which is nothing except you. What are you doing here?"

"Checking my flower bulbs. Like I said, I work at night, especially now."

"Did you hear that Vance was arrested today? And Quick left town to avoid being caught, or so I was told. There's a warrant out for him so he won't be hanging around here. That should make it safer."

"Safe? Nothing's safe anymore. Who told you the kid got arrested?"

"The city juvenile officer. He confirmed that there was a gang of kids, though he said it had been 'cleared up.'"

"Confirmed! I don't need any confirmation except my own eyes. They aren't going to admit anything about gangs. Gangs are bad for business and business is what this town's all about." Lyle turned, walked swiftly across the courtyard, and disappeared into the shrubbery.

Sidling in at the back of the hall where even the standing room was packed, Neva had trouble at first shifting her thoughts away from the gardener to what was being said into the microphone way up front. She had handled the encounter clumsily, no doubt about it. Naturally McRae would be offended by the word "confirmed," and he was a touchy sort in any case. She must be more careful about what she said to him, especially if she was to have any hope of doing a story about the greenhouse somewhere down the line.

When at last she did tune in to what citizens were saying, they were hammering away at the same old points that had been made at the two previous meetings and it was not worth writing down. Testimony droned on, gradually the crowd thinned, and after an hour she settled in a free chair halfway up the aisle. She didn't like to be in such a conspicuous spot in case she wanted to slip out, but at the moment, sitting down was even more attractive than being unobserved.

The limit per speaker was three minutes, and the mayor's hammer allowed no exceptions. Even so, there were still speakers waiting at midnight and they probably could have kept it up until dawn had everyone with fire in their eyes been allowed to speak. SORE came out ahead in numbers, though one City proponent pointed out that the "silent majority" in the community had already approved the riverfront plan by passing the bond levy and he saw no reason to "flog a moving horse."

Though voters had approved a bond measure to pay for the project, SORE argued, citizens had been misinformed about what the plan really entailed and should be given another chance to evaluate it along with a less drastic alternative.

No dice, was the official answer. Any delay in construction could jeopardize the City's bond rating. The plan had been five years in the works, with plenty of opportunity for citizen input.

Though little new was said, Neva had enough good quotes by the end to turn into something, and this was comforting—like finally being able to see the top of the hill on a hike, you know you can get there from here. It was a column in the bag, even if a ho-hum column. Before the last speaker was done, she slipped out to avoid being cornered by someone with more ire to spill and was home by half-past twelve. In the dim hall, the telephone message light again was blinking.

Ethan. It must be. He generally called every two or three days but so far this week she had not heard from him. But the Caller I.D. window did not show her son's phone number—"Unidentified caller" it said—and it was not her son's voice that wailed into her ear. The caller was a woman, her words rushed and anguished.

"Jeneva Leopold? I'm sorry, I can't give my name, but I had to call. There's been a terrible mistake. You're the only one I can think of that can do something about it. I really am upset and beg you to get justice. The wrong man has been arrested. When I heard it on the radio I couldn't believe it, not Vance Fowler, he'd never kill anyone. He's got some problems, and he'd be the first to tell you that, but I've worked with him in a social service capacity and I know he's gentle on the inside. Just listen to his songs, he's a musician you know. Ask him to sing you, 'Dreaming of Carlie,' and you'll know what I mean. He has his old aunt in town, Wygelia Chance, over on Thirteenth Street, I think, or maybe Twelfth. His great aunt, I should say. Call her, she'll tell you about Vancie. I'm just so upset I don't know if I'm making sense, but please do something."

Neva rummaged for a pen on the cluttered table, pushed the replay button and wrote fast. Despite her distress, the woman's voice was strong and clear, and it took just two playings to get the words down. *Wygelia. . .* she had spelled it like the shrub but added a note to check. Standing for a moment with the message in hand, Neva felt her initial interest give way to irritation. Such calls were essential to her work but it was frustrating that so many of the distraught people who begged her to "do something" lacked the courage and courtesy to leave their name and number. What were they afraid of? They trusted her enough to get in touch but not enough to make it possible for her to call back, to ask essential questions. Sometimes she felt like the town puppet, hanging out there ready for anybody to jerk her strings and make her dance in a new direction. She welcomed the dance, of course—or her telephone number wouldn't be in the directory and printed three times a week at the end of her column along with her email address—but it would be nice to have more confident partners.

The directory on the hall table listed a W. Chance on Twelfth Place, a cul-de-sac off Twelfth Street, according to the foldout city map. Just five blocks from downtown, in one of Willamette's oldest neighborhoods, the street appeared to be little more than a long driveway. She would call Wygelia after breakfast, and mention the telephone message—no, on second thought, this would not be necessary and it was best to keep things simple. Enough to say that she wanted to talk with her about the arrest of her great nephew. With luck, she would get a column out of it and not have to write about the riverfront after all. Old women rarely failed her as material. Whatever they may have been like in youth, in old age women tended toward startling frankness, and nearly always managed to be quotable. And now that Vance Fowler had been arrested, he had become a public figure, fair game for comment.

Twelfth Place turned out to be a very short street with just two houses standing side-by-side at the end. Both were modest Victorians, but this was all they had in common. One house was immaculate enough for a magazine cover. The other was a perfect haunted house, right in every detail down to the ancient figure waiting on the porch. The old woman did not fit the robust voice that had answered the telephone and said to come on over, and she did not respond to Neva's wave through the open car window.

Puzzled, Neva reached for her bag and notebook, glanced at the address she'd jotted on the open page, and shook her head. She should know better than to jump to conclusions—the accused murderer's great aunt did not live in the ruin, she lived in the show place. This was disappointing, as the crone looked an interesting nut to crack.

But as she headed up the walkway that was flanked by pansies rather than the one flanked by hawkweed, Neva felt a sudden flush of pleasure at the attractive order. The lawn was plush, the white camellias were large and spotless, the gingerbread house trim was crisply painted.

Either Vance's great aunt was on the young side or she had young help to keep the place in beautiful order. Maybe the helper was Vance?

"Vance doesn't live here," Wygelia volunteered as she drew Neva into a hallway redolent with furniture oil and fresh pastry. "He likes his independence. What I can't do myself I pay for. I was lucky enough to marry a very good provider who has passed on, bless his dear heart, but then, I don't imagine young women like you care to think of men as providers anymore."

Not accustomed to thinking of her forty-six years as young, Neva had no ready reply apart from a smile. Wygelia was just what her telephone voice had promised, and just what a great aunt should be, from the print dress to the tea and homemade lemon bars waiting on a table next to the channel-back chair. Even her persistence in the subject of matrimony was in character. Seated on the sofa, she said with a bright-eyed tilt of the head, "I hope you're well married?"

"I was well married. Thank you." Neva raised the white porcelain cup, but added before sipping, "Carlo died in a boating accident years ago, when our son was just four. There's never been anyone else, not really." Surprised—she rarely talked even to friends about this definitive disaster of her life—she wondered whether she'd said it to gain her hostess's sympathy and trust. But Wygelia was not a woman who needed winning or drawing out.

"That's a shame, a real shame," she said. "Vance's mother, my niece, died when he was three and I suppose that's where the trouble started. When I saw the officer on the porch I knew it was Vancie he'd come about. For some kids life is one long party. Others just seem doomed from their first breath. Everything goes wrong. Vance tried hard. It still wrings my heart to remember the day he helped me weed the garden when he was about six. He got the carrots mixed up with the dog fennel we were pulling out, both being feathery on top, you know, and I didn't realize it until he'd done a whole row. When I told him, he took all the little carrot seedlings out of the weed basket and tried to replant them. Of course, they died. I found him crying out there after supper. Poor little boots, he took everything to heart."

Tender child driven to crime by ill fate and a harsh world . . . Neva set down her tea.

"They teased him in school, that is, until he got his growth."

"I understand your nephew is musical?"

"Oh, yes, Vancie has a lovely voice. It was so sad when he left the choir. Father Nelson said he had such promise, but then he did come back to it, not the choir, he was too old for that, but he did come back to music in the hospital."

"He was ill?"

"No, not exactly. He was in Clarendon, the state mental hospital, back before it closed. He was never a danger to anyone but himself. I told them so. They finally realized it was true and let him out. He was just depressed, but maybe it was a good thing he went in because he learned guitar. I have a tape if you'd like to borrow it. I don't dare listen to it now myself, not with him back in jail."

"Vance has been in jail before this?"

"Only a few times, and only for sleeping in the park. He has a perfectly good bed here any time he wants but he says he gets claustrophobic and needs the fresh air. I understand. Sometimes I feel like I'm stuck in a closet myself." Wygelia looked around the handsome room with the appraising eyes of a prospective buyer rather than a homeowner. "I was born here and I expect I'll die here. Did you ever go to France? I always wanted to go to France but it looks like I never will. As for the death of that street person, I never heard such nonsense. Vance saved his life, he never killed him."

"But Angel is dead."

"That was before, three weeks ago, when Angel was drunk and fell in the river. Vance jumped in and pulled him out or he would have drowned, the police said so. Vance was down there feeding those cats. He had a regular route, you know, feeding the wild cats. Ferals, he called them. He always has loved cats. He couldn't stand to see anything suffer, not my Vancie. He was really worried, you know, last time he was here. He said that riverfront project they're all talking about was going to destroy the cat colony. I told him cats are better survivors than that, but he was worried just the same."

"Do you have any idea why he would be arrested in connection with the murder? Was the missing money found on him?"

"I don't know anything at all, I'm afraid, other than that it's just the kind of thing that happened to Vancie all his unfortunate life. I'm just so glad you're going to write about this, Ms. Leopold. I'll sleep better knowing he's going to get fair treatment from somebody, at least."

Chapter Four

"Well, what did you think?" Ambrose settled back in the old swivel chair, fingers laced behind his head, an expectant look on his lean face.

Wary, Neva said nothing as she ran her eye over his desktop and the bulletin board where he often pinned up the day's news pages. The pages were marked with emphatic circles, lines and exclamation marks denoting the good, the bad and the ugly. Today's front page hung in the middle of the board, a photo of the crowd at Angel's memorial service filling half the space above the fold.

"Fine job," she said.

Ambrose raised an eyebrow.

"Very fine job?"

The other eyebrow went up.

"Prize-winning job!"

"If there was a dry eye in town I'll eat my socks. And that's just the kick-off. We're going for the whole enchilada on this one. Angel's story from birth, what put him on the streets and so on. And Frankie's working on the profile of a killer. What kind of man could beat a harmless drunk to death so violently they had to get a fire truck to wash down the sidewalk? It seems they were perfectly friendly in the past, no bad feelings between them, no prior difficulties other than the usual wino spats, although Fowler was a bad egg from the get-go by all accounts. The story on the arrest wasn't much, as you no doubt noticed, but Frankie's fleshing that out, too."

"Are you sure it's a good idea to profile a 'killer' before he's even been arraigned? The press release said 'in connection with the investigation.' That's a long way from a conviction. And there is the matter of a possible accomplice."

Sitting forward, Ambrose placed both hands flat on the desk and fixed her with a fervent look. "What we've got is not only an arrest but a video. That's news to you, I see. The security film at the Dari-Mart where they buy their booze. They got Fowler hassling Angel, trying to get money off him and threatening him. A couple hours later he's dead."

"You know that wouldn't be enough to convict anyone with a decent attorney. And they are looking for a second man, a man who's said to be the real tough customer."

"If and when they arrest him we'll report it. The point here is contrast. You have two street people, both the dregs of society, so to speak, but they handled their outcast status completely differently. One a saint and one a killer. A great story."

"If it's true. I've heard conflicting accounts. I heard Fowler's just a sidekick to the real murderer and not really a bad sort at all, while Angel's less than angelic. Fowler isn't really homeless, he simply chooses to sleep in the park sometimes. And I heard that Fowler actually saved Angel's life not long ago by pulling him out of the river."

"I knew you'd been poking around, Leopold. Could you at least tell Frankie what you've heard? He's out right now trying to track down some relative of Fowler's, some old lady."

"That would be Wygelia Chance, the great aunt."

"You heard about her?"

"I spent the morning with her."

"Damn it, Neva!"

The editor was truly angry this time, with no hint of joking. Surprised, her usual playful response frozen half-formed, Neva also felt sudden anger. She was tired of this game. For years she had soft-footed and pulled punches to allow Ambrose's reporters to catch up, not only in the interests of keeping the editor happy but to maintain the proper order: news stories give the facts while columns and editorials comment on facts. To have to provide the information and then comment on it in the same seven-hundred-and-fifty words was a tall order. She rarely set out to scoop the news team, but young reporters tended to be ambitious and rarely stayed longer than a few years on the modest little Willamette *Current*. They no sooner got to know their beats intimately than they moved on, while she dug in deeper year by year. Plus she had a knack for recognizing tips of significant icebergs—it was one of her few real talents, something innate like perfect musical pitch. She worked hard, as hard as anyone in the newsroom with the possible exception of the city editor who, as one newsroom wag had put it, "went to bed at night with her arms around the city directory." Neva had earned her position as the mostly benign bloodhound in the kennel and she was proud of it.

"Damn it yourself," she said flatly. "We've been through this too many times, and frankly I'm sick of it. What am I supposed to do, funnel my tips to your puppies and let them run all over the trail? Am I supposed to tell the people who call me that they should give their story to some twenty-three-year-old just arrived from J school, who's more interested in that future Pulitzer than spelling their name right? Maybe you've forgotten how many good tips I have passed along, how many reporters I've rescued from charging down the wrong track and falling into pits full of enough egg to smear us all. You know and I know that there is plenty of news out there waiting to be found, plenty of rocks to be turned over, and no one has prior rights to any of it. You were a reporter. You worked a beat. You know what it takes and I don't believe for a minute that you would have let yourself be scooped by a columnist pushing fifty, and you wouldn't have wanted to be hand fed, either. I've been patient about this for years but I've had enough."

She stopped, not because there wasn't more to say but because of the faces looking in through the editor's glass wall. Reaching behind her without turning, she shut the door. Ambrose still sat with his hands flat on the desk. Beyond the glass, J.D. shooed away the newsroom audience, though she made no attempt to hide her delight. The number of times Neva and the editor had seriously fallen out could be counted on one finger, and predated J.D.'s arrival at the paper. At the time of their only other serious showdown, Neva had been working at the *Current* for five years already. Ambrose had been on the job less than six months, and had been hired direct from the metro desk of the San Diego Union-Tribune. Ethan, then in kindergarten, had developed scarlet fever and naturally Neva stayed home with him. When she returned to work after a week, Ambrose had told her bluntly that the job came first and next time she was to get someone else to do sick duty.

With the worry of her only child's serious illness still fresh in her very cells, Neva had left his office and the building without saying a word. She did not return to work. Ambrose waited three days before calling her at home. Is something wrong? Her anger spent by then, she had told him calmly and precisely what was wrong, from the personal to the universal, from enduring values to changing times—and managed to conclude without screaming No intelligent person should have to be told that kids come before jobs. To Ambrose's credit, he had listened, understood, and soon afterward instituted a new family leave policy.

Since then, their disagreements had been friendly spats resolved through humor. Even now she had not quite shouted, and already felt the anger ebbing—regrettably. The outburst had been a long time coming and she felt terrific.

Ambrose cleared his throat. "Are you writing about Angel?"

Amazed—he was obsessed with the murder, blind and deaf to anything else—Neva was about to turn on her heel and stalk out for the second time in their long working partnership when he continued, "The reason I ask is because you're right. I get carried away, as you know. Write whatever you want." The editor's hands strayed over his desk, lifting papers at random, straightening a stack of Oregon Newspaper Publishers Association newsletters, closing a desk calendar and opening it again.

"Thank you," she said, waiting.

"No need. Is everything all right at home?"

Her laughter erupted as suddenly as the anger. "That's a terrible cliché, Ambrose. Trouble at home! You know my home has been as calm as a mountain monastery since Ethan left."

"It was a bit out of character."

"I didn't even yell."

"You don't have to. That was like anybody else throwing furniture and punching the walls. So what is the deal?"

"If anything, I'm frustrated at having done three good interviews in two days and seeing no way to use them, not without a lot more information. Even the conversation with the great aunt this morning can't be used, not as is anyway, and maybe not at all since it was mainly a plea for his innocence. And though I think it's way too early to condemn anyone for murder, I'm not quite prepared to declare him innocent on the strength of a relative's testimonial."

"Couldn't you let her just speak for herself?"

"She won't do it. She says it wouldn't help. She had the idea that I would take what she said and somehow make it my own, give it some authority. Looks like I'm going to have to write about the damned riverfront again. Don't bother to read it."

"Would you mind just checking in with Frankie, to see if you got anything out of the old lady that he didn't?"

"You really are incorrigible, Ambrose. Next time I will throw furniture. But he'll do fine. She's a lamb."

Before settling down to write, Neva did a quick web search on flagstone patio. She got 167,000 hits, which seemed sufficient for the job. The first two were for rock suppliers, the third and fourth offered "how to" advice, just what she needed. It didn't look too tricky to set flagstones in sand. She sent the simplest, clearest set of directions to the printer, retrieved the two pages, put them into her bag to study later, and got out the meeting notes.

For some time she sat with her hands on the keyboard while nothing happened, not even a whisper of inspiration reaching her brain. The meeting had produced no new information, no surprises, no flamboyant new characters . . . but there had been plenty of human drama: the fiery crowd; the impatient mayor who could barely restrain herself from cutting off speakers who repeated what the last one had said; the exhausted Council members who squirmed in their chairs like preschoolers; the self-righteous woman who herded her six children to the microphone and accused the City of "killing the trees they grew up with. It's stealing part of their childhood, it's a betrayal."

Stealing their childhood! Neva laughed aloud and her fingers began to dance over the keys.

An hour later, she left the building, walked to the Beanery, bought a slice of cold quiche and coffee and carried them one block east to the riverfront. Though she could see only a small bit of river from the bench at the foot of Dolley Avenue, the bench sat in full sun. She could hear the light swoosh of the current along with the muttering of small birds in the underbrush between the bike path and the bank. For a long, lovely moment she sat with her eyes closed and let heat and tranquility seep inward.

The quiche was bacon and cheddar, a bit soggy but she was too hungry to care. She took a bite. As though triggered by this simple act, a heavy crash split the silence. She glanced around but saw nothing that could have made such a sound. Setting the food aside, she stood up for a better look along the bike path. A second crash led her to the left, downriver, to a small platform that extended from the bank to give a view of the water. Braced against the railing that surrounded the platform, she leaned out and looked downstream. About a hundred yards away a small barge was pulled up close to shore, its deck mounded with boulders. A crane mounted on the deck picked up a huge rock, swung it toward the bank and dropped it onto a heap of others just above the water line.

"You could set them down," Neva said into the air.

Surely, that was riprap they were laying?

But it couldn't be. The city wasn't authorized to begin any work on the riverfront yet, not until the park showdown was settled.

The dropped boulder had rolled over several others already in place and though it had stopped it looked precarious, as though it might just roll into the river and disappear. The crane hooks hovered above it, eased down, took hold again, and swung the great rock back to the top of the line. Whatever was going on here, it was a very neat job, though it had ruined her quiet lunch spot.

She was turning away when the door to the crane operator's cab opened. He climbed down a short ladder and walked up the deck to join two fellow bargemen who were already seated near the bow on folding chairs, lunchboxes at their feet.

Relieved, Neva returned to the bench, made short work of the quiche and coffee, then stretched out her legs and closed her eyes. Six lovely months of bright weather lay ahead. Willamette Valley winters could depress a healthy frog but spring was long and exquisite, summer was warm without humidity, and fall was reliably brilliant. It was not a bad bargain as weather goes, especially now when the gray was behind and blue lay ahead.

And in a few weeks she would have a sunny patio to go home to after work. The building instructions called for a rectangular shape but hers would be curving and irregular though she could not yet picture the stone other than it must be a warm color. The website had mentioned slate, quartz and sandstone but she'd have to see and touch the rock to make a decision. There were several landscape rock suppliers in the area, businesses she'd noticed in the past but driven by without particular interest. Where did the bargemen get their rock? There were gravel quarries upriver but it didn't seem likely that those could produce such boulders. When she called Alexandrova or one of the other city engineers to find out what was going on here, she must remember to ask the source of the rock as well.

But that could wait. She was in no hurry to go back indoors. Without opening her eyes, she laced her fingers behind her head and raised her face to the sky.

"Hello," said a voice.

Too drowsy and comfortable to be startled, Neva opened her eyes, blinked at the woman who stood gazing down at her, and replied, "Hello."

Though she was close enough to touch had Neva sat up, the woman gave no sign of awareness that she might be intruding on another's immediate private space. After a long silent moment, she shifted her scrutiny from Neva to the black shoulder bag that sat near her on the bench. "I was thinking of taking your purse."

"There's not much in it, I'm afraid. Mostly scraps of paper with old notes."

"I wouldn't have kept it. Just for a lesson, so you'd be more careful."

"Your bag looks more interesting."

"This thing?" The woman shrugged her left shoulder, which supported a maroon knapsack. "Anyway, it isn't mine."

Tall and large-boned, with alert dark eyes and the clear skin of a girl, she could have passed for almost anything from the shoulders up—businesswoman, artist, homemaker—but from the shoulders down she was unmistakably indigent. The worn jeans, stained nylon jacket, and sport shoes without laces likely came from the free bin at Vina Moses, and she smelled like musty leaves, as though she had risen from the riverbank itself. Earthy and rich, the smell was not unpleasant.

"Nice day, isn't it?" she said.

"Very nice. Why do you think I should be more careful?"

"You weren't watching. You have to watch now. The river used to be a good place but not anymore. I don't stay here now." The woman squatted as though by a campfire and let the knapsack rest on the ground.

"Where do you stay now?"

The woman's shrug suggested lack of interest in the question rather than evasion.

"Do you ever sleep in the park, Azalea Park, I mean?"

"They don't like it at the City. The police want to talk to me but I'm tired of them. They never believe me anyway. I'm just a 51/50 to them. I may be mentally ill but I'm not crazy, only they're too dumb to know the difference."

Neva looked into the woman's calm eyes and smiled with sudden deep interest as she extended her hand. "I'm Jeneva Leopold."

"I can read. I find a paper most days in the trash. I'm Reba Winner." She released Neva's hand, regarded her expectantly for a moment, then said as though prompting, "You're supposed to say, 'You look more like Reba Loser to me.'"

"Is that what usually happens?"

"Often enough. I thought of changing my name to Reba Winsomelosesome but I took pity on the hospital folks and the jail folks. Just think of all that paperwork they have to fill out. With a name ten feet long it would take them all night. Of course, that might be a good thing, keep them from hassling other people for a while. That's what you call quiet heroism. That's me all over, the quiet hero, so quiet nobody even knows. Someday they'll be surprised. Or not."

Rather than reply with her usual quick ease, Neva hesitated, feeling her way. One false step and she would lose this extraordinary woman, she was sure of it. "What's a 51/50?"

"Police for crazy."

"Ah, unbalanced. I see."

"I think it's some legal code number. Out of California, I heard."

"Hmm, interesting." After a silence that was expectant rather than uncomfortable, Neva ventured, "I came down to the river to try to clear my thoughts. I have to go back to the office and finish writing my column for tomorrow. It's about the riverfront project but so far it seems pretty boring."

"That's because you don't know the river. You just go to meetings like everybody else. I went to a writing class at the library one time and they said, 'Write what you know.' It made sense to me."

"I used to know the river, in a way. When my son was little we spent a lot of time at Willamette Park swimming and playing around. But that was years ago."

"The nude beach?"

"Sometimes. It had the best sand."

"It's too late to know the river. They already killed it. They killed Beavis, Half Tom, Little Whitey, Stork, and Meow, and scared off everybody else. That's why I don't sleep down here anymore. All the good company's gone. And now they got Vance, and Angel, too. They think it's just some trees that are threatened, but it's the soul of this town. Believe me, it's nothing to do with trees. Come on, then, if you want to see. If you're not embarrassed to be with me."

Reba Winner started upriver along the bike path before Neva could gather her things but she soon caught up and they walked in silence to the foot of Martha Street. Here a gap in the cottonwoods and willow brush gave a more open view of the water than from most spots along the path. The bank was also visible—and it was heaped with gray boulders. There was no railing here for support but by bracing against an alder trunk, Neva was able to lean out far enough to see thirty yards of new riprap extending upriver. There was no sign of a bank cave-in, no obvious reason for the heavy covering of rock.

"When did they lay down the riprap, do you know?"

"They smashed the beaver house." Reba pointed down the bank. Small branches with pale, chewed tips stuck out from under the tumbled rock at the edge of the water. "Beavis was inside when they did it. I found him and buried him. He was the biggest old buck beaver I ever saw." In addition to killing the beaver, the barge work had driven away three pair of nesting mallards, one pair of mergansers, a great blue heron, and most of the feral cats. Some of the cats had been hit by cars when they fled and one was torn apart by a Doberman. "I buried the pieces. There's one or two cats left but they won't come out anymore, they're scared, and who wouldn't be."

"I had no idea there was so much wildlife close to downtown. Someone told me Vance Fowler also fed the cats down here."

"A lot of us fed them. Did you see those guys on the barge? They call me the cat queen and throw stuff at me, apple cores and other trash. It used to be good people down here. They drank and acted stupid, but they weren't bad people. I never felt unsafe. But now, well, it doesn't matter anymore. I don't care with the cats gone. I don't know why they need so much rock. They have the boulders coming in by barge and the gravel in dump trucks."

"Where are they putting the gravel?"

"That's an interesting question, Jeneva Leopold." Reba raised one fine eyebrow and shrugged her broad shoulders. She pointed to a small level spot halfway down the bank, a few feet above the riprap. "I used to sleep down there, where I could hear the beaver. The only trouble I ever had was cops. They'd shine their lights in my eyes so I couldn't see to get up the bank. I got so I just stuck my arms out when I saw them coming because I knew the handcuffs weren't far behind. But, hey, somebody has to keep them entertained. Seriously, there's not enough crime in Willamette to keep them busy. They thought it was funny to drop me off across town in the middle of the night. I always walked back and sometimes they'd do it again the same night. You see what I mean, I did my part for this community keeping the cops out of trouble. I'm not too 51/50 to figure out how to do that." Her voice had turned playful but her expression as she looked at the river remained unhappy.

"Where do you stay now?"

"Here, there, everywhere, like the cats. Anyway, my life isn't interesting like yours. You have important people to talk to, Jeneva Leopold. You should take my advice and watch out. Watch your bag. I wish somebody would steal this one. My shoulder's getting sore, but I don't guess they'll let him out any time soon."

Neva walked a full block before the homeless woman's last words took proper hold in her brain. *I don't guess they'll let him out any time soon* . . . Was she talking about Vance? Was she carrying Vance Fowler's knapsack around?

Hurrying back to the bike path, she walked up and down calling for the homeless woman in a low voice and peering down into the bank shrubbery, but Reba was not to be found. Irritated with herself for not being more alert in the first place, she started again toward the *Current* but decided to go past the bench where Angel used to hold court, and turned right up Second Street at the post office. The bench, half a block up in front of the main entrance, was visible from the corner, or should have been visible.

Instead of a bench there was a heap of trash, as though one of the city garbage trucks had tipped half its load onto the spot.

And standing in front of the heap with her back to Neva was a young woman.

Walking fast now, Neva studied the girl's back and was quite sure she was the one who had left the rose on the table at Angel's memorial gathering. She took something from her pocket, leaned forward—adding it to the heap, it appeared—then stepped onto a skateboard and sped away.

"Hello!" Neva shouted after her. "Wait, please."

But the clattering wheels must have drowned out her words for the girl did not slow down, glance back or give any sign of having heard. It was probably just as well—what could she have said to the girl apart from Tell me about Angel, the sort of open-ended question that rarely yielded interesting answers.

In the next instant, she forgot the girl and simply gazed in amazement at the buried bench. It was not heaped with trash; it had become a shrine.

The centerpiece was the framed picture of the murdered man that had stood on the table at the church. Around it were piled such a miscellany of weird objects that she took out her notebook and began to list them: three plaster saints, daffodils in a spaghetti sauce jar, new socks still in the package, a striped blanket, a 40-ounce can of Lucky Lager Beer, a pack of Old Gold cigarettes, York peppermint patties, a coffee can full of marbles and buttons, an incense burner with a half-burned stick, a balloon animal that could have been a dog or a horse, a fire-blackened coffee pot, a stack of comic books held together with rubber bands, a plush elephant with rhinestone eyes, a basketball covered in scrawled signatures, a copy of the *Current* story about the memorial service with hearts drawn around it, a toy shopping cart half-covered in stick-on silver stars—and at the end of the bench, the real shopping cart, Angel's "chrome Cadillac" glinting with stars made of gum wrapper silver.

Neva put away her notebook after listing a dozen offerings but continued to study the motley assemblage. The beer, cigarettes, mints and socks must be coveted by other street people but had not been touched. Which of the small objects had the girl left, the smooth stone, the whistle of carved bone, the lone gold hoop earring?

It really was extraordinary, not just the number and variety of offerings but that they'd been allowed to remain here. Willamette was a tidy town, with strong feelings about clear sidewalks. This sort of obstructive jumble would generally not be tolerated, especially on public property. For that matter, it was remarkable that Angel's own presence here on the post office bench had been allowed to go on and on.

Some, at least, of the post office workers must have got to know him, maybe even know him well. Neva turned, ran lightly up the steps, and got in line for a window. As the line edged past the rack of supplies, she chose a manila envelope. Four of the six postal windows were open for business, with the usual familiar faces at their usual spots. The one she wanted was at the far window. For a moment it appeared that luck was with her, that he would be free just as she reached the head of the line, but then his customer remembered a further need and a different window came open. Neva waved the woman behind her to go ahead.

Tom's customer completed his business and Neva hurried to take her place. She had known Tom for years, known him, that is, as well as it's possible to know someone you see once a month for five minutes while stamps are bought, parcels weighed, packaging jobs tidied up with stout tape. His first name was on his shirt or she would not know even this about him. As she approached the window, he glanced up and favored her with the usual grin. Most people do not truly grin. Tom was one of the few who could be counted on to produce that good-humored stretch of the mouth that was not really a smile so much as a trademark signal that no matter how long the line might grow, at Christmas say, or on tax day, he would not be rushed or impatient. He would grin and say, "Hey, how's it going?"

"Well enough." She placed the envelope on the counter. "Just buying this. Amazing monument you've got out front."

"Isn't it something." He glanced at the sticker on the back of the envelope and tapped the price into the keyboard. Compact and round-headed apart from the flattop haircut that hadn't changed in twenty years, he gave the impression of just passing through, of having been called in to work only for the day, of knowing that tomorrow he would be out hiking again, or throwing a stick into the waves for his dog.

"I'm impressed that they're letting it block the sidewalk. Where's the good old paranoia about lawsuits gone?"

Tom's chuckle was followed by a sorrowful headshake. "Angel was like family. Not your usual panhandler."

"Could you add a sheet of stamps to that and let me see what you've got, please. Did you know him very well, talk to him much?"

"Oh, sure. Everybody talked to him. Like I said, he wasn't the usual panhandler we get outside the doors here. Come to that, he wasn't really a panhandler at all even though lots of people gave him money. He turned around and gave it to the next guy." Tom took a sheaf of stamps from a drawer and spread them on the counter. "Flowers, flags, cancer, presidents, bugs, sea creatures."

"I hate to admit it, but I'd barely noticed him out there." Neva picked up the sheet of flower stamps, studied it for a moment, put it down. "Some people say he wasn't such a nice guy after all."

"Who is truly nice in this world? He had a great shtick. Kids loved him, and you know how it is—if kids and dogs like you, hey, you must be okay."

"Too true. I think I'll take the bugs this time." Surely, after two years, it was okay to go for something other than breast cancer stamps. "Sounds like you saw through him though, saw something else there."

Tom accepted the twenty dollar bill and half-turned to make change. "If you're writing about Angel, all I can say is good luck. I guess I knew him as well as anybody here, and what I can tell you for sure is he never said a mean word about anybody, even the cops, not that they gave him any trouble. Promise not to give us away if I tell you something else? It's just, you know, Angel hardly got any mail, but when he did, like his disability check, one of us delivered it to him."

He paused to enjoy Neva's expectant look, then concluded. "We delivered it to him—to the bench. You want to bet that was the only regular postal delivery to a sidewalk bench in the whole friggin' country?"

Back at her desk once more, Neva made a note of Tom's charming confession. It was too good to let go. Somewhere, somehow, it would provide a lovely detail and, when the time came, she'd deal with his request to keep it under her hat.

She also jotted down two pages of notes about Reba Winner while the encounter was still fresh.

Next she dialed the city engineer's office but Alexandrova didn't answer, and Neva clicked off before the recorded message came on. Anyone in the department should be able to answer her simple question. She dialed the main office and was connected to a cheerful young man who explained that the two sections of riprap were emergency measures to shore up damaged slopes, and that no more would be done until the park dispute was settled.

"Can I fax you the relevant page from the City Council packet?" he offered as though proffering treats.

"No thank you—actually, on second thought, sure, please send it over."

Unable to put it off longer, she returned to her draft of the riverfront column. The riprap provided a paragraph of new information, though it did nothing to add life, and she wasn't willing to use any of Reba's comments piecemeal. Deadline came and went. With her fingers resting on the keyboard, she sat on, unable to send the column to the copy desk without some spark in it.

You don't know the river . . . Was this how Reba had put it?

Most of us live for years on the banks of the Willamette without really knowing it as a river, she typed. We pedal along the bike path, drive over the bridges, and run the water out of our taps by the gallon. But we don't know the river the way the beaver knows it, or the heron, or those few souls who canoe or bird-watch at dawn, or even those who, for whatever reason, end up homeless and camped on the river's edge.

Her fingers moved as though on their own until she had three new lead paragraphs. She read the whole column through, sent it on to the copy desk for a headline, stood up and stretched toward the ceiling, then bent at the hips to rest her hands on the floor. Gravity tugged at her head and her spine opened like a string of boxcars pulled from both ends. She drew and released a long, blissful breath.

As usual after submitting a column she felt physically lighter, with an opulent sense of time lying open ahead. Her next deadline was two full days distant, an age. Before checking for calls that might have been diverted to the message center while she was writing, she opened the telephone book and found the landscape supply section. There were a dozen listings but only two in town that advertised decorative rock, Herman's Hardscape, and Riverearth Stone. She dialed Herman's Hardscape.

"Yellow?" a man's voice rasped as though gargling gravel. "You want yellow you say? You won't find any rock that's yellow, not the whole thing. You have your quartzite in a range of colors from gray to green to red, with some yellow and gold in. You said it's for a patio? Desert colors, you said? Well, the best thing is to come on out and look at it. I do have one called Lone Pine Gold that might do the job for you."

Lone Pine Gold! She had a great feeling about this.

"I'll be out soon to take a look," she said, and stood up as she set the phone down, ready to rush straight to the rockery—messages be damned.

But self-discipline won out over impulse, forcing her to sit down once more and dial the retrieval code. There were six new messages. Only one was of interest, and at first she listened without hearing the individual words, struck by the warm, musical quality of the voice, a trained voice, surely, meant for music, radio, or stage. She found a pen and hit replay.

"This is Carter Grey speaking. We've never met but I'm a faithful reader. I won't say I always agree with you, but you do get my blood moving in the morning, and at my age that's a gift. I recently opened Winton & Grey Fine Antique Prints on Second Street which, as you would know, is just a block from the riverfront. Naturally, I have become interested in the riverfront park issue. I've appreciated your columns on the situation and just wanted to put a bee in your bonnet. Have you looked into the insurance question? I've heard from reliable sources that the riverbank work is being driven by insurance requirements. In other words, they want to put some four-story buildings on the west side of First Street but they've been told by insurance folks that the costs for coverage will go through the roof if they don't do the whole stabilization scenario, stripping off all the trees and laying down that appalling geofabric or geotextile or whatever it's called, plus riprap and the rest of it. That would explain the City's stubbornness on this issue, wouldn't it?

Frankly, I haven't heard any other explanation that really makes sense. Feel free to call me, but that's really all I had to say, and I'm sure you can take it from here."

Grey ended with his telephone number. She called back immediately and left a message in turn, and had just hung up when a quick rap sounded on the half-open door.

"You beat me to Great Aunt Wygelia," Frankie said, frankly accusatory. "I thought you said you weren't writing about Angel."

"Sit down, Youth." With a smile of welcome, Neva waved at the small armchair in the corner and watched with amusement as the young man inserted his lanky frame into it. His scratchy voice made him sound even younger than he looked, and the way his hands dangled from long arms reinforced the impression of a kid just off the farm.

"Investigations not going well?" she asked with genuine sympathy. It had been many years since she had to chase ambulances or dance to an editor's tune but the memory remained potent.

"I'm running like a scared chicken but even with Ambrose hot on my tail there's not much to show for it. He said you talked to the old lady already. What did you get out of her?"

"Some yummy lemon bars and truly sad history. She says her Vance was a good boy with bad luck, who was misunderstood and tormented. She was emphatic about his innocence, and frankly, I'm inclined to believe her. What did you get?"

"The door in my face."

"Not from Wygelia! She's a lamb."

"The devil's own. She said how come there wasn't even a notice on the back page when he saved Angel's life but now the paper had sent two people in one day because of the arrest for a murder he didn't do. Then I got the door in my face. I was so pissed off I went over to see if the neighbor could tell me anything. Another old lady was sitting on the porch, but you'd never guess she's related to Wygelia. She'd be a sure bet for burning at the stake, to look at anyway, but she was really nice."

"How is she related to Wygelia?"

"They're sisters. She's Fowler's grandmother."

"Why was he raised by his great aunt?"

"Granny didn't want him. She said he's the worst little shit that ever drew breath, and if she'd had her way he would have been stuffed in a sack and drowned."

"You call that nice?"

"She was nice to me. But wait, that's not all. She said she hopes he's convicted before those bleeding-heart sapheads get rid of the death penalty. She wanted to know what you were snooping around for. She said, and this is word for word, 'Tell Jeneva Leopold this—if she wants the real story I'll give it to her for five hundred dollars.'"

"Do you think I could claim it as a business expense?"

"You aren't going to play along with her!"

"Wouldn't you be tempted? Come on, Frankie, where's your curiosity? It's cheaper than a weekend in San Francisco and sure to be great theater."

"If I didn't know better I'd believe you. Anyway, you'll probably talk her out of it for free."

"I'll do my best. Any other goodies?"

"Not from granny, but Marcum was pretty helpful, for a change. Vance has a record going back to middle school. Marcum actually volunteered that."

"Record for what?"

"It sounds like a bit of everything. I'm headed over to get the details."

"Wygelia said he's been arrested a few times but only for sleeping out where he's not wanted."

"There must be more than that. Marcum was really worked up. He said Angel was a prince among beggars and he'd still be alive if we had a decent jail. He almost said straight out that your columns killed Angel. What do you think of that? He said it's your fault that everybody rejected the first jail bond, and Angel's death should give them a more realistic view."

"If my columns have the power to kill, I'm going to insist on combat pay. Really, Frankie, that's too weird."

"Actually, I'm not sure what he meant."

"No doubt he was referring to the second suspect, Ernold Quick, who was let out of jail because it was too crowded. On the day Angel died, as it happens. I told you there was a second suspect, remember? Are they still keeping that quiet?"

Frankie's headshake was glum. "And here I thought he was being cooperative. I don't know why I bother. I'm the one on the cop beat and I've done my best to get their trust, all of them, from the sheriff down to the dispatchers, but they still play cat and mouse with me. If you hadn't told me I wouldn't even know there was a second suspect, and they wouldn't give me his name when I asked. I didn't know you had his name already. You didn't mention that before. How do you rate?"

"I don't rate, not with the police. I had Quick's name already when I went to see Captain Oleander. As you know, information draws information, and of course you always pretend to know more than you do. Oleander asked me to keep Quick's name quiet for the time being, but you should know, especially if Marcum's trying to link Vance

Fowler with the jail bond situation. It was Quick who was let out of jail the day Angel died, not Fowler."

"They must think I'm a moron, that I'll swallow any old bait."

"Don't be discouraged, Frankie. You're a good reporter. The only thing you don't have that I do is nearly twenty years of building a loyal readership that loves nothing better than to tell me what's really going on. This is invaluable even when they're wrong, which is at least half the time."

"You don't think they could have arranged the whole thing to make the point about the jail? It's ridiculous, I know. I wouldn't mention it to anyone else, but you've reminded me often enough that truth is stranger than anything we could invent."

Neva looked at her young colleague thoughtfully. Could he have hit on something? But it was unthinkable that an assistant police chief in a small Oregon city would engineer a murder in order to win a new jail, and even if it weren't unthinkable, he never would employ street people for the job, or try to pin it on a street person. She said, "Not in this case, I think."

"Marcum also said it's one of the cleanest murder cases he's ever seen. He said the D.A. will have an easy job of it, with the Dari-Mart video and everything. You know Angel was an honors student before he dropped out of high school down in Arizona? The family tried hard to get him off the streets, but he didn't want help. Ambrose seems to think this is Pulitzer material and maybe he's right, but so far it looks like nothing except a nasty street crime that wouldn't get anybody's attention in Seattle or even Portland. Unless you've got some other ideas?"

"But when she got there, the cupboard was bare."

Frankie's laugh was closer to a giggle than a manly chuckle. He soon left the office looking almost cheerful again, and Neva was about to follow when she noticed the stack of letters in her in-basket. She had not read her regular mail for several days, in fact, had got into a bad habit of letting it go since most of the interesting stuff now came in by email. But it would be a serious mistake to grow too indifferent to the regular post—in this business, the message or phone call you miss is bound to be the one with the tip to end all tips.

Sorting rapidly through the stack, she winnowed out bulk mail and business envelopes. This left five proper, hand-addressed envelopes from actual humans. Four were notes from readers responding to specific columns, which she scanned and put aside to read more carefully when it came time to do her periodic column on reader comments. The fifth envelope lacked a stamp or postage mark, which meant it had been delivered by hand to the mailbox beside the front door. This had been fairly common before email took hold, but now most correspondents who were in a hurry used the computer.

The envelope was addressed in printed block letters to Ms. J. Leopold, *Willamette Current*. The return address said only "A Friend." Folded inside was a single sheet of white paper, a photocopy of a memo on police department letterhead.

The handwritten memo was brief: "Kitty, The situation seems to be going as hoped, despite JL sticking her nose in. I'm taking steps to deal with possible bad press. Don't worry, the thing's tight. This is one round we're going to win. G"

Stuck to the page below the memo was a pink Post-It bearing a note scrawled in green ink: "I thought you should see this. 'G' is Gale Marcum. You won't have to guess who JL is. Please keep this to yourself as I could get in BIG trouble."

The note was not signed.

Chapter Five

How she got out of the building without anyone noticing her expression she didn't know, but she cursed all the way across the parking lot, slammed the car door, and slapped the steering wheel furiously.
Hell!
Goddamn double hell!
What a fool she was. What a damned stupid fool—to think she'd actually believed in the possibility of trust between the news and the law!
She had truly believed Kitty Fiori was a friend.
A friend!
Angry blood scorched her face and back. She threw open the door, slammed it again, opened the window, then got out and paced up the parking lot. How many times had she been fooled? How many times had the chief pretended to cooperate while scheming in secret? How many notes like this one had been passed around the cop shop while she went smugly on her way believing whatever story she'd been fed?
It didn't matter that Kitty hadn't written the note. Assistant Chief Gale Marcum had done that, and he was clearly masterminding whatever game was afoot, but the chief must have full knowledge of it, must have approved and agreed that JL who was *sticking her nose in* was a nuisance and should be stonewalled and deceived along with the rest of the press.
For years, ever since Fiori was hired to bring Willamette's good ol' boy police department into the modern age, Neva had supported the chief, had nurtured what she believed to be mutual trust and regard, had stood by her through tough times. Against the howls of paunchy patrolmen in love with cushy cars, she had backed the chief's campaign for increased officer fitness training and neighborhood bicycle patrols. She had sent flowers to Kitty's hospital room following knee surgery, and had met her for drinks to talk over community issues, always convivially.
It was Kitty she cared about, not Marcum, and Kitty was going to hear about this, right now. The thing must be dealt with openly . . . but

how to account for having the note in her possession? The anonymous friend who had passed it along must work in the department, and had asked her to be discreet. She could not confront the chief without showing the memo, and then it would be easy work to find the leak. Somehow, she had to devise a way to challenge the chief on the facts of the situation without exposing her informant, which probably meant not revealing that she had the note. She must think of some other means by which she could have heard that they were plotting to keep her in the dark, a rumor maybe, or someone having overheard a conversation in the hall.

Her head was shaking even as she cast about for plausible explanations. She couldn't do this. She could not put on such a false face to Fiori or anyone else, no matter the circumstances. She could not play such games no matter that the chief was conspiring to cast her as a busybody, accusing her of *sticking her nose in . . .JL is sticking her nose in. . . sticking her nosy nose in . . .* Neva stopped suddenly, threw her head back, and laughed.

Of course she stuck her nose in. This was her job description. Her nose was her main asset, her tool, her passport, even her privilege. Her nose led her anywhere and everywhere, invited and uninvited. Yes, indeed, she was a Nosey Parker of the first order and now, thanks to the memo, she would do her utmost to stick her nose into the Angel de Silva situation as far as it would go.

But "bad press" was another subject altogether. The only truly bad press is inaccurate press and accuracy was her holy creed. To describe the kind of writing she did about community issues as "bad press" was a shot across the bow she could not ignore.

No doubt Marcum was behind the whole mess. Since he had joined the department five years ago, she had not liked or trusted him. Now, it appeared, her instincts had proven sound. Marcum was a schemer who clearly returned her dislike and distrust.

But what were he and the police chief up to? *Don't worry, the thing's tight. This is one round we're going to win.* They would know about her conversation with Oleander, of course, and something about it must have sparked a defensive reaction . . . or was this all about the jail bond? But then *bad press* would make no sense. The press, at least in the form of her columns, had already been about as bad as it could be. No chance now to stave off "possible bad press" about the jail. The first bond measure had been put forward already and lost.

Something must be done, she must take some action and she had to do it immediately or she'd lie awake all night fuming.

With no idea yet what she might do or say, she returned to the car, drove up Sixth Street and cruised past the law enforcement building. Looking hard at the ugly concrete wall that faced the street, she was struck by a revelation: she and the police chief did not live in the same town. The chief's office was buried deep in that mausoleum, secured behind walls that could withstand a small bomb and that stood between her and the people of Willamette. Neva's working world was out here, on the streets, in the parks, the businesses, the schools and private homes. Chief Fiori's main stock in trade was bad behavior. Neva wrote mainly about the good, the humorous, and the endearingly quirky.

Both she and the chief were deluded, no doubt. The true picture of the community must lie somewhere between their views.

Speculating, she continued to drive and soon found herself crossing the bridge that led out of town toward the east—the road to Herman's Hardscape. Well, she would soothe her riled feelings by looking at flagstone and then decide what to do for the evening.

The small parking area at Herman's was empty. She pulled into a spot next to the prefab hut that housed the office but she did not go inside. The rocks drew her straight out to the gravel flat covered in bins and stacked pallets. Huge slabs of rose sandstone stood upright like vinyl records in a rack. Wire hoops were stacked full of ledge stone in red, brown, ochre, and white. A wooden crate divided into compartments gleamed with polished green and white rocks from China. Cobblestones, tumbled stones, naturally polished river rock, turquoise flakes, decomposed granite, red and black basalt. . . And then there were the wonderful names: glacier green, sockeye, Pennsylvania bluestone, New Mexico buff, Molalla, camas, three rivers, bitterroot, Mt. Moriah, chocolate charcoal, gold rush, limelight. And here, shining under the pale spring sun, was the Lone Pine Gold that "might do the job."

Even without Herman's suggestion Neva would have stopped at this pile. The step stones were two inches thick and colored like the quartz in the Dry River hills of eastern Oregon. Yellow, gold, orange, rust, cream, white, and silver, with many of the silver pieces sparkling with mica. The stone was warm to the eye and the hand. In summer it would sparkle, in winter it would glow like wet sunshine.

Standing with both hands flat on a trapezoidal yellow stone two feet across, Neva said, "Yes!"

It was nearly six when she left Herman's Hardscape elated and hungry. Five yards—twelve thousand pounds—of river sand would be delivered to the house on Friday. Once she cleared and leveled the patio site, she would cover it with sand, pack the sand down hard, then return here to choose her flagstones rock by rock, picking out the yellow and leaving the silver and gray apart from the occasional contrast piece.

"Like the yellow, do you?" Herman had mused. He was a small man, compact, weathered, wearing a cap with the ear flaps down despite the balmy late afternoon.

"Love the yellow ones."

"Most people prefer the gray."

"Gray's the color we need to get away from around here."

Herman shrugged and spit sideways onto the gravel. "Each his own, I say."

"Great, then I won't feel guilty taking the yellow."

"Guilty? You're payin' for it just the same."

A crusty character for sure, but she'd win him over. She'd woo him when she came back to pick out her rocks, and she'd bet there was a column in it. There was a good story somewhere under that crust.

An hour of daylight remained, an hour that could be put to good use clearing ivy, but she was hungry and suddenly longed for a delicious, leisurely meal in some new and interesting place, ideally shared with a comfortable friend. Driving slowly back toward town she ran through a mental list of friends who might be willing to join her for dinner, but every single one, male and female, had partners, children, dogs, and other complications. They could not simply get a telephone call, put on a jacket and walk out the door for a meal.

Well, she would eat alone, and the obvious spot was Willamette's only new restaurant, *Au Courant, Fine French/Northwest/Asian Cuisine*, at the south end of First Street. The first of many restaurants that were expected to follow once the riverfront makeover was done, *Au Courant* occupied half the ground floor of what had been the town's earliest farm supply store, and would soon be a warren of shops and eateries. For now, the restaurant was the only tenant of the newly restored brick building.

It was early yet for dinner and she found a parking spot a few steps from the door, and inside, a nice corner table that let her face the room.

Two nearby tables soon filled with familiar faces, not friends but people she knew well enough to exchange a few pleasantries before they all settled to the business of ordering. She had got as far as the baked scallops with spicy kimchee, ikura, kobayaki, and truffle oil, with shichimi togareshi/beurre blanc appetizer—she made notes to look it all up later rather than ask the waiter; more fun to see how much she could figure out simply by tasting—when a second waiter arrived with a bottle of wine. Before she could explain that she had not ordered it and wanted only a glass, he nodded toward the two elderly couples sitting to her right and said, "Compliments of the next table." One of the couples had lived up the street from her years ago, and the other had owned the main toy store in town before retiring. With regret, she addressed the other table: *Thank you thank you, but she could not possibly accept the gift as this was against newspaper policy.* Followed by the usual sort of exchange: *Nothing to do with the newspaper, just an expression of personal appreciation/ But it's too much for one person/ Drink what you want and take the rest home/ Won't you share it with me?/ We've ordered the same for us/ You're really too kind/ Our pleasure.*

She had learned when it was futile and even rude to protest too far, and once that obligatory point was passed, she was delighted with the gift, a rich Merlot she would have ruled out as too heavy. Tonight it was perfect, deeply warming and restorative. The temptation to slip the waiter a special dessert order for the other table was only fleeting—as her Great Aunt Elizabeth Dewar had gently insisted, *Knowing how to receive gracefully is as important as knowing how to give.*

Knowing when to stop eating and drinking was another matter. It was full dark when she left *Au Courant*, having behaved herself by ordering the splendid appetizer, a simple salad, and a New York steak, without the port deglazing. "Nothing but the meat," she had said, "rare and preferably fatty." All would have been well, even splendid, had she not poured that second glass of Merlot and been bowled over by the dessert menu, which included the dangerous option of a "taste" of all six multi-layered and much-frosted-and-creamed offerings. The "tastes" being clearly meant for heroic folk, she had risen mightily to the occasion and should now be lying down.

Instead, she was out on the sidewalk with the half bottle of wine stuck in her shoulder bag and bumping against her hip. Breathing deeply, feeling better after opening her belt a notch, she set off to walk a few blocks in the hope of further revival. First she went toward the south end of town but turned after a few paces and headed in the opposite direction, away from the knots of smokers clustered outside Mad Molly's, the lone bar on the riverfront. Ahead, up First Street toward Lyle's warehouse, all was tranquil, the few street lamps spotlighting the blank faces of old buildings awaiting their turn to be sawed, hammered, plastered and painted into new respectability.

She had no plan, certainly no intention of visiting the gardener, though thinking about Lyle McRae reminded her of the police memo she had managed to put out of her thoughts all evening. Fresh irritation quickened her step. Maybe she should call Kitty tonight, from home. They could talk it out woman to woman—but just what "situation" was it that Marcum claimed to have under control? If she could puzzle that out it might give her some leverage for confronting the police chief. And she still had not thought of a way to broach the subject to Fiori while also protecting her source.

The sidewalk ahead was deserted, though across the street a couple strolled along the bike path. As she glanced that way, the pair passed from the shadows into the range of a streetlight. They were not a couple, but two men, one strikingly tall. The tall one stumbled, bumping into his stocky companion, and in the next moment both men lurched out of sight into the shrubbery on the river side of the path. There was no trail down to the water at that spot, nothing but a steep bank. Braced for the sound of crashing bodies, Neva heard only a light clatter of rocks.

Were these some of Reba's "good people" looking for a place to sleep where they would not be rousted out and deported across town? The night was not cold but neither was it warm, and the ground would be damp. She would not want to sleep outdoors on the riverfront—or even in Lyle's warehouse, jungle or no jungle. The closest streetlamp was on the corner and the light bulb must be failing because the front of the warehouse was a dark wall, the door a black rectangle. Neva stopped in front of it, then felt for the lock.

The lock was gone. As she fumbled for the hasp to see whether it was off the staple, her hand touched the door and it swung open into darkness as black and dense as wet asphalt. Air flowed around her as it had the first time, but now the flow was into the warehouse rather than out.

"Lyle?"

Gripping the doorjamb on both sides, she leaned inward to look toward the stairs. As before, mild greenish light illuminated the top steps, though now it had to be from a lamp shining through leaves rather than from the windows.

"Lyle?" she called, louder this time. "It's me, Neva."

There was no answer but she was not surprised. Lyle would be out in the park tending his bulbs, though why he had left the lock off the door and the hasp off the staple was a puzzle.

Feeling in her bag, she located the small flashlight that had once been attached to her key chain and played the narrow beam over the plank floor and pillars that were close enough to see. They were just as she remembered. She closed and latched the door, hesitated, then continued up the sidewalk, turned left at the corner, and walked to the mouth of the alley that ran behind the warehouse. The alley was darker than the street, not a place she cared to walk, but the flashlight beam was strong enough to pick out a narrow back door with a dumpster beyond it.

Unlike the solid front of the warehouse, the rear wall was softly lighted along the second floor by the bank of greenhouse windows, though Lyle's apartment windows just above her were dark. As she stared upward, wondering what sort of home the gardener would have made for himself in this deserted corner of the old downtown, a light flickered within. She exclaimed, then laughed softly. Of course, it had been the beam from her own flashlight, which she had turned upward without thinking.

Nonetheless, a sudden feeling of discomfort, of being in the wrong place, made her walk briskly back around the corner. Dinner had been perfect, the walk had done its job of settling the heavy meal, and now she was ready for home and bed.

In the morning she would decide what to do about the memo—Lyle's door was hanging open again! Standing in front of the black opening she looked up and down the sidewalk. Not a person in sight. The door had been closed securely, no question about it. She had pulled it tight against the frame and pressed the latch into place, then tested it with a gentle push as she had learned to do growing up in old houses with sloppy hardware.

No sudden gust could have blown it open, and there had been no gusts, in any case. The air was still, the street quiet apart from the mild whoosh of traffic on the bridge two blocks downriver.

"Lyle!"

This time she shouted the gardener's name, pitching her voice toward the rear of the warehouse. "Lyle, are you there? It's Neva Leopold."

There was only silence in reply.

She called again and as though in answer, the night was rent by the wail of a siren. A car squealed around the corner and slammed to a stop at the curb. Two officers leaped out and pinned her with their flashlight beams.

"Where is he?" An officer barked as a second car sped around the corner.

"What are you doing here?" A voice demanded close beside her. "Did you call 911?"

"I can't see." Neva held her hands in front of her face and shut her eyes. "Take your lights away."

The lights were withdrawn, someone said, "Sorry," and she found that she was surrounded by police officers.

"I'm Jeneva Leopold. Is there a problem?"

"Maybe you should tell us," a pugnacious young woman said in fine gangster-movie style.

"It's all right. Hello, Jeneva," said a familiar man's voice.

It was Assistant Chief Gale Marcum, speaking as genially as though they were meeting at a party and he'd never in his lifetime written a rude memo about her. "Sorry about all this, but we've had a report of a homicide at this warehouse."

"Oh, Christ!" She started for the door.

Marcum stepped in front of her. "You know who's in there?"

"Lyle McRae. It's his place, his garden."

"Sorry, you can't go in." He turned to address the policewoman. "Better get on with it."

The woman spoke in an undertone to the officers around her and then things happened fast. Several circled around back, one stood at the door, two went inside shining powerful lights ahead of them and two others followed with drawn handguns.

"I suppose you have a reason to be here." Marcum studied the bottle protruding from her bag. "We'll need a statement."

"There's nothing to state. I had dinner at the new restaurant down the street and then walked up this way. When I passed here, the door was closed. When I came back a few minutes later the door was open. Then you arrived."

A car shot up First Street and slid to a halt at the curb pointing the wrong direction. Out leaped reporter Shawna Deagan and photographer Kelly Redpath. Neva closed her eyes. The newsroom scanner, of course. They had heard it on the scanner. Now she would have some real explaining to do.

Half an hour later, driving home through empty streets, Neva began to shiver violently and pulled over to sit with the heater blasting and her head on the steering wheel. She must not think about it now. She must get home. She would take a very hot shower and drink whiskey, a lot of whiskey, fast. She would not think about it now. She would sleep and think in the morning.

A sudden pounding on the car made her look up sharply. A pale face hung in the passenger's side window. She shuddered, closed her eyes, then opened the window.

"Hey,' Reba said when the window was only half down. "Sorry to scare you. I didn't think I was that scary."

"No, no, it's not you. I've just had a shock, a terrible shock. Please, get in."

"I don't need a ride."

"Just get in. I don't want to talk through the window."

Reba got in awkwardly, hunching as though not used to small spaces. "What's the matter, anyway? You look sick. It's hot in here."

"There's been another death, another murder. Tonight, just now."

"You were there!"

"No, not there, I mean not exactly. I was outside the warehouse, Lyle McRae's warehouse. You must know Lyle."

"He wouldn't kill anybody."

"No, it was Lyle who died, Lyle was killed. In his greenhouse."

"I'll have to feed his cats."

"Cats?"

"There are two in the alley, a little Manx girl and a Kleinfelter male. I can probably find a home for him. They're rare you know, the calico males."

"Are they?" Neva studied the calm profile that stood out clearly against the glow of the streetlight on the opposite sidewalk. A man had been murdered, a man Reba knew, yet she showed no reaction to the news apart from concern about the cats.

"Did you find him?" The homeless asked as though requesting a match.

"No, I was just there by coincidence, walking by, walking up the street. I'd had dinner at a restaurant, that new place. I needed some air."

"What did you eat?"

"Eat? You want to know what I ate? Really, Reba, I'm sorry, I can't think about that, about food, right now. You said I look sick and you were right. I've got to get home. Where are you going?"

"To Bald Hill Park, if you have to know."

"Is that where you're sleeping?"

"Sometimes. At least they don't have patrols out there."

"I can take you, but why don't you stay at my house tonight? I have a spare room ready to go. I hate the thought of you sleeping out tonight."

"It's no different from any other night. Not for me. I'm not going to get killed, if that's what you mean, Jeneva Leopold. I'm not worth the trouble of killing, you know."

"Oh, for heaven's sake, Reba!"

"No kidding. Anyway, I wouldn't mind staying with you but not when there's trouble. That's a waste, isn't it? I don't get to visit people very often and I'd rather do it right. He was a good gardener."

Chapter Six

They have killed a beautiful thing...
Neva woke with the words in her mind and wondered at them, repeating them in thought as she listened to the jays in some early morning squabble outside the window. Something beautiful. What had she been dreaming—the greenhouse. The gardener, Lyle McRae, dead. It had happened, the thing he predicted, the thing she had not really believed. She had not believed him and now he was dead, murdered in the lovely greenhouse.

And her head hurt, it hurt terribly. The pale morning light seared the inside of her skull. The whiskey had done its job, had put her to sleep and kept her there until dawn, but now it would make her suffer for the favor. She couldn't think and wouldn't think until after coffee. She felt for slippers with her feet, pulled on her robe, eased down the stairs one step at a time. On the front porch she stooped with care to collect the newspaper and carried it to the kitchen still folded.

She never opened the *Current* before coffee, and today, in particular, she needed to be prepared. She already knew the worst, but headlines and pictures deal blows of a specific kind. A name, a face, a few words summing up horror. It was a form of hyper-reality, a direct shot at the heart, concentrated, focused, irrefutable.

Letting the water run to clear the taste of old pipes, she squinted against the bright morning light that was usually one of the best things about the kitchen. She set the kettle on the burner, reached for the jar of coffee beans, and swore softly. The jar was empty. This was so rare, so unlike her to run out of roasted beans, that she stood for some time looking stupidly at nothing before turning off the burner and heading resignedly down the basement stairs. Roasting beans required less than ten minutes, including the cool-down at the end, but no task should have to be done before coffee, especially today.

The roaster sat on the workbench amid a scattering of papery chaff that had escaped the filter basket on top. Small sacks of green beans lay about. She reached first for the new Guatemalan beans but decided instead on the reliable Yirgacheffe. Three scoops into the small glass roasting chamber, filter top in place, turn on heat dial, stare at dancing beans . . . With sudden decision she turned back to the stairs, climbed carefully to the kitchen, and opened the newspaper.

Gardener strangled in warehouse.

Under the banner headline were two color photos, one of a covered body being carried by emergency personnel, the other of a young Lyle McRae with a mustache and a fringe of red bangs. The story was brief and dry and said nothing about her—mercifully, Ambrose had accepted the argument that she should not be mentioned. The story included only two bits of new information, but one was a dilly. Three years ago, Lyle McRae had won two million dollars in the Oregon lottery.

Lyle McRae a millionaire?

It could not be true.

It must be true. Reporters make plenty of errors, but not errors concerning major public facts like this one, information that could easily be verified. Lyle was wealthy . . . or had been wealthy in the recent past. Surely, a man who could afford to live anywhere would not choose an old warehouse, even one with a jungle, for he could have recreated that in a magnificent glass house on his own grounds. And certainly a man who could afford to flee would not stick around town if he feared for his life. Maybe she had misunderstood and he did not live at the warehouse, but used the apartment only casually, as needed, though it was also true that money can't change nature. A solitary eccentric is likely to remain a solitary eccentric regardless of sudden riches.

The money would explain one thing—how he could afford to garden for the City without being on the payroll.

The other new bit was that the anonymous 911 call had been traced to a downtown telephone booth and was made at 9:14. McRae had been dead for less than an hour when police arrived at 9:45. Neva had left the restaurant somewhat after nine. This meant that McRae had been killed just before she got to the warehouse or while she was standing outside.

A sudden smell of smoke reached the kitchen. Neva dropped the paper and dashed down the stairs. She turned off the roaster and ran back upstairs carrying the small roasting chamber. The back door stuck, as usual. She yanked it open and flung the charred beans into the flowerbed. Leaving the door open for a draft, she descended back into the smoke, measured three scoops of fresh beans, and stood with one hand against the side of her throbbing head as she waited for the beans to darken.

When at last the coffee was roasted, ground, and drip-brewed, she settled at the kitchen table and drank half a cup, slowly, before looking again at the newspaper. Using the notebook and pen that were always lying ready on the table, she made a time-line of the events at the warehouse as described in the story. It was true, no way to dodge—if she had resisted the dessert menu and left the restaurant half an hour earlier, she might have saved the gardener simply by her presence, by knocking on the door and shouting into the cavernous interior. As it was, the killer had very likely been looking out at her from that silent darkness as she peered in, calling Lyle's name.

Lyle McRae was not just a paranoid nutcase. His cry for help had been real and warranted, and she had failed him as thoroughly as it's possible to fail a fellow human being.

The new killing had pushed the Angel stories below the fold, including the one about his childhood in Arizona. Frankie's story about Vance Fowler jumped to Page 5 after the third paragraph, and was thin thanks to Wygelia's refusal to cooperate. Frankie had, however, tracked down two of Fowler's former teachers who managed to appear discreet while making it clear that no one had expected anything good of the boy. "You can lead a horse to water but you can't make him drink," one teacher had said, thereby settling blame neatly on Vance.

As usual, the only thing Neva did not even glance at was her own column, which she avoided so thoroughly that she skipped the entire page to keep from being drawn in by whatever headline—apt or otherwise—the copy editor had slapped on it. Once in print it was too late to change anything, and if there were blunders she would hear about them soon enough.

It was too late to help Lyle McRae. How she might have helped him was not clear—a column wouldn't have done any good because he died before the next one was due to appear, and a determined killer would not have been stopped by words, in any case—but now she was bound to see his sad story through to wherever it led. She would follow every thread he had dangled. She must visit Happ's Hardware to talk with Debo, who had doled out Angel's monthly disability checks. She must find Win Niagra, the man from the craft center who had reputedly taken the gang's bait. She must try to find someone other than Reba who knew Fowler and Quick. Making rapid notes, she was able to cover just half a page, but a list is only a starting place, a set of entryways into paths that would branch in their turn. Studying it, she wondered which of the notes would prove dead-ends, which, if any, would prove crucial—but this was futile speculation.

The day was perfect for walking the two miles to work but she would not enjoy the stroll today, and half the morning was gone already. The car felt clammy inside compared with the soft spring air outside and the old faux leather upholstery was stiff. She turned on the heat, backed out of the short gravel driveway, and headed down Spring Street. Before she'd gone a block the car filled with a strange musty smell, heavily floral but artificial enough to be gagging. Pulling over, she lowered all the windows but the car continued to reek.

She got out to look around, but could see no obvious source of a flowery smell in the nearby yards, no Daphne or hyacinth gone crazy. In fact, the air was marvelously fresh. Spring Street, as usual, was as quiet as a country lane because it led only to a dead-end with a flight of steps going up to the next street on the hill. Turning back to the car, she opened the two doors on the curb side, and was reminded suddenly of Reba—surely the pungent smell had come into the car with the homeless woman but she had been too distressed to remark on it last night.

A black strap lay on the floor. A light tug on the strap and out came the maroon knapsack. The pack had been shoved up out of sight, directly under a heat vent as it happened, and now she recognized the smell. Patchouli oil. Lots of patchouli oil. The pack was light, and for an instant she thought it must be empty, but then the front flap gaped open and the contents tumbled out at her feet.

A flannel shirt, a thermal cup, a notebook, a flashlight, matches, and a bottle of pills.

The cup had no lid. The pills were a mix of white aspirin, red decongestant, and large chewable Vitamin C. The flashlight had batteries but didn't work. The shirt was damp and wadded into a ball that she left as it was. The notebook had landed open, with the covers facing up. Both front and back were solid with doodles that had been worked into three-dimensional patterns like the graffiti on alley walls and boxcars. Big numbers, letters, abstract shapes, the words love, hate, cat.

Neva turned the notebook over. Reba Winner looked up at her from the right-hand page. The likeness was good, so good the homeless woman seemed to return Neva's startled look with one of amused recognition. Above her head floated a halo of tiny cat faces, each with a different accessory—one sunglasses, another a baseball cap on backwards, another with a jeweled ear stud. The cats were both winsome and disturbing, more like impish feline spirits than domestic cats.

A sudden sense of being watched made Neva glance around, but there was no one, of course, and it struck her even as she picked up the notebook that she was the hidden watcher, the trespasser. These things were not hers. The right and proper thing to do was to put them all back into the pack with no further prying and return them to Reba somehow.

But already she was turning the pages, studying the faces that were revealed at every turn, sometimes one to a page, sometimes several, some suggested by a few lines and others detailed down to individual hairs and wrinkles. Apart from Reba, she did not know their names, though many were familiar because they were regulars at the Beanery. Here was the barista with the dreadlocks, and the man who drank only hot water because of his bad stomach, and the woman who wore shorts winter and summer, and the guy in the cowboy hat and tobacco-stained mustache. Here was the bearded man who had recited at Angel's memorial gathering, his eyes closed as though in sleep and—she almost dropped the notebook in surprise.

Her own face looked up at her from the page.

She was looking down at herself and up at herself at the same time.

And it was her as she appeared now, today, with hair falling almost to the shoulders rather than cut short as it was in the photograph that ran with her column. Someone had examined her very recently, carefully enough to get a striking likeness and discreetly enough that she had not noticed when it happened.

At the Beanery? Well, why not? She was a regular there, just like most of the other subjects in the notebook.

But they were all characters!

Laughing, delighted, Neva closed the notebook and thought back through her recent visits to the coffee shop. She could not recall having seen an artist at work. People read, talked, used laptops, stared into space. It was true that she generally tried to avoid eye contact because catching someone's eye could be taken as an invitation to talk. She didn't want to be sociable at the Beanery. She went there for a break—like the old British men's clubs, the Beanery was a communal haven, a place to be solitary without being alone—but surely she would have noticed the kind of intense scrutiny required for such good drawings.

The artist was not Reba. Reba was never in the Beanery, plus the drawing of her was no self-portrait.

With the notebook open again, she was disappointed to find that her portrait was the last one in the book. Beyond it were only blank pages. Turning through them, she soon reached the back cover. Unlike the outside of the cover, the inside was unmarked apart from a line of neat writing in one corner.

All morning the morning has been blackening. Poem by SP.

All morning the morning has been blackening . . . Gloomy, very gloomy. Sylvia Plath? Lady Gloom personified. It would be easy to confirm by Googling, but she would call her son in Berkeley instead. Ethan was not so long out of the gloomy poetry phase himself, and though she needed no excuse to talk with her son it gave her a reason to call during the day rather than wait for the usual evening chats they managed at least once a week.

The immediate question was what to do with the notebook and pack. Reba had implied on the riverfront that the knapsack was not hers and that she wished to be free of it. That it might be Vance Fowler's still seemed a possibility, in which case it should go to the police.

On the other hand, Reba might have left it behind on purpose, for safekeeping, trusting Neva to hold onto it. If she turned it in, she would have to tell how it had come into her possession, which could expose the homeless woman to yet more hassling. It also would destroy any hope of getting to know Reba better, of discovering her story and turning it into a column.

And she felt no sense of obligation or allegiance to law enforcement this morning. She had not forgotten Marcum's memo.

If Reba had left the pack by accident, she would retrieve it sometime, discreetly. If she had left it in the car on purpose, then it would stay put until there was a good reason to move it. Neva restored the contents and pinned the broken zipper shut with the large safety pin that had come undone but remained stuck in the canvas. She walked the half block back to the house, put the pack in a heavy plastic bag with a twist-tie around the top, and continued driving with the windows open to the *Current* building where she scrubbed her hands free of patchouli oil in the lunchroom sink.

Journalists, in general, can't remember their own names before noon but this morning the newsroom was a battle scene. Reporters hunched over telephones and keyboards, editors paced like starving tigers, the printer spewed copy, a news clerk bustled in with ancient clip files from before the digital revolution. Ambrose was in his command chamber, feet on desk, phone clamped to right ear, left hand gesticulating, his entire body radiating gleeful energy. Rather than thread her way through the lines of reporters' desks, Neva moved casually around the perimeter, thinking *I am invisible*. Though Ambrose had kept her out of the initial story, everyone must know by now that she had been at the warehouse, and no reporter worth a bean would let her off without attempting some "background" questions at the least. Slipping between the wall and a couple of ailing rubber plants, keeping a particular eye on Frankie and Shawna whose desks mercifully faced the other way, Neva managed to reach her office unnoticed.

Before opening email or checking phone messages, she pulled up Wikipedia and searched for patchouli oil. Ah, she should have known, it was in the mint family. *Pogostemon cablin* was a bushy herb up to two feet tall, with small pink-white flowers. The name derived from Tamil for "green leaf." Native to tropical regions, it has been cultivated and used in perfumes for centuries. "The scent of patchouli oil is heavy and strong." No kidding.

Next she called her son.

"S.P.?" he said drowsily after confessing to a late night. "Sylvia Plath?"

"That was my first thought. Do you recognize the line?"

"I could find it and call you back tonight. What are you up to, oh unpredictable Mother? I sense a puzzle."

The two had shared a love of puzzles throughout Ethan's childhood, and had got into a habit of arranging small mysteries around the house for the other to solve. These could be simple, like swapping one picture for another on the wall to see how long it would take to be noticed, or complicated enough to require a series of discoveries, a trail of clues that added up to a message. Several times over the years he had helped her work out real-life puzzles, but when she finished describing the current situation, especially the events of last night, his young voice grew stern. "Stay out of it, Mom. This is nasty, very nasty, and no business of yours. I know I'm spitting into the wind and might as well save my breath—"

"Saliva."

"What's that?"

"If you're spitting you want to save saliva, not breath."

Ethan groaned, laughed and promised to look up the poem when he was fully awake. "Meanwhile, don't take any candy from strangers. Or was that wooden nickels."

Neva's smile lasted only a few seconds into her first telephone message. It was from Anya Alexandrova, who said she had enjoyed that morning's column about the riverfront and found it "even-handed."

In other words, wishy-washy, which was worse than being accused of bias.

The next call was better. A member of the SORE contingent, who identified himself only as Pete, accused her of "waffling" on her previous questioning of the City plan. "You were too easy on the bureaucrats," he said. "I just hope you don't go soft on their inflated jail bond as well. I'd like to sit down and discuss this with you over coffee."

Neva noted down the three telephone numbers he repeated with slow care, though she would not meet him. She tried to return all reasonable calls, but if she met with everyone who wanted to "discuss this over coffee," she would spend her days talking about columns rather than writing them. Fast-forwarding through two messages that had been misdirected to her line, she came to one from Marcum stating that he

expected her at his office at eleven o'clock.
"Hell," she said, and reached for her bag. It was 10:54.

Gale Marcum did not look like a police officer. Fit and trim, dressed for drinks at the golf club, he looked at the world through blue eyes striking enough to raise the question of colored contact lenses. With that clear skin that seemed never to need shaving he would have been altogether too pretty except for a nose that turned up enough to show open nostrils.

Seated in a leather and steel chair, he rested his elbows on the desk with his chin on laced fingers and regarded Neva in silence. She had not taken off her jacket, and sat with her right hand in the pocket curled around the memo. She would not speak first.

"You've been hard on us, Ms. Leopold," he said at last.

Neva cocked her head a fraction but did not reply.

"Two homicides in less than two weeks. It made the Portland TV news. So much for our low crime rate. Tell me, is there any aspect of the proposed jail that you deign to like? As I recall, you said it's too expensive, too far out of town, too many beds for our low crime rate and, in fact, the real object is to make money by renting beds to neighboring counties and why should Willamette County taxpayers have to foot the bill to house nonresident offenders? In fact, it would be more like a prison in size and character than like a jail. Have I missed anything?"

"Columns are a matter of personal viewpoint. After studying the proposal and talking with people on both sides, that is how the situation looks to me." Neva hesitated only for an instant before pressing on. "Surely you're aware of the recent study that named Willamette the safest town in the country? This doesn't just refer to the crime rates, of course, but to everything—natural disasters, traffic accidents and everything else. But still it's considered the safest small city in the whole country. This has to mean something."

"You and I both know that numbers don't mean anything compared to what's really out there. Now, just what were you doing at that warehouse? You were not, and I repeat were not, simply strolling past by coincidence just after a man you interviewed two days ago was killed inside. I want the truth about what you were doing there at that exact moment. You looked upset when we arrived. Why?"

"You'd be upset too if you were out for an evening walk and a pair of squad cars screeched to a halt next to you and lights were shoved in your face. But it's true that there was more to it than that. When I left the restaurant I felt too restless to go right home and I thought of Lyle just up the street. I walked up that way with no definite idea about what to do when I got there. I called his name and I suppose I would have gone in if he'd answered. But there was no answer, and it was so dark inside that I decided not to go in."

"Inside? *You* opened the door? You said last night that you found it open."

"I opened it by accident when I first got there because the usual lock was gone from the hasp. I closed it and went behind the warehouse to look up at the windows, checking for lights. When I came back around to the front, the door was standing open again. And I did close it the first time, no doubt about that. I pushed to be sure the latch caught."

"I see this is complicated. Tell me exactly what happened, in order, while you were in the vicinity of the warehouse." Marcum listened without reaction until she described the light beam flashing inside the apartment, for she was now certain it had not been a reflection of her own flashlight after all. "You're sure it was inside?"

"It's impossible to be one hundred percent certain, but I think it was inside, probably a flashlight."

"What did you hear? You must have heard something."

"There was not a sound from the warehouse, nothing at all."

"And you saw no one?"

She thought of the two homeless men shuffling along the bike path. Those two feeble, staggering derelicts had not killed Lyle, and wouldn't have recognized a suspicious circumstance if they'd tripped over it. She said, "No one."

"Who did you see?"

"No one."

"Who do you think killed Lyle McRae?"

"I have no idea other than that he was afraid of Ernold Quick. Do you know where he is?"

"I realize you're used to asking the questions, but that doesn't mean anything here." The telephone rang. Keeping stern eyes on Neva, he picked up the receiver and snapped, "Marcum." In an instant, his face changed. He smiled, chuckled, nodded and said, "Nothing could be easier. Don't give it another thought, Kitty. I'm just finishing up here. See you in a jiffy."

With the smile still in his voice and on his face, he addressed Neva as he hung up. "I'm afraid this is all the time we have for now. My notes will be typed and you'll need to read and sign the statement. Someone will call you. And if you think of anything significant you will of course let me know." He stood and came around the side of the desk.

Neva also stood up so that they were face to face with the chair between them.

"And now I really can't let you go without putting it to you straight one more time, Ms. Leopold. A lot of us are concerned at the way you've misled the community about our need for a jail."

"A lot of us?"

"In the department, Chief Fiori, the sheriff, members of city government. We're in a dangerous situation here. We've got a revolving door. We might as well be running a bed and breakfast for the violent and insane. You talk about 'enlightened law enforcement,' well, there's nothing enlightened about turning the court and incarceration system into a joke. Lowlifes around the state know they can come here, sell meth or break into cars or whatever, and if they're caught they'll be let out in a week to make way for the next crop. Kitty has turned this department around from a good-old-boy club to a model law enforcement team, against all odds, I might add. The crowning piece is a new jail, and without the jail, well, you get the picture. Why you think you can hold us up single-handed I don't know, but this department is going to get a jail, come hell or high water."

"Single-handed?" Neva looked at the assistant chief with genuine surprise. "All I do is write. Citizens vote the way they choose to vote. They rejected the jail bond the first time around because they found it a bad plan, not because I said it was a bad plan. If they vote for it the second time around, it will be because you scale it down, or persuade them it's a good plan. Anything that would cost as much as the library, the swimming pool, and the whole city parks system combined has to be a really good fit to be acceptable to this community."

"Which you pointed out."

"Naturally. That's my job. But I don't tell anyone how to vote."

"Don't you feel any sense of responsibility at all for what's happened?"

"Responsibility in what way?"

"Quick was released from jail due to crowding and killed a man the same night. He'd still be in there now if we had the new jail. If we hadn't been short on beds, nobody would have died that night. He's still on the loose, and now we have a second one. Can I say it any plainer?"

Chapter Seven

Marcum's problem was being second-in-command. Chief Fiori never took things personally and never threw her weight around. She and Neva had long ago agreed to disagree, although, striding around the Azalea Park loop to blow off steam, Neva wondered whether the jail column had angered the chief as well as her right-hand man. She had not had occasion to speak with Fiori since it came out. Maybe Kitty, too, blamed her for the failed bond levy. There was the memo, and Marcum had claimed that the entire department was upset. Oleander had been civil enough, but he was not the type to put the personal ahead of the professional.

The rule of the game in journalism and politics is that, no matter how you spar in public, you remain civil in private, everyone recognizing that the public behavior is dictated by the role and not necessarily by personal inclination. Civility is in everyone's best interest, for information sharing, for calling in favors later, for keeping the rough machinery of government and journalism clanking along. If the rule really had broken down in the police department, her job was going to be tougher until things blew over or the regime changed, though losing Fiori could bring far worse. She was hot stuff in the law enforcement world and likely to be tempted away any day, which could leave them with Marcum in charge.

If, that is, he didn't follow his heart and go with her.

Recalling the transformation in the assistant chief as he talked with his boss on the phone, Neva felt suddenly embarrassed on his behalf. Could his passion about the jail bond be a bizarre form of courting?

A shout brought her attention back to the park. Three boys on bicycles with high handlebars were racing around the far side of the loop. They appeared to be a hard lot, although the hard look was cultivated by so many kids you really couldn't tell which were dealing crack and which were headed home to do algebra. They pedaled fast and skidded to a stop in front of a man sitting on a bench near the rose bed.

Neva headed that way, straining to hear what was said, but the distance was too great and by the time she drew close enough for a good look the boys had ridden on. The man gazed after them, a paperback open in his lap.

"Good morning," she said.

He nodded.

"I'm Jeneva Leopold, a columnist for the *Willamette Current*. I wonder if you could tell me who those boys are?"

"Just boys," he said, and looked down at his book, but lifted his head again instantly to add, "Sorry if that sounded terse. What I meant was that I don't know them. One asked if I had a match and I said no. I haven't smoked in years."

"You look familiar. Have we met?"

"I don't believe so, though of course I recognize you. I'm often in the park so maybe you've seen me here. I'm Win Niagra. I run the craft center across the park there."

"It's good to meet you. May I sit down?"

Niagra gestured at the space beside him on the bench, his manner pleasant though not welcoming.

Turned half toward him on the bench, Neva said in a musing tone, "It's odd to meet you by chance like this because you're on my list of people to talk to today. Your name has come up in connection with something rather difficult." She paused for a reaction, could detect no change, and went on. "You read that Lyle McRae was killed last night? You must know him, the thin, sandy-haired man who tended the flowerbeds here and around the courthouse. Two days ago he told me about a situation he said he'd observed while working in this park."

"I was so sorry to read about his death, and shocked, of course. I had seen him in the park sometimes, mostly in the evening."

Neva nodded in somber acknowledgement, watching his face. His eyes were tired, and sad in a way that made her speak with yet more care. "It was because of Angel's murder that Lyle called me. He said he thought he knew who had done it, and it had to do with a gang of kids run by two men, Vance Fowler and Ernold Quick."

Niagra looked away toward the east end of the park with a sudden turn of his head that brought a ponytail into view. It was rare for a man to grow such a long ponytail, and the gray streaks suggested he was older than he looked. After waiting for a moment to see whether he would face her again, Neva addressed the back of his head.

"Lyle said the gang included a few girls as well as boys. They cruised around on bicycles. He said the main job the kids do, or did, was to carry cell phones and report on the whereabouts of patrol cars so the two leaders could do their deals and other business without being caught. Right here, in Azalea Park. Lyle said the two leaders also used the kids as bait for setting up men looking for under-age sex. Then they blackmailed the men."

She waited but Niagra said nothing and still did not turn around. If Lyle were alive she would not be doing this, not be pressing such questions on a near stranger, but she was bound now to persist. "This is unbelievably awkward, but his murder gives extra weight to everything he said that day. He trusted me to help him and I failed. Now I feel compelled to check everything he told me, no matter how difficult or unlikely. So here goes. He said you were one of the men being blackmailed."

Niagra turned now, swiveling his body rather than moving only his head. His face was set, almost expressionless, and his voice was level and unemotional. "Blackmail, yes, that part's true, but it's the only part."

Unprepared for such a reply or for his calm delivery, Neva had no ready response and simply waited for the rest of the story. When he offered no further explanation, she said, "Could you please help me understand?"

"You have a graceful way of trying to get people's secrets. It's almost enough to make me bare my soul—almost. But as it happens, I can't, and it wouldn't be any use to you anyway. What I can tell you is two things. My situation has nothing to do with sex. I like children, I don't love them. And I don't know anything about gangs or drug deals or what happened to Lyle. My situation is entirely personal, with no relevance for anyone else."

"I see," Neva said with genuine relief. "Whew."

"And one other thing. No facts, just instinct. I've seen Vance Fowler around quite a bit and a less likely murderer would be hard to find. Or blackmailer. He's a good kid at heart and with half a chance he'd make a fine adult. And that's all I have to say."

They didn't speak as two joggers and two mothers with strollers went by. Niagra sat with the book in his lap, his legs in worn sage-green pants resting neatly together like a woman's, the ponytail hanging forward over his shoulder, his feet bare in heavy leather sandals. That he was an artisan or artist she assumed because he managed the craft center. She could see no paint on his hands or clothes. A smell of linseed oil suggested woodwork.

His calm refusal to tell her the full story was striking because it was rare. Although experience led her to expect cooperation, she had often been puzzled by people's readiness to expose their lives, to reveal just about any detail she requested regardless of how personal and potentially embarrassing or compromising it might be. As useful as this was for a journalist, she sometimes felt the urge—and occasionally followed it—to say, *You don't have to tell me these things, you know. I'm not the law, or a priest.*

Most people appeared to lack whatever it was that made Win Niagra able to recognize that he, not Jeneva Leopold or any other inquisitor, was in charge of information about his own life. Because she asked a question didn't put him under an obligation to answer. And that he could hold onto his privacy without being rude put him in a very small club of secret keepers who had withstood her manipulation over the years. That something in the description of the gang had upset him was obvious, but he had it under control and she was inclined to believe his claim to innocence—though how, then, to account for blackmail? He was being blackmailed, he said, but not by Quick and Fowler, well not Fowler at any rate, and not for supposed gang activities.

"I enjoyed your column about spending the summer in the desert, at that gold mine," he said. "I suppose most of us fantasize about running away to solitude like that, but not so many can actually untangle themselves and go. And that kind of solitude isn't for everyone. You have to be able to live with your own thoughts. You must have a happy conscience."

"Happy conscience. What a nice line. I'm not sure it's true, though. My regrets are as serious as anyone's but I enjoy the present so much, the little things in daily life, that it keeps me pretty cheerful. Kind of like a dog, I guess. Biscuits now! That's my motto."

Niagra smiled at this. The next moment his face lit up with delight. A gaggle of rosy-cheeked preschoolers trotted toward them up the path, cheered on by three teachers, one chanting, "Run, run, catch the sun, shed those growlies one by one." As the kids passed the bench, a girl with pigtails dropped her buddy's hand, ran to Niagra, was swept up in a bear hug and deposited again on the walkway in one smooth movement that sent her back to the line giggling.

The chanting teacher beamed at Niagra as she passed and said as though speaking with a friend, "These little jumping beans are so squirrely today they can't even sit still for stories."

When they'd rounded the curve of the walkway and were out of sight, Niagra said, "My granddaughter. The little one, that is."

"She's darling. I'm not quite into that phase of life, but I certainly hope to be some day. I have one son, still in college."

"I know. Remember, I read your column, like everybody else."

"Then you know the sort of thing I write. That is, I seem to get drawn into just about every kind of local subject. Sometimes I'm not sure where

I'm going, which is certainly true at the moment. Is there anything you can tell me about the kids on bikes, or about Ernold Quick and Vance Fowler that might help me understand the situation? Or about Angel de Silva?"

Something shifted in the artist, some internal twitch or tick, but he only stood up, inclined his head in a suggestion of a bow, and said, "I've got a fifth grade class coming in for a pot-throwing session. I'm glad to have met you."

With the door shut politely in her face, Neva watched him walk away with the easy stride of the fit and well-formed. Just before rounding the bend that had hidden the children, he stopped and looked down at a flowerbed. It was a solid wash of newly opened daffodils. Lyle's daffodils, no doubt. From bulbs that had been pressed into the earth by the strong, warm hands that had held hers just three days ago.

Debo Happ was weighing out six-penny nails, digging them from a bin with a galvanized scoop and pouring them thunderously into the scale bucket. She transferred two more scoops before answering Neva's question, seeming more puzzled than upset to be talking about the dead man whose disability money she had managed for the past year.

"Angel said he was going to buy a car to live in and needed all his cash at once. I reminded him what happened last time and he said he'd found a legal place to park it."

"What did happen last time?" Neva leaned in the doorway that connected the main room of Happ's Hardware with the back room where nails, screws, hinges and other small essential home and machinery repair items were kept in bins and could be bought singly. She still recalled with pleasure her first visit to the old, wood-floored store soon after she bought the house on Spring Street. She had needed a washer for the kitchen faucet, and had gone first to one of the mega stores on the town's only business strip, but washers there came in packages of ten different sizes at a cost of $4.99. Although she couldn't imagine ever needing the other nine washers, she was about to buy the multi-pack when an elderly man addressed her.

"Go to Happ's on Second Street. They'll give you just what you need and without that plastic packaging it takes an axe to get into. I only come in here for the birdseed sales."

Narrow and pleasantly dim, the store was crowded from floor to ceiling with parts and tools you didn't know you wanted or needed until you saw them, as well as such traditional offerings as oil lamps, real straw brooms, and spools of rope, the buyer being invited to cut off the desired length like ribbon in a fabric shop. The store smelled of a different era, a time before plastic and fluorescent lights. Neva had identified a few of the ingredients in the redolent mix, mainly oiled wood, hemp rope, burlap, and smoke from the old wood-burning stove in the middle of the store with its ever-present enamelware pot full of free coffee.

On that first visit she had been sold a single washer for three cents and since then had not set foot in any hardware store but Happ's. Debo had been a schoolgirl with big teeth then, helping her father by scrambling up the ladder to retrieve goods stored on high shelves. Recalling with startling accuracy what a customer had purchased last time, she was likely to inquire about the outcome of the particular plumbing or wiring project. Now Debo managed the store on her own, her rangy form striding about in overalls, her knowledge of where to find a three-inch eye bolt or beeswax toilet bowl seal impressing Neva anew every time she needed something.

This was the first time she had needed information, but she wasn't sure, despite what could be described in old-fashioned terms as their longstanding mercantile relationship, that Debo would talk. Apart from hardware, she had never appeared to have interests or much inclination toward conversation despite Neva's efforts to draw her out. She hadn't married, though she was handsome in a farm-girl way, smelled of fresh air despite the long hours in the store, and her teeth were now in proportion to her considerable height. She ran the store, kept a big dog, drove a pickup, and had lived alone since her parents died.

As earnest as a young girl determined not to waver from the story line, Debo said, "Angel never could drive, he never learned, which was a funny thing when he told me three years ago he bought a car. It was an old, orange Chevy station wagon, big as a hearse. Not to drive, you know, to live in. The second night he got it he was sleeping in there and this officer wakes him up. He says he can't stay there because it's illegal parking on that block. That was over there on Martha Street between Fifth and Sixth. Or maybe Third and Fourth, I disremember. Anyway, the guy he bought it off drove it there for him. Angel never drove it. He'd been drinking, too, nothing new for Angel, but you think about that, he was drunk and never knew how to drive either, but when the officer says he has to move the car, he gets in the front seat and starts it up."

Now she smiled, though the expression on her long face remained sympathetic. "It was in reverse. When he stepped on the gas it went backwards and smashed into the police car. Then he got it into first somehow and took off up the street. The police car could still run and the officer caught up with him in the next block and arrested him for drunk driving and hit and run."

The two women exchanged baffled looks, then laughed irresistibly.

"It is funny, but we were all kind of cheesed about it," Debo said. "A couple of us went to court and I have to say Judge Wyzack did his best. He knew Angel didn't have anything, and it was no good putting him in jail. I mean it just took up a bed and didn't make any difference in how he lived after. They took away the car, it wasn't licensed anyhow and you can't just park a car downtown and live in it, although it wasn't hurting anything. He had to do twelve hours community service."

"What did he do?"

Debo's face twitched, though this time she controlled the laughter. "He had to pick up trash around the park and courthouse and down on the river, which is what he does anyway. That's where he got the gum foil for all those stars. So of course I tried to talk him out of buying a car this time but I've been thinking about it, and I guess he just said that to get me to give him the money. He'd tried damn near everything else."

"You refused to give him his own money?"

"That was our deal. He made me promise that, no matter what he said, I wouldn't give him more than his daily allowance for those forty-ouncers and food. He tried the job on a couple other people before me, but it's not easy, you know, when he comes staggering in and demands a hundred dollars. He used to get pretty tricky, saying he had to get medicine or buy shoes. He never bought any clothes, I knew that, he got them from the free bin over there at Vina Moses. He came in one time and said he needed twenty bucks to buy a notebook to write his memoirs. Twenty bucks! I just laughed and told him to take a walk and come back when he could talk sense. We got along."

"Why did you give in this time?"

"I don't know. I've been asking myself that. It's not as if I believed he was really going to buy a car."

"Was he alone?"

"As far as I know. He left his cart outside, as usual, and sat on that stool the way he did and had a coffee. He said he was thinking of making some changes in his life and first thing he needed was a car. I asked him did he have a license and he said no, he had to have the car first but anyway, he'd learned his lesson about parking on the street."

"Did you read about Lyle McRae in this morning's paper?"

Debo nodded, then shook her head in disbelief.

Neva let a brief silence pass before pressing on. "As it happened, I met with Lyle a few days ago and he claimed that Angel got the money from you that day on purpose because he knew Ernold Quick was looking for him, and was bound to take the money and that would help prove him guilty. Does that sound likely to you?"

"It's the kind of harebrained idea Angel would come up with, but it sounds pretty stupid. Kind of like shutting the gate after the cows are out, only a lot worse. I thought it was that guy, Vance something or other, that killed him."

"That's who's been arrested, but they're looking for Quick."

"Good luck—you could lose that guy in a closet with the light on. But I thought he was a friend of Angel's. I used to see them walking along the river. You know street people, they kind of hang together, especially when it comes to the law. They're all in the same boat, so to speak. It's kind of strange not to have Angel coming in for his daily allowance. Like I said, we got along."

Debo hesitated, a scoopful of nails poised above the scales, then continued with an air of reluctance, "I was at that memorial. It doesn't seem quite right now he's dead but I guess the truth still means something. I mean, it wasn't true, what they said. No, that's not right either. It was true but it wasn't the whole story. I mean, I don't know all he was up to, but sometimes Angel had way too much money and it didn't come from his disability. I didn't ask and he didn't tell. I guess he was just a human like you or me."

"No angel?"

"No angel." The nails crashed onto the worn metal scales, Debo poured them neatly into a bag, rolled the top, and set it with the others. "Special order." Looking at the neat cluster of sacks, she reflected, "No angel but no devil either, I guess. I don't know. Someplace between the best and the worst, like the rest of us. I don't like to judge, although I did hear stories."

"Stories?"

"You know, stories. I don't guess they mean anything, especially now."

"They might help explain what happened, how he died."

"They know what happened. It was in the paper."

How often Neva had heard this over the years—the claim that something was true because it had been *in the paper*. Knowing how fast a newspaper is put together, the pressure driving reporters and editors, the reliance on official sources with a definite agenda . . . well, it had been a long time since Neva believed that "truth" had much to do with "news" though she did believe that most of her colleagues wanted to get things right. They certainly worked hard enough, and were by far the best news source going despite the growing delusion that it could all be found online. That the information has to be dug out in the first place, by someone who can distinguish between information and rumor, seemed not to have occurred to an awful lot of people who should know better.

"Sometimes things are more complicated than they may look in news reports," she said, smiling to counteract any tone of preachiness. "Journalists are expected to turn everything into a tidy story, with a beginning, middle and end. Life, as you know, doesn't often follow such a neat pattern."

Debo nodded thoughtfully. "You can say that again. So there's more to this than somebody's telling. No surprise I guess. All's I can say is that if I had a kid I don't guess I'd feel too comfortable with them hanging around Angel. I mean, he was a street person when you come right down to it. Speaking of streets, I wish they'd get done with those gravel trucks. They go right by here, and yesterday a lamp chimney got shook off the shelf and went smash."

"If they're driving too fast, you should report them."

"It's not that, not speeding. They're just big and shaking things up. One of them ran over Angel's shopping cart a while back."

"When was that? Did you see it?"

"I heard it, not the crash but the yelling, so I ran out. Angel was standing there screaming at the driver."

"I thought that was his cart over by the post office bench."

"He got a new one from the Safeway parking lot, like always. The driver got out and looked at the cart and turned around to get back in the truck like it was nothing. And Angel's stuff was in there, too. Squashed flat."

"The driver didn't apologize or try to help in any way?"

"Not a bit. Lyle was out there, too. He'd just bought a short-handled shovel and I was afraid he was going to go after that guy with it, but he just yelled."

"Did he threaten the dump truck driver?"

"I wouldn't call it that exactly. It was more calling him names which I won't repeat if you don't mind. And he said something about street people not being trash and not being as dumb as some people think. They have eyes and ears and know what's going on."

"What did the driver do?"

"Ignored him. He got back in the gravel truck. That's when the other guy, a city engineer or something, got out of one of those little white trucks they all drive. He gave Angel some money. Angel told me it was a hundred dollars, as if I'd believe that. Anyway, he was happy and that was the end of it. As long as they're filling potholes out there, I hope they hurry up and do the ones in front of my door."

Chapter Eight

As though in answer to Debo's complaint, a gravel truck passed the hardware store just when Neva was leaving, though it didn't stop to fill the single large pothole out front. She watched it disappear up the street, then she considered the pothole. The street was just a block from the riverfront and was to be repaved as part of the park plan so it would make no sense to fill the holes now. But where was the gravel going? Apart from the two patches of riprap, there was no work underway yet on the waterfront, and no other major City project in progress anywhere that she knew of.

Neva took out her pad and made a note to call the city works and engineering office again.

The immediate question was what to do next, return to the *Current* to see what the day's letters and messages might offer, call Carter Grey again to follow up his insurance hint, visit Vance's furious grandmother in the hope that she would spill whatever beans she had to spill even without a payoff, or check county records to find out who owned *Au Courant*. She had not managed to get a sensible answer out of the waiter or anyone else last night, and the restaurant was worth a column.

Like the riverfront column, it would be easy to write one on the restaurant—as long as she could keep from dwelling on the other events of the evening—and it would buy her a few days to keep poking into more serious business. Already she was heading for the steepled Victorian courthouse where the land records were kept in basement rooms with walls of gray stone. It was the same stone that had been used for the entire building, as could be seen in the historic photographs that hung in the foyer. One picture showed the courthouse just after it was built in 1886, when the exterior stone was the natural gray. But a gray courthouse had not suited turn-of-the-century judge Bertram K. Dixon. According to the brief history that hung with the photos, Dixon had ordered white paint, to be delivered from the East by train, but he had not reckoned on the porosity of local stone. The entire first shipment, which had used up the annual budget for courthouse maintenance, had been sucked into the surface of the south face of the three-story building. The paint job had required ten years to complete, but now the outside was a crisp, New England white that did very well on postcards.

The interior of the property office had been left with the original untreated gray stone. Vault-like and comfortable no matter the season, it felt full of secrets that would yield to those with patience and a proper feeling for complex human stories. Neva, however, was in the usual hurry. She hoisted the volume of platting maps onto the viewing table, found the four maps that listed riverfront lots, carried the heavy book to the counter, and requested copies plus the landowner keys for these pages. The stout clerk disappeared through a door and soon returned bearing four legal-size sheets of paper. Neva paid two dollars and was on her way, the errand having taken less than ten minutes.

Pleased by the efficiency of the transaction, she walked with brisk good cheer down the hall toward the exit. Ahead of her a burly police officer suddenly stepped into view as though he had walked through the wall. Close behind him was a young man in orange pajamas and handcuffs, followed even closer by a second officer. The young man's head was deeply bowed, his face hidden by long hair.

The three turned up the hall with the prisoner between the two officers, forcing Neva to stand against the wall as they passed. She watched until they reached the stairs to the second floor courtrooms, then turned to examine the doorway. It was gone. Had she not seen an opening, she would have no idea that the plain wood panel was anything but a wood panel.

The jail had been built before she moved to Willamette. Had she lived here then, had she been writing columns, she would have fought that jail as hard as she was fighting the current proposal, but for a different reason—location. The squat, concrete set of cell blocks had been built against the north side of the lovely old courthouse and was like a big wart on an otherwise perfect face. Why they needed a secret tunnel connecting the two was puzzling since they shared a wall, but maybe this, too, was a result of Sixties paranoia about the budding youth revolution.

She had heard of the passage but never wondered about it particularly. She took out her notebook and jotted *ask re jail passage, maybe get self 'arrested' and spend night in cell?*

"I've never seen you at an arraignment before."

Neva turned to find Gale Marcum standing behind her, a folder of papers in one hand, a briefcase in the other. He must have come from an office farther up the hall though she had not heard a door open or close.

"You people sure are getting good mileage out of this," he said. "It's interesting, isn't it, that no matter what happens it's good for the newspaper business. I counted three homicide-related stories in today's paper. By the way, just so you know, I sent the *Current* a Readertorial signed by Kitty and me, telling how it really stands with the jail."

"Thanks for the warning," Neva said dryly, but did not add *And thanks for the tip about Vance.*

Marcum strode up the hall with Neva not far behind, but rather than follow him up the stairs she went to the telephone across from the elections office, one of the few in town that had so far survived the cell phone revolution, and dialed the newsroom. Yes, J.D. assured her, Frankie was covering the court appearance. "What are you doing over there?"

"Digging through dusty property records."

"Property? What does property have to do with a murder arraignment?"

"Property drives everything," Neva teased.

"Oh, come on. What are you doing?"

"I got curious about property ownership downtown. Nothing to do with crime, sorry."

"Anything interesting?"

"I haven't had a chance to look at the stuff yet."

"Well, enjoy."

For some moments after hanging up, Neva stood by the foot of the stairs, tempted to slip into the courtroom for a better look at Vance Fowler, but she was unlikely to learn much just by looking and she needed a break from painful experiences. She had no proof that the backpack and sketchbook were his, but Reba had made it clear they were not hers. *I hope they let him out soon.* Vance, too, had fed the feral cats on the riverfront, surely grounds for a special bond between the homeless woman and the accused man. Whether the young man was guilty or innocent, his boyish head bowed over handcuffs had been a disturbing sight. She was not ready to look him in the eye.

The property maps were confusing at first as maps generally are, the schematic version of the world bearing little resemblance to the real thing. Rearranging them on her desk to line up properly, east/west and north/south, Neva at last located the *Au Courant* property. It was quick work to compare the lot number with the list of owners, but her triumph turned to disappointment and a disgusted, "Damn!"

The "owner" was a corporation, Left Bank, Inc. No names, no address, only a post office box. *Damn damn damn.* Most likely the property owners didn't own the restaurant—most downtown businesses leased their spaces, as far as she knew—but the property owners would have been able to tell her who did own *Au Courant*. They also could have answered her other questions, mainly about potential tenants for the rest of the old warehouse. She would have to return to the restaurant and persist until she found someone with more knowledge than the waiter she had asked last night.

"Don't know who owns it," he had said with a shrug. "I just started yesterday. The cook gives the orders but she's no owner. Too young."

"Who hired you?" she had pressed.

"The manager, but he's in Hawaii for a wedding or something."

Left Bank, Inc. could consist of one person or a dozen, though it seemed unlikely that a lone individual would declare himself a corporation. If it was a large group, it might well have extensive holdings. She made a list of the lot numbers to the south, north, and west of the restaurant, checked the key, sat back for a moment in surprise, then compared lot numbers for several blocks in each direction.

Left Bank owned them all, including Lyle's warehouse.

It was no secret that downtown was owned mainly by a few families, most no longer living in the area, but still the size of Left Bank's holdings was unusual, and their location was highly suggestive—the corporation owned roughly a third of the property facing First Street and the river, plus a good two blocks on Second Street.

This was worth a column in itself, especially with the riverfront park controversy raging. It was an easy bet that the owners were on the city's side but she'd like to know for sure. Casting about for likely owners, she thought of Lyle McRae. Is this where his lottery millions had gone? Buying up property around his warehouse? It would help explain his reluctance to leave despite the sense of threat that had turned out to be all too real.

Other business owners might know who owned the land but there weren't many businesses on First Street, and she didn't know the owners. On Second Street she knew only Debo at the hardware store and the nice couple who owned the green coffee bean store. . . But there was no reason to go beating the bushes. They would know the answer at the Downtown Willamette Association.

A crisp, recorded voice answered the call and said with no apology, "The Downtown Willamette Association office is closed until April 30th for remodeling. If you need to speak to someone immediately, please contact the city manager's office."

The call had taken less than a minute but when she hung up, the telephone message light was blinking. Really, it defied the laws of probability how often calls came in when she was on the line or out of the room for five minutes making tea or using the toilet. She should start keeping a record and calculate the ratio. It might make an amusing column.

The message was from Ethan. "You were right," said his strong young voice. "The line is from Plath, from 'Sheep in Fog,' which I guess could describe how most of us feel most of the time. I'll read it. 'The hills steep off into whiteness. People or stars, regard me sadly. I have disappointed them . . .' "

I have disappointed them.

Recalling Vance's ducked head and shackled hands as he went down the courthouse hall, Neva could not help picturing a small figure replanting doomed carrots in the twilight. We all let others down, we disappoint family and friends, but someone like Vance Fowler might well go through life feeling like a walking embodiment of failed hopes. . . . Listening to the poem twice more, she got down the words, hung up, and discovered the message light blinking yet again. This time the call was from the antiquities dealer, Carter Grey. Yes, he would be happy to talk with her about the insurance situation on the riverfront, had she been to the new restaurant *Au Courant* yet, and could she meet him there for a drink after work today?

Her first reaction as she hung up the phone was *No, not today, not back to that restaurant so soon.*

True, she had just been thinking that she needed to go back there to try again to find out the name of the owner or owners, but faced with an invitation to go there in a matter of hours she shrank from the prospect. Working hard, keeping busy, she had managed not to dwell on the events of last night, not to let thoughts of the gardener and the timing of her own visit to the warehouse overwhelm the day. There were plenty of other places to meet Grey, even if less interesting than *Au Courant*.

And yet, how could she write a column about the restaurant if she avoided going there or thinking about it? Her memories of last night were barely below the surface as it was, and to return would make little difference—and the restaurant part of the evening had been marvelous.

Though Grey had called just minutes before, he did not answer when she called back, but this was fine, even a relief. Talking to a machine was quicker and simpler. She would meet him at the restaurant at 6, she said, and hung up.

A Google search for Left Bank came up empty, not one single mention, which was almost unheard of these days. Even her five-year-old neighbor boy was on the Web and had told her so proudly the other day as she walked by on her way home. *I Googled me, Georgie Capro*, he had chirped, *and got two hits.*

Congratulations! She had said after a moment's perplexity—the new coming of age?

Google did better for Winslow Niagra, though only three of the 234,000 hits were for the sculptor, including a notice for an art show last year and two schedules for pottery classes.

Next she pulled up the *Current's* own online archives and easily found the news item about Angel's arrest for drunk driving. It was just as Debo had related except for an additional detail—Angel had not been alone in the station wagon when he was told to move on. When the officer pounded on the door, Angel had been asleep in back of the station wagon, while the middle seat was occupied by a homeless woman with a crippled leg. "Angel gave me a place to sleep out of the cold," she had told Judge Wyzack. "Didn't anybody else do that."

"Good grief," Neva said aloud. Debo had said he was no Angel, but he'd had some kind of good heart.

The meeting with Carter Grey was not a date, definitely not a date. Even so, the prospect of spending a pleasant hour over drinks with a well-spoken man who had said her columns got his blood moving helped Neva survive a weary afternoon of catching up on mail. She was in no fit condition today to tackle Wygelia's sharp-tongued sister or anyone else. And by the time she left the office, even the meeting over drinks seemed a mistake. She wanted only to be at home working in the yard, thinking about nothing except sand and flagstones. And it seemed foolish after all to return to that restaurant so soon, or to go anywhere on First Street.

It was now just five minutes to the hour, too late to call Grey at his shop. She could call the restaurant and leave a message. Standing in the parking next to her car, she considered the consequences of not keeping the appointment. He might be offended, which would mean the end of whatever information or revelations he was prepared to offer. Even if he was not offended and agreed to meet another day, it would mean going through the arrangements all over again, and putting off what might turn out to be good, immediate column material.

She had not used the car since arriving at work and had forgotten about the pack, but when she opened the door the smell of patchouli oil brought it back instantly. Then she saw the plastic bag on the front passenger's seat, neatly folded with the straightened twist tie lying on top. Reba had retrieved the pack already. At some point during this long day Reba had located Neva's car in the lot, opened the door that was rarely locked, and collected what it was clear now she had not meant to leave behind.

Imagining the scene, she felt her mood lift for reasons she could not have explained apart from a general feeling of interest in the homeless woman. Thinking about her, she drove the five blocks to First Street with no more hesitation. The air when she got out of the car smelled of river and spicy cottonwood buds, which buoyed her up further. Briskly walking up the block to the restaurant, she allowed herself no more than a glance toward Lyle's warehouse.

The restaurant door opened directly into the single large dining room. Only three tables were occupied and only one by a single man—but what a man. Why had she not gone home and changed?

At least she could get rid of the old windbreaker. She waved back at Grey and turned to hang the jacket on the coat stand by the door. Her lace-up leather shoes were scuffed, the blue shirt, which had never encountered an iron in its life, had obviously been through an active day, the cotton pants were bagged out at the knees. Would he notice her flat chest? Her entire lack of female frontal equipment? She tucked the shirt in with a brusque shove. This was not a date, and anyway, from now on any man interested in her would have to accept the surgery or move on.

Grey stood up to take her hand. Lightly tanned, his face suffused with healthy pink, he gave the impression of having just stepped in from a walk down a leafy lane, though the linen jacket over a black turtleneck was more urban hip than country gentleman, and the trim middle suggested gym workouts rather than gardening or dog walking. His age was tricky, but she would have bet he had never married or had children, never lost a close family member too young, never struggled through a life-threatening illness in himself or a beloved. She'd known others like this, men and women who had never suffered anything worse than the death of a pet parakeet, whose faces remained strangely childlike and uncut by grief. Those the Fates had treated less kindly carried the signs. A cold or a poor night's sleep were enough to make the flimsy repair work fall away, exposing pain around the eyes and mouth. In the past, she had found such unmarked faces disconcerting, even somewhat unreal, but tonight she welcomed her host's untroubled air.

Carter Grey radiated contented geniality as he squeezed her hand. "You're better looking than your picture."

Twenty years' worth of such remarks had not conditioned Neva to be ready with a graceful response. As always, she wondered whether he meant that she was good looking or that her picture was particularly bad. "That's certainly preferable to the other way around," she said.

"You're also taller than I expected."

"Well, you're not at all what I expected from your silver-toned voice. I expected a suave fellow in a black turtleneck and cream linen jacket who would size me up like a job applicant."

After a startled moment, Grey chuckled and released her hand. "Forgive me, it's just so interesting to meet you for real when I feel as though I know you already from your work. Now, what will you have? This is a very nice Syrah from a small winery in the Applegate Valley."

Neva would have been happy with the Syrah but his self-possession piqued her into an independent choice. And, for the sake of the column, it made sense to try the bar. "A Manhattan would be fine."

Grey ordered the drink, regarded her gravely, and said, "Terrible business down here last night. I hope you didn't mind meeting so close to the scene of tragedy."

"I thought I might but it seems to be okay." The words *I was here last night, at the warehouse* hovered for a moment, ready to be spoken, but she said, "This is a really pleasant place, isn't it? And here comes my drink already."

She picked up the cold glass and Grey raised his in a salute. "To spring, if I may."

"To spring and sweet cottonwood sap."

"Cottonwood sap. Is that what it is? I can actually taste it."

"The sticky buds are all over the ground along the bike path." A moment's silence allowed them a chance to sip and glance around. A poster showing grape harvesting on the wall behind Grey reminded her of his unusual business. She said, "What sort of prints do you deal in?"

"Any sort. Or maybe I should say any sort that take my eye. I buy and sell what I love. Right now, I'm on an antique map kick. My latest gem is a lovely seventeenth century map by Abraham Ortelius, covered with galleons and sea-monsters, yours for $3,500."

"A bargain, I'd say. These are originals?"

"I don't deal in reproductions. I've also recently acquired a lovely map of the world from the late fourteen hundreds, based on a much earlier geography work by Ptolemy. The idea that everyone in the Middle Ages thought the earth was flat is wrong, you know. Those who could read the ancient manuscripts knew the world was round."

"When was that, how ancient?"

"Around 200 B.C. The Greeks living in Egypt actually measured the Earth's circumference and got it more or less right, using the Greek sports stadium as the unit of length. I hope I'm not telling you more than you want to know?"

"Heavens, no. Please continue."

"Well, then. Unfortunately, when Ptolemy was compiling his geography book three hundred years later, he didn't actually measure the curvature of the earth himself. He copied the old information but got it wrong because his sports stadium was smaller."

Neva laughed with delight, and felt a sudden current of relief wash through her like a shift in temperature. "This is wonderful. I had no idea."

"It gets better. Christopher Columbus used Ptolemy's erroneous calculations, which of course made the world seem smaller than it was and the voyage more feasible. The correct measurements would have put India beyond the range of his vessels, and he would have had a lot tougher time getting sponsorship from dear Isabella. Thus, no 1492."

Again she laughed and observed Grey with a different eye than she had mere moments before. Naturally he appeared carefree and unmarked by life—he lived calmly among antiquities, buffered from the troubled present by his love for the benign ancient.

"This is a particularly fine map. It's on the studio wall at the moment, should you care to see it."

"You really sell things out of a shop on Second Street that are over five hundred years old?"

"*Sell* is too energetic a word at the moment, but I'm optimistic. I'm gambling on the theory that reproductions of just about anything are too easy to get now. With so much that's copied, the genuine becomes all the more precious and desirable. Anyone with money can buy a classic Jaguar, but there's only one *Cattleya mossiae* by Augusta Withers."

"And you own this particular one and only?"

"Once upon a time I did. I sold it through my online business. Part of me would like to keep everything, but even if I didn't have to earn a living, I've discovered that you can only enjoy a few pieces at a time. Really enjoy, really see. I cycle favorites in and out."

Neva's hand dropped toward her bag but drew back before grasping the notebook. Grey was definitely column material, but this must wait its turn. "I'll be in soon to see the real and genuine, and I'd love to do a column on the antiquities trade sometime in the future, if you're willing, when other things have settled down."

Grey made a low sound, though whether of assent or demurral was not clear. Neva was watching a waiter just behind him manage an alarmingly large tray, and only when he landed it successfully on a table did she continue. "Before we get into the subject of insurance, I have a question for you as a downtown business owner. I'm afraid it's pretty humdrum after Ptolemy, but have you heard of Left Bank, Inc.? They appear to own quite a bit of property along First Street, including this building. I'm trying to find out who the partners are."

Sitting comfortably back from the table with his legs crossed, Grey smiled thoughtfully and twirled the wine in his glass. "As it happens, your question brings us right to that very subject of insurance. Real estate's a funny business, but insurance is even stranger. In some ways, you could say insurance drives modern life. When we were kids, did anybody think twice about some neighbor boy falling out of a tree in our yard? Or of our father having a stroke at forty and being unable to support the family? Or losing our baggage, or any of the hundreds of other things people insure for now? I don't believe my father carried any kind of insurance, even on his car. I wouldn't go down my driveway without at least collision coverage."

"What do you think, have we become more fearful or more prudent?"

"Both, I'd say. Whether it adds up to good or bad for society is too big a question for me. But you can bet insurance is a big deal in the business world. I'm sure your newspaper company's insured for every conceivable circumstance, from a gunman crashing in and killing everybody to a hurricane taking the roof off. Now, consider First Street. You have a city building code that favors density over sprawl, a good thing in my book, but the significant point here is that it calls for multi-story buildings on the riverfront where it's mostly warehouses now, with mixed zoning, the object being to get back to the days when people actually lived downtown. That's all well and good in principle, but you have property owners who've been waiting for years for something to happen down here. You have city government sitting on a pile of bond money kindly approved by voters for a major park overhaul. You have, in fact, a major river flowing a hundred feet away from the front doors of existing and future businesses, a river that is as unpredictable as rivers always are. It could flood, take out the bank, destroy the new street and plazas and what have you, all in one swoop."

"Which it has shown no sign of doing since the town was founded more than a hundred-and-fifty years ago," Neva could not help pointing out. "The bank has hardly moved, according to photographs. Even the recent bank slide was no big deal despite what some people say."

"True, but is prudence always logical or justified? Look, I don't mean to argue with you, I read your columns and essentially agree with you on most subjects, including this one. But what I'm saying would explain why the city's pushing the radical bank stabilization thing on a community that doesn't seem to want it. The insurance companies won't insure multi-story buildings down here, with retail on the ground floor and apartments above, unless the riverbank is engineered to be disaster-proof. City government isn't telling what's really driving this because so many people don't want big development down here anyway. It would just make them madder and more determined to stop the project. You see the reasoning. They could say the whole problem could be solved by keeping development back from the bank, in other words leave it as grass and trees, which is what the opposition wants. If you don't do all that building, you don't need the insurance."

"That would explain a lot, but how could they keep that kind of conspiracy secret?"

"It's not exactly like that. You've served on committees and gone to a thousand hearings. Are you ready for another one?" Grey indicated her empty glass.

"Well, that went down nicely, but no, not another mixed drink. I think I will take a glass of that wine now, thank you."

"Then we may as well have a bottle."

Grey ordered the wine, plus a mixed appetizer tray that included most of the yummy things she had passed up last night. This had not been meant as a dinner meeting but the order sounded substantial, and she was prepared to do it justice

"No conspiracy is necessary if you have persuasive people at the top," Grey continued in a voice that carried easily above the din of the now packed restaurant. "There's nothing easier to sway than a committee, and as for the City Council, well, they're a well-meaning bunch but no match for the professionals. When you talk to the Council they say they're following staff recommendations. When you talk to planners or other staff, they say they're following the Council's wishes. Rather a merry-go-round, um?" He chuckled, raised his glass in a salute, and swallowed with his eyes closed and a look of intense savoring on his smooth face.

Chapter Nine

They said goodnight at the restaurant door. Just why she had declined his invitation to stroll along the path—upriver, away from Lyle's warehouse—she wasn't sure. She had enjoyed his company and was ready for a walk after the closeness of the restaurant, but echoes of last night were still too strong, plus there was something about the antiquities dealer, a certain smug confidence or maybe a prissy tidiness and polish, that made her feel contrary just as she had when deciding on a Manhattan rather than the wine he had chosen.

She watched him out of sight around the corner, bound for his shop, he had said, then headed for her car. The cottonwood perfume was heavier on the air than before, sweet and nostalgic as summer memories. Rain must be moving in again. Though stars showed overhead she walked faster at the thought, and became aware that two figures that had been crossing toward her from the bike path also speeded up. That they meant to intercept her was clear enough to trigger an even brisker stride, though she felt no fear. Hurrying was a reflex. She was not interested in conversation with strangers tonight, or even a panhandling encounter with what she could now tell were street people. One stumbled and was steadied by the other as they reached the car, all three at the same time.

"Jeneva Leopold?" said a muffled rumble, as though the words came from inside a barrel rather than from the barrel-shaped man. "You better come."

"Excuse me?" She could smell them now. Smoke, pee, sweat, earth.

"Come with us. Now."

"Are you asking me to go somewhere with you? Right now?"

The simple questions were too much for the speaker and had to be repeated , but at length Neva understood that some unnamed person wanted to meet with her right now, tonight, close by, over there on the bike path. They had been told to bring her, they had to hurry, she had to come.

"Couldn't whoever wants to see me come here?"

No. She must go with them, that's what they had been told, to be sure to bring her back. It was important, very important.

"Most people call me on the telephone."

It hadn't been meant as a joke but the remark got a laugh, followed by a coughing fit from the speaker. His friend slapped him hard on the back, so hard he was knocked forward, stumbling. Neva caught him by the arms and set him up straight again like a soggy Teddy bear. He was surprisingly light and even fragile inside the puffy jacket, and she knew now who he was. He was the drunk who had recited the poem at Angel's memorial gathering.

"Asthma," he gasped. "It's bad this time of year."

"You shouldn't be down here on the river, not with so much pollen."

"Live here," he said, waving an arm out toward the water.

"You know, I really can't go with you," she said, reasonable and conversational. "I'm sure you can understand that. I don't know your names, or where you want to take me, and it's late. There are people coming and going at the restaurant so I don't mind talking to you or anyone right here. On the other hand, if you could tell me who sent you it might help."

"She said not to tell."

"Ah, I see. Maybe she was too busy feeding cats to come herself?"

The spokesman chortled and elbowed his very tall friend. "Did you get that, Tomasino?" And then to Neva, "Don't tell her you know. She'll be mad. But I didn't tell, did I?"

"No, you didn't tell. You did your job just fine. Is she up the bike path somewhere?"

"Those fishermen go there. We better go or she'll be mad."

"Sounds like she has quite a temper."

Again the chortle and elbowing of Tomasino, who made a low sound that could have been a laugh. Without consciously deciding to go along, Neva found herself walking between them, the spokesman on her left, shuffling, and Tomasino on her right, dragging one leg. They crossed the street and turned upriver on the bike path.

"Did you write the poem you recited at Angel's memorial service?" Neva asked, more to keep talk going than because she had any doubt. "What is your name, by the way?"

"Hogan," he said, lurching to a halt and striking a declamatory stance. "When the flowers came out in color, Willamette lost its little brother . . ."

"That's a fine tribute to a friend," Neva said when he reached the end of what seemed like considerably more verses than he'd recited in the church. "Do you have any idea who would have wanted to kill Angel?"

"That's. What. They. All. Ask." Tomasino's words, the first he'd spoken, came out one at a time like separate productions in his brain.

"We have to go," Hogan urged and again they fell into step three abreast on the bike path.

"Who asks?" Neva said, and touched Tomasino on the jacket sleeve. He towered above her, thin and swaying like a plant starved for light.

Wordless sounds came in reply, but before she could press for a clearer answer, Hogan turned off the paved path and led the way down a narrow dirt track. Blackberry vines grabbed at her jacket. The last street lamp was far behind. Descending into the smell of river with Hogan ahead and Tomasino following, Neva felt suddenly like a sacrificial victim being led to a site of ritual drowning. This was a ludicrous thing to be doing—anyone could be waiting down here. Hogan had not actually said it was Reba. Maybe he had just played along with her guess . . . Ahead of her he stumbled and her hand flashed out automatically to catch him by the back of the jacket. These two were about as capable of plotting as a pair of newborn puppies.

The path leveled and led into a small clearing bounded by a half-circle of willows that faced the river. A sturdy figure stepped out from among the bushes on the far side. "Hello, Jeneva Leopold."

"Hello, Reba Winner."

"You're going to get into trouble someday, taking up with homeless guys on the riverfront."

"These aren't just any old homeless guys, they're Tomasino and Hogan the Verse Writer."

"You know them?"

"I do now."

"Sshh!" Reba said when the men hooted, although she also sounded amused. "I'm trying to stay out of sight, remember? They patrol the bike path just like everyplace else. Tomasino, come here."

Tomasino stepped forward, turned to face Neva, and cleared his throat. He cleared it again, and a third time.

"Tell her," urged Reba. "You said you wanted to tell somebody, so here's your chance."

"My, legs, hurt, bad," Tomasino began, again speaking each word individually. "My legs hurt bad. My hips are real bad, too. I can't hardly sleep at night. So I went to lay down. In the bushes. I was laying there. Maybe I went to sleep. I don't know. It didn't feel like it. I heard talking. There was people talking. I didn't say nothing. I just laid there. Somebody was on the bike path. On that bench. Sitting on that bench. Talking. I could hear them. They couldn't see me but I could hear them. A man talked. He said somebody made a plan. The plan was for Angel to be dead soon. How could he be dead? That's what the other man said. Trust me on this. He will be dead soon. Real soon. Then they left. I got up. My legs hurt. I looked for Angel. To tell him about it. I went to his bench. He had some people there. So I waited and they went away. I told him about it. He laughed. Then he was killed. That's what happened."

The quiet that followed Tomasino's lengthy and painful recitation was broken only by the whisper of the wide, black river. The air that had tasted sweet as they descended the trail now felt thick and overripe. At last, with an effort, as though Tomasino's brain pattern had taken partial hold of her own mental workings, Neva said, "Did you recognize the voices? Of the men?"

"It. Was. Far." A pause. "Maybe. I. Heard. One. Before."

"One seemed familiar?"

"I. Guess. So."

"Which one?"

This confused him until Reba said with slow precision, "There were two men talking. The first man said that Angel would be dead soon. Was that the voice you maybe heard before?"

"No. I. Never. Heard. That. One."

"So it was the voice of the second man that you thought you might have heard before? The one who asked how the other one could know that Angel would be dead?"

The big head nodded, yes, it was the second man.

"A man has been arrested for the murder and another man is wanted by the police. The man who was arrested is Vance Fowler. Do you know Vance?"

Another nod.

"Was it Vance's voice you heard, the familiar voice?"

The thin shoulders went up in a shrug while the head did a slow shake.

"The man who is wanted is Ernold Quick, the one they call Quickie. Do you know Ernold Quick?"

A nod.

"Was it Quick's voice that was familiar?"

Another shrug. "It. Was. Far." A pause. "I. Was. Scared."

"I can understand that." Neva felt an urge to rock the poor, wounded creature in her arms. Could he have turned out differently with different raising? The height and stressed joints were in the genes, but there must be treatments to relieve the pain, and the terrible, halting speech might have been trainable into something less frustrating—for the speaker and hearers alike. "Thank you, Tomasino. This is extremely important and I appreciate being told. Just a few more questions, if you don't mind, to help me know what to do with the information. I need to know when the conversation took place. Was it the night Angel was killed?"

"No."

"Was it the day before Angel was killed?"

"No."

"Was it several days before Angel was killed?"

"No."

Tomasino was shaking his big head so hard it made his body sway alarmingly. Reba gripped his arm. "Tom-Tom, it's okay. We'll figure it out. Think back. Think of when you heard the two men talking. Then say a few words about how long it was until Angel died."

"That day," he said without having to think.

"Oh, that day," Neva said. "Not that night. I'm sorry, I don't mean to be confusing. You heard the conversation during the day, and that night Angel was killed. Is that right?"

"That's. It."

"When the man said it that Angel would be dead soon, did you think he meant he would be killed by someone?"

"Seems. Like. It."

"Did you talk about this to anyone else, anyone besides Hogan and Reba? And now me."

"I. Did. Not. Talk."

"Was anyone else there when you told Angel."

"No."

"Did the two men see you?"

"No. Way."

"Good. At least we don't have to worry about that."

"What are you going to do?" Reba demanded. "Do you think this is just drunks bullshitting?"

"Of course not." Neva hesitated, wondering why she wasn't very excited by Tomasino's story. She had been more galvanized by Carter Grey's insurance lead even though the riverfront project was trivial compared with two violent deaths. Was she, as Reba suggested, less impressed by the information because it came from a confused wino or druggie? And now she would worry about Tomasino as well as Reba, about his leg pain and the possibility that he might have been seen by the men he overheard.

"I'm not sure what I'll do with this information even though it seems very significant," she said, feeling only a little false. In the morning things would no doubt be clearer. "I really don't know what to make of it all, of this and other things. If he recognized one of the men, one of the voices, we would need to figure out how to tell the police."

"No. Police." Again Tomasino was shaking his head.

"Oh, sorry, Tomasino, I'm not suggesting this, I mean I'm not suggesting that you should talk to the police. But if you could identify who it was you heard talking, someone should pass that information along. I'd be glad to do this, but at the moment I'm not thinking very clearly about any of it. Do you have any ideas, Reba?"

"I have so many ideas I can't sleep nights. Why do you think I'm out here all the time? That's my big problem, obsessing about everything. What are you going to do about this?"

"As I said, I'm not really sure. I need to think about it when I'm not so tired. And right now I'm wondering about Tomasino's joint pains. I've read about this kind of thing, about people who grow too fast and tall for their joints to keep up. Is he getting any medical help?"

"Hear that, Tomasino?" Reba sounded amused. "He smokes his meds, don't you Tomasino? He had a medical marijuana card but it got lost. Twice."

"Maybe he should have Debo keep it the way she used to keep Angel's disability money."

This amused them all. The giggle was followed by a brief silence that Reba broke. "We better get going. I'll take you. You guys stay here until I get back."

"I can find my own way," Neva protested.

But Reba was striding toward the path, and Neva followed after saying goodnight to the men, who had collapsed on some scraps of bedding already. Reba led the way in silence nearly to the bike path, where she stopped abruptly and backed into Neva, whispering, "Get down."

Light streaked the darkness and the sound of an engine swelled.

"Cops," Reba whispered.

"There's no road."

"They go on the bike trail. All the way down to the point. You don't expect them to walk?"

To be hiding from police was such a new experience that it felt like a game. On her own, Neva would have walked openly on the path, hoping the officer would stop so she could inquire about the surprising practice of driving on bicycle trails, but this was Reba's world, not hers, and her role was to follow. When the sound of the car vanished upriver, Reba led the way out of the blackberries and back toward the lights of downtown.

"You're okay now," she said, stopping beyond the reach of the first streetlamp.

"My car is just up the street. Is there some way I can find you if I have questions? Which I'm sure to in the morning."

"I don't hide. I'm out and about."

"Right. Though so far you have found me rather than the other way around. Did you take the pack out of my car today?"

"Sorry about that, but it wasn't locked."

"No problem. I half expected that you'd come back for it. Can I give you a ride somewhere?"

"I have to go back. Those two are making me worried, especially Tomasino. I heard one time that God protects drunks and babies, but that's just drunks with bank accounts. And *little* babies, not big babies with bad knees."

Chapter Ten

In the morning, Neva arrived on Twelfth Place early, so early the cobwebs strung between weeds in the front yard of the old house shone with dew. Even so, Vance's grandmother was already in her rocking chair scowling out at the world through the twisted trunk and dangling flowers of a wisteria that engulfed her porch. Now that Neva knew of the family connection between the two old women, the vine's messy abundance, like the uncut grass and riotous shrubbery, seemed a calculated affront to the meticulous home-maintenance next door. Were these two radically different women sisters or sisters-in-law?

"Good morning," Neva said as she started up the steps. "I'm Jeneva Leopold from the *Willamette Current*."

"Tell me something I don't know." The words were ruder than either the tone or the voice itself, which was surprisingly pleasant in timbre.

"No, no, that's your job," Neva replied cheerfully. "Remember, I'm the nosy journalist and you're the source who sent word you have a story to tell."

The old woman's lip twitched though she didn't smile or speak. She did, however, wave Neva to a straight-backed chair. The chair had no seat. Neva looked at it, scanned the miscellaneous tools and trash strewn the length of the porch, retrieved a stout gray cedar shingle from a stack, put it across the seat opening, placed what looked like the back of an old life vest on top, sat on it, frowned, stood up, turned the vest over, and sat again.

"Nice view," she said, looking into the wisteria trunk.

Her reward was a snort, but this was as encouraging as a belly laugh and allowed her to begin. "I had a strange experience last night. Actually, it kept me awake for quite a while after I got home, and I thought of you."

She said nothing more until her listener moved her feet impatiently. Although Neva hadn't looked directly at her while speaking, she had tallied the details of the old woman's appearance, which was opposite to Wygelia's in every way. Lean, opulently wrinkled, wound up in sweaters and shawls like a refugee, hair hidden under a black and pink stocking cap, slippers swaddling her feet below baggy trousers tucked into thick socks, a smell of old wool and Campbell's soup.

"I'm going to tell you what happened to me last night," she said, still gazing out at the yard rather than at her audience of one. "And I've decided not to charge you five hundred dollars even though it's a good story. As you apparently know, I write columns for the paper about all kinds of subjects, some personal but most having to do with community issues. Yesterday's column was on the big public hearing about the riverfront park. Readers often call me with ideas or information, and sometimes they invite me to have a drink, coffee, or even dinner."

She paused and glanced at the old woman, who was paying close attention, with no presence of indifference.

"Yesterday, a man I didn't know called and said he had some interesting information about the riverfront and would I meet him for a drink so we could talk it over. Most of the time I try to persuade such callers just to talk to me on the telephone, but for some reason I said yes to this man, maybe because I was feeling emotionally wrung out and he had a lovely voice. He's an antique prints and documents dealer named Carter Grey who recently opened a shop downtown. We met at a new restaurant called *Au Currant* and talked for quite a while, in part about a very interesting theory that may explain why the city wants to do such massive bank stabilization just for a park. We ended up eating a whole tray of appetizers, and by the time we finished it was after dark. We said goodnight outside the restaurant and he went down the street and I went back to my car. Just as I got there, two men came over from the bike path. It was easy to see they were street people. They said someone wanted to talk to me and I should go with them immediately, on foot up the dark bike path."

"You didn't!"

"I did. The really dangerous situations take you by surprise, they don't walk up and rumble conversationally at you, plus I used to work at a soup kitchen. Believe me, people who have trouble standing up are no threat. And I had a pretty good idea who wanted to talk to me. I went with them just about to where Coffee Creek flows in, down below the Beanery. We took a side path there." Neva continued the tale, spinning it out, pausing for dramatic effect, embellishing a little, paraphrasing Tomasino's account, and concluding, "What this suggests is that Angel's murder was not a random street crime, or triggered by the money he was carrying. Someone planned this. And there was more than one person in the plan, by the sound of it. I don't know what that might say about Lyle McRae's death. Did you read about Lyle in yesterday's paper?"

Her listener nodded.

"My point is that this seems to be a lot more complicated than it looks from the news stories. It also makes me wonder whether any others could be in danger, as well, because of what Lyle said about being on a list. The police have gone off on a very specific track and don't seem interested in any other possibilities. I've been drawn in, you see, but don't really know what I'm doing."

The long silence that followed nearly persuaded Neva that her strategy had failed, but at last the old woman said, "My sister's a fool, in case you didn't notice. She destroyed my daughter and I haven't talked to her since except when it couldn't be avoided. That's the story."

"Your daughter?"

"Vance's mother. She was only fifteen and that woman made her have the baby, made her think only a criminal would have an abortion. After, she was never the same, and then she was dead."

The flatness of the old woman's voice did not disguise her anguish. About to murmur sympathetic words, Neva was struck by the realization that her companion didn't want to give up any part of her pain to a near stranger, not even to the extent of accepting sympathy.

"How old was your daughter when she died?" The question was crisp, even businesslike.

"Eighteen. They found her in the river. They said suicide but they didn't care enough to look, not really look."

"Then Vance was around three when it happened?"

"I wouldn't have him," she rasped, twisting her hands.

"He grew up with Wygelia?"

"If you can call it that. She spoiled him. I tell you, she's a fool and always was and look what's to show for it!" Her hands grasped the arms of the rocker and her body quivered. "He was only fourteen the first time he was arrested. She wanted me to pay bail but I shut the door in her face."

After a silence, she cried, "I'm too old for this! I'm too old."

"You think Vance did kill Angel de Silva?"

The old woman stared, then exploded. "Of course not! She thinks so, I know she does, she raised him and now she's throwing him away like she threw away my baby. But not this time. Not this time!"

Neva reached instinctively to take hold of the older woman as she half rose from the rocker but she collapsed back again with a groan, shrinking from Neva's touch. Waving help away, she composed herself into a rigid figure of judgment. "Sleeping in the park isn't murder. Taking drugs isn't murder. His father was a crazy young skunk, not a killer."

"I thought you said to Charlie Frank, the young reporter who was here, that Vance was a no-good character and deserved the death penalty."

"I was angry. At her, at him, at the whole stupid lot of them. They ruined my life. But that's still not murder, is it? Anyway, he says he didn't do it and he never was a liar."

"You've seen him?"

Neva's surprise appeared to please the other woman, who nodded. "I went down to the jail but she wouldn't go. She said this family's reputation is ruined. This family never had any reputation since they found my Sheila in the river!" Trembling again, she said, "I don't have any more to say. I saw you over there at her house, and I just wanted you to know he didn't do it. His father was a skunk and I wouldn't have him to raise, but he didn't do it. That's all. Goodbye."

"Two things before I go, please. I just realized I don't know your name?"

"Arva Beatrice Jacoby Fowler."

"Thank you. And why did you tell Frankie I had to pay five hundred dollars for your story?"

Arva Fowler showed a glint of real amusement. "Anything you pay for is more valuable than what you get for nothing. It got you here anyway."

From Arva's house to the *Current* building was just eight blocks, a quick trip on foot, but still Neva stopped at the first bench in Azalea Park to write down everything she could recall of the old woman's story, in her own words as near as possible. That Arva remained furious and bitter all these years later she understood easily, but that she had turned her back on her grandson, on her beloved daughter's child, had left him to be raised by the despised sister-in-law she blamed for her daughter's death, was beyond comprehension. What must it have been like for Vance to be raised at Wygelia's while being banned from his grandmother's house next door? Wygelia, domestic, motherly, sympathetic . . . *I found him crying out there after supper. Poor little boots, he took everything to heart* . . . Had Arva been looking out the window that evening when her grandson tried to replant the limp carrot seedlings?

When the note-making was done, Neva sat on for some minutes longer, allowing confused sympathy to run its course. Things are always more complicated in families than they appear from outside, it was not her place to judge, especially while knowing so little, but really it was too, too sad.

When she walked on it was no longer toward the office but in the direction of the river. At First Street she turned left toward the warehouse, resolutely, without hesitating, though the sight of the empty sidewalk in front of Lyle's door made her pause. It had been less than 48 hours since the murder, yet there was no sign that anything had happened here, no yellow crime scene tape barring the way in, no investigators, cars or equipment, not even, she saw with real surprise, a lock on the door. It remained as she had found it two nights ago, with the small difference that the hasp had been hooked over the staple. The door would not blow open or yield to a stray cat or light touch of the fingers, but anyone could walk in.

Something else was wrong as well. Uneasy, standing back with her arms crossed, she waited, listening, feeling the air. Nothing, there was nothing happening here at all, and this was the troubling thing. Not only was there no sign of a crime scene, no securing of the premises, but there was no evidence of any sort that a terrible event had occurred here. Angel's bench had been smothered in offerings from people who had known him only as the friendly spirit of the post office. Lyle McRae, who had created enduring beauty in the heart of the community, had not been remembered, honored or recognized with a single daffodil.

And she, too, had come with empty hands.

It didn't matter that to bring flowers here was like taking sand to the beach. Lyle had loved flowers and their stark absence from his doorstep at this time was a second crime against him. Tomorrow she would cut whatever was blooming in her yard, hyacinth, quince, camellias, and leave them here in a bucket of water.

And maybe she should write about the gardener, should remind readers of just what he had given them all and continued to give as his daffodils, tulips and perennials bloomed on for months and even years. Maybe this is what had drawn her back here, an underlying sense that something more was needed than the pat description of the gardener in the news stories.

She unhooked the latch and pushed the door open. The earthy current that flowed out was even more intense than on her first visit, as though the air had been pent up and waiting like a healthy creature to get out. Standing with her eyes closed, Neva tasted the complex brew of soil, leaves, blossom, and wood. Nothing was out of place, nothing had been disturbed apart from the loss of the man who had created it all.

She stepped over the sill and walked to the edge of the light patch cast by the open doorway. Here she waited for her eyes to adjust and the mood of the warehouse to enter into her. Despite the open door, it was deeply quiet. Pillars took shape in the gloom, solid and handsome just as she remembered.

NO ANGEL

And as before, the topmost steps were bathed in pale green light. Placing her feet with care, she crossed the dim room and climbed toward Lyle's hidden world. As her head cleared the floor of the greenhouse a tingling ran down her spine and she tensed as though in preparation for a challenge or a shock of some kind, but turning quickly at the top she saw only plants. Looking hard at the crowded trees, shrubs, and ferns she was struck by their perfection. They were too perfect, too green and robust. The hands that had planted and tended them were cold and dead, yet not a stem or leaf drooped.

This seemed wrong, somehow, like children showing indifference to the death of a parent—and yet it would have been worse to find the plants wilting and dying. The greenhouse was a community treasure, but the plants could not thrive here for long on their own. Without careful tending they would die, some very soon. Many were too large to move even if new homes could be found, and it would be a great loss to break up the garden.

Neva went to the chair and settled in it again, her gaze moving over leaves, bark, vines, blossoms. Who was responsible for all this now? Lyle had no known living relatives, and certainly no heirs. Whoever owned the building must now own the plants by default. When she tracked down the partners in Left Bank her first question would be about the plants. Was there a way to keep the place intact? A nursery? A garden restaurant? Would they consider donating it to the community, maybe in memory of the gardener? As an indoor park?

An indoor park. . . An indoor park!

What a comforting place it would be to visit on those gray January days that smother the heart and chill the soul. It would be far better than the local garden nursery greenhouses she sometimes sought out for relief in the winter, so much bigger, the plants mature rather than in small pots waiting for new homes. Here it was always warm, always summer, always sunny—she looked around, puzzled. Though it was not sunny outside at the moment the light in here was distinctly golden as well as green. She stood up and stepped over to where she had a clear view of the windows. The glass in the top third was rich yellow, a touch she had not noticed on her first visit. Any light coming through would take on a sunshine cast even on the grayest of days.

"Well done, Lyle," she murmured. Turning back to the plants, she went to the vanilla orchid, then to a tree trunk covered in ferns like shaggy green fur, then to a plant with deep crimson leaves. What was it? What were they all? Despite years of gardening she recognized almost nothing, and not a single plant was labeled. One of the first steps would be to invite a horticulturist over from campus to identify things, and maybe this would be the way to begin her campaign for an indoor park. Her first column in a series would describe the greenhouse and give a rough tally of the number and types of plants, including what was rare and unusual. No doubt the official reaction would be negative at first. *Parks are outdoors, not indoors. The city is not in the business of maintaining warehouses for public use. It would be too expensive to keep up.* . . . though if some of the lottery money still existed in an account somewhere, maybe it could be used to sustain Lyle's legacy—an interesting legal question in its own right.

The key thing was to rouse public enthusiasm by letting people see this wonder for themselves. It was a perfect situation for an open house, with the whole town invited to walk through the greenhouse and imagine it as a public park. They could have horticulturists and botanists on hand for guides, serve refreshments, invite suggestions and donations to a park fund. It would be a memorial to Lyle McRae, the ultimate bouquet, to keep his own flowers blooming forever. She could picture it so easily that it seemed real already, even inevitable, though she knew such a campaign would require months to carry out and might well fail.

Meanwhile the plants must be cared for. Excited, happy to have a useful task, she went to the standpipe in the main path. The hose that had been coiled next to it on her first visit now lay stretched in loops down the path with a watering wand attached to the end. She picked up the wand. It dripped on her shoe.

Beside her was a tropical-looking tree with a fleshy-leaved creeper spilling from the lip of the pot to the floor. Working her fingers in under the creeper, she felt the soil. It was saturated.

Wind rattled a loose pane of glass. Neva let her gaze travel down the length of the windows to the far end, to the wall with a door that must lead to Lyle's private quarters. Simple and elegant, the door had been painted a dark terra cotta, and pots of white geraniums on low ceramic columns bloomed on either side as though on a porch. The door stood slightly open. She started toward it but stopped after two steps. The door had moved, surely it had moved. Slowly and steadily the gap between the door and the frame grew smaller until it was gone.

Watching the door, unable to imagine who could be on the other side, in Lyle's apartment, Neva stood rooted to the spot like the trees. Apart from the water that continued to drip from the wand she had set across the edge of a pot, there was only the calm silence of motionless leaves. Whoever had watered the plants was still here, and must have heard her open the door downstairs and had retreated to the apartment, and very likely had been watching her. A prickling chill ran down her back but even as she shivered, a reasonable interior voice said that anyone who came to water Lyle's plants could not be an enemy, could not be dangerous. They must feel kindly toward him—and they must have known him well, to care about his living treasures.

Without looking away from the door, Neva felt for the notebook in her bag, eased a page free, wrote two lines, placed the note on the floor in clear sight with a small rock on it, and ran down the stairs.

The newsroom was back to its usual deserted morning silence when Neva arrived after a rapid walk that had started as a run. Her heart was beating too fast but her thoughts had grown clearer, maybe from adrenalin, and she now realized that it would have been better to put her office phone number in the note rather than her home number. And she should have said why she wanted to talk, that she wanted details about the gardener that would help her create a real portrait, something more than the "familiar figure working in the flowerbeds around the park and courthouse." The column was due in four hours. It would be the first of two or three on the greenhouse and its creator, and even without talking to McRae's mystery friend, she could write tomorrow's column well enough. She would focus mainly on the garden, and hope the unseen plant-waterer could provide richer material on the man for a second installment in her campaign.

Zigzagging between empty desks, lost in thought, she didn't hear anyone come in behind her but as she was passing the coffee maker a voice said, "Some people think coffee's supposed to taste good." It was Frankie, and before she could turn around, his long arm reached around her for the pot. "My brain is a flock of sheep, and coffee is the sheepdog. Until the dog is in there, herding thoughts into place, I'm useless, lost, mentally adrift in the meadows of stupidity."

"Wow."

"That was original—and I've only had one cup. Think what I can do after this one." He poured a black stream into a cup big enough to boil corn. "I turned up something interesting about Lyle McRae. He didn't really win the lottery, that is, he won it for someone else. He bought the ticket. Nobody knows who for, I mean for whom, well, whatever. The thing is, he wasn't rich after all."

"Are you certain?"

"Afraid so."

"That really is disappointing."

"It is kind of a weird letdown, isn't it? But to be honest, I'm glad to have something new to report. I haven't found anybody who admits to knowing him more than passing. He was just somebody you saw pulling weeds."

"You're writing it for tomorrow?"

"It's all I've got going. Any particular reason you want to know?"

"I'm doing a column about my visit with him and what's going to happen to his plants. I'm going to suggest that the warehouse be turned into an indoor city park, and I had thought the lottery money might come in handy if it could be worked out legally. Scrub that part. How does an indoor park grab you?"

"Nice," he said with no pretense at real interest. "Neva, tell the truth, you're not going to spring new information on us, are you? Like, there was a witness and you found him and he turned out to be your long-lost brother and McRae actually strangled himself?"

"Frankie, you're a genius. You're so clever you can have the story."

"Seriously now. No shocks in tomorrow's column? Come on, spill it," he said when she hesitated.

"There's nothing to spill yet, not in this one, but I may have stumbled onto an interesting source, a possible friend of Lyle's. We haven't actually met yet, and it may come to nothing. And one other thing. I've been told by a homeless man that he overheard two men talking the day Angel died. One was apparently telling the other that 'someone' had made a plan and that Angel would be dead soon. He has no idea who they were, didn't see them. If true, it would mean it was no random street crime and not for the sake of the money. I can't see any way to use this given the source and the vagueness of it, though I'm certainly going to try to follow it up. At this point, I'm actually more interested in Lyle the gardener than Lyle the murder victim, so how about if I focus on his life and pass along anything that seems to bear directly on his death. Anything solid, I mean."

The young reporter continued to regard her with suspicion.

"You've done remarkably well so far with limited material," she said. "Truly, Frankie."

"Thanks, Mom."

"No problem, Son. Did you find out what he did live on, since he wasn't rich after all?"

"He earned a little bit selling exotic plants to nurseries, but that wouldn't keep a monk in rice, or whatever they eat."

"Any news on Quick?"

Frankie's headshake was slow and thoughtful. "I get a funny feeling about that, almost as though the cops aren't really trying to find him. You always say to trust those feelings, so the question is, what's their game? They're playing it really close. They're treating me just like the rest of the media, Portland TV, radio, the Salem and Eugene papers. No special breaks for the locals at all. You know what I think? I think they're having a blast. They finally get to use their special investigations squad and they're playing the drama for all it's worth."

For three hours, Neva resisted email, put a hold on calls, pushed all other thoughts out of mind, and wrote about Lyle and his private green world. The words came slowly, the lead alone taking half an hour. It was one of those columns that required the right opening before she could move on to the rest of the story, but at last she had it: "When he led me into his greenhouse two days before he died, Lyle McRae's hands on mine were strong and warm. A gardener's hands, nurturing hands . . ."

After the lead, her primary stumbling block was what to say about Angel, for she couldn't write about one killing without at least referring to the other, particularly when Angel had been so much better known than Lyle. The solution, she realized, was simply to say it was difficult to believe the two weren't connected but no link between them had been established. Reading the passage over she felt like a traitor—it was precisely to connect his own possible death with Angel's murder that Lyle had arranged to meet her—but she also felt a pulse of satisfaction. This was just the sort of seemingly innocuous observation that could nudge a reader with uncomfortable information into coming forward. Oftentimes, all that was wanted was an opening, an indirect invitation to spill the heavy beans, and she knew from experience that she was viewed by many as a far less frightening confidante than the police.

It was a full hour past her deadline by the time Neva forced herself to let the column go, and rather than wait around for possible questions from the section editor, she attached a note saying to call her at home. Before leaving, however, she had to make one final call of her own.

"Alexandrova," came the engineer's robust voice.

After the obligatory chat about the riverfront meeting and subsequent column, Neva got to the point: what about all those gravel trucks heading down to the riverfront?

"Gravel trucks? Well, gravel trucks. Yes." A pause and then, "We were concerned about the trucks from the beginning. If there'd been any way to route them other than through downtown you can bet we'd have done it."

"I guess I'm not being clear. I'm not concerned about traffic or noise problems. I just want to know

where the gravel is being dumped. What is it being used for in this phase of the project?"

"Ah, a good question, but not so simple to answer. Gravel has many uses. One moment, please." Her voice became small as though she had looked away from the telephone. "What's that? Of course, sorry, I lost track of time. I'll be right there." And then into the phone again, "Neva? Listen, I'd love to discuss this with you but they're waiting for me in the conference room. Could we talk another time?"

"Certainly. Tomorrow would be fine."

"Well, it looks to be quite a day, but how about I give you a ring when I can break free?"

Gravel has many uses, indeed!

Neva set the telephone down gently, as though to avoid alerting the woman at the other end to her own consternation. The usually direct and telegraphically informative engineer had been thrown by a question that should have a simple answer: *The gravel's being used to fill a culvert ditch at the foot of Abigail,* or, *It's being dumped behind the old shingle mill to use in mixing concrete.*

Hired three years ago from the San Francisco public works department, Anya Alexandrova had the rare power to make Neva feel like a school child called in for a scolding. Highly efficient people prone to sarcasm put her on the defensive, and to have the tables turn like this—to have Alexandrova flustered—should have been pleasant. Instead, she felt worried. The riverfront controversy was hot enough already without some mix-up about gravel that would no doubt turn out to be tedious but still inflammatory to one faction or another.

The only gravel she really wanted to concern herself with right now was decomposed granite—the best filler for the gaps between flagstones, according to the Oracle of Herman's Hardscape.

Chapter Eleven

It had been a long time since Neva waited through an evening for a telephone call, but at first the slashing and digging occupied her enough to keep impatience under control. With the cordless telephone on the back porch where she couldn't miss the ring, she managed to forget for minutes at a stretch that she was waiting for anything. The chicken stuffed hastily with rosemary and shoved into the oven sent tempting smells out the back door, and by the time she stopped to eat, the yard-waste recycling cart was crammed full of ivy, Virginia creeper, honeysuckle, and trumpet vines, and the pile next to the cart was nearly as tall as the cart itself.

Dinner was the chicken and raw baby turnips eaten whole like apples. Though the sun was down, she had worked up enough body heat to be able to sit out comfortably on the porch to eat. Pulling pieces off the bird, which sat in its roasting pan, she ate with her fingers while studying the mess she had made of her once-green haven of a yard. The small lawn was trampled to mud. Walls and fences were bare apart from feathery patterns where ivy and Virginia creeper rootlets had been left behind or had pulled away paint. A corner that had been filled with two straggling old rhododendrons was empty, the old rhodies sacrificed at last to light and order. A dozen small laurels, self-sown and tenacious, lay on the heap. A bamboo clump was a quarter of its former size and would be gone altogether if only she were a lumberjack with a stump router—it was slow going with the Pulaski though not nearly as slow as a shovel would have been.

Truly, it was a mess.

Best mess she'd made in a long time. And terrific roast chicken.

The silent phone caught her eye. There had not been a single call since she got home, not from work, or friends, or even pollsters. She had checked twice to be sure the phone was plugged in and the dial tone working, and that no messages had been left while she was hacking too hard to hear the ringer. It would take mere minutes to drive to the warehouse, but she would not find Lyle's friend there now, and, equally certain, the call would come in as soon as she left the house.

The simple meal ended in deep twilight. With the phone beside her, she settled in the armchair by the window to watch the last of the light go and to organize her thoughts. In the notepad she had started fresh the day of Angel's memorial service, she wrote headings at the top of four pages: Angel, Lyle, Riverfront, Left Bank/greenhouse. Left Bank presented the most obvious course of action. She must track down the names of the partners who were buying up the riverfront, who owned Lyle's greenhouse, and who might or might not also own Au Courant—the conversation with Grey had been so entertaining she'd forgotten to question the waiter. Now she listed research purchase history, find out where corporation details are listed and if public record, call DeeDee at Mentor Properties, ask her to snoop? question restaurant staff again, talk with other downtown business owners, chat up chamber of commerce clerk? She had used this ploy before with good results. Dropping by the Chamber office on the pretext of picking up a brochure about, say, local wineries, she would chat with whatever bouncy young thing was behind the counter. It was wonderful how office help picked up information without knowing, or perhaps caring, that it might be sensitive and not meant to be passed blithely along through casual conversation.

On the riverfront page, her notes included following up the gravel question with Anya Alexandrova, and stopping in to see her own insurance agent at Wellford's. She would pay her biennial premium, then lead the conversation into the hazards of building near water. She had learned not to ask certain kinds of questions directly, not to reveal the actual nature of her interest, since even sources with nothing to hide would sometimes turn coy if they thought they possessed useful and hard-to-get information. And the very fact that she had inquired about something could get talked around and cause a stir.

The Angel and Lyle pages of her list were uninspiring and brief. She must look up old news stories about the death of Arva Fowler's daughter, find Tomasino and question him more closely about the overheard conversation, and locate some memorial speakers other than Hogan. Her expectation that a few, at least, would be quoted by name in Frankie's memorial service news story had been disappointed. Some of the remarks were there, in italics, scattered through the story without attribution as though they were fragments of song or ancient verses. For editors to allow this was extraordinary, but it and had succeeded in conveying the power and emotion of the event more effectively than the usual, "'Blah blah blah,' said So-and-So, bowing her head in grief."

But it had failed to help in tracking down Angel's particular friends.

She set aside the notebook, stood up to stretch, yawned violently, and sat down again to consider a troubling question. What to tell the police? Never before had there been doubt in a question of reporting versus law enforcement; the line between journalism and police work was clear, or always had been clear. But now the line had become uncertain and she didn't know what to pass along. Tomasino's story would likely be dismissed as useless rumor from a druggie, just as Lyle's fears had been dismissed, while the business of the squashed shopping cart and Angel's remark about not being as dumb as some people think would be seen as a mere incident, without relevance to anything else, certainly not murder. The weight she gave things—for instance, the fact that Vance had saved Angel's life mere weeks ago—was not the same weight that official investigators were likely to give the same information. Rather than help, passing her random gleanings along could simply add confusion and bring unwanted attention down on vulnerable heads.

Or was she simply choosing to see things this way because of Marcum's memo—had it stung her enough to make her less willing than usual to cooperate with the proper investigators?

No. She was not that vulnerable to insult, not after twenty year's worth of letters from readers.

Night blackened the windows. With an irritated glance at the telephone as though it were to blame for failing to ring, she said, "All right then, forget it," and went down to the basement to roast coffee. She chose, as she so often did, the Ethiopian Yirgacheffe. After her first taste of the bean, she had looked it up online and printed the description to pin up on the wall by the workbench: "It is said that in 850 AD an Ethiopian goat herder named Kaldi discovered coffee when his flock began to dance around sleeplessly in the night. Curious, he discovered that his flock had been eating the cherries of coffee trees, and the rest is history. Ethiopian beans feature a fragrant aroma with hints of citrus and floral undertones. The subtle fruity taste of this bean is accompanied by a moderate acidity and light body. Excellent at any roast level."

Now, that was the sort of origin myth she could happily embrace. Bow down to Kaldi!

In the morning, Neva got up early, eager to put in an hour or two of patio prep. Before going to bed, she had placed the telephone back on its cradle and now she stopped in consternation halfway down the stairs—the message light was blinking. This was impossible. She had never slept through a ringing telephone in her life.

She ran down the remaining steps, snatched up the handset and scrolled through the recent list on the Caller I.D. Four calls had come in during the last hour, all from "Unknown." She punched in the message retrieval code and listened with chilled disbelief to the recorded voice.

"You have no new messages."

Sinking onto the hall chair, she sat still as the wave of disappointment crested. It was followed by disgust. She knew what had happened. She had not missed hearing the telephone. Two nights ago she had turned off the ringer to make sure of a solid sleep after being jerked awake by automated sales calls two mornings in a row. She had waited in vain through the evening and night for a call she couldn't hear because the ringer had been silenced by her own hand.

Truly ridiculous.

The caller had tried four times at roughly fifteen-minute intervals, and thanks to Caller I.D. she knew the calls had come from a pay phone. The last call had been made just ten minutes ago. Somewhere in downtown Willamette a figure stood hunched against the predawn chill near one of the few remaining public telephones wondering why Neva didn't answer. By the Safeway? At one of the two gas stations on Fourth Street? The Beanery telephone had vanished some years ago—but at least this meant there weren't many left to check. If she were to drive downtown and cruise through the empty morning streets . . . but surely, a fifth call would come soon. Anyone who had tried four times would try again.

Maybe it was time to break down and get a cell phone, or go whole hog and convert to an iPhone?

No, not worth it for the sake of rare missed calls like this. She did not want to be available every second of the day and night. It was a noisy, crowded, busy, distracting, intense world, a marvelously interesting world to be sure, but one that must be controlled where possible. She was free to choose. Her choice was for quiet and at least a sliver of privacy. She was not a reporter and did not need to be just a jingle away from the happening world every second of the day.

Still, it was frustrating, terribly frustrating, and even worrisome. Why had the caller not tried to reach her last evening? Had it taken all night to work up the courage? Or maybe he'd had no money for the pay phone and had collected bottles from recycling bins along the street?

A powerful wish to apologize to the caller, to comfort the caller, to reassure the caller made her want, again, to rush out into the dawn to find him. She would wait half an hour.

After checking to be sure the ringer was now on—the sound turned to maximum volume—she collected the newspaper from the porch, filled the kettle, ground beans, and read the *Current* from end to end, including all the wire service stories she usually skimmed or ignored. The telephone did not ring. She swept the kitchen, gathered the dirty dishtowels, washrag, and potholders and started a load of laundry. She turned on NPR but turned it off again immediately, preferring a waiting silence to voices that were not what she craved to hear. Afraid of making too much noise and drowning out the ringer, she resisted yard work until 8 o'clock, and then stuffed her feet into boots, yanked on gloves and attacked the last of the ivy with the telephone on a chair within reach.

The morning was sweet and clear. Finished too soon with the ivy, she got a basket and snippers to cut daffodils. Most were still buds but by going from bed to bed she found enough that were about to open to make a good bouquet. Working her way around from the back to the front yard, with the phone in the basket, she was crossing toward the flower border between the street and the lawn when she glanced toward the driveway. It was separated from the shaggy grass by a line of shrubs that had only partially leafed out. Her car stood in fairly clear view and on the windshield, tucked under the wiper blade, was a piece of blue paper.

Moving fast, sure of what she would find, Neva crossed the grass, went sideways between the lilac and mock orange, and retrieved the damp paper. It was a flier for a concert in the park, folded in half with the announcement showing on the outside. Inside, on the back of the flier, was a message written in pencil in a cramped, uneven hand: "I got your note. I red what you wrote about Lyle in the paper today but you should realize something and hears what it is. He always ment well but he was confuzed about some things. Im' sorry he got killed but its' better for some peeple. That's all I can say I gess. I hope it helps."

Neva read the note three times, stood looking into the air for a bit, folded the paper into eighths to go in her pocket and returned indoors. She plunked the daffodils into a canning jar, grabbed her bag and jacket, and left in the car. Minutes later she pulled up in front of Arva's ruin. The old woman was not in her usual seat, which, after a pang at this further disappointment, seemed for the best. She left the jar of flowers at the top of the porch steps and didn't bother with a note. The daffodils had been meant for Lyle McRae's door but the message on the flier had taken the heart out of that impulse.

Chapter Twelve

"Good column this morning, Neva."

Ambrose didn't just call out as Neva passed his office door, but stood up and came out to meet her. "Did I pick up the situation right? Were you *in* the warehouse? Since the murder?"

"Yesterday. In the early afternoon. I was drawn back there and I think it must have been subconscious concern about the plants, and then I got to thinking about what McRae has contributed to this town. The door's not locked, which seems strange."

"Umm, yes, well, if I'd realized he had a whole jungle in there, not just a greenhouse, we'd have done a feature, at the least a picture spread," the editor said with regret.

"It's not too late. It could help the park idea. Tours would be good as well, but I'm thinking it's too soon. Better to wait a bit before inviting the public in."

"You'd have a circus. What are you working on now?"

"I was going to do another column on Lyle, focused just on him rather than the park idea, but I may wait a bit on that, too. Frankie's story this morning is probably enough for now."

"Interesting about the lottery. Did you know he didn't get the money?"

"Nope. Frankie beat me fair and square. It's hard to believe there's no record of the real winner."

"The money was paid to Lyle." Ambrose shook his head, then nodded thoughtfully. "Whoever actually got it covered his tracks, but Frankie's not letting it go. He's really got his teeth into this one."

"You mean your teeth."

The first telephone call of the day, to Neva's realtor buddy DeeDee at Mentor Properties, bore instant fruit. DeeDee had been in real estate since the day she graduated from business college and joined her mother's two-person office. Now the owner of the largest realty company in town, she was Neva's guru on anything having to do with

NO ANGEL

property, and she needed no softening up before the question. "DeeDee, is there a way to find out who the partners are in a corporation listed as a property owner?"

"That's an easy one. That kind of corporate information is public record. Just check with the State Corporation Division in Salem. Who's the victim?"

"Something called Left Bank, Inc., that owns three blocks of riverfront and more."

"Hmmm, that rings a bell but only a dim one. I'll let it stew around in the back-brain closet and if anything pops out I'll let you know. On another subject, if you've got a minute, are you maybe being a little hard on the city over the jail bond? We really are short on beds."

"We?"

"The community." A pause. "I am on the jail siting committee, you know."

"I didn't know. Does this mean you're one of the crazy people trying to persuade us to quadruple the size, triple the staff, and spend more on it than we spend on parks, the youth club, the new fire station, and the City Hall remodel combined?"

DeeDee laughed merrily. "Well, it's hard to argue when you put it like that, but believe me, the situation isn't pretty. Criminals are coming here from all over because they know they'll get bumped back onto the streets in no time."

"What criminals?"

"All kinds, burglars, rapists, drug dealers."

"When was the last arrest for rape in Willamette? How can anyone claim we have more burglars flooding in when burglary rates have dropped in the county over the past two years? Didn't you hear the recent news report about Willamette being rated the safest small city in the country?"

"Well, yes, but you know how easy it is to twist figures any which-a-way. We have no idea how they reached that conclusion. Your column was persuasive, I admit, but when you look at it from the inside, it really does seem different. Just look at the jail. It's crammed. It's a disaster waiting to happen. And what about these murders? Two in a week, I mean, since when did we have that kind of crime?"

"We don't really know what kind of crimes they were, DeeDee. That's the thing to remember. If the police are right, Angel was killed by someone who grew up here."

"But the other one, the one they're looking for, he's a drifter who was let out of jail just before it happened. We had a breakfast meeting about it this morning."

"Your committee?" Neva hesitated, reminded herself that she and DeeDee always played it straight, and said, "Is Gale Marcum on the committee, by any chance?"

"Well, as it happens, he is the departmental liaison. He's very good. I wouldn't be surprised if he takes over as chief when Kitty Fiori moves on, as she's sure to one of these days. Have you interviewed him?"

Criminals flooding in from out of town! Looking unhappily at the telephone she had set down a little harder than usual, Neva regretted not pointing out to DeeDee that the guest column in today's *Current*, signed by Marcum and Fiori, had said nothing about an invasion of thugs. They wouldn't dare to air such tripe in a public forum, knowing they would be pounced on by readers who knew how to find real information on crime statistics. It's one thing to present bogus figures at a committee breakfast meeting and quite another to announce them in the newspaper. The fact was that in the past year crime in all areas except domestic violence had dropped in the county as well as the state as a whole. Even methamphetamine operations were scarcer with the new controls on ingredients.

The county did need a better and somewhat bigger jail. The puzzle was why the police and sheriff's departments were so determined to build what amounted to a small prison ten miles out of town. Was it a simple case of empire building? Fiori didn't seem the type for this, although she was campaigning hard for the jail, characterizing it as a prudent step toward protecting the community for years to come. Evidently, she had failed to notice a basic truth about this town—people here didn't much like locking up citizens. Except for really dangerous types, who belong in the state pen, they favor alternatives like home detention, treatment programs, work training, job placement and legalizing marijuana. She had lost count of the letters to the editor that made the same point: if you have lots of jail beds you're bound to fill them up, but if you don't have them, you're forced to find more humane and progressive alternatives. It had been a long time since "penitentiaries" were designed for repenting one's sins.

For a police chief who had wrenched a good ol' boy department out of its rut and turned it into a community-based agency featuring cops on bicycles, Fiori showed a strange blindness on the subject.

Before making another call, Neva allowed herself to dip into email, where she found six messages from senders she didn't recognize, all responding to the column on Lyle McRae. Three said roughly the same thing, that they had long appreciated his contributions to the beauty of the park and courthouse grounds, were horrified by what had happened, and were moved by her tribute and liked the indoor park suggestion. The fourth was so enthusiastic about the proposal that he'd already called some friends to arrange a meeting and would Neva be willing to address them about her idea? The fifth writer said why was the newspaper making such a big deal out of the deaths of a nutcase sicko gardener and an alcoholic panhandler when there were real issues needing investigation, like the conspiracy to take away our right to own guns. Refreshed by a good giggle, she pulled up the sixth message, from Hero@power.com.

"Some people should be dead."

Five simple words but they hit her like a slap. Flinching away from the screen, she sat back but leaned forward instantly to read them again. *Some people should be dead . . .* She felt for the note that had been left on her windshield and smoothed it out, still damp, on the desk. *Im' sorry he got killed but its' better for some people.* Same idea but a different writer, definitely a different writer, and though both must have known McRae pretty well, the windshield writer sounded regretful while the email message dripped bile. Something was festering here, ready to burst. Could it be Ernold Quick surfacing, full of the anger that McRae had feared? But these weren't the words of a killer, not one who had succeeded at any rate. A killer, surely, would have got vengeance enough in the deed.

Typing rapidly, Neva replied, "Your note was obviously written in response to my column about Lyle McRae. As I said in the column, I didn't know Lyle well, and visited him only once at the warehouse. The column was based on impressions from that visit, but I would welcome learning more about him from someone who knew him better, including someone who considers him better dead."

After sending this without allowing herself time for second thoughts, she returned to the message about the upcoming meeting and replied that she would be happy to talk with the group, and maybe they should also invite the director of city parks. As she hit the send button, the telephone rang and she snatched it up half expecting to hear the writer of the nasty note responding already to her message, but instead she heard the smooth voice of Carter Grey.

"Did I catch you at a bad time? I just wondered if you'd followed up on the insurance angle."

"It's on my list. I'm hoping to get to it today. How are you doing?"

Just fine, and he wanted her to know how much he had enjoyed the other evening and would she be free for dinner sometime this week, any night was fine, the sooner the better.

"Dinner?" she said, surprised into parroting the word though she'd heard it clearly. She was free tonight but she needed time to think. How was she to treat Carter Grey? Her male friends were all buddies, men she had known for years, and dinner with them didn't feel like a Date. Grey's invitation bore echoes of high school, as though some boy two rows over in Spanish class had called.

Her life could have been different. There had been plenty of opportunities for romance after Carlo died, but when Ethan was little, just thinking about the possibility of a powerful new romantic bond had felt wrong. What if her new man failed to love her son? It hadn't been worth the risk when he was young, and now being single was a settled habit, if a sometimes lonely one. At forty-six, she was still attractive enough—give or take a mastectomy or two—to draw a second look, and thanks to the summer at the mine, as fit as she'd ever been.

Was it time to let romantic love back into her life?

Possibly. But Carter Grey was not the man to provide it, though he might be a good subject to practice on, to help her rediscover how to behave as an interested woman. And as she recalled his confident and graceful attendance to her comfort at *Au Courant*, she thought she recognized the hallmarks of a committed flirt. The game was the object, and this suited her fine just now. In his company she could bask in sexual warmth without being required to extend herself emotionally or physically.

And then, who knows, she might find that she was ready for the real thing one of these days.

"Neva?" said Grey, "You still there?"

"Yes, I'm here. And yes, dinner would be lovely. How about tomorrow?"

Unable to regain her momentum after hanging up, she sat listening to the hubbub coming from the newsroom through her narrowly open door. Voices, phones, police scanner, laughter, the printer spewing out copy. It was a busy, familiar clatter, and struck her at that moment as a thing she would recall with nostalgia in the future when she no longer occupied this privileged seat . . . but that time was still years away.

Her call to the State Corporation Division got the usual lengthy recorded message about options. She punched five for corporation names and information, waited through another recording and several minutes of limp violin music, and at last was rewarded by a real and robust male voice. "Hello, this is John. How can I help you?"

NO ANGEL

Yes, he said, he could give her information about Left Bank, Inc., including the name of the corporate president, secretary, and registered agent for legal service of process. He would fax it to her for a dollar.

"Can I also get the names of the partners, just in case they're not the same as the officers?"

Yes, he thought the public had a right to see corporate reports, which should list the partners. He didn't have the details at hand, but the rules spelling out just what the public could request were in Chapter 60 of the Oregon Revised Statutes.

"Is that on the Web?"

"Right you are," John said, and read her the Web address.

Pleased by his sane, cooperative response—he could just as easily have played the game of bureaucratic impenetrability—she typed in the Web address, scrolled down the document, and stopped smiling. The sections went on and on, detailing every conceivable aspect of forming, running, and dissolving a corporation. To find the information she needed would take long, careful reading, more than she had time for during the day. It also would be hell on her eyes to read so much on a screen, but to print it would be a huge waste of paper. She tried a word search, but "partners" was in every other paragraph. The telephone rang and with relief she book-marked the site to peruse further if the faxed information didn't do the job.

"Leopold," she said in what struck her own ears as a cross tone of voice. She added sweetly, "This is Neva."

"Lars Oleander." The captain cleared his throat, said, "Sorry, just a bit of a cough, but do you have a minute? That was quite a piece you did on Lyle McRae."

"Thank you," she said automatically, though "quite a piece" was not necessarily a compliment. Was Oleander regretting his contemptuous dismissal of nearly everything the gardener had said?

"It did set me to wondering if you picked up anything else that you didn't include in the piece, anything that might help us with the investigation. A man will say some strange things when he's hysterical."

"Hysterical isn't really the right word. I'd say he was afraid and somewhat irrational in dealing with it, but not hysterical. You already got the whole story, everything he said to me. And now I don't know how to put this other than bluntly, but he was certainly right about being in danger. If you remember, you said he was just a nutcase."

"He was a nutcase." The words were flat and unapologetic, though followed immediately by a gentler tone. "That probably sounds terrible considering what happened, but some things are just true and you have to face it. This department doesn't have the resources to protect someone

120

like that, even for good reason, which there wasn't. Or didn't seem to be. But I don't want to get into a big discussion, just see if there's anything McRae told you that we should know, that you didn't mention."

"I can't think of anything, I'm sorry. I would like to ask you something, though. You say McRae was a nutcase. Is there more to that than his odd life in the warehouse, and doing his park work at night?"

"What do you mean, 'more'?"

"Other behaviors, things he did or was involved in. I've heard from two separate sources now that he was, well, I'm not sure just how to put it. Actually, one said that 'it's better for some people' that he's dead and the other one said 'some people should be dead.' Do you have any idea why anyone would say such things about Lyle McRae?"

"Now, who told you that?" The captain's voice had changed instantly. The hard tone was gone, replaced by the sort of voice that might be used to coax a child to eat. *Come now, just one little bite...*

"I don't know. That is, they didn't give their names."

"What were they like? What kind of people?"

"I'm afraid I have no idea. They're just anonymous notes. Readers send me notes all the time."

"And is that all they said?"

"Yes." It was not quite the truth, but nothing in the notes would help the police investigation. What tenuous possibilities they offered would be useful for her only, and she already regretted admitting their existence. She really needed to watch herself better.

"We'll need the originals. I was on my way out the door anyway."

"Originals? Are you asking for the notes?" Of course he was asking for the notes, but there must be a way to resist. She could say they both came by email and she'd deleted them because they were unpleasant, or simply refuse to turn them over without a court order since they were her private correspondence—and yet, why make a fuss, just out of principle. Oleander was right that anything related to the murder should be part of the official investigation. The note on the flier would require further explanations, but again, the mysterious plant waterer had known Lyle and should be interviewed. Why, then, did the prospect of police doing the interviewing make her feel like a traitor? To whom? The pitiful-sounding unseen author of the windshield note? Surely not the vicious writer of the email message. Her allegiance was to Lyle McRae, at least to the extent of making up for failing to protect him, or even trying seriously to help before it was too late, and surely this included giving police every scrap of possible evidence that came her way—except that her instincts recoiled from sharing the notes with anyone. Not now, not yet, not until she'd had time to feel for the path forward in her own way.

But was it worth the grand hoo-haw that would result from refusing, especially without good rational reasons?

No.

"They really say very little," she said into the silence on the telephone. "One came by email. It says only, 'Some people should be dead.' The other note was handwritten and left on the windshield of my car this morning. When I was at the warehouse yesterday I was going to water the plants but someone else had already done it, so I left a note on the floor asking them to call me. I figured they must have been a friend of Lyle's to be taking over the plant care like that. The note was on the back of an old concert poster. It's misspelled and really messy but readable. It says, 'I got your note. I read what you wrote about Lyle in the paper today but you should realize something and here's what it is. He always meant well but he was confused about some things. I'm sorry he got killed but it's better for some people. That's all I can say I guess. I hope it helps.'"

"That's it? Nothing more at all?"

"Nothing more, on either of them. Certainly no names."

"Well, it isn't much, but we'll have to have them. Did you answer the email?"

"Yes. I asked for more information."

"Then I'll need a copy of your message as well."

"Whatever for?"

"And copies of any replies. And if he does answer, don't write back. Call me."

The call left her feeling irritated and ineffectual. Of course Oleander would demand the notes, and had she thought for two seconds before speaking she would have avoided any mention of them. Her usual policy of complete openness in most situations needed amending here; extra care was needed on this one, not blundering honesty at every turn.

She photocopied the windshield note for herself and left the original copy along with a printout of the email message at the front desk for the captain to pick up. The library was not next on her list but it would give her a walk across the park to get there and she needed the outdoors to calm down. Striding vigorously, she did the figure eight loops twice but still she felt too restless for the small, picky business of looking for old news stories on microfilm. But here was the library and the task would soon be done. She'd take a longer walk when she was done.

Pausing outside the glass doors only long enough for a few breaths of sweet air, she was soon sitting in the basement at a microfiche reader. Why was it that turning through old yellowing newspaper pages was a thrill, a treasure hunt through tangible history, while speeding through plastic reels enlarged on a screen was cold and clinical—truly like a visit to a morgue—and generally left her feeling dizzy rather than richly rewarded?

By calculating backward using Vance Fowler's age as a marker, she determined the year of his mother's death, found the section of reels beginning in January, and began checking front pages. January, February, March . . . She found it in a Sunday edition at the end of April, three brief paragraphs at the bottom right of the page. The body of Sheila Margarita Fowler, 18, had been found lodged in willow brush on the bank of the Willamette River two miles downstream from town. Clothed in shorts and a T-shirt, the body had shown no marks of violence or recent sexual activity. No note was found but suicide had not been ruled out given that the deceased was prone to depression, according to Wygelia Chance, her aunt.

Searching for follow-up, she skimmed through two weeks' worth of news sections before finding an even smaller notice on an inside page. The investigation into the death of Sheila Margarita Fowler had been closed. Cause of death was by drowning. How the victim ended up in the river was inconclusive.

Inconclusive? A drowned puppy might get more notice than this on a slow day at the *Current.* Deaths of young people, accidental or otherwise, weren't common here. Sheila must have been known already to the police as a girl headed for trouble, which should have made no difference, but there was a distinct echo here of Oleander's attitude about Angel and McRae. No wonder Arva remained bitter as well as grieving.

And now the baby that young Sheila had left motherless was in jail on a charge of murder.

With photocopies of the depressing articles folded in her bag, Neva headed back up the stairs but rather than making for the front door she turned spontaneously into the reading room. A stained glass window cast rich light on a double row of wingback chairs and dark wood tables. Beautiful and still, the room offered a monastic-like sanctuary that had often soothed her troubled thoughts. And she wasn't the only one who came here for comfort. After the library expansion and remodel three years ago, street people had taken to sleeping in the capacious chairs, slumped, reeking, and snoring.

Naturally there were complaints, but still it had been a surprise when the library board had taken the severe step of banning the homeless. To head off protest—vain hope, it turned out—the library had issued a press release saying that the problem was not the use of the reading room as a daytime dormitory so much as the use of the restroom sinks for bathing. Young readers, in particular, should not have to find half-naked winos sponging off with 50 feet of paper toweling, which ended up sodden in the sinks, clogging drains and costing taxpayers.

Neva had led the opposition, arguing in a series of columns that the rule was discriminatory, harsh, unnecessary, and unworthy of Willamette, but to no avail. The ban had gone forward, barring sleeping, sponging off in the toilets, and otherwise "carrying on in ways unsuitable to a public library." The problem now, as one librarian had since confided, was that staff members had to check the reading room during the day to see whether anyone was in violation, which then triggered a call to police if the violator refused to leave.

"The worst," the librarian had said, leaning across the checkout counter and dropping her voice, "was when I called the police on a man I couldn't wake up. He looked like he hadn't slept in a bed in weeks and his snoring was driving people out of the reading room. You know who he was? A botany professor. A full professor. I could have died."

Surveying the current occupants of the wing chairs to see how good she might be at sorting the plain riffraff from the credentialed riffraff, Neva discovered a pair of eyes that sent a shock of recognition through her, though she'd never seen the man before, she was certain. She could not have forgotten those yellow-brown cat eyes, or the raw quality of the skin and hair, as though he'd been coarsely manufactured and let go into the world without finishing touches.

They locked gazes for a long moment. His eyes dropped first, to the magazine folded in his hands. He set it on the side table, picked up a knapsack from the floor by his feet, and strode out of the room through a door at the far end.

Neva went to the chair and picked up the magazine. What had such a man found of interest in the *New Yorker*?

"I've never been the patient type but it's amazing what prison can do to tame a mind and body that were born in racing mode," she read at the top of the open page. "For the first three years it was all anger and punishment, but then something changed deep inside. If no one on earth was interested in getting justice for me, then I must get justice for myself. I began to study law."

The article had been written in prison by a convicted kidnapper who claimed to be innocent. She sat down in the chair, which was still warm, and began to read from the beginning. A sudden internal jolt stopped her. The man with cat eyes had written the repulsive email message about Lyle McRae. She knew this with the clarity of memory. She had not a scrap of evidence apart from what had been in his eyes when they recognized her, yet she would have bet anything that he had used a library computer to send the note.

She dropped the magazine and ran, out the reading room door, through the lobby, through the double front doors, across the entryway patio and down the steps. Less than two minutes had passed but there was no lean figure with a knapsack and coarse hair hurrying down the sidewalk, unlocking a bike, or pulling away in a car. She dashed across the street to the park, crossed the walkway and strode out into the middle of the first circle of grass. The park shrubbery, still mostly leafless, was not sufficient to hide a cat. A woman stood at the base of the slide to catch a small boy in a red cape, and a young couple held hands on a sunny bench. That was it.

The man had vanished and so, abruptly, did her confidence that he had written the note. It was nothing short of ridiculous. That he had recognized her was beyond question, but this was usual rather than unusual given how often her mug was in the paper. His flight could have any number of explanations. It had happened before, that look of surprised recognition followed by anger, irritation, or alarm, though far more often she received a look of interest from strangers who recognized her. Though she worked hard to be accurate, and gentle even in criticism, there was no way to keep from offending certain readers and subjects, or wounding them in unforeseeable ways that could get even their friends, relations and neighbors mad at Neva. And once angry with her, some readers tended to stay that way for years.

It was a mercy that he'd simply departed rather than confronting her in the library, though now she was left wondering just what had triggered that flash of emotion in the yellow-brown eyes or why she had felt a responsive wrench of familiarity. Could he have been the watcher from behind the door of Lyle's apartment? He would know her on sight though she would not know him . . . She was shaking her head. No, this man was not a lover of plants.

This one was going to puzzle her for days, but she must set it aside for the moment and clear her mind for the next task on the list: a visit to her insurance agent.

Wellford had been Neva's insurance company since she arrived in Willamette, with the same two agents handling the business for the entire time, but the office had relocated a few years ago from commercial quarters downtown to a grand old home west of the park. Each time she visited the handsomely restored Victorian on insurance business, Neva had the same conflicting reactions. Such well-proportioned rooms were meant to be lived in, not filled with desks and computers. On the other hand, Wellford had rescued the house from decrepitude, and possibly the wrecking ball, so the company could hardly be faulted for abuse of fine architecture.

"May I help you?" inquired a young woman she'd not seen before. Tall, hollow-cheeked, too tan for the season, cased in something white and stretchy, she reached purple fingernails to pick up a ringing telephone and informed the caller coolly that the office always closed at five sharp and would not be open at 5:15. The papers should be dropped through the mail slot.

"Is Tom in?" Neva inquired

"Mr. Seerio has a luncheon engagement."

"How about Lurleen?"

"Whom may I say is wishing to have an interview?"

"Please let her know that Jeneva Leopold would like to see her."

Lurleen Studebaker drew Neva into an office packed with sports memorabilia. That she looked more like a dorm mother than a jock would have led an uninitiated visitor to conclude that the display represented pride in her children's achievements. But the trophies were for Lurleen's own softball prowess, from her days as a player to her current role as the top women's league coach in the valley. She was also an enthusiastic supporter of women's basketball, rowing, and triathlon.

"Hey, young lady, there's still time for spring tryouts," she teased, taking up where she always did, that is, in the middle of her perennial insistence that Neva was a born pitcher, she could tell by the set of her shoulders.

"Sorry, I'm already signed with the Blazers."

"They play basketball, dear heart."

Their laughter was easy and light. Neva saw Lurleen only on rare insurance business or casually around town but the meetings were always as congenial as though they had an actual friendship. She had asked to see Lurleen's partner, Tom Seerio, because she would have felt less devious trying to finesse information out of him than Lurleen, but maybe this was a happy turn of events. Maybe she should simply play it straight with Lurleen, with the emphasis on play.

"I'm here under false pretenses," she said, and was encouraged by the other woman's look of quickened interest. "I'm pretending that I came to pay my six-month premium—oh, I am going to pay it, don't worry about that—but my secret object is to tease information out of you. Are you ready for the serve?"

Lurleen rolled her chair back a few feet and struck a defensive posture. "Ready."

"You know that the city's riverfront redevelopment plan calls for cutting down all the trees and shrubs and terracing the bank with something called geotextile in order to keep it from collapsing."

"Right."

"And that an opposition citizen's group has formed, claiming the riparian destruction and geotextile covering weren't spelled out in the bond measure. They've enlisted the expertise of river researchers who say the bank is stable the way it is and cutting down the trees could actually destabilize it."

"Right."

"The town is up in arms but the mayor, City Council and staff are refusing to change the plan, insisting it's the only way to go because we all approved it by voting for the bond measure in September."

"Right."

"And if you ask for explanations from city staffers, they say, 'We're doing what the elected councilors tell us to do.' And if you ask the councilors, they say, 'We're following staff recommendations and we trust our staff.'"

"Right." And then, with a chuckle, "I love it."

"But if you talk to the right people they say the real reason the city's being so stubborn is because insurance companies have said they won't insure riverfront buildings over two stories high unless the bank is reinforced through engineering."

Lurleen gave her a long look. "Oh, tricksy, tricksy. I always knew you were a sportswoman but I think, maybe, you're a poker player rather than softball." Despite the playful words, her expression was thoughtful, and when she spoke her tone was serious. "I'd like to know who set you off on that track, but I won't ask. I admit it sounds juicy, and you did make me wonder for a minute whether it could be right. But it's not. I hate to disappoint you, especially after the great setup, but it's just not true. We insure for the risks, whatever they are. We don't dictate standards, those are in the building code. I don't think city code has any such restrictions specific to riverbanks, but multi-story buildings have to have certain reinforcements for earthquakes and whatever. Frankly, that riverbank hasn't gone anywhere in the last hundred years so I doubt it's going anywhere in the next hundred. I'm with the team that says if it ain't broke don't fix it. Now, the real question is, who won?"

Though disappointed, Neva had to laugh. "You, of course. I didn't even begin to sneak one by."

"In that case, I'll ask around. Maybe I've missed something. I'm awful damn clever but I don't know everything."

Chapter Thirteen

Rather than return to her office, Neva picked up the car from the *Current* parking lot and headed for Herman's Hardscape. She needed to deal with something solid and material, something she could get her hands on without having to wonder what it was all about.

Herman was driving around the crowded lot in a small front-end loader. He waved and shouted something she couldn't make out, but his sweeping arm gesture was surely an invitation to go ahead and pick her own rock, as they'd discussed last time. She hadn't planned to do this today—the sand still had to be spread—and she had not come prepared with gloves, but Herman was an old hand at this business and kept a bin of heavy canvas work gloves next to the office door.

She grabbed a pair, gritty inside with fine sand, and headed for the pallets of Lone Pine Gold.

Herman was heading that way with an empty pallet on the loader tines. He set it down and roared off to a new task, and for a moment she stood uncertainly considering the two neat stacks of rock and the empty wood slats of the new pallet. Evidently, the pallet was intended for stacking the rocks she wanted—but she didn't know anything about rocks. She didn't know how to choose a rock, handle a rock, place a rock in a patio.

How could she have been so blithe about this monumental project?

The sensible course was to stop right here and hire an expert. It was not too late. She had nearly finished clearing the way, she could specify yellow rock, and in short order she would have a perfect patio . . . but it would have been built by other hands. This was not what she wanted. She wanted a patio built with her own hands and all it had to be was good enough.

As for choosing the rock, well, Herman had said last time that she should simply take a pallet and use whatever flagstones were in it. "You can bring back what you don't want," he'd said as though sweetening a deal, but added, "You'll use it all. They always do."

The two stacks appeared untouched, and so neatly arranged that the corners were square. The rocks on top of the nearest stack were gray. One, a long, rectangular piece, glinted with mica. With sudden determination, she grasped it by the ends and hoisted it into the air.

And set it down, hard. The rock was shockingly heavy. *Dead weight. Lift with your legs.*

With her knees slightly bent, she gripped the rock again and straightened her legs. Three careful steps to the second stack, ease the rock down on top, straighten the legs again. Not so difficult after all.

"What's wrong with that one?" Herman stepped up and patted the rejected stone.

"It's not yellow, not even in spots."

"Turn it over." Without waiting for a response, he flipped the flagstone with ease, as though it were a piece of dry wood. The underside was rich yellow-ochre with swirls of red at one end. "You have to check both sides."

"No kidding. It's gorgeous."

"Anyway, a little gray wouldn't hurt. Gray rocks in with the yellow. You don't want to mix different kinds of rock but the same kind in different colors is okay. You get your contrast and variation."

"That makes sense, though I really do want mostly yellow." She picked up the rectangular rock, which felt lighter now that she'd seen Herman handle it so easily, and squatted to place it on the empty pallet.

"You've got your work cut out for you," he said.

"I'm in the mood for hard labor, or I wouldn't be doing it."

"Most people hire contractors."

"Does that mean most of your customers are contractors?"

"Umm, maybe half. A lot of folks do paths and such, easier stuff."

"Do contractors take more care than amateurs in choosing rocks? Or less? Or no difference?"

"Hooey, now there's a question." Herman turned around in a complete circle, surveying his stone yard with a surprised air, as though seeing it for the first time. "That is a question. A real question."

A green pickup pulled into a parking spot near the office and two young men climbed out. Herman considered them for a moment, grunted, and went to meet them.

The website with the patio building instructions had recommended steel-toed boots "because you will drop at least one fifty-pound rock on your foot before you're done," but Neva had no such thing, even at home. She would have to mind her grip. Working with slow care, she now turned over every piece no matter how drab on top. The rocks were about two inches thick, though they were otherwise so irregular—square, rectangular, triangular, trapezoidal, randomly curved—that fitting them together might take the whole summer. No matter. Her pleasure in the stone grew steadily as she went down through the layers, exposing whole slabs of yellow, swirls of sienna and gold, and mixed pieces with gray, gold and glittering mica all in one.

She was about halfway through the first pallet when Herman returned.

"Cheap," he called out. "Contractors pick out cheap and charge more. See there? Contractors. Patios and such. They said 'What's your best deal today, Herman?' And I said, 'Depends what you want,' and they said, 'Depends what you're charging,' and I said, 'Like I said, depends what you want.'"

"What do they want?" Neva scanned the rock yard and spotted one of the men studying pink sandstone slabs and the other considering the pea gravel.

"Stepstones. Buildin' some walkways for a lady over by Scio."

"With what kind of rock?"

"Cheap. Like I said. They charge a price. Subtract costs, keep the rest."

"Makes sense in a business sort of way, as long as the customer's happy. I'm seeing some gorgeous rockwork around town these days. Who buys your most expensive stones?"

"Contractors."

Neva looked at him quizzically but before she could protest, *You just said contractors are cheap*, he said, "Picky people like you are expensive, taking out the best pieces."

"You said most people don't want yellow. You also said, if I remember right, that it doesn't matter because I pay for it just the same."

"I said that, did I? Well, then." Herman tugged his cap down tighter, stepped up to the pallet, picked up a stone, said, "Here's a beauty," and added it to her stack without waiting for approval.

In the morning, having forgotten all about the fax from the State Corporation Division, Neva plucked the two pages from her newsroom in-basket with no particular interest. Walking on, she scanned the top page and froze with one foot half lifted for the next step. It simply wasn't possible. It was not possible—yet here it was in black and white. Left Bank's only corporate officer was the president.

The president of Left Bank was Carter Grey.

Carter Grey was Left Bank and Left Bank was Carter Grey.

Casting back through her conversation with the antiquities dealer at *Au Courant* she felt a slow flush spread down her back. She had asked him outright about Left Bank, she was certain of it. Sitting convivially over food and wine, enjoying a man's company in a way she had not done for too long, laughing, expressing interest in his business and his knowledge—all this while she had been hoodwinked.

Incredible.

And what sort of game was he up to with the insurance farce? As a major riverfront property owner, he had to know that the insurance issue was a bogus tip, a false trail, as Lurleen had made clear. And, as the owner of the warehouse where Lyle had lived, he must have known the gardener, yet he had not mentioned him during their restaurant conversation apart from a general comment that it was a terrible business, and he had said nothing further on the telephone yesterday despite her morning column. And as for the restaurant, she would now be willing to bet that he owned it as well as the building. She recalled his ease, his familiarity with the menu and—the crowning exhibit—the fact that he had not been given a check. She had gone to the restroom and when she returned he was standing by the door with her jacket in hand. Struck by the fact that he had known which was hers and collected it already, she had not mentioned money. He was too obviously the gallant to allow her even to raise the question of paying her share but now she was certain there had been no bill.

Truly, it strained belief.

And she had agreed to meet this schemer for dinner. Tonight.

He must take her for an extraordinary fool.

She strode into her office, snatched up the telephone directory, and flipped through to Art Galleries without bothering to sit down. Winton & Grey Fine Original Antique Prints was the last entry. She copied the number onto her Post-it pad but in the few seconds required for the writing her thoughts sped in a different direction. Canceling the dinner would be satisfying but what would it accomplish apart from salving her feelings? Maybe the best way to even this score was to blow Grey's cover, to devote her Saturday column to property ownership on the riverfront, detailing the extent of Grey's holdings and featuring the restaurant. That he preferred to keep his business secret in general was not difficult to understand—for a newcomer to buy up a significant portion of downtown would not be well received—but he should have been honest with her. He had lost the privilege of claiming her discretion. She would see that he drank plenty of wine to loosen his tongue, and then maneuver him into telling all, about the restaurant as well as the Left Bank Corporation and its plans for the riverfront holdings. With community attention now focused on the redevelopment project, his telephone would ring for days with calls from partisans on both sides demanding his support.

It was possible that he owned only the building and someone else owned *Au Courant* and he had some special arrangement with them for his own bills, in which case he must have felt amused and pleased with his little game, deliberately leading her away from the question about Left Bank . . . and yet it was puzzling. He was an intelligent man and must know the game would be short-lived, that she would flush out the truth sooner rather than later. He had contacted her, not the other way around, and had as good as invited her to dig into a supposed rumor that was bound to turn up his own deep involvement. It really was baffling.

She had not yet looked at the second page of the fax and turned to it now. Titled "Name Change History," it was as spare as the first in its contents though without particular interest. From it she learned only that the name, Left Bank, Inc., dated back just six months. Before that the company had been called Northwestern Redevelopment, Inc. What anyone stood to gain from such a name change, she couldn't imagine. She had assumed that Left Bank was a playful nod to *Rive Gauche*, inspired by Willamette's position on the west side of the river. Northwestern Redevelopment was a good deal less interesting but surely it would be a rare businessman who would change a name for this reason.

Another angle suddenly struck her. Since it was Grey who owned Lyle's warehouse, she would broach the subject of the indoor park, and if he proved enthusiastic—if he proved enthusiastic and helpful—she would spare him the full exposure. If he found difficulties and opposed the plan, preferring some other use for the property, she would get what leverage she could from the threatened column. To use her column in this way was unprecedented, but then so was the entire situation. The beauty lay in the possibility of settling the score while pursuing something truly worthwhile for the community.

Almost cheerful again, Neva closed the office door and sat down at the keyboard. Her next column deadline wasn't for twenty-four hours, but if she could produce a quickie, something she could write out of her head without legwork—a MacColumn, as Ambrose had rather unoriginally dubbed her easy outs—it would give her a free day tomorrow for more digging.

Without having to think, she typed, "The farmer buried deep within me woke up yesterday morning as I harvested the season's first daffodils . . ."

Two hours later, with a publishable draft filed, she left the office, walked to the new gluten free bakery just to give it a try, and bought a cranberry cornmeal biscuit, warmed and buttered. Eating as she walked on, she turned upriver along the bike path. The afternoon light was somber despite an airy canopy of tender new cottonwood leaves and maple racemes overhead. Few strollers were out. A man and a dog lay on a sunny patch of grass, a young woman practiced juggling red and blue balls, a boy and a woman pedaled past on a tandem bike. Near the south end of town where the path ran into trees and shrubs a familiar figure approached from upriver.

Win Niagra raised a hand in greeting and would have passed without a word had she not said, "Hello, Win. I'm hoping to find Tomasino, a tall, skinny guy who goes around with Hogan. They have a camp somewhere along the river. Do you know him?"

"I do."

"Do you have any idea where he is right now?"

"I thought your business was writing about the community."

"Tomasino is part of this community."

"Is he? Do you really think these street people play a civic role? How enlightened of you."

Surprised and offended by the blunt animosity, so different from his graceful conduct on their first meeting, she looked at him without speaking until he said in a less resentful tone, "Tomasino's harmless. If you think he had anything to do with the Angel business, you're on the wrong trail. Street people are a surprising lot, you know. They're as complicated as anybody else and not human freaks, to be made into stories and then forgotten."

"Is that what you think I'm doing?"

He shrugged, looked away, and addressed his next words to the riverbank trees. "I lived on the streets before I got myself together. I know the hopelessness but also the sheer, fuck-the-establishment freedom of it. You don't have to give a rat's ass about what anyone thinks. You're not afraid. You do what you want and people feel sorry for you and give you money and you laugh at them for their fear and their safe, bourgeois lives. That shocks you."

"No, I'm afraid it doesn't. Was it something that happened during your street life that made you vulnerable to blackmail?"

Had he not been rude she wouldn't have asked the question, at least not so bluntly. As soon as the words were out she regretted them, but Niagra appeared amused rather than angry. "You're like one of those things, what do they call them, that you get in your socks out hiking. A tickseed, that's what you are, a sticky little tickseed. I begin to see how you get some of the surprising stuff in your columns. As it happens, though, the blackmail has nothing to do with my years on the street. It's a family matter, that's all, a family matter, and nobody's business at all."

Bobbing his head in a curiously old-fashioned gesture of parting, he went on his way. Turning to watch him go, Neva experienced the cartoon jolt of seeing him turn simultaneously to look back at her. That he handled it better than she did, coolly flashing the peace sign, gave sudden authority to his unflattering view of her behavior.

Did she regard Tomasino and Hogan and even Reba as mere story material?

Possibly. But this was how she viewed the entire world. Every sight, sound, smell, encounter, thought, and occurrence as she went through the day was potential column fodder. It wasn't pleasant to think of herself in this way, as a mere conduit for impressions to be assembled into 16 inches of text with a punch line . . . and yet, botanists notice plants, artists observe shape and color, psychiatrists analyze friends' behavior.

The man with a hammer sees nails everywhere.

And she did have one small piece of information to pass along to Tomasino. A call to county health had turned up a program that would help with anti-inflammatory drug treatments. It wasn't much, and she couldn't imagine Tomasino keeping track of daily doses, but maybe it would lead to more solid help.

Walking on, she came to the path that Hogan had led her down to meet Reba in the small clearing. Now the clearing was deserted, although just offshore a fisherman in waders stood casting into the current.

"Any luck?" She called.

"Don't expect any." The fisherman looked over his shoulder with a smile. "It's just an excuse to be on the river."

"Do you often come down here?"

"Regular would be a better word than often. Depends."

"Have you seen a tall, skinny man named Tomasino? His head kind of wobbles like it's too heavy for his neck. He's a sort of regular along the river."

"One of the bums, you mean? To be honest, I can't tell one wino from another. Seen one bum you've seen 'em all."

Bum . . . *Hallelujah, I'm a bum, hallelujah bum again, hallelujah give us a handout to revive us again.* You didn't hear them called bums so often these days. Homeless, indigent, street people. Why had they ever been called bums? She must remember to look it up.

Neva climbed the short trail back to the bike path and continued walking to the point where Coffee Creek flowed into the wide Willamette. Here the path turned to follow the creek upstream. A few hundred yards along, the path ducked under a railroad bridge where there was a dry camp used by drifters and the homeless. The hard ground was littered with cardboard, a sleeping bag, grimy lumps of clothing and blankets. A coffee pot with no lid sat on a rock next to the black remains of a fire. It was a dismal scene, and she didn't linger. Hogan had said the permanent camp was across the river, but she had suspected he was misleading her, most likely out of habit. Now she would have to try the other side after all.

Rather than follow the river back, Neva cut through the skateboard park that had been built some years ago thanks to successful lobbying by certain well-spoken skaters, who won over the city council and the community in general. Located under the highway bypass south of downtown, the entire thing was sunken, a great hemisphere of concrete set into the earth and humped with ramps and jumps where a dozen boys and one lone girl whizzed around. Intent on perfecting their moves, each one might have been the sole skater in the park, oblivious of the other hurtling figures no matter how close they came. Watching with appreciation, Neva made her way around the rim until she came to a large sign next to the parking lot:

OREGON LAW REQUIRES ALL PERSONS UNDER THE AGE OF 16 TO WEAR HELMETS WHILE RIDING A BICYCLE, SKATE BOARD, SCOOTER, OR ROLLERBLADES.
Failure to obey could land a fine of $25.
Next to the sign was a bulletin board bearing a large notice:
The Rider Code.
1. *Respect. Respect. Respect. No bad attitudes! Use respectful language, turn music volume down. Keep the respect you've fought so hard to earn.*
2. *Watch out for the other guy or girl. Nobody "rules" the park, not the best riders, not the biggest riders, not the majority.*
3. *Yield to riders in the front of the line.*
4. *When the park is crowded call out your obstacle.*

A flier on the bulletin board announced the *13th Annual SK8R Bash, Big Air, Board Grabs, Rockin' Music.*

As Neva turned to see whether the skaters obeyed the helmet rule, the girl skater popped onto the rim and caught the board that flew up behind her. With fluid grace that made it seem all one movement, she hooked the board onto the back of a bicycle and wheeled the bike around in Neva's direction.

It was, again, the girl from Angel's memorial gathering.

NO ANGEL

"Hello!" Neva said and stepped into the path.

The girl swung a leg over the seat, then sat waiting without expression for whatever Neva would say or do next. Lean and athletic, she had a fresh wholesomeness that didn't go with the graffiti spray can in her shirt pocket.

"I'm Neva Leopold. I write columns for the *Willamette Current* about all sorts of subjects. This is my first close look at the skate park since it was finished, though I supported the idea from the start, in writing I mean. Is it a good one, do you think, as skate parks go?"

"Definitely."

"What makes a good skate park?"

"Plenty of ramps. Room so you don't crash." She shrugged. "The whole thing, you know."

"I was just reading the notice about the skate bash. Did you go to that?"

"No way. Can't handle the egos."

Neva laughed and nodded. "I can imagine. Sometime, if you were willing, I'd love to talk to you about girl skaters. It would make a very good column, I think. I haven't seen that many girl skaters around town." She paused for confirmation or disagreement but the girl did not respond. "I'd suggest we do an interview now if you had time but I'm really involved with some other subjects. As it happens, you may know something about one of them. You were at Angel de Silva's memorial service, I think? At the beginning, anyway. You left him a rose."

A nod.

"I'm looking for people who knew Angel, particularly the people who spoke or left offerings there or on his bench."

The girl watched her with a steady gaze that seemed mature for her age, not hardened exactly but without any sign of shyness or silliness. Like Win Niagra she volunteered nothing into the silence that Neva left open.

"You were a friend?"

One shoulder went up and her head canted toward it in a gesture that was more quizzical than either affirmative or negative. She looked down as though considering what to say but still didn't speak.

"I hear such different things about Angel that I'm really puzzled," Neva pressed. "Some people say he was kind and helpful, and others say he was usually drunk and had other problems. Can you help me understand what he really was like?"

"He was just Angel, that's all. Somebody to talk to. Everybody talked to him, not just me. He didn't tell you what to do. He told good stories. Sorry, I have to go now." Pushing off hard with one foot, the girl sped away before Neva could think of the right words to hold her.

You're getting nowhere, fast, Leopold. Never before in her years as a journalist had she struck out so consistently. What was it about Angel and the whole situation that made everyone so close-mouthed? Some weird loyalty? All she got were generalizations and hints that he was both bad and good. The girl had shown no signs of distress, embarrassment, shame or any other such emotion that might suggest that she'd engaged in questionable activities, as a gang member or otherwise. And yet, she had not been at ease. Steady, yes. At ease, no.

What had she said about Angel? *He didn't tell you what to do . . .* Was there any conceivable reason why he should? He wasn't a parent, a teacher, a bossy older brother, but just a guy on a bench with a winning personality.

Walking on, preoccupied, Neva was halfway across the new parking lot that had been built at the south end of downtown in anticipation of the riverfront renovation when the close rumble of an engine made her look up. A gravel truck pulled into the lot and stopped in the far corner next to a man with a clipboard. Her first thought was to wonder whether it was the same driver who had run over Angel's cart. The next was a satisfied internal nod that here, at least, was one little mystery explained. The gravel was for the new parking lot—except that the lot was already paved and the truck did not dump its load. At a wave from the clipboard man the driver circled back onto First Street, traveled one block north, and turned left away from the riverfront.

Neva approached the man with the clipboard, and said with a smile, "The work's really coming along down here."

"About time." He pulled a thermos from a bag by his feet and unscrewed the top. Taller than Neva by at least a head, he was layered in multiple shirts under a down vest that gave him the bulk of a football player. He watched the coffee stream into his cup, sipped, nodded, and looked down at Neva. "Anyway, it's supposed to weather in good by the weekend."

"Rain?"

"And then some. I was going to put in my garden peas but looks like I'll have to take a rain check." He swallowed his chuckle along with another swig from the thermos cup.

"You're keeping the gravel trucks busy." Neva stood as though planted for the day, her hands in her pockets, her eyes casually taking in the small mobile construction office, the Best Pots outhouse, and a stack of black PVC pipe.

Bending easily from the waist, the man set his thermos and cup on the ground and flipped through the pages on the clipboard. "Twelve so far today. There should be one more coming."

"Do they have to haul it far?"

He shrugged. "There's more than one quarry around here, but I'd guess this comes from close by."

"Where's it going, I mean, where are they dumping it today?"

"Today? Let's see now." Again he consulted the clipboard, shook his head. "Don't rightly know. Could be north, could be south."

"Not on the riverfront?"

"Not this lot, no. We're all done here. They just check in for the record. Ah, here comes the last one, right on time."

The truck pulled up, claiming his attention.

"Good luck with your peas," she said as he turned away.

"Oregon sugar peas, that's the ticket," he called over his shoulder. "Like eating green candy."

Walking on, she stopped abruptly at the edge of the new parking lot and turned back, cursing her idiocy—the driver would know where he was taking the load.

But it was too late. The truck was pulling out already on the opposite side of the lot and the man with the clipboard was gathering his things to leave for the day.

"I can't deny it, Ms. Leopold. You caught me fair and square." Carter threw his hands up in mock surrender, then reached for his glass and raised it toward Neva. "To the future of a beautiful and thriving riverfront."

Neva touched her glass to his and brought it to her lips, but didn't drink. She had managed to make the wine he poured at the beginning stretch halfway through dinner while Carter consumed three glasses, commenting on her restraint but not pressing her to drink more. He was in a fine mood, witty, flirtatious, talkative. She had waited until his third glass was poured, and then had needed only to hint at her knowledge of his ownership of the three riverfront blocks to make him 'fess up, as he put it.

"Score one for you," he said. "I suppose you think I'm quite terrible for making you dig that out instead of simply telling you the facts?"

"Naturally, I wonder why." At ease, sitting back with her legs crossed, Neva felt ready for whatever this dodgy character might dish out. Despite his apparent surrender to candor she could not assume he would now be straightforward. Clearly a game player, he had some motive in all this that she needed to understand. "And why didn't you mention your connection to Lyle McRae? You must have known him pretty well. Did he pay rent for the greenhouse? When we thought he'd won the lottery, it seemed strange to live in a warehouse, but the winning ticket actually belonged to someone else. But you no doubt already knew that. Or maybe—" she raised an eyebrow—"maybe he bought the winning ticket for you?"

Carter set down his fork and dabbed his mouth with the gold napkin. "I suppose you won't believe this now. I was going to tell you that as soon as you brought up the subject but you beat me to the punch line. Yes, Lyle McRae won the lottery for me. I gave him the money to buy ten tickets and said to keep any five for himself. The winning number was in the lot he handed to me. We let his name go out as the winner. No special reason. He got a kick out of it."

Five chances out of ten to pick the winning ticket . . . Carter, already blessed with personal advantages, had won. Lyle, who had been served a bad hand from the beginning, had lost. It made no difference that Carter had paid the pittance for the tickets, the Fates were simply unfathomable and not in the least lovable.

"It does raise strange questions," Grey said, somber for the moment. "It wasn't comfortable for me. I would have given him half, a quarter, a monthly stipend, whatever he wanted. He wouldn't have it. The only thing he would accept was a lifetime home in the greenhouse. Money was just trouble, he said. What he really wanted from life couldn't be bought, not outright. He wanted to be recognized as a landscape architect rather than a gardener. I paid for the schooling, but he had a falling out with a teacher and didn't finish the program. He was temperamental, unpredictable. A moody man, though never mean that I know."

"Why didn't you say anything when it was reported in one of the news stories that he had won the lottery?"

"Do you think Lyle would rather have the town believe he had died an eccentric millionaire whose money couldn't be found or just a penniless weirdo who planted flowers? It didn't make any real difference. He has no heirs."

"Did you buy up the riverfront with lottery money?"

"I am a long way from 'buying up the riverfront.' Three blocks does not a riverfront make." He cocked his head as though listening to his own words, then chuckled. "Sound like a pompous ass, don't I? What else are you dying to ask? May as well get the cross-examination done so you can give some attention to this very fine dinner."

"Are you aware that someone is staying in Lyle's room, or at least, going there to water the plants?"

"I've been watering the plants. Ah, another surprise, I see. Sorry. I haven't actually set out to be mysterious but it never occurred to me that anyone would care what happened at the warehouse after Lyle was gone. I've been wondering what to do with the plants. Your suggestion for an indoor park is intriguing, and I might be willing to donate the property, but it would take money to run such a thing. A lot of money, I should think. Unlike an outdoor park, you'd need at least one staff person there during open hours."

Neva was no longer listening. She was back at the greenhouse watching the door ease shut. That it might have been Grey hiding in there she dismissed without serious thought. The fact that made her squirm internally was that she had jumped to conclusions, had assumed that the silent watcher was benign because he had watered Lyle's plants. Whoever had eased the door closed could have been there for any sort of reason—for shelter, in search of something, hiding evidence—though she had not been entirely wrong in her conclusions. Whoever left the note on her windshield had certainly known McRae, had been close to McRae in some way, even if their attitude was not entirely sympathetic. *It's better for some people if he's dead...*

"Neva? Attenzione?"

"Sorry, Carter, just thinking about what you said. I'm afraid I really can't see it, I mean you hauling hoses around. Out of character."

"I'm not sure I like that," he said with a pained expression that reflected the most genuine emotion he'd shown in her presence yet. "But you can't really think Lyle used hoses to keep that jungle lush. It's automated. He used the hose only for a few pots out of reach of his system. When I say I've been watering, I mean I've checked to see that everything's working properly, the water turning on, and maybe even more critical, off when it's supposed to. I do have a small garden of my own. Which I water by hose."

"Oh, dear. I've trodden on toes. Sorry. It had occurred to me that some things might be automated, but when I found the hose dripping and the pots newly wet, well, there seemed only one explanation. I suppose it would take all day to water it by hand. I really didn't mean to imply you wouldn't be up to the job. I've never liked hoses myself. Even the supposed non-kink varieties get into a mess." To be apologizing to Grey felt wrong, a reversal of what she had intended for the evening, and she did not give him a chance to reply before pressing on. "And now for your bogus insurance tale. I'm ready for explanations."

"It wasn't a bogus tale." From the inside breast pocket of his jacket Carter pulled a folded paper. "This came a week ago. I checked with my agent, who said it isn't true, but, well, see what you think."

The letter was typed on plain bond with no letterhead and no signature.

Dear Mr. Grey:

As a major riverfront property owner you will no doubt be interested in an item of information that I am passing along because I care about the future of this community. You know that the city is trying to clean up and improve our riverfront after many years of neglect, and that a group of self-appointed and self-righteous folks calling themselves SORE is doing everything it can to stop the project. I have sat in on a couple of their meetings, and believe me, some alarming things are being said and planned. They claim to know that the real reason the city is seeking such big improvements to the bank is that insurance companies are insisting on it if there is to be major construction on the west side of First Street. They say they are going to break this story to the press when they're ready, that is, when it would do the most damage to the city's project. I have talked to one insurance company and they say they don't know anything about it, but this isn't their area of specialty. I have been unable to get other information.

I am writing to you because, as a property owner down there, you will be able to check with your insurance agent to see if there is any truth in this story. If it gets into the newspaper it won't matter whether it's true or not, as you know. Once something is printed you never can convince people it isn't true even if it was only an accusation, which I have learned from experience. But if you find out the truth before it's too late, maybe you could talk to Jeneva Leopold and she would print the real story. She wrote some columns against the riverfront project but she would be interested in something like this, I think, because she likes to stir things up. Sometimes that's a good thing even though I don't agree with her most of the time.

Sorry I can't sign my name but who I am isn't important to the issue. Good luck.

Amused by the reference to herself, Neva read the letter again, slowly this time.

"As you've realized, I got you involved in a rather different way than the writer suggested," Carter said when she looked up. "I thought you might be able to get to the bottom of the insurance question yourself, and might be more motivated if you thought it was true. My agent pooh-

poohed it but it still makes me uneasy. Where would such a story come from?"

"People love conspiracy theories and seem able to pull them out of the air. As it happens, my agent also said there was nothing to it. Did any other property owners get this?"

"I haven't asked. I like to keep a low profile, as you've discovered, though evidently whoever sent this letter has found me out, about owning property that is. Come now, eat up. I've ordered something really special for afters. I hope you like fine port. This wasn't meant to be a business occasion, you know."

"May I keep this?"

"I'll get a copy to you." Reaching across the litter of plates and glasses he took hold of the letter in such a way that his large hand half-enfolded hers in a warm grasp. She let go of the paper.

This time, Neva accepted Carter's suggestion that they stroll together along the river path after dinner, although first she spent half an hour in the kitchen making notes for the column, which he now appeared to be taking in good grace and admitted could be useful publicity for the restaurant. Despite her resolution to keep Grey at the distance he deserved, she found this difficult once the confessions were made and his wit kept her laughing. They walked for about twenty minutes, talking easily, mainly about why he had chosen to settle in Willamette after years of restless moving among the world's major cities.

"You'll laugh but what first caught my attention was a news story about gay rights. Do you remember, well of course you do, way back when your county commissioners said the Oregon Constitution required equal treatment of citizens so they were going to allow gay marriage. That was before the domestic partnership act or whatever it's called. As I recall, the state told the county they couldn't do this until a lawsuit in another county was settled, so the commissioners put a stop on all applications for marriage licenses for the time being, gay and straight. I may have the details wrong, but it was the gesture that impressed me. And I'm not even gay. I was in Krakow at the time looking for posters, and it made the front page of the English language paper."

"I'm agog. That it made news so far away, I mean. And that it impressed you enough to move here."

"It wasn't just that. It got me started reading the *Current* online and lots of things struck me. I first read your column, for instance, in an Internet café in the old city square, the Rynek Główny. Is that a person or a bear coming out of the bushes?"

A bulky figure emerged from the dark undergrowth alongside the path and started toward them, calling out, "Hello, Jeneva Leopold." It was Reba, carrying a white sack. She approached to within a few feet and looked at Carter. "A bodyguard. You're getting smarter."

"To be honest, I thought she was protecting me," Grey confided in a conspiratorial whisper, leaning toward the homeless woman. "She's tougher."

Surprised by their joint giggles, Neva was about to say *You know each other?* when the question was answered in the negative by Carter extending a hand.

"Carter Grey."

"Reba Winner." Reba's handshake was tentative but she did not add the line about Reba Loser.

"So you're the one feeding the cats." Carter nodded at the sack in Reba's hand. "That calico's unusual."

"You know Spitty?"

"A distant acquaintance. Who's the new one with the white patch around one eye?"

"Half Tom! Where?"

"In the alley. He turned up yesterday."

"How did he look?"

"Like half a Tom, but a dose of Iams perked him up."

"Iams! Now you've done it. He'll never be happy with C-rations again." Reba held up the white sack and the two studied it as though judging the authenticity of an antique.

"I once read that underfed rats live longer," observed Carter. "Maybe it's true of cats, too."

"It just seems longer. I stole that line but it's funny anyway."

"What do you call the other one, the one with Spitty?"

"Loose Thing."

"Hmm, nice. I suppose you know what happened to Lyle's cats?"

"It was easy to find homes for those two. Fancy-pants."

"Glad to hear it. How about I leave the Iams in a five-gallon can outside my back door, I mean my shop door. You can shorten all the cats' lives with it. If it runs out and I forget the refill, let me know." Carter took a card from his jacket pocket and handed it to Reba.

She looked at it, nodded, put it into her sweatshirt pouch, and said, "I'll leave you two to get on with it, then. Take care of her, okay? She thinks people are nice."

Reba crossed First Street and slipped through a gap in a cyclone fence that had been put up around a storage building bound for demolition. When she was gone, Neva turned to look at Carter Grey with new eyes.

NO ANGEL

She had not said one word since Reba came out of the bushes, not even hello. Her contributions had not been needed. Either Grey was enough of a smoothie to fool even Reba, or there was something solid and real behind the game playing and the urbane façade.

Chapter Fourteen

Scrub jays yammering outside the open window woke Neva early, as they often did during the nesting season. The two young birds in the family were already as large as the adults, distinguishable by the extra gray on their backs and a certain bumbling quality. They pecked at almost anything to test it for edibility. Pansy blossoms, bits of bark, her gardening gloves left out on a stump. But the instant one of the parents approached they reverted to pitiable helplessness, fluttering their wings and crying with open beaks for a tasty tidbit.

This morning they were all in the hawthorn tree outside her window, bouncing from limb to limb and knocking down showers of white petals. That the white showers were the object of the game she didn't doubt, not after watching their ancestors for twenty years, a new family every spring from the same line. These four seemed to have even better humorous faculties than most, teasing the squirrels that passed through, landing in a line on a loose telephone wire and making it swing wildly until only one was left clinging after the others tumbled off, opening one wing and then another in a sort of slow fan dance to catch the sun's heat while balanced on the back of a bench. And of course, most charmingly, bouncing around in the hawthorn to make it snow white flowers.

Her restraint on the wine last night probably had not been necessary for getting straight answers out of Grey, but her head was certainly happier this morning as a consequence. She made quick work of coffee and breakfast and was out the door by eight. The distance to the *Current* building was less than two miles through the town's oldest neighborhoods, usually a brisk twenty-minute walk, but after barreling along for a few blocks she slowed to a stroll despite her impatience to be at work. The landscaping here, like the houses, was venerable, with big old lime and sweet gum trees, rhododendrons as tall as a second story window, and glossy-leaved magnolias with colossal pink and white flowers. In summer, the streets were green tunnels, but now the canopy was an open lattice of branches and tender new leaves that let in plenty of light.

Despite slowing down, she reached Azalea Park by 8:30. As usual, it was the picture of tranquility, nothing remarkable or untoward to be seen, only two boys on a bench. Their bikes stood propped against a nearby cottonwood trunk.

"Good morning," Neva said with no particular strategy in mind. "I'm Jeneva Leopold, from the *Willamette Current*."

One grunted, the other nodded.

"I write a column that comes out three times a week. You might have seen it. It runs with a picture of me, although my hair's quite a bit longer now than when the picture was taken." She paused for an indication of whether they recognized her. None came. She went on pleasantly, "I write about all kinds of subjects, from dead cats to politics. One of the subjects I'm interested in right now is youth homelessness, specifically teenagers." Recalling an article that had run a while back in the *Current*, she added, "I don't just mean kids living on the streets, but also the ones they call couch surfers."

That got double nods.

"Looks like you know something about that. Do you know anyone who's living like that, anyone who's living around on couches at the moment?"

They looked at each other, back at her. "I guess so," said the one with the most hair, although neither one had much, both having shaved their heads at some recent date. "Yeah, I know some guys, some couch surfers."

"Do they couch surf because they can't go home or don't want to or don't have a home to go to?"

"Yeah, I guess so," the same boy replied.

The other one elbowed him in the ribs. "You're supposed to say 'all of the above,' or 'none of the above.'"

"All of the above," the first said promptly.

Neva's attention focused on the second and evidently sharper of the two. "In journalism we use a method called personalizing the story, which means telling about the situation of a real, specific individual in order to help readers identify with some general subject like homelessness. What I'm looking for is someone around your age who lives on the street or couch surfs. Do you know anyone who might talk to me? I wouldn't use their name unless they wanted me to."

The boys frowned as though she had asked a tough philosophical question, and then the second one said that he was sort of a couch surfer.

"I don't actually sleep much, though," he said. "I mostly watch TV. They wouldn't let me watch late TV at home."

"Why was that?"

"Inappropriate for my age."

His deadpan delivery made her smile. "What do you watch?"

"He's an old movie freak," said his companion.

"Bogart's the best. I'll watch anything but he's the best. Have you heard of Humphrey Bogart?"

"I have, indeed, and seen a number of his films. Whose couch are you staying on?

"His."

"Ah, I see."

"If I had a car I'd sleep in it, even without a TV," the couch surfer volunteered. "A big, shiny black Rolls Royce, that's what I'd like."

"You've ridden in a Rolls?"

"No way, but I've seen lots in movies."

"I wonder why you don't see Rolls Royces around here?"

"You can't get service. I mean, I don't know for sure, but that's what I'd say. No parts, no service. It isn't practical, you know? But I'd still get one. I'm not practical. I've been told that often enough."

"Maybe you're creative. Creative people have a reputation for not being practical."

"He's just lazy," the other boy said, and was promptly whacked on the shoulder.

Silence prevailed for a bit after they finished shoving each other, and Neva realized that she didn't want to pry into their lives. Maybe it was cowardice, but she didn't want to know anything bad about these two. They weren't street kids, and not members of a park gang, if such existed. Ready to turn away, she hesitated. "There's a girl around town who rides a skateboard and does graffiti, or at least I think she does. She carries a can of spray paint in her pocket. Her hair's short, almost like a boy's. I talked to her yesterday but forgot to get her name. Do you know her?"

"That's Pet. Everybody knows Pet," said the couch surfer. "Cool skater."

"She went to the memorial service for that homeless man who was killed a little while ago. They must have been good friends."

The change in the boys was subtle. An exchange of glances, a silence, and the flat tone of voice again from the couch surfer. "Yeah, I guess so." They stood up as one.

"Sorry," the couch-surfer said courteously. "We have to go. We're late."

With sudden energy, they were on the bikes and gone before she could try to tease out what had made them bolt—the mention of Angel or something about the girl, Pet.

NO ANGEL

Walking on, she found herself composing the lead to a column about a boy with an unlikely taste for a vintage actor and a classic British car . . . *They may look like clones, those rangy teens in low-rider pants, but what's happening under the buzz haircut is often surprising. . .* Several variations, none quite right, carried her to the staff door, where she paused for her ritual moment of appreciative breathing.

The door flew open and Frankie dashed out. "Hey, there you are," he cried, one arm jabbing for a jacket sleeve that flapped behind him. "There's another one. I'm on my way."

"Another what?"

"Body. It's a fucking epidemic."

"Where?"

"On the river. Another street person."

"Which street person?"

"Don't know."

Without making a conscious decision to go with Frankie, Neva turned to cross the parking lot with him. "Just push that stuff onto the floor," he said as she stood with the passenger's side door open, considering the heap of notebooks and papers on the seat.

He sped the five blocks to First Street while Neva gripped the armrest. *Please not Reba . . .* "Do you know if it's male or female?"

"Nope. No info at all. Just dead."

Frankie hit the brakes in front of Lyle's warehouse and stopped with two wheels well up on the riverfront park grass. The bike path downriver was taped off but the officer on guard let them through at a signal from Gale Marcum who stood behind the barrier. Frankie bee-lined to Marcum, but Neva didn't want to hear this from the assistant chief, and made for the ambulance and the knot of people in bright yellow standing farther down the path.

"Hey, Neva," called a woman's voice.

Her former neighbor, Jolene Murchisie, left the cluster of emergency medical technicians and came to meet her.

"Jolene, hello. Do they know who it is yet?"

"No name, but it looks like she drank herself into a coma and died out here sometime in the night. A real mess. Oh dear, sorry, you're not used to this."

"It's okay. I need to know. Is she large, with dark hair?"

"Definitely not. Just a little thing."

"A girl!"

"No way. I meant a small woman. I only saw her for a few seconds but she looked pretty well along. Of course, you can't really tell, not when they've been living like that. We used to get them like that up in

Portland at the shelter and you'd swear they were sixty and then find out they weren't even forty yet." Jolene put an arm around Neva's shoulder and squeezed. "You don't want to stick around here. There's nothing to see and you don't want to see it anyway."

Neva turned away, relieved and ashamed of her relief—a woman was dead, after all, even if it wasn't Reba—and saw Marcum and Charlie Frank approaching. Despite the grim situation and the unpleasantness of their last meeting, the assistant chief addressed Neva in an arch tone that was almost coy. "Well, you have caught the crime bug."

"Crime? I thought it was alcohol."

"We won't know for sure until the lab reports are in. Given the others, we aren't jumping to conclusions. It's getting to be quite the thing to find bodies down here. Some good lighting wouldn't be amiss."

"Lighting?"

"Streetlights. Shine a light on evil and it slinks away. Now, if you'll excuse me."

With Frankie stuck to his side like a nursing calf, Marcum strode cheerfully toward the ambulance as though heading for a party while Neva looked after him in consternation. There was something truly disturbing about this man that she couldn't pinpoint, and today he struck her as outright dotty. No, not dotty. Dotty was far too charming a word, suitable for certain old English ladies but not for a scheming officer of the law. He was fixated. Nothing really seemed to register with him outside his campaign for a jail, although the reference to streetlights suggested that he'd caught the riverfront renovation bug as well. The city's plan called for dozens of faux antique pole lights along First Street, far too many, according to the opposition, enough to show from outer space like the Great Wall of China.

Watching Frankie trail Marcum, Neva made a mental note to remind the calf that the best information comes from underlings in an organization, not from the brass, particularly brass on a bandwagon. She started after them but soon turned and strode away. There would be pictures of the dead woman back at the *Current*, probably before she got there, and a picture would be more than enough to have to take in.

But she did not return to the newspaper building, not directly. With a glance around to be sure no one was watching, she pushed open the door to Lyle's warehouse, slipped inside, and stood waiting for her eyes to adjust. She also needed to gather her courage, she realized. Two deaths at this end of First Street within less than a week had to be more than a coincidence, even if one was a murder and the other death by alcohol.

"Hello?" She pitched her voice toward the stairs though she did not expect a reply. "Is anyone here? It's Jeneva Leopold, from the *Current.* Carter, are you there?"

The opening at the top of the steps was particularly bright today, and as she climbed, the air warmed and thickened. She could sense nothing amiss here as her head cleared the hatch, but as soon as she stepped out onto the main path and looked toward Lyle's apartment she could see that something was wrong. The door stood open and beyond it a chair lay on its back with a lamp leaning against one leg. What sort of home Lyle would have created for himself she could not have imagined but two things were instantly clear as she reached the open doorway: the room had been beautiful and it was now a mess.

The ceiling was high, the windows tall, the walls white. Large botanical prints in rich hues hung in the spaces between the windows. Against the back wall stood a loft bed flanked by bookshelves made of dark wood. In the kitchen area to the right of the door gleaming pans hung from a circular rack and jars of beans, flour, nuts, and raisins stood in colorful rows behind glass cupboard doors.

None of this had been touched, but from the windowsills down the room had been hit by a hurricane. Cushions, towels, clothes, magazines, bedding, newspapers, toilet paper, dishes, cans, bottles, pizza boxes, and crusted paper plates covered the floor between upended lamps, end tables, two armchairs, a crushed lampshade, and a couch with wooden arms. The wastebasket lay on its side next to trash that had spilled out in an ugly mound on the straw floor mat.

One step into the room and the lush perfume of living plants was overwhelmed by the smell of stale grease and something sharp and vaguely medicinal that suggested a biology lab.

Neva stepped carefully through the litter to a window and opened it with a brass crank. Propped against the windowsill with her arms crossed and the breeze around her, she studied the room. The mess was surely deliberate. This was no casual accumulation from careless squatters who had discovered the door unlocked. And yet so much more damage could have been done. A real enemy or vandal would have knocked the books from the shelves and smashed the glass in the kitchen cabinets along with the jars of beans.

Someone had been staying here since McRae died. Lyle would never have left pizza boxes and greasy paper plates around even if he did eat fast food, which seemed unlikely given the wholesome contents of his cupboards. The person who had observed her through the door crack and left the note on her windshield must have used the apartment for at least a little while—but had that same person wrought this destruction?

The mess could have been caused by a struggle, by drunken shoving and pushing, which would mean it was accidental and not aimed at McRae. This also would explain why worse had not been done.

The trash basket lay close by. Neva set it upright but could not bring herself to pick up anything else without gloves despite a contrary urge to set everything in order. It would not take much to make the room beautiful again.

One of the white chair cushions was tilted at an angle, an end resting on something dark red that showed an edge of coarse fabric. It was Reba's knapsack, but even as she knelt for a closer look she dismissed the possibility that it was Reba who had stayed here or trashed the apartment. She must have given the bag to someone else, or lost it, or got careless as she had been when she left it in Neva's car.

The clinical smell was stronger near the floor, clearly detectable over the sickly sweet patchouli oil. On her hands and knees, she searched the area close by, lifting food wrappers and pushing aside chair cushions and towels. The empty bottle was lying on its side next to an overturned chair. Oregon Springs Vodka, the cheapest of the cheap, better for pickling lab specimens than drinking. A good bit of it must have landed on the floor to make such a stench.

The bottle lay against a crumpled black sweater. Neva did not pick up the bottle, but pushed it with one finger so that it rolled away from the sweater. Gingerly, using two fingers this time, she spread the sweater out on the floor mat. It was a cardigan, cashmere surprisingly, but heavily worn and missing most of the shell buttons. Small enough to fit a child, it gave off a delicate smell of smoke. Not cigarettes, she decided after lowering her face to within a few inches of the fabric, but outdoorsy smoke, campfire smoke.

Homeless camp smoke?

She sat back on her heels and considered the sweater for a long, thoughtful moment before looking around once more. Beyond the overturned chair, magazines spilled from an upside-down basket. In the loose pile was a notebook with a spiral binding. Unsurprised now, she pushed aside magazines and picked up the notebook—*the* notebook—and slipped it into her bag.

Chapter Fifteen

"You were smart to leave without seeing her." Frankie looked up from his keyboard with unhappy eyes. "Sodden's the only word for it, inside and out. How do people get like that?"

The dead woman had carried no identification but one of the EMT's had recognized her from an earlier incident. She was Lisette LaBruce, no known relations, though known to county mental health. Some months ago, they'd given her a subsidized apartment at the Gregorian, a grand hotel converted to handicapped housing, but she'd lost it because of letting other street people flop there and had ended up back on the streets. And that was about all for now. No one at the health department had worked closely enough with her to tell him much, though he still had a few calls out that might turn up something. As far as he could tell, she was just an old babe who had fallen through the cracks.

"Sorry if that sounds callous. I'm not enjoying this."

Neva gave a sympathetic smile but her thoughts were casting back—she had heard this name before. "Wasn't one of the women who spoke at Angel's memorial service called Lisette? The one who said he gave her money for food and she'd never forget it as long as she lived? There can't be that many Lisette's around."

"Could be. Street people hang together. The hair was about right. And build. I don't think I got her name at the service but I'll check my notes. There might be a quote there, so thanks for the reminder. I've got to get this in now, then go look for more. Why did I ever think crime reporting would be edgy? It's just sad."

Neva dropped her bag on the office floor, sank into the armchair, and curled up with her head on her arms and her eyes closed. Intuitive leaps had served her well many times, but she'd also been wrong often enough to make her cautious. Letting her thoughts drift and mull, she tried to avoid the painful fact of the missed phone calls but everything circled back. The dead woman, Lisette LaBruce, had been staying at Lyle's, she was all but certain. She had died near the warehouse, she had been wearing a black sweater at the memorial service, a full bottle of cheap vodka in a small body might well be lethal, she had known Angel and therefore likely knew McRae . . . but most of all, instinct said it was true, that it was Lisette who had been staying at the warehouse and Lisette who had tried four times to reach her by telephone and Lisette who had left the note on her car—and, not twenty-four hours later, Lisette lay dead on the bike path.

If the call had reached her and Neva had talked with Lisette, would she still be alive?

There was no logical reason to think so. She had no particular power to save lives—she had failed a direct appeal from Lyle McRae—and a drunk is a drunk regardless of what anyone else says or does. And yet, Lisette had not looked like a drunk at the memorial event. Hogan swayed on his feet and mumbled but the thin blond woman had been steady and clear.

My name is Lisette. Her voice had been as light and breakable as her narrow shoulders. She had been in jail and had no friend when she got out. Angel had given her a little money for food, making her feel cared for and rescued. *I won't never forget that as long as I live . . .* She had lived for another two weeks and two days. .

Was there anything here that should be passed along to the police? What, exactly, could she say? I was snooping around the warehouse and found an empty vodka bottle and a small woman's sweater that smelled of campfire smoke. The dead woman spoke at Angel's service and did not look like an alcoholic. I believe she was a friend of Lyle's. This means she was connected to both of the murdered men. There must be something here that's more than coincidence. Are you certain she died of drink?

She imagined saying this to the chief, to Oleander, to Marcum, to a nameless duty officer. All regarded her with flat, unresponsive faces. *We'll look into it.*

Neva's copy deadline was looming again, and the property ownership column was ready to write. . . She could not write about property with Lisette LaBruce filling all the space in her mind—but she could not write about Lisette because she didn't know enough, and there wasn't time to dig for more information.

Just get on with it, Leopold.

With determined effort, she stood up, stretched toward the ceiling, sat down at the keyboard and began to type. Rather than beginning with a direct statement about Carter's property empire, she would open with a description of the surprising cook at *Au Courant,* Lucy Gambol. Just twenty-seven, Lucy would have been memorable simply for her white fish consommé with a pastry boat afloat in the bowl. Add to this the fact that her left foot had been bitten off by a shark while she was on vacation from culinary school and, as a consequence, she sped around the kitchen on high-tech wheels, and she was star material.

"Such a waste," Lucy had quipped. "He ate my foot raw and unseasoned."

Ambrose would have a fit that she'd wasted such material on a column when it would make a great feature with a photo spread. Cheered by this thought, Neva felt the words begin to flow.

The first draft was soon done and she was contemplating her next move when there was a knock on the door. Without waiting for an invitation, Frankie came in and collapsed toward the armchair.

"Tired of the dead beat?" she teased and was rewarded by an amused "Ha!" And then, gazing around her small sanctuary as though it were gilded, he said mournfully, "You don't know how lucky you are. Or maybe you do. Anyway, I hope you appreciate it. Ambrose's gone crazy with story angles. I never thought I'd say this but I'm missing my daily beat. I'd be happy to write a do-gooder feature about old ladies, rose gardens—anything."

"You want to swap jobs for a week? I wouldn't mind being an investigative reporter right now."

"So what would you do in my place, if you don't mind saying."

"What I wonder, well, more than wonder, I have a strong hunch that Lisette LaBruce had been staying in Lyle McRae's apartment. It's close to where she was found, and a drinker certainly had been there. The place reeks of alcohol and there's an empty vodka bottle, and it's a terrible mess, the sort of mess that could be caused by a fight."

"How do you know that?"

"I was there this morning, after I left you."

"You have a key?"

"It's not locked."

"That's weird. You'd think after a murder, well, they must have got everything they need already. You already did a column on the place. What are you poking around for?"

"I don't really know, but I'm drawn back there for some reason. It might just be the plants."

"Do you think your indoor park idea has a chance?"

"Yes, I do. But the point now is that someone had definitely been staying there. I think it was Lisette. That would make a link between those two deaths and we're already pretty sure she's the woman who spoke at Angel's memorial, so that's another link."

"I see what you mean, but those people all know each other anyway and she died of drink so what's the point? I mean if she'd been murdered, too, it would be different. So she was at McRae's—hey, you won't believe this." He sat up with sudden energy. "You remember that he never won the lottery after all, he bought the tickets for somebody else? Well, I found out who did get the money. Ambrose wouldn't let it rest. He said there had to be a record somewhere, so I kept digging. It's that antique art dealer, Carter Grey. He owns the warehouse, too. They met at the state nuthouse. He's a really nice guy. It's not like it sounds. He did everything he could for Lyle, let him stay in the greenhouse—what's wrong? What did I say?"

"How did you find out?"

"I hung around the state lottery office and there was this woman who—"

"Not about the money. I mean that they were both in Clarendon."

"You knew about the money?"

"Sorry, I was going to tell you, but this morning threw everything off. I just heard about it last night. You're sure they were both in Clarendon?"

"Oh no, not Grey. He taught there, photography and printmaking, and in the state prison, too. He told me himself."

Frankie's voice went on but Neva didn't take in the words. Grey was still not being honest with her. He was, incredibly, still playing games. They had talked at length about McRae last night, yet he had said nothing about knowing the gardener at Clarendon, and this despite making a show of openness—how had he put it? *What else are you dying to ask? May as well get the cross-examination done so you can enjoy this fine dinner.* To carry on in such a frank and confiding manner and still omit significant details was diabolical. And hadn't he said that he'd come to Willamette because of reading about it when he was in Krakow? He had to have been living in Oregon for years to have worked at Clarendon when Lyle was there—Lyle had been gardening in town for a long time.

Aware, suddenly, that Frankie's voice had stopped and that he was looking at her quizzically, she said, "I had dinner with Grey last night, as it happens, and he's not quite as straightforward as he seems at first."

"He sure puts on a good show, then. Dinner was on him, I hope?"

"Definitely—he owns the restaurant. I just wrote a column about it."

Frankie chuckled as he heaved himself up. "You get all the fun, don't you. I'd like to hear about it but I've got a dragon breathing down my neck. I'm afraid it's back to the dead beat. Thanks for that, by the way."

Getting a reasonable column draft done should have had a calming effect but the information about Clarendon undid the tonic. True, it might mean nothing at all. Carter had to have met McRae somewhere, so why not at the mental hospital? He might not have considered it worth mentioning—or maybe he had been protecting Lyle's privacy again, just as he had refrained earlier from mentioning that Lyle was not a millionaire—but that still left questions about his charming tale of being drawn to Willamette by the county commissioners' stand on gay marriage.

What possible reason could Grey have for inventing such cockamamie?

Reba had appeared to trust Grey instantly, but maybe she was wrong to put such stock in the homeless woman's instincts. On an impulse, she returned to the draft of the restaurant column, scrolled to the bottom, and added: "To Reba: I need to talk with you about something important. Please contact me as soon as possible."

In the past, there had been occasions when she was tempted to use her soapbox for specific purposes, to find lost objects for readers, encourage family reconciliations, even once as a clue in a treasure hunt, but she had resisted. Though Willamette was small enough for such folksy touches in the newspaper, it had felt like taking unfair advantage of her position. No one else in town had such a high-profile bulletin board at their command, at least in actual newsprint. But now her sense of urgency drove out other considerations. She had to find Reba Winner, and though Reba said she was easy to find she generally turned up when she chose to and was never seen, at least by Neva, the rest of the time. The alternative was to wait for her near where she was feeding Half Tom and the others, but that could be any time, day or night, given the homeless woman's habits. It was unlikely that Reba read the newspaper regularly now that she no longer hung around the riverfront and the Beanery, but one of the other regulars down there might see the appeal and pass it along.

Years ago, the editors on the copy desk would have intercepted and questioned such a ploy, but now, trusting her long experience, whoever was responsible for the page read only enough of the column to write a headline. By the time anyone discovered her little trick, the message would be out there doing its work.

The rest of the work day was taken up with correspondence, phone calls and simply staring into space with a notebook at hand, waiting for inspiration that never arrived. From the *Current* she drove to the co-op and bought fresh linguini and anchovies. At home she went straight to the kitchen, tied on the red apron, turned on *NPR*, and reached for the garlic. Listening to the news, not letting herself think, she tipped olive oil into the cast iron skillet and set it on medium heat, minced salt-cured capers, kalamata olives, eight cloves of garlic, and half the can of anchovies, and added the mixture to the hot oil along with a generous sprinkle of red pepper flakes. The frying pan sizzled, pasta water steamed, the kitchen filled with pungent vapor. Working fast, she drained the pasta, added it to the pan, mixed it into the fiery, salty, tangy sauce, scraped every last savory bit onto a plate, and set it on the kitchen table. She poured a large glass of Cabernet, lit two candles, turned off the lights and the radio, put on a CD of Cecilia Bartoli singing the songs of Pauline Viardot, and sat down to eat.

The ferocious pasta forte worked its usual magic, helped by the heavy wine. Distracted by pure gustatory sensation, she forgot about human complexity for half an hour. Leaving the dishes, she settled on the couch with only the flames from the fireplace for light. Her mind was clear despite her physical ease, and she was able to think about Lisette without pain.

The Lisette of the memorial service had been thin, careworn, pale. But she had not been a wreck, not been shaky, not been a figure in search of death via ethanol. Moving her like a piece in a mental chess game, Neva walked that Lisette through the front door of the warehouse, among the shadowy pillars, up the stairs, through the greenhouse, into Lyle's trashed apartment—but she wouldn't go. She stopped at the door and refused to budge. She looked at the mess with a woeful shake of her narrow head and turned away.

Something was out of place in the picture she was trying to shape, something was seriously wrong. The mess was the problem. Lisette would not be meticulous, as Lyle must have been, but she would not actively trash the room. It had offered her a haven, after all. Someone else had done the trashing. Her first thought that there had been a fight or struggle in the room gave way for the moment to another possibility; maybe someone else had joined Lisette at the apartment, a person who had not known, or had not liked Lyle, or was simply too far gone to notice or care what sort of mess was made. Lisette had, after all, allowed fellow drifters to stay in her subsidized room at the Gregorian, leading to her eviction. There might have been half a dozen of them squatting at Lyle's, strewing trash about . . . Neva turned to consider her bag, which she'd dropped on the couch while hurrying through the living room before dinner.

She had forgotten about the notebook.

A faint smell of patchouli rose from the purse as she opened it. Leaving it open to air, she slipped off the couch onto the floor in the full light of the fire and turned to her own portrait. The artist had failed to give her real life as he had done for Reba and Win Niagra, though he had noticed details, the permanent corkscrew in a chunk of hair that she habitually twisted on one finger, the look of quizzical amusement that cameras sometimes caught or she would not know it was characteristic.

Her hope that the artist would have added drawings was disappointed. Her portrait was still the final one in the notebook, but the very last page was no longer blank. Loose handwriting filled it.

One thing about life you never know when you've got it good until its too late, not that I ever realy had it good but you know what I mean. If only I could get out of this town. Look what happened to Lyle. This world is full of crazys and I don't just mean the ones that talk to themselves and eat garbage. Iv'e been called crazy myself but then Im' used to it. Im' used to just about everything except one thing that bothers me is Im' so lonely and sometimes its scarey. I wonder what Lyle would say if he new I was here but when somebuddys dead who cares. If I ever had a baby somebuddy would care if Im' dead but thank GOD I never brought a inosent child into this world like some people I could name. Youd be surprised if I told you but I promised not to tell. You draw real nice. If I could draw maybe I wouldn't of had this life of trubble and care. Sorry about my writeing but I never finished grade 8, they didn't have any use for me and I din't have any use for them so same diffrence I gess. I keep hereing funny noises but I never slept with so many plants before. Do you think plants talk? I can almost here what there saying sometimes. I gess that's all I have to say. Have a nice life.

Neva looked into the fire for a pained moment, set the notebook down, and reached again for her bag. This time she felt for a side pocket and pulled out the photocopy of the flier that had been left on her windshield. Smoothing the sheet out flat next to the notebook page, she looked back and forth, but it did not require particular study to recognize that these were the work of the same writer. The handwriting was the same. The strange spelling and punctuation were the same, at least in the manner of their idiosyncrasy.

Whoever had been staying in Lyle's room had written the note as well as the wretched paragraph. Lisette's high voice sounded in her head like a voice heard at a distance over water, faint but clear. *I won't never forget that as long as I live.* The words on the page turned to speech in the same high voice. *If I ever had a baby somebuddy would care if Im' dead...*

It was a bad night, the worst she'd suffered in a long time. The red wine had been a mistake, leaving her legs twitchy and her skin flushed. This along with churning thoughts would have been enough trouble, but there was more—the uphill neighbors had left their porch light on again. She had thought this little matter was solved but, clearly, the students' memories were weaker than their neighborly vows.

Though she lived at the base of a hill dotted with houses, only one was visible from hers. It was a ramshackle, two-story affair that had been occupied for years by old Jessie Hockstone who had kept her blinds drawn and her lights frugally off. The house had been in such bad shape when she died two years ago that naturally a landlord got hold of it, and, naturally, he filled it with students. To Neva's surprise, they were generally quiet apart from an occasional Thirsty Thursday party—"We don't have classes on Friday, which means we can party on Thursday and sleep it off the next day and still have the weekend for homework"—but a different sort of problem had plagued her with this latest bunch. They could not remember to switch off the light above the deck, which then beamed right down through her bedroom window. She had been up there three times in as many months, always polite of course, and was always assured that it would never happen again.

Well, tomorrow she would take a different tack. She would employ the stealth method.

When daylight came at last, she left the stuffy bed with relief. As she was pouring water through the coffee grounds she heard the rumble of an unfamiliar vehicle and the crunch of tires on the driveway gravel. For a befuddled moment she thought it must be Reba responding already to the note at the end of her column—but that column hadn't run yet and Reba had no car.

A heavy door slammed. Drawing her robe closer and cinching the belt, she hurried into the front hall. Footsteps thumped across the porch and a gaunt silhouette showed through the window in the top half of the door.

It was Debo Happ, hunched against the dawn chill and dressed only in the usual overalls and T-shirt. "It's kind of early, I know, but I have to open the store," she said without a greeting.

"Come in, please." Neva stepped back with a welcoming gesture. Despite a long history of random visitors turning up at her door, generally in response to specific columns, she was surprised to see the reclusive Debo.

"No, thanks all the same. It won't take long. I thought of something Angel said. It was when he came to get his money. He was sitting there with his coffee, working on me the way he did. I wasn't paying much attention. I had something on my mind, which I guess is how he got around me for once. Anyway, he said, 'If somebody that was a friend of yours was hurting all the time and you could do something about it with all the money you had, would you do it?' I disremember what I said, and when I talked to you the other day, I said I gave him the money to buy a car. He talked about that, too, and it stuck in my mind more than the other thing. I don't expect it means anything, but you did ask."

"Do you have any idea who he was talking about?"

"I don't at all. Sorry."

"Do you think it could have been Tomasino, the tall guy who goes around with Hogan? He has really painful joints."

Debo shrugged and shook her head. "Could be. Beats me. Five hundred dollars wouldn't get you through the hospital door these days, but Angel didn't think that way."

Watching Debo's bony frame charge down the walkway as if to attack her own pickup truck, Neva smiled and wished yet again that this one-of-a-kind hardware maven would agree to a column. *Fine*, she'd said before. *Write about the store but not me. I'm not interesting. I'm just me.*

Half an hour later, with coffee and breakfast done, Neva took a 25 watt bulb from an upstairs hall lamp she rarely used and left the house on foot. Spring Street ended after a couple of bends at a short flight of steps that led to another street above. It was just one block long. At the end of it she turned left on the street that looped up the hill, and then left again on the next street up. More of a lane than a street, it wandered across the hill above her house, the houses on it widely spaced among oaks.

Jessie's house was the fourth from the turn, and to Neva's amusement, it looked better under student care than it had when the old woman lived there, though garbage and recycling bins stood on the small front lawn, and the flower pot by the front porch was full of cigarette butts. The usual cars and bicycles were gone, which was as she had expected—certainly hoped—on a school day.

The house was a typical hillside design, with the front door leading from the street into the second floor and main living area. The bottom floor was built into the hill and invisible from the street. The deck at the back stood on stilts and ran the full length of the top floor. The only way around was an overgrown gravel walkway that led down to the left away from the entry door.

She followed it to a gate with no latch, stepped through into the steep back yard, and looked down in surprise at her own little mess of a garden. It not only was torn up and raw, but she had not considered how exposed it would be without the tangled vines. When she finished the patio she would build a bamboo screen or some such thing to get some privacy back, and meanwhile, maybe it was a good thing students lived here—they wouldn't care what she did to their view.

Turning to go up onto the deck, she discovered that there were no stairs. The only access was through the house.

The deck was high but sturdily built, with cross struts every few feet between two of the four-by-four support posts at either end. After studying it for a few moments, she tucked the light bulb into a shirt pocket, took hold of a strut with her right hand and put her left foot on another. Climbing fast, she was soon at deck level and then over the railing, which was the only tricky bit. There were no chairs on the deck so she dragged over a flower pot full of dry soil as hard as pavement. Standing on it, she unscrewed the 100 watt bulb and put in the 25. Even if they noticed a difference, the students would never bother to change the bulb as long as it put out any light at all, just as they didn't bother to turn it off during the day.

A small victory, but satisfying.

"You didn't have to bring flowers," Arva Fowler said, deeply accusatory.

Confused, Neva looked down at her empty hands as though a bouquet might appear there, and then remembered the jar she had set at the top of the porch steps some days ago. "Those weren't flowers, they were daffodils," she said, aware of the illogic but not bothering to clarify as she sat down on the straight-backed chair.

Confused in turn, the old woman demanded, "Well, why did you bring daffodils?"

"I cut them to leave for Lyle, the man who was killed at the warehouse, but then changed my mind. You weren't on the porch so I left them. How did you know they were from me?"

"I can read, can't I?"

This was not going well. Neva knew for certain that she had left no note with the flowers. Stumped, she said nothing and neither did the old woman. The sound of a vacuum cleaner running next door came clearly out to them through an open window. Why she sought out the grandmother and had not revisited Great-Aunt Wygelia Chance Neva could not have said, and at the moment it seemed a mistake to be in the neighborhood for any reason. "Did Vance carry a maroon pack with a skull and crossbones on it?"

"How would I know? He never came here." Arva took wadded tissue from her sweater sleeve, swiped the end of her nose, and shoved the tissue savagely back up the sleeve.

"Was he good at drawing?"

"He wasn't good at anything except getting into trouble." She slapped the arm of her chair. "Not true. He could sing. Yes, he could sing. He's good enough to sing at his own funeral, and if I know her, that's how it will be. She's got tapes, I do know that."

Neva's hands went to her jacket pocket where she remembered putting the tape Wygelia had given her, but it wasn't there. She must have set it on the dresser. "He didn't draw, didn't sketch people?"

"He took up pottery, but you don't have to draw to stick clay together. He made that there." Arva nodded toward the trash at the other end of the porch.

After some searching, Neva made out a terra cotta object half-covered by an old curtain. On pulling away the curtain, she found an unglazed clay figure that struck her for a moment as grotesque, but then she got the joke. It had the body of Buddha and the head of Jesus.

"It's striking. Very clever, and well done, too."

Arva snorted. "I'm not a churchgoer but there's nothing wrong with respect. You might as well take it. No, never mind, leave it be."

Seated again, Neva found nothing to say and soon departed with vague excuses that got no response. Striding past Wygelia's, she admired a bed of crisp daffodils. A few paces farther on she stopped, smiled, and shook her head. *I can read, can't I?* Arva had read her column on gardening, which opened with a mention of picking daffodils, and had put two and two together about the bouquet in the jar. The old woman's offspring had gone disastrously off track, but there was nothing wrong with her gray matter.

Chapter Sixteen

Neva managed to reach her office without speaking to anyone in the newsroom, always the best thing in the morning. There was just one telephone message, from Lurleen Studebaker, and it made her smile: "Ring me, kiddo. You'll like it."

Before she could call the realtor back, however, Ambrose put his head in the door. "Could you join us in the conference room? Now?"

To be summoned like this, in such a tone of command, was unheard of in Neva's years at the *Current*—and what did he mean by "us"? Mystified but not in the least uneasy, she followed the editor to the conference room where daily news meetings were held, and discovered Himself sitting at the head of the long and otherwise unoccupied table.

Hardy Hightower was young for a publisher, and he had not come up through the ranks of reporters and editors but rather from the business end of the newspaper world, from advertising and circulation. When "Corporate" first sent him to take the helm, the newsroom had been in despair, everyone in the industry knowing full well that publishers from the news side and publishers from sales are two different breeds. No one expects a publisher from sales to understand that the worth of a newspaper isn't measured by its advertising revenue—by the ratio of its ad hole to its news hole—but rather by its editorial scope and integrity. The last thing seasoned news jockeys want is a boss who rates the bottom line way above the byline, and who worries about advertisers' tender feelings.

Hardy Hightower, however, had surprised them all. Tall, beefy, loud, and fond of knock-knock jokes, he had arrived from Arizona with all the subtlety of a boxcar-load of longhorn cattle. And promptly charmed them all before disappearing into his office, rarely to invade the newsroom thereafter except for the yearly Christmas party. He managed the business of publishing and left the content of publishing to Ambrose.

Ninety-nine percent of the time, that is.

"Knock-knock," he said, drumming big fingers on the table.

"Who's there?" Neva took a seat across the table.

"Aloyshius."

"Aloyshius who?"

"Aloyshius you'd stop bugging the police chief so she'd stop bugging me."

What a shame that this kooky publisher was not fair game as a column subject!

"I mean," he continued affably, "what have you got against a nice new jail? I toured our current edifice yesterday. They've set up cots in the common room. Your arguments are all very well for the future, but right now we're facing a crisis. The *Current* is endorsing the scaled-down plan they're going to announce soon. That's the official editorial position and it's damned awkward to have you hammering away from the other end. It will be better for all of us if you stop. I'm not asking you to praise it, you understand, just to keep a polite silence. Thank you."

The publisher moved as though to stand up.

"Half the prisoners are drug and mental cases, you know," Neva said as though he really might know this and simply needed a reminder. "If they took them out of the criminal justice system, where they don't belong in the first place, we'd have two cells for every legitimate prisoner. And don't forget last week's report from the Pew Center that the U.S. now imprisons one out of every hundred people. And that Oregon spends a higher percentage of its general fund on so-called corrections than any other state. We're spending more on prisons than schools in Oregon. As for disagreeing with the editorial position, it has never been the policy here that I have to stay in line with the *Current'*s official point of view. I write what I think. That's the mission of the columnist, and it's half the fun, for me and for readers. It underlines the fact that the newspaper is made up of individuals with distinctive ideas and points of view. Take my Sally Hemings argument. Nobody around here but Ambrose likes the idea, and last time I wrote about it there was a screaming editorial the next day. Now that got some real mail. Great fun."

"Sally Hemings?"

"Neva used to beat the drums to name a street for Hemings. You know, Jefferson's slave girlfriend," Ambrose said, speaking for the only time during the meeting. "There's logic in it—Martha Jefferson got a street even though she was dead by the time he reached the White House. Or was that for Martha Washington? Whatever, there'd be justice in it, and like Neva says, it sure gets attention."

The publisher was shaking his head. "All the same, some issues are different."

"You mean some issues get lobbied more effectively."

"Chief Fiori did damn near talk my ear off. But I made up my own mind based on the facts."

"Knock-knock," said Neva.

Ambrose's eyebrows shot up.

"Who's there?" The publisher sounded suddenly more alert.

"Canoe."

"Canoe who?"

"Canoe honestly say it wasn't Kitty's blue eyes that won the argument?"

Ambrose escorted her back to her office and lingered a moment in the doorway. "You've got some nerve."

"He laughed, didn't he. Anyway, what's he going to do, fire me? I could retire tomorrow and be perfectly comfortable as a cranky old widow. Without cats."

"Your bank account might allow it, but your prying, busybody self would go nuts and you know it."

"I'd write letters to the editor every day, in rhyme, with lots of references to God and UFOs. And I did make a concession, after all. It's the first time a publisher will read my columns before they go to press. I don't mind—I don't plan to write about the jail again anyway, at least no time soon. Maybe he'll turn out to be a great editor and give me some good suggestions. It will give him something to do for a change."

Ambrose's chuckle was followed by a moment of serious scrutiny and a subtle headshake. "I'm not going to ask what you're up to, but I almost hope you're a couple jumps in front of us on this one. I've never seen the cop shop play one so close to the chest before. There's a rumor that Ernold Quick's back in town but we can't even confirm that. They won't say no and they won't say yes. I suppose Frankie's told you he thinks something smells about this whole investigation."

"I agree, but I think the difference is that Marcum's more involved in this one than usual, and he's paranoid right up to his beady eyeballs. I'd say there is some sort of strategy afoot that we're not being told." At his look of anticipation, she made a sudden decision, opened a folder, and handed him the assistant police chief's memo to his boss, the note on the back of the flier, and the vicious email message about McRae. Since the police now had the two anonymous notes, the news team should have them as well.

"I knew it," he said, foregoing the usual explosion.

Half an hour later, after the necessary bargaining—Ambrose would consider the import of the new material in deploying his troops but would not mention the memo or notes outright—she promised to give him daily reports on her findings. "But not my guesses and reasoning and so on. Only the tangibles."

"Fair enough. You can keep your Leopold leaps to yourself. For now, anyway." Urging her to remember that there had been two murders and this was not a nice business, the editor left at last. She did not suggest that there may have been *three* murders, and her hand was on the telephone before the door shut.

Lurleen answered with her usual, "Studebaker," followed instantly by, "Score one for you, Honey Pie. I'm not saying there's fact behind the insurance rumor. There isn't. But the rumor's for real. Someone's putting this about for their own purposes and a lot of people are believing it. You could do everyone a favor with a debunking column."

"Can I use you as a source if I do? I'll need someone with the right professional connection if I say there's nothing to it."

"Named or unnamed?"

"Named is always stronger."

"Let me think about it, okay? At the moment I doubt there'd be a problem but I'd like to see whether I wake up in the middle of the night sweating. Then I'll know for sure. I'll call you."

"If you don't, I'll call you."

"Natch."

Neva tried again to reach the city engineer but got an answering machine. She stood up to ask city government reporter Shawna Deagan whether she knew of any projects requiring gravel, but sat down again, and instead called the city planning department. No, said the new young planner who happened to be in the office, nothing was happening at the moment, only the riverfront and that was on hold until "everybody's finished throwing rocks at each other and we can get on with it." Clearly, the young man had not connected Neva's name with the newspaper or he would have been more discreet. Neva made a note. With luck, she was done writing riverfront park columns, but you never know.

She called Kitty Fiori's office but reached only a clerk who said the chief was out and her schedule was full for the coming week.

"Tell her I called and it's important."

"It's always important." The clerk sounded more weary than rude.

Yes, but I'm Jeneva Leopold and she'll want to see me! . . . Or maybe not.

Relieved more than disappointed not to be meeting with the police chief in the next few hours—such meetings took energy that she didn't have today—Neva left the building and walked to the parking lot where she'd seen the gravel trucks. No jolly man with a clipboard was there to talk about planting peas and not a single gravel truck rumbled by. She continued to the skateboard park but failed to find Pet, though she was treated to the sight of a very small boy doing breathtaking aerial flips at the top of a half-pipe, which she watched until he stopped to rest.

Heading up Second Street toward the post office, she could tell from a block away that the inevitable had happened. Each time she had checked Angel's bench, more things were missing, first the socks, then the beer and cigarettes, then the nicest of the plaster saints. Since her last visit, everything had been cleared away, including the shopping cart. She stood for a moment wondering who had decided it was time to move on, whose hands had collected the offerings, where they had ended up. Most likely in the trash, even the picture, which had become streaked and wrinkled from rain.

She turned to leave but was stopped by the sight of a woman on the post office steps. Though the woman stood no more than ten feet away, she was in a world of her own, hunched into a yellow rain parka despite the blue sky, her face so openly grieving that Neva's own head dropped automatically in sympathy and respect for the woman's privacy. The next instant she looked up, wrenched by a terrible thought. This was Angel's mother making a pilgrimage to the spot her son had called home for the last years of his life . . . The woman turned her head, trancelike, looked into Neva's eyes for a long, blank moment, and then lit up with a startling smile.

"Jeneva Leopold," she said simply, without question. "I enjoy your pieces in the paper so very much."

"Thank you. Thank you, deeply."

"You always write true about families, the best and the worst. I've saved quite a few of them. How is Ethan?"

As usual, it jolted Neva to hear her son's name spoken in this way by a stranger, though now that the woman's face had relaxed it seemed familiar, and it certainly was not Angel's mother. Relieved, she said with an answering smile, "My son's doing well, thank you. It's nice of you to ask."

"I saved the piece you wrote about the first time he took the car and didn't come home. You waited up all night. You didn't know he was helping somebody in trouble. That's something you can still hold close, knowing he was helping. You thought the worst."

"I was sure of the worst. I could see the car upside down in a ditch without even closing my eyes. It can still give me the midnight panic if I let it. I'm not sure I've had a really sound sleep ever since."

Neva had meant to lighten the moment, to make it easy for them to laugh over the obsessive bonds with children that they clearly shared.

But the woman's face had collapsed again into private sorrow; she shook her head and murmured, "So good to meet you," and walked away down the handicapped ramp on the other side of the post office porch.

Pulled after her as though by a cord fixed between their hearts, Neva ran up the steps but stopped at the top. There was nothing to be done, nothing she could say. Had the woman wanted to, she could have spilled her sorrow as many readers had done before, responding to columns that had moved them deeply, usually because Neva had described some powerful experience that echoed something in their own lives. This reader was not ready to speak in words despite the grief that spoke so clearly through her eyes.

Photographer Kelly Redpath scrambled down the steep trail, camera bag bouncing on her hip. The trail to the homeless camp was just off the east end of the Hannah Avenue Bridge, and easier to find than to navigate. Either there was an easier way down, or Hogan & Co. must suffer a lot of drunken tumbles. Neva grabbed for a willow branch as her feet slid in the mud.

"You okay there?" Kelly stood safely at the bottom, her sturdy legs planted wide, the tripod resting neatly on her shoulder. "Looks pretty well used. What do you think, upriver or down?"

"Up. Across from downtown."

"What about campfire smoke? Dead giveaway."

"I'd be surprised if they were organized enough to manage fires very often. That takes dry wood, matches, getting it together in daylight. It's not likely to be much of a camp."

About this, however, she was wrong. Trails branched all through the scrubby woods along the river but one was distinctly more traveled than the others, and five minutes walking brought them to a small clearing. Kelly, an eager scout, led the way and soon stopped short with a loud, "Whoa!"

The camp filled a sizable clearing and included three rakish dwellings assembled from tarps, poles, plywood, and sheets of corrugated plastic. In the middle of the clearing, half a dozen log rounds, an old car seat, and two metal folding chairs were arranged around a ring of fire-blackened rocks. Sunlight picked out a mirror fixed to a cottonwood trunk. One of the shelters had a rusted stovepipe sticking through the roof.

"Home sweet home," Kelly murmured, and unzipped the camera bag.

Neva approached the fire ring, which showed the usual half-burned cans and foil among charred wood remnants. She set the paper sack containing coffee and scones on a stump. "Hello? Anyone home? Hogan? Tomasino? It's Jeneva, from the newspaper."

Only a distant crow calling and the hum of traffic crossing the bridge downriver broke the afternoon stillness. Though the camp was more substantial than she'd expected, it was bleak enough, and stank of sodden ashes and sour pee. Approaching the canvas flap that served for a door to the largest of the shelters, she called out again, then pulled the flap aside.

A sudden scrambling at the back of the shelter made her draw back sharply.

"What is it?" Kelly was behind her in an instant, then darted to the right around the side of the shelter. "Hey! Stop! We're okay, not police."

Recovered from her surprise, Neva ducked through the low door but even from inside she could hear the crash of underbrush as whoever had dodged out the back fled through the woods. Kelly soon returned and pushed aside the flap to peer in.

"I didn't even get a good look," she said in disgust. "Anybody still in here?"

"In a manner of speaking."

An old-style metal bedspring took up most of the space in the shelter, and taking up most of the bed was a huge roll of blankets with two feet in socks sticking out the bottom. The roll was inert and silent.

"Hello!" Boomed Kelly. "Are you awake?" There was no response even when she shook one of the feet and shouted, "Hey!"

Holding her breath against the smell, Neva leaned to look at the face at the opposite end from the feet. The sleeper was an unfamiliar man with a coarse blond beard. "I don't know this one."

Kelly had already pushed through a curtain that led into a small back room, and said over her shoulder, "This must be where our escaped bird was hanging out. Not bad."

The room was almost homey, with a carpet floor, a cot and sleeping bag, and a table, chair and oil lamp. The lamp was lit and a *Sports Illustrated* magazine lay open on the table.

"A reader," Kelly said just before her flash went off. "I suppose we don't need a written release to take pictures. Ha, ha. That's the current issue, by the way."

On their way out she photographed the human bedroll, then got the shelter from the outside with the door flap hooked half open. "Don't know that they'll be any use, but just in case. Maybe it's time for a general feature on the homeless. What we need is a couple inches of snow to make it really pitiful."

Neva was heading for the other shelter and only laughed at the photographer's cynicism. Kelly Redpath had been hired a year ago by the sports editor and had taken so many good pictures of fans, cheerleaders, coaches, kids, parents, even food venders that Ambrose wooed her to the news side. She was bound for big things, no doubt about it, and Neva had sought her out for the expedition, knowing that Kelly not only would make good illustrative use of whatever they encountered, but would remain unfazed and even have a good time—and she was no pushover physically.

The second shelter was smaller but had a bed with a proper mattress and a plywood floor. Bits of clothing lay about, and half filled a shopping cart in the corner.

"Anything?"

"Nope." Neva backed out and scanned the camp and the surrounding woods. "That wasn't Tomasino or Hogan we scared away. They're not up to running, and they wouldn't bother anyway. They must be in town somewhere. I can't help wondering if it was Ernold Quick. Ambrose said there's a rumor he's back in town, and he'd have a good reason to run."

"The guy who killed Angel? Great. Remind me to say no next time you come knocking." Kelly squatted to repack the camera bag, her manner untroubled.

"Sorry to waste your time."

"No waste. I'm glad to know about this place. If my roof keeps leaking I might just move over here—after they catch that guy."

"BYOT."

They walked single file back up the trail for a minute or more in silence before Kelly said, "Sorry. Guess I'm kind of dim today. Could you translate?"

"Bring your own tent."

It was late afternoon when they arrived back at the newsroom, and early twilight by the time Neva got home. A solitary Friday evening lay ahead and this was just fine, especially given the pallet of magnificent quartzite waiting in her driveway. Before going indoors she pulled away the bands of plastic Herman had wrapped around the stacked stone to keep it in place. The top layer looked almost peach-toned in the evening light and felt warm as she rested her cheek against the rock.

A pile of sand—an enormous, daunting pile of sand—had also been delivered. It would take only minutes to lay down the landscaping fabric, leaving more than an hour until dark to trundle wheelbarrow loads of sand around to the back. A full day's work on Saturday should finish the job, leaving Sunday to begin laying stones.

The first step was to get out of slacks and into jeans, but on her way through the hall she was stopped by the blinking of the phone message light. If it had been any number but Ethan's in the Caller I.D. window she would have let it wait. Her son's voice brought the usual smile but his words made her turn a quizzical eye to the calendar that hung above the telephone table.

"You didn't tell me what the talk was about, but I hope it's something fun," he was saying as she found the scrawled reminder: *7 p. remarks at Pearl—brief.*

"Hell!"

It was now 6:30. In half an hour she was expected at The Pearl, Willamette's newest art gallery. She had agreed to speak at the opening exhibit and celebration, which meant dressing in something other than mud-spattered cotton pants. Unbuttoning her shirt as she went, she dashed up the stairs and yanked a linen blouse from a hanger. Too pale. She tossed it on a chair, put on a scoop-neck emerald stretch top that she hadn't worn since before the cancer, stepped into a calf-length, slim-cut skirt and considered her reflection in the mirror.

Turning sideways, she continued to study her shape for a long, still moment. In the snug top, her chest was as flat as new pavement. Some might call it chic. Tonight, for the first time since her torso was reduced to a rib cage wrapped in skin, she would stand in front of an audience wearing a fitted top.

She was ready.

With a half-peeled banana in hand, she was out the door.

The gallery was at the foot of Martha Street, at the opposite end of the riverfront from Lyle's warehouse. It had been carved from one corner of a former logging supply store dating back to the 1890s. Neva had not yet seen the inside, but the outside was festive, with strings of small white lights framing the windows and people clustered by the door. Scanning the crowd, looking for familiar faces, she drove past and circled the block. Pulling into an empty parking spot at the opposite end of the block from the gallery, she was still paying more attention to the crowd ahead than to driving. With a jarring ram, her front wheel went up on the curb, then slammed down onto the pavement again so hard it hurt her teeth.

After a shocked moment, she sprang out and squatted to look under the right front corner of the car. The dusky twilight made it impossible to see anything in detail, but at least no parts had fallen off and no oil or brake fluid was pouring down.

She straightened and turned to head for the gallery.

"No damage done, I hope," a cheery voice called out behind her.

A smiling Carter Grey took her arm. "Sometimes they put curbs in the most inconvenient places. Did you really say you were writing a column about the restaurant?"

"I did, and I did." Neva smoothly withdrew her arm.

"Well, what judgment did you pass on my humble eatery?"

"Just what I told you. It's a winner, though naturally I had to have a little fun with it. Your cook's shark story is in there, along with her peg leg and roller skate."

"Yes, well, that sounds very good." A pause. "Did you, by chance, mention that I own three blocks?"

"Is that in partnership or all by your lonesome? I forgot to ask."

"I'm the only partner who counts given that the other two are my parents, both in a nursing home in Indiana. Did you mention it?"

"I did not."

A small breath escaped him.

"It wasn't significant in terms of the restaurant column. I'm saving that bit for a column about riverfront property ownership in general. You still haven't given a good reason for why you didn't confess when I asked you straight out about Left Bank at our first meeting, or why you're so concerned about it being known that you own extensive property down here."

"No real reason, except that I'm in business and I've learned that the more you keep your affairs to yourself the better. Also, though it may be cowardly, I'd rather duck the whole redevelopment question and just let things fall out the way they fall out. I've never been a comfortable team player."

"You also didn't tell me you had met Lyle McRae in Clarendon."

"You didn't ask where we met. Does it matter?"

"I'm also wondering about your real reason for moving to Oregon. You said you'd read about Willamette and got interested while living in Krakow."

They had reached the open gallery door and before Grey could reply, Ambrose stepped up. "Neva, there you are. You've got to see this."

"Half a second," she said, and turned to look squarely at Carter. "I'm ready for answers any time except now."

"Of course. It's simple—but we'll talk later."

Ambrose led the way through the press of bodies to the far side of the room and stopped in front of a sculpture on a low stand. The figure was a reclining nude woman with the head of a deer, about half life-size and intricately graceful.

"What do you think?" He demanded. "I love it. I'd buy it for the front hall at home if I didn't know Annie would have a fit."

"Amazing," Neva said. "But I don't know that I'd want to look at it every day."

"Why not?" said a voice behind her.

Glancing around, she found Win Niagra.

"I haven't had time to think," she replied. "My first impression is that it's beautifully done but it unnerves me because, well, the deer looks unhappy, trapped maybe, with this lovely but unsuitable body. It has all kinds of possibilities for symbolism, but I react to art esthetically and emotionally more than intellectually and it leaves me feeling uneasy. What do you think?"

"It's the best thing I've ever done."

Unable to speak, Neva looked back and forth between the sculptor and his creation. What an appalling blunder—but the man was a potter, wasn't he? "My god, I had no idea," she managed at last. "I don't know what to say."

"No problem," Niagra said coolly. "You reacted with feeling and that's a compliment to the work even if you hate it."

"I don't hate it, not a bit."

"I didn't mean to say you did, I was just trying to make a point."

They regarded each other warily. Niagra wore spotless white overalls over a purple shirt with rolled sleeves, which struck her as affected attire for the occasion, particularly for an artist who must be in his fifties, for now she knew he was an artist rather than an artisan, if there is a difference.

"Well, I love it," Ambrose said with hearty good cheer. "Red wine or white, Jeneva?"

"Red, please, as you've known for years." Neva did not look away from Niagra. "I didn't know you were a sculptor. Are the paintings yours too?"

"They're a mix, three different artists. I work only in the round, not on canvas. These are all mine."

She considered what the crowd allowed her to see of the half dozen other pieces, all variants on the same idea, that is, figures made of combined human and beast body features. Every one was formed with skill, but the others didn't affect her like the deer-woman. "Highly original," she said. "I need to look at them individually, sometime when the gallery isn't so packed. I thought you were a potter."

"I teach pottery and sculpture. Did you find Tomasino?"

"Not yet."

"He may have left town. They do that. Excuse me." He turned away to intercept a tall woman carrying a clipboard.

"I seemed to recall you prefer red," said Carter Grey, reappearing at her side. He handed her a glass just as Ambrose arrived with her wine.

Neva accepted both glasses and drank two-fisted while making a circuit of the gallery and doing her best to avoid conversation. Putting the Niagra incident out of her mind for the moment, she focused on what to say about art in Willamette. Her brief turn on the platform came and went. Mingling now, merry from the wine and relieved that her remarks had been reasonable if not brilliant, she was ready to hear Carter's explanations.

But he was not to be found, and for a moment she felt strangely let down—had he left before she spoke? Had he run away from her questions?

Niagra, on the other hand, was all too evident and several times she caught him watching her. When their eyes met she nodded but she was not up to resuming their conversation, though she made a point of staying until only a few others remained. Weariness, and no doubt the double dose of wine late in the evening, caught up with her as she was preparing to leave. On her way out, she stopped to admire a watercolor that caught a particular quality of wet, spring light, and then she was out the door and breathing deeply. The air was damp and redolent with cottonwood perfume. Her head cleared, and strolling back to the car, she felt at ease and pleased with the evening—with the convivial mood, her own small role, even the art despite the faux pas with Niagra.

If it weren't for her job as a columnist, would she ever attend such events?

Probably not. If left to herself, she would turn into Arva Fowler

Neva almost laughed as she slid in behind the steering wheel. Yes, she would be a recluse in no time, though she'd grow hot peppers in the front yard rather than hawkweed.

Still smiling, she turned the key in the ignition.

Nothing happened.

She tried again. And again. Each time there was a click and then silence. The starter did not turn over, the engine didn't cough or sputter, only a click and silence.

Surely, the jolt from ramming the wheel could not have damaged the starter? But it must have done something, must have knocked loose a wire or other connection. The car was twelve years old but it never failed to start. She would look under the hood in case there was an obvious problem and then call for help.

Rather than dig the little flashlight out of her purse, she lifted the hood and tried to see by the light from a distant street lamp. It was almost black in the engine compartment. Gingerly, she felt for the battery posts, which seemed to be clean and solidly connected.

"Having trouble?"

The low voice came from close by, but when she turned to look there was no one in sight. The sidewalk was deserted all the way down to the riverfront, and the lights were now off at the gallery.

"Hello?" She said, scanning the narrow shadow cast by the building next to the sidewalk.

"Car trouble," a man's voice mused from the shadow, pleasant and low. "What a nuisance, and now they've all gone home and there's no one to help."

"Where are you? Do you know anything about mechanics?"

"I know a lot about cars, enough to keep one from starting when I want to."

"Why would you want to do that?"

"To keep somebody from driving away when I want to talk to them."

"It would be easier just to ask them to stay."

"Why would anybody do what I ask them?"

"Why wouldn't they if you had a good reason?"

"All right then. How about the death of Angel de Silva—you call that a good reason?"

"A very good reason. I'd like to talk with you, but please tell me who you are. And where. I'm not comfortable talking to someone I don't know and can't see. I'm sure you can understand that."

"Sorry. No name. And we can't talk here, not with the cops cruising by. You're going to close the hood of your car, then go down the sidewalk into the alley and stand in the first doorway until you hear my voice again. Got it?"

"I can't do that, you know." Neva reached up and lowered the hood, casually, then dusted her fingers. "Think about it. I have no idea who you are, it's the middle of the night, I'm a lone woman. I'm not leaving this spot, believe me. I will talk to you right here. And if you try force I will scream bloody hell and put up a fight that might surprise you."

The only response was a scraping sound.

"Listen, please," she said. "I really do want to talk to you, but I'm cold and I've been standing up talking for the past two hours. You'll probably laugh, but here's my suggestion. You stay where you are, out of sight, and I'll get into the back seat of the car where my jacket is and roll down the window. You know enough about cars to know I'm telling the truth that this one is old enough to have hand crank windows. Right? We can talk fine, and if a car comes by I'll put my head down." Disregarding the snort from the shadows, she went on firmly as she moved to the back door on the passenger's side, "Now I'm going to open the door and roll down the window and get in. You're going to have to trust me not to hide in there with the doors locked just as I have to trust you not to hit me on the head, which wouldn't do you any good, would it? Believe me, there's no other way this is going to happen."

Not waiting for a response, she opened the car door, her back tensed and tingling, ready for a blow. She rolled down the window, sat on the cold seat, swung her legs in, and closed the door. "Now I'm going to put on my jacket," she said facing out the window and adding in a conversational tone, "It's not very warm, unfortunately, but better than this thin shirt." Resting her forearm on the bottom of the open window, she pitched her voice toward the shadowed wall to the right where his voice had come from. "First I have a question for you," she said with enough volume to cover the sound of the lock button clicking. "What made you think I wouldn't just ask someone at the gallery to help start the car or give me a ride?"

"I didn't know, but most people fool around for a while. They think it's going to start if they just keep cranking it. I would. But they all left, anyway. So here's the deal."

The words now came from the left rather than the right, from the dense black rectangle of what must be a doorway. There was the quick flare of a match and glow of a cigarette tip, though the man had turned away so the light revealed only a momentary silhouette of a bent head. An inhalation, a sighing exhalation. "Listen. You have to listen to me real good, you understand? I heard you've been talking to people. You want to know what really happened. Well, first you have to know something else. The whole thing about Angel is bogus, it's not like they said about him at the so-called memorial. I wasn't there but I heard about it. And those two guys never did it. They took the money, okay, but they never beat him, never hardly touched him at all. He was so drunk they didn't have to do nothing but empty his pockets."

"How do you know this for sure?" She thought she knew the answer, but wanted to hear it from him.

"I just do, that's all."

"You are Ernold Quick, aren't you?"

"That's right," he said without hesitation, and then with vehemence, "He deserved what he got. He was a snitch, a dirty lying snitch. A lot of people wanted him dead, you got that?"

"So which one killed him?"

"How should I know? It's a frame job, a pure frame job. Angel wasn't no angel. Sure he helped some folks, but he got what he wanted out of it."

"Why did you come back?"

"I never left. I never run from a fight. I never ran from anything in my life. That's just more of the bullshit that's going around. And Lyle McRae, the way you wrote about him, he's not what you think either."

"I met him just once and must have got it wrong. That's one of the hazards of doing what I do. I often have to make snap judgments, to trust my instincts."

"He was blackmailing that guy, Win Niagra. That's dirty shit, doing blackmail. Go ask Win for yourself, if you don't believe it. He'll tell you."

"Lyle said you and Vance were the ones doing the blackmailing, not just Win but others as well."

"Oh, yeah, what for?"

"For having sex with kids that you provided from your gang."

Quickie's laughter was harsh and wheezing, and ended in a fit of coughing. At last he said, "Creative guy, that McRae. What else did he say about me?"

"That you and Vance ran the gang out of Azalea Park and the kids kept watch for police on bicycles while you arranged drug deals and other nasty business."

The laughter was almost merry this time, though followed again by coughing. "Oh, Jesus. That's good. But kids today, they don't need any help to get into bad shit. Not from me, anyway. Kids on bicycles, that's too much. Looks like he deserved what he got, too."

"Do you have any idea who did that?"

"No way. Well, anybody's got ideas but I don't know."

"What are your ideas?"

"I guess you'd like to know that, wouldn't you?"

Neva did not reply and at length his impatient voice came again. "You've been talking to everybody. You've been asking questions. Are you some kind of undercover cop?"

"Definitely not. My job would be easier if I were because then I'd know what the police know as well as what I'm able to find out. But I'm just a nosy journalist who got involved in this without really wanting to be. Is that why you wanted to talk to me? And how did you know I'd be here tonight?"

"I saw that flier about the gallery. You were at the top of the list, like the big event. I didn't really believe you're a cop. Do you think I'd mess with a cop car? Only, somebody said it so I thought I'd ask."

"Who said it?"

"I don't really care about that. All I want to say is that me and Vance found Angel drunk. We took his money without any fight or nothing. Since you're so curious you might as well know. Vance had the money when they caught him so they think they can pin it on us. Could have been anybody. I mean, he was dead drunk."

"There's also a videotape."

"What's that?"

"At the store where you buy beer, the Dari-Mart. It shows Vance threatening Angel just a few hours before he was killed."

"They got Vance on there, with pictures? Well, what do you know." After a brief silence, Quick mused as though to himself, "He must have gone back after."

"What do you mean, after?"

"Maybe he went back after we ran, you know, back to where Angel was at. We saw a cop car coming and took off."

"But you didn't stay together?"

"No way. The kid runs like a duck. You know I just got out of the hole and I don't plan on going back in. I left him in the dust. We were going to meet in the morning and split the money but then I heard about Angel. And he got arrested."

"A week later. You didn't see him for a whole week?"

"We were both hiding, only he wasn't very good at it. He should have stashed the money, the dumb shit."

"Why did he end up with all the money?"

"He took it off Angel. It was his idea."

"Do you know anything about Lisette? You probably heard she had a huge amount of alcohol in her. They're calling it death by alcohol poisoning."

"That doesn't sound right to me. Lisette was a stoner from way back. She was a stupid slut but I never saw her drunk."

"Was she staying at Lyle's greenhouse?"

"She did before sometimes, when he was alive."

"Lyle and Lisette were close friends?"

"Lisette had a lot of guy friends, if you get my drift."

Quickie's account had the ring of truth, and he could no doubt tell her a great deal more if she could just think of the right questions. "Listen, I'd really like to talk to you some more but I've been working hard all day and it was a tiring evening. I don't think clearly when I'm tired. Could we talk again, soon? And I will talk to you, I promise, any time you want. It's my business to talk to people."

"What do you want to talk about?"

"I don't quite know, as I said. I have to think about it, about what you've said."

"Okay then. But if it's a trick, if you tell anybody—"

"Oh, for heaven's sake. Just fix the car, please. I really need to sleep."

"Get in front then."

"What about talking again?"

"You leave that to me."

"Wait, there is one question I've got to ask. Did you send me an email message about Lyle McRae?"

A silence was followed by a low chuckle. "Yeah, I sent a message. And I meant every word."

Chapter Seventeen

Saturday morning brought heavy clouds and rain that blew in under the eaves and struck the windows. Neva woke up with no transition between sleep and full consciousness.

"Hell," she said and swung her legs out from under the blankets.

Damn the rain. How could she shovel sand in the rain?

Sand! How could she think about sand after last night?

But no. Too early. She would not think about Ernold Quick, not now, not on Saturday morning, not before coffee.

The front hall was dim and full of the sound of water. She opened the door to find a cascade pouring from the roof on the left side of the porch. The gutter was overflowing, flattening the newly opened daffodils below. Neva pulled her bathrobe close, considered the daffodils, considered the downspout that must have clogged, then picked up the newspaper. She would see to the mess later—now she wanted a civilized hour by a bright fire.

The dry fir kindling caught easily and burned with a happy snap. Though she had not roasted beans last night there were enough left from the day before and she was soon sitting in a chair drawn close to the hearth, coffee and *Current* in hand. She looked at the front page. Her eyes found words but their meaning did not reach her mind. Two paragraphs into the lead article she stopped resisting and let the clamoring scenes from last evening have their way. She expected Ernold Quick to take over but it was not Quick who grabbed the first opening, it was Win Niagra as she had last seen him, watching her through a break in the gallery crowd, his face set and troubled. Why? Why had he looked so gloomy on such an occasion? Apart from her gaff, the evening had been a triumph for the sculptor, with red "sold" stickers blooming on one piece after another. He should have been delighted by the public reaction to his work, should have celebrated and rejoiced, yet each time she caught sight of him throughout the evening he appeared somber and sad, not in the least like the artist hero of the hour. She had stepped on his toes, certainly, but not hard enough to ruin his big night. She had said clearly that the piece moved her deeply, and this was a compliment of a particular kind, though he had not appeared to take it as complimentary.

Though she could not believe she'd been the sole cause of his gloom, she certainly should make amends, the sooner the better. If the rain kept up, she would have to put off hauling the sand and might as well make a quick trip to the craft center. If the sculptor wasn't there she would try the gallery . . . the gallery. The Pearl of Martha Street where Ernold Quick had disabled her car.

Had he really done this? Snug by the fire, she could not believe the scene as it replayed in her mind. No one—no sane person—would use such a ploy merely to talk with her. He had sent her one email message. Surely, he could have sent another note to ask for a meeting. . . But he would be crazy to do that because he was wanted for murder and had no way of knowing whether she could be trusted not to set him up for the police. Still, to disable her car was extreme and melodramatic. And what had been the point? Casting back she could not recall clearly all that he'd said, though the main message had seemed to be that he'd robbed an unconscious drunk but had not killed him. Why had he felt driven to tell her this? Because she was talking to everyone else and everyone else was mostly lying. It's a pure frame job, he'd said.

It might well be true that he had only robbed Angel, but what about all the rest of it, the youth gang, drug dealing, blackmail . . . *Creative guy, that McRae* . . . He had laughed at the whole tale. Only once had his certainty and self-possession slipped. The mention of the Dari-Mart security film had thrown him off for a few heartbeats, though he'd appeared puzzled more than worried. If she believed Quick, it put in question everything McRae had said, even his claim that Quick had a vicious violent streak and held a powerful grudge against him and Angel, a grudge ferocious enough for murder.

As for her own part in the pageant, she had handled it well—or else with foolhardy bravado. Her cool had been no bluff, but now she had to wonder how much this was due to the wine. And yet, what else could she have done? To go with Quick as he'd demanded would have been far riskier than refusing and even turning her back on him to get into the car. She could have run, but he might have been armed and reacted with sudden violence to her flight. And that part of town was deserted for at least two blocks in every direction at that hour, so she could not have brought help by screaming despite her threat to do just that.

The fire settled suddenly, flinging up sparks. Almost at the same moment, a hollow thump came from the direction of the front door. The thump was followed by heavy footsteps and a pounding knock. Already on her feet, Neva kicked a stray ember back into the fire and went eagerly to the hall expecting to see the lean figure of Debo Happ again through the door window. But the silhouette that filled the thinly curtained frame was bulky and hunched, and rather than Debo's mild rat-a-tat the second burst of knocking was fierce.

"I don't appreciate being put in the newspaper," Reba protested before the door was fully open.

"Reba! You're wet. Come in."

Neva opened the door wide but the homeless woman merely glowered from inside the hood of her sodden sweatshirt. "Did I ever say I wanted attention from this town? Now I've got everybody and their brother telling me I'm supposed to talk to you."

The distance from the front door to the armchair could be covered in seconds but it took a good ten minutes of apologizing and coaxing to move Reba, and then she refused to take off the wet sweatshirt. And rather than sink into the warm comfort of the chair, she sat up straight with her feet flat on the floor, and instead of holding her bare hands out to the flames she clasped them hard in her lap.

No, she was not cold. No, she was not hungry. No, she didn't want coffee or tea. What did Jeneva want with her?

"Have something hot to drink at least. Then we can talk."

Okay, she would have tea. With sugar.

When Neva returned with a tray bearing oatmeal cookies as well the tea, Reba was still sitting up like a rigid sentry on duty. She accepted the tea with reluctance, but once it was in her hand she gulped it and put the cookies in her mouth whole.

Neva sat on the couch watching the cookies disappear and wishing she had made a sandwich.

"Well, I'm here," Reba said when the last cookie was gone. "What was such a big deal that you had to advertise me? You may as well get on with it. Don't bother beating around the bush."

"All right then, here it is. The morning Lisette LaBruce died I went to Lyle's room in the warehouse. It was a wreck, completely trashed. Your maroon pack was there."

"Is that what you wanted to ask me about?"

"One of many questions. You know things no one else does, and I believe what you say."

"You don't have to butter me up."

"No butter, just the truth. Is the pack yours?"

Reba shrugged and looked away, but instantly looked back and said simply. "No."

"Is it Vance Fowler's?"

"I found it at the camp where he stayed. I took it to keep for him, mostly because of his pictures. After I got it out of your car, I carried it for a while, but I got real tired. I'm big but I don't like carrying anything more than my own self around. My own self gets real heavy sometimes, especially on slow days. Do you ever get slow days, Jeneva Leopold?"

"Yes, at times. Then I don't want to do anything, not even get out of bed. I'm not very good at giving in to it, but I feel it."

Reba eyed her skeptically but went on, "I was going to put it back in your car but I gave it to Lisette to keep for Vance since she had a place to stay."

"Lyle's apartment?"

"That's right."

"I've heard she wasn't a drinker. Kind of strange, considering she died of alcohol poisoning."

"She drank beer once in a while, to be sociable, but she smoked to feel good. She was like the cats, she never hurt anybody."

"Has anyone told the police she wasn't a drinker?"

"They could figure it out for themselves if they did a proper medical, but they won't. You know why? Because she was homeless and homeless means trash. If I was found dead they'd probably call it cat poisoning."

Neva's laughter made her guest smile for the first time. She sat back in the chair and turned her fine dark eyes to Neva. "Well?"

"Do you have any idea why anyone would want to kill Lisette?"

"Maybe she saw something."

"Something such as?"

"I don't know in particular, but we see things. People who live inside walls all the time don't realize what goes on out there."

Neva waited but nothing more was offered. She said conversationally, "Last night something pretty strange happened to me. I was downtown and my car wouldn't start and it turned out that Ernold Quick had tampered with it. He said he wanted to talk."

Reba nodded.

"You knew he was in town?"

"I figured."

"He said he and Vance robbed Angel but didn't hurt him. He said he was passed out and they just took the money out of his pocket, then ran away when they saw a police car. What he said had the ring of truth somehow, but it doesn't fit at all with what Lyle McRae said. I can't remember whether I mentioned this before, but he said Quick had it in for both him and Angel and now both of them are dead. My question for you is which one do we believe, Lyle or Quick?"

"What do you mean?"

"They can't both be telling the truth, and Lyle was right, at least, about his life being in danger."

"I told you already, Vance and Quickie didn't kill Angel. That's the whole point."

"I don't think you ever said that. Not to me."

"I did. Why do you think I had Tomasino talk to you? You don't believe me any more than anybody else does. You sure had me fooled." Reba heaved herself out of the chair, shook like a large dog flinging off something disgusting, and headed for the door.

"Wait! Reba, please. Please stop."

Reba was already in the hall and did not slow down. Neva dodged around her and stood in front of the door with her hands lifted in a pleading gesture. "That came out wrong. I know I'm saying clumsy things, but I'm very confused and also concerned. We don't know if this is the last of it, if anyone else might be killed."

Reba stood with her arms crossed and her face set.

"There has to be a connection between the murders." Neva also crossed her arms and stood as tall as possible, but still she had to look up to meet her visitor's gaze. "I seem to have got involved without really wanting to, but I need help. I keep thinking I should just leave it alone, leave it to the police, but then something else happens. Or somebody tells me something and it makes sense but not the kind of sense to pass along to law enforcement, or the reporters. You know what I mean. Too much gut feeling in this, too much instinct working and not enough information."

Reba's manner remained fierce, but she gave a slight nod.

"What I need is some definite link that connects the three deaths, something more than the victims all being street people, or almost, in Lyle's case. Can you think of any link that would connect them?"

"Maybe it's me."

"You? But, Reba, I don't—what do you mean?"

"Maybe I'm the link. I knew them all for a hundred years, ever since Clarendon."

"They were all in the mental hospital? You too? And Lisette?"

"Hospital! Whoever came up with that? More like Auschwitz for the weird and unwanted. It was a great day for the state of Oregon when they closed that place down. I just wonder what they did with all the straightjackets and shock machines."

"If they all knew you at Clarendon they probably knew each other too."

"And every other so-called nut in the state. We're not talking killers here, we're talking chemical imbalance, and a sick treatment system."

"I'm not suggesting a fellow resident killed them, but maybe that connection is a key."

"Then maybe I'm next on the list. You always do cheer me up, Jeneva Leopold."

"Did you ever see Carter Grey at Clarendon?"

"He wasn't there!"

"Not as a patient. He taught photography."

"I never saw him. Now leave me out of the paper, ok? I have enough trouble as it is. If I think of anything I'll let you know."

Chapter Eighteen

Rain fell all day Saturday, but Neva did not have the heart to go looking for Win Niagra, though in addition to owing him some sort of apology she now had a double reason to follow up the claims of blackmail involving the sculptor and the gardener. When Niagra had said it was family business and had nothing to do with what was happening, she had allowed herself to believe it—Lyle was still alive then. But after last night, trying to get the truth out of Niagra was going to be all the more unpleasant and most likely impossible. She did not want to think about it. Reba's visit had deepened the gloom of the day and it felt natural to go for an antidote rather than struggle. She kept the fire going, made a pie with the last of the frozen summer blueberries, read the whole of Isherwood's *Prater Violet* and found herself laughing aloud. She finished her day of retreat by watching the ever-reliable *Cold Comfort Farm* while eating a quarter of the pie. She went to bed feeling fine.

Sunday dawned clear. The air was scrubbed clean, the new spring leaves glowed as though lighted from within. The ground where the lawn had been was a mud slick, and at first Neva's rubber boots slithered and the wheelbarrow made heavy grooves wherever it went, but she started shoveling before breakfast and soon covered the whole patch in a thin layer of sand for easier walking. Then it was an endless round of filling the wheelbarrow, trundling it to the back yard, tipping the sand out in a small heap, kneeling to smooth it to a depth of six inches, going back for another load.

The robotic chore left her mind free, and after the day of rest, her thoughts were clearer than they had been for many days. It had been wrong to put Reba Winner on the spot as she had done, but she could not really regret it. Though the homeless woman had not proved to be the treasure house of information she'd hoped, she had at least confirmed a number of things: Lisette had been staying at Lyle's and she was not known as a drinker; the maroon pack and notebook belonged to Vance; Quickie and Vance had not killed Angel, or at least Reba was convinced they were innocent. And there was the Clarendon connection, which must mean something.

Her only regret was handling the visit so badly. She had failed to make a proper breakfast for Reba, had failed to make her feel at home, had driven her back out into the rain by her clumsy questioning. With different handling, they might have spent the day together by the fire. Who knows what she might have learned from a well-fed, warm, relaxed Reba—and Reba would have left the house dry and possibly even smiling. That she might get another opportunity, a second chance to make up for her blunders, seemed very unlikely.

The sky was still clear on Monday morning and she was out before breakfast, stiff and sore but determined to haul the final barrow-loads of sand. When she made herself stop at last, only a small heap remained, but it was Monday, after all, and she was now ready for what had to be done. She brushed off her jeans, pulled a blue sweater on over the T-shirt, and was on her way.

The parking lot on the south side of the First Church of Christ was empty apart from a battered pickup. The craft center was in the basement, reached from outdoors by a short flight of concrete stairs. A sign invited visitors to *Walk In* but still Neva knocked first, then pushed open the door without waiting for a response. The large room was pleasantly warm and crowded with potter's wheels and tables, and nearly every surface was covered in clay bowls, mugs, pots, plates, and fanciful figures.

Win Niagra was alone. He sat on a stool at a high table with a ceramic mug before him, and though he looked up as she entered, he didn't greet her or say a word.

"Your coffee's cold," she said, and slid onto a stool across the table.

Win touched his cup with two fingers. "How did you know?"

"The skin of milk on top. I still feel funny about Friday."

"Some people loved them. I sold five and got orders. Who am I to want more than that?" Neva waited without speaking until he said, "Okay, no problem. Forget it. What's up?"

"I want to show you something. A drawing." From her bag she pulled Vance's notebook and set it in front of him open to the sketch of Niagra leaning over a potter's wheel.

With a wordless exclamation, he snatched up the notebook, snapped it shut, and clamped it under his arm. "What are you doing with this?"

"It was Vance Fowler's."

"What do you mean *was*?"

"It was in a knapsack found in his camp after he was arrested. There's a sketch of me in there too, and a lot of other people, but they all appear to be in public places like coffee shops, all except for one. The exception is that drawing of you, which must have been done here. Are you a friend of Vance's?"

Win stood, crossed to a wall cabinet, opened a wide, flat drawer, took out a sheet of watercolor paper and placed it on the table. It was a charcoal study of a little girl—Win's granddaughter, she saw after a moment's scrutiny.

"I was teaching him. This was his best yet, but that's no business of yours. It's nobody's business. I know I sound like an asshole, but that's all some people seem to understand. Nobody wants you in this." He picked up the drawing, returned it to the drawer, set the notebook on top, and locked the drawer though it had not been locked before.

Unprepared for the sculptor's emotional and possessive reaction, Neva regarded him with troubled amazement. She had no rightful claim to the notebook while he at least had the claim of knowing Vance and having been his teacher, but even so she felt robbed of something important, with no explanation or apology. "You don't care that he could spend the next twenty years in prison, possibly even get the death penalty?"

"You think you can save him? Give me a break." And then, without warning, Win Niagra began to cry. Turning away without another word, he crossed the room, opened a door, and stepped out of sight into the darkness beyond.

Back outside, Neva did not return to her car but, moving as though in a trance, she crossed the small square to the park, dropped onto a bench, and stared at the ground between her feet. What was she failing to see and understand?

Everything, it seemed.

She must be flat-out blind. Something was right there in front of her and she couldn't see even its approximate shape. Everything seemed to be linked in layers of connections but she could not see the connectors, only the end points.

How long she sat she could not have said later, but at last she felt the cold press of the wooden bench slats through the worn fabric of her jeans. She heard chickadees, smelled fragrant tobacco, and looked up to see Tolbert White standing on the walkway, observing her thoughtfully through smoke that curled from his pipe. Her smile was automatic. Without being a close friend, Tolbert was nearly as familiar as one. Since her first year at the *Current*, she had seen the defense attorney almost every day, nearly always in the park, which he crossed to get from his law office to the county courthouse. In the early years he had walked, limping slightly from a knee injury for which he made use of a briar cane with a carved handle. Three years ago he'd given up the cane for a recumbent bicycle that he pedaled with a leisurely air, the pipe trailing a fragrant plume.

"Mind if I join you?" He sat beside her with the comfortable settling motions of a solidly built man at home in the world. "You walked right by me just now you know. Looked right through me."

"Sorry. I didn't see you."

"Obviously not. The question is, what demons have got hold of you? If I'm not prying. But it isn't like you to walk around blind."

"Not demons, just strangeness that I don't understand. Do you know Win Niagra?"

"What's he up to now?"

"Up to? What does that mean?"

Tolbert pushed big hands into the pockets of his baggy suit jacket, stretched his legs out straight, crossed them at the ankles, and looked at his leather shoes. "Ummm. What to say. In the law we have statutes of limitation, but life in general isn't so considerate. How many years are enough years to clean a man's moral slate? And then, there are so many unknowns."

Neva's determined silence was soon rewarded.

"I didn't recognize him when he came back, and if he'd changed his name I probably still wouldn't. Talk about a transformation. You have to give credit, whatever the catalyst was. I've thought of asking him but, well, he doesn't invite it, does he. But I'm not helping you."

"I take it Niagra lived here in the past, something happened and he left, then he came back a very different person?"

"That sums it up."

"Don't be coy, Tolbert. What happened?"

"That's the odd bit. We don't know what happened. When I first opened up shop in Willamette he was one of the regulars around town, you know the type, spend all their time in coffee shops and bars without ever visibly working or seeming to need money. You couldn't help wondering, and then he was such a freak, big hair and the whole bit. I always expected to see him in court but never did. Then one day they found him standing on a street corner with nothing on, jabbering like a crazy man. He was a crazy man as far as that goes, no memory, couldn't talk a straight sentence. He did a week in the hospital and then it was the nuthouse and I didn't think about him again until, oh, maybe twenty years later. I was at a fundraiser for something or other and up gets this

NO ANGEL

solid, calm guy to make a pitch. And it was him, Niagra. Normal as toast. A solid citizen, artist, a daughter and after a while a granddaughter. Why'd he go nuts? Don't know. How'd he straighten out? Don't know. End of story, such as it is."

"When you say nuthouse, do you mean Clarendon?"

"That's right, our one and only before it closed. Now, what's your story, why are you asking about Niagra?"

"Not really a story, just odd behavior." Neva described the gallery episode but said nothing of the notebook, or the fact that Niagra had admitted to being blackmailed, or that Ernold Quick had said the blackmailer was Lyle McRae. "You're back and forth through this park every day of the year. Have you ever seen what looked like a youth gang?"

Tolbert filled his pipe from a leather pouch as he considered the question. "Yes and no. To some eyes, more than one teenager of any stripe gathered in the same spot is a gang. But I can't say I've seen anything I'd call a serious gang."

"Oleander said there was significant gang activity here some years ago but it was cleared up."

"Did he now. And he should know, shouldn't he."

Neva studied the defense attorney's fleshy but still somehow boyish profile. Tolbert White gazed straight out across the lawn, the pipe angling toward her from the corner of his mouth, his complacency suggesting a rich store of pleasurable secrets.

"He is the juvenile officer. Tolbert, what are you hinting at?"

"You really don't know?"

"I don't even know what category of information it might be that I don't know."

"His boy was the worst of the lot. It's really not so surprising. Teacher's kid gets expelled, professor's kid drives a garbage truck, policeman's kid deals pills. By rights all three of mine should have ended up behind bars. None did—I got lucky with girls." He removed the pipe to chuckle. "Of course, one of mine did worse. She became a prosecutor and now butter wouldn't melt in her mouth. I just hope I never have to go up against her in court."

Neva was paying little attention to the attorney's pleasantries. She was trying to fit Captain Oleander's calm presence into the same frame with a dope-dealing kid—the sporty little boy in the family photo on his office wall—but the picture would not hold.

"What happened to the boy?"

"They got him into some program over around Bend. It looked like he was going to straighten out, but then he died. I'm surprised you don't remember. It wasn't even a year ago. He had that infection, MRSA, that thing that resists antibiotics. He was already in pretty bad shape from the bad habits. In a week it was all over."

Back in her office, Neva sat with her fingers resting on the keyboard. Had she ignored the story about the boy's death out of cowardice? It must have been in the *Current*, but her habit was to skip unbearable reports about children suffering or dying. And how could she have missed the signs in Oleander, big solid Lars Oleander? Such a loss had to show somewhere, around his mouth, his eyes, in his voice. He would assume she knew, that everyone knew—but she would not have let such a loss go unacknowledged had she known. She would have said something, maybe in reference to the photograph on his wall. No matter what kind of face he presented to the world now, he was no longer the man pictured in that happy family of four and she should have known. Somehow, she should have known.

She certainly had read about MRSA, but it had seemed distant and unlikely, like those rare reports of bubonic plague and weird viruses that appeared out of nowhere to kill people on a cruise or in a hotel.

She typed "MRSA" into Google and clicked on the first of the 4,780,000 hits.

"MRSA, the so-called 'super bug,' is an acronym for 'Methicillin Resistant *Staphylococcus aureus.*' *S. aureus* is a strain of bacteria that is resistant to antibiotics known as beta-lactams, the main group of antibiotics in use today, including amoxicillin and penicillin as well as methicillin . . . The bug has surpassed AIDS in yearly deaths in the U.S. and, according to some estimates, now kills one in five affected patients. MRSA is a serious problem in hospitals, and often lives in the noses and on the skin of healthy people and spreads from person to person on contaminated hands, skin, and objects."

Neva pulled her hands off the keyboard and looked at them in consternation. What public objects had she touched so far today? Door knobs, park bench, the lunch room water dispenser . . . She had no open cuts to let bacteria in but there was a sizable blister on her left palm from shoveling and it was sure to burst. Was soap any use against it?

She read on, skipping from one alarming site to another, until at last she hit "MRSA-Killing Paint Created," an article from *Science Daily*. "Building on an enzyme found in nature, researchers at Rensselaer Polytechnic Institute have created a nanoscale coating for surgical equipment, hospital walls, and other surfaces which safely eradicates methicillin resistant *Staphylococcus aureus* (MRSA). In tests, 100 percent of MRSA in solution were killed within 20 minutes of contact with a surface painted with latex paint laced with the coating. Unlike other antimicrobial coatings, it is toxic only to MRSA, does not rely on antibiotics, and does not leach chemicals into the environment or become clogged over time."

Paint . . . not much good after the fact, but then, nothing on earth could help after the loss of a child.

She did not look up the news story about the boy's death. Maybe another day.

Chapter Nineteen

Unlike her second in command, Chief Fiori was every inch an officer. She was also physically fit, alert, and not distinctly masculine or feminine. It was as easy to picture her fluting pastry as handcuffing bad guys.

"What took you so long?" she said, seating herself in the second of two armchairs rather than returning behind the desk after their handshake. "I hear you've been everywhere but here. I was beginning to feel left out."

"It's embarrassing to admit but I had the foolish idea that I might actually get some information if I talked to just about anyone but you."

"You might have been right, but you drew Lars. If I'm a safe deposit box, he's Fort Knox."

Their laughter was easy and privileged, the shared mirth of women at home with each other and with their influential, though very different, roles. Relieved to find the chief apparently unchanged in her regard—the memo notwithstanding—Neva would have liked to extend the convivial moment, but mention of the captain made this impossible. She said, "I just learned about his son. I don't know how people survive such things."

"He left the job for a week, and when he came back the only change I could see was lunch. He stopped eating with the others in the break room. He doesn't ever talk about it—closed curtain. Now, what are you after, my girl?"

Another laugh—the chief had called her "my girl" since they met though Neva was older by three years. "Well, my good woman, to be perfectly blunt, we're tired of being kept in the dark. And I don't mean just me. Frankie can't get anything but official press releases out of your scout troop and it makes me wonder, Kitty, it really makes me wonder. Are you playing a close hand or are you really in the dark too?"

"First, I don't believe for one second that you're actually 'in the dark.' Second, I'd like to know what you plan to do with the information.

I won't make the mistake of saying it's not column material, but still, I find it hard to see what your object is, and how or why you got involved at all."

"I got pulled in despite myself. You may have noticed that I haven't written about Angel except in passing, in the piece on Lyle McRae, and I wrote that only because he called me two days before he died. Most of what he told me is being called into question by what I've heard since, but he asked me for help that I couldn't give, and said he was in danger. Then he was dead. You see how it is. Now I have to do what I should have done before, I have to turn over every rock. Obviously I hope for some good columns out of it, but also to stop feeling guilty, and possibly even to help in some way. So now, for starters, what's the connection between Angel and Lyle?"

The chief did not waste time pretending there was no link between the killings. "We have ideas but no good evidence yet, nothing that should be made public."

"Since when do you consider me public?"

"Sorry, sorry. What I meant was nothing solid enough to let out of the shop, even to you. What have you turned up?"

"The main thing is that no one believes Quick and Fowler are guilty. People who know them pretty well are saying you've arrested the wrong man, and what's more, you know it and did it as a ploy of some kind."

"I won't ask you which 'people' are saying this but they're wrong. We don't arrest people for the sake of the game. You know that. There is evidence. I won't say it's strong but it's there."

"Okay, moving on. Is there any suspicion that Lisette LaBruce didn't die of drinking, but was actually killed as well?"

"Well, naturally that had to be considered but she was a known drunk."

"On the street they say she was a doper."

"One doesn't rule out the other. Two murders are more than enough for this town, Neva."

"Do you know where Lisette was living before she died?"

"Either at the Gregorian with a friend, or—and I hesitate to say this because you'll jump to conclusions—at Lyle McRae's place. She was in and out of both at different times."

"I'm not jumping to conclusions, Kitty. I know she was staying at Lyle's."

"You *know*?"

The women looked at each other, blue eyes and brown openly calculating.

"My sources aren't necessarily ones you would trust but I do."

The chief nodded.

"It's a tangle of bits and pieces," Neva continued, closely watching the other woman. "Frankly, I've been surprised to find the place unlocked. I've been back several times, and the last time I went was right after they found Lisette. The apartment had been trashed, and there were some things there, like a small black sweater that smelled like wood smoke and could have been the one she wore at the memorial service. Other things struck me, too, so I started asking around and a reliable person confirmed that Lisette had been staying there. There's more, and I'm almost prepared to tell you the whole story but not quite. There are some obstacles, including your buddy Marcum. He's not behaving himself, Kitty. He's telling the whole planet that I as much as caused the murders by opposing the jail bond. I can't believe you agree, but I'm wondering why you're letting him get away with it."

The police chief was shaking her head, though her expression was amused rather than displeased. "He's gone round the bend a bit, hasn't he? Though I have to say I was disappointed myself. I'd somehow thought we'd have your support. Of course I don't think that you or the jail bond had anything to do with the death of Angel or McRae, but I see nothing wrong in letting what happened anyway help the cause—the incarceration crisis is real. If Gale's overdoing it, well, there's no real harm. It certainly won't hurt you. My guess is that deep down you enjoy it."

"In other circumstances, I probably would. But I strongly suspect there were three murders, and how do we know there won't be more? This isn't just a battle of words. To make it seem like that, to drag issues like the jail bond and riverfront project out in front skews everything. Our reporters feel thwarted by your department, which is all the more puzzling after the cooperative atmosphere we've all worked hard to establish. You know as well as I do that good press reports can help an investigation."

"As well as interfere with it. There are some peculiar circumstances here that require extra care, Neva. I hope you'll believe me that the last thing I want is any permanent damage to relations between the department and the *Current*."

Neva's smile was thin—*What about that memo?* If she were to pull it out of her bag and set it on the table, what then? To see the chief nonplussed for five seconds would be a relief and a pleasure, for even the wily Fiori would have a tough time explaining that one away. But if informants couldn't trust her absolutely, she would soon have none, and as for paraphrasing, there seemed no useful way to do it. Do you really think I've *stuck my nose in* where it shouldn't be?

"Why didn't you do a column about Angel?" The chief said. "I'd think it was a natural."

"I didn't know him. Were you a fan?"

"He affected a lot of people."

"Was he an angel?"

"Depends on the definition. If you mean, was he never in trouble, then no, he was far from an angel. He was a homeless panhandler with some drug issues, mostly marijuana. If you mean, did he make a lot of people smile and feel good over the course of a day, then yes, he was pretty angelic. And no, I was not a fan. Like you, I didn't know him particularly. I always use the north branch of the post office, closer to home. What have you got against Angel?"

"Not me. It's what I hear on the streets, a tale of Jekyll and Hyde. I'm sure that's no surprise to you but I've picked up a few other tidbits that might be new. If you were willing to give me even a little real information I'd give some back."

The police chief remained silent long enough for hope to stir, but when she spoke it was with regret. "I'm sorry, Neva. You know I value your friendship, and I don't doubt for a second that you've got good information that we may not have. But I can't budge on this one. You would serve the community best by telling me what you know and think you know, but I can't make you do that without taking legal action, which I'm not prepared to do. Not yet. And I'm not prepared to horse trade."

The newsroom was deserted as though abandoned in crisis. Chairs faced every which-way, blank screens stared out over shaggy heaps of paper, the air stank of forbidden cigarette smoke. Hurrying through, revolted by the graceless disorder and frustrated by her failure with Fiori, Neva opened the door to her own tidy office with relief. Desk, telephone, keyboard, notebooks, calendar, Post-its, the tools of her peculiar trade, all arranged and ready for action. What if she had continued studying water rather than switching to journalism when Carlo died? As an expert on water rather than human foibles, she would be on the cusp of the environmental movement now, working with solid facts of nature that did not involve individual human misery, did not require treading on the mysterious private grief of artisans or playing pussyfoot with close-mouthed police chiefs.

She must have handled the meeting with Fiori particularly badly to get nothing at all.

And what on earth was Win Niagra's story?

The telephone rang. Her hand went out, hovered, waited for a second ring. If it was the police chief calling to apologize and invite her right back for a proper heart-to-heart, would she accept or stand on dignity? *Thank you, Kitty, but I'm awfully busy* . . . Game-playing was for children. Her business was to get information wherever and however she could.

"This is Neva."

"Alexandrova here," said the city engineer's crisp voice. "Sorry I didn't get back to you earlier, as promised. You haven't written anything on the gravel question yet? Good. Could you meet me in, say, half an hour? The Beanery?"

"Fine," Neva said. "That would be just fine."

Well, well, well. This was something different, something very different indeed. Never before had the city engineer suggested a meeting, and until this moment Neva could not have imagined her apologizing for anything. Her usual style was to save precious time by giving information by telephone or Fax. Something was afoot that trumped efficiency. Some kind of door was about to open at last.

Alexandrova was waiting for her at a corner table in the large coffee shop. Though empty tables were scattered about, the engineer had chosen a tiny table jammed against the back wall behind shelves displaying coffee makers, mugs, and kettles. It was the room's most private spot.

The opening chitchat did not last long. They agreed that it had been a wet and gloomy Saturday but the weekend had been more than redeemed by glorious Sunday. Then the engineer said, "To be honest, Jeneva, we've got a bit of an awkward situation here. We're counting on you to understand."

"I'll do my best." Neva smiled inwardly at the uncharacteristic "we." Something good was coming.

"I don't know how you manage it, but you do seem to have a nose for glitches and irregularities, even small, unintentional ones."

"Thank you. That's a compliment in my business."

"Yes, I see that. Well, here goes then. As you know, the riverfront project is budgeted at $6.4 million, the work to stretch over two building seasons. What you may not know is that, by the end, it will have involved more than a dozen contractors and subcontractors, from pipe-fitters to horticulturists. That's a lot of budgeting and a lot of contracts. It wouldn't be surprising if they got screwed up once in a while, would it?" And this is just what had happened, though how it had come about had not yet been determined, Alexandrova said as though considering the diagnosis of a rare disease. Specifically, the gravel order had been doubled from one hundred thousand dollars to two hundred thousand, twice what was needed for the project, though still no huge sum, after all. The gravel contractor was actually the hauler rather than the quarryman, so he had subcontracted in turn to the quarry to supply the aggregate. The quarry was small, and the owner had hired extra help to run the crusher and other equipment necessary to fill the order.

"The quarry's local, Neva. We like to buy locally when we can, you know. By the time the over-buy was discovered, we had a whole string of folks depending on that contract. People with families. About half the blasting had been done. What to do? Now, I wasn't involved in any of this—hey, I'm not trying to pass the buck, just telling it like it is. All the paperwork is done over in finance. In fact, I didn't really look into the details myself until you called, although I'd heard that there'd been some adjustments."

"Adjustments?" Neva prompted after a silence.

"Right." Another silence. "Of course, the public fuss over design issues is largely to blame for delays. Delays are never good in construction projects. You have bonding deadlines to meet and building seasons to contend with. When work gets off-schedule, it's hell. And costly."

Neva looked at her informant without replying. Such a shoddy attempt to blame staff errors on citizen activism was not worthy of an answer.

"Okay, okay." Alexandrova raised both hands as though to ward off something more ferocious than Neva's raised eyebrows. "You can't blame me for looking for cracks to hide in. This is rather embarrassing."

"In the newspaper business, we make our mistakes in front of thousands of readers. If I misuse a semicolon in my column, I get reproving letters from retired English teachers. At least most of your disasters happen in private."

"I never thought of it like that before. I see what you mean, but then, you're used to looking stupid." Alexandrova went very still for a moment and then her face flamed red. For the first time in their acquaintance, she appeared deeply flustered. "I mean, oh Christ, I didn't mean it the way it sounded. I didn't mean you personally."

Neva laughed whole-heartedly, and felt some of the morning's weight lift from her shoulders. "Never mind, Anya. If I took offense easily I'd be a bitter old recluse by now. Just finish the story, please. It's very interesting."

Still red-faced, Alexandrova said that rather than being cancelled, the mistaken "overbuy" order was being sent to the site of a future construction project.

"What site?"

"What's that?"

"What site is the gravel going to?"

Alexandrova cleared her throat, picked up her pen, riffled through the papers she had placed next to her cup, and at last said, "Out in south county."

"Where in south county?"

"Glenn Creek Road. Surprise."

The little word "surprise" was, in a way, the most intriguing part of this conversation. It was so out of character for the dry, businesslike engineer that Neva felt a pulse of sympathy—only a pulse. "Ummm," she said.

"It's not as bad as it looks, you know. There's nothing deliberate here, no attempt to cheat taxpayers. Anyone was free to look at the project budget, it's a public document. The two-hundred-thousand-dollar figure was in there. This was a human solution to human error."

"Ummmmm," Neva said again. And then, musingly, "The proposed jail site. Thousands of dollars' worth of gravel for a controversial project that hasn't been approved by voters. My, my."

"It will be approved. Eventually."

"Is Gale Marcum involved in any of this?"

"Marcum? Well, I don't know. I suppose he might have been at some level. Someone in law enforcement had to be."

"Do you have documentation?"

Alexandrova pushed the stack of papers across the table. "It's all there. I've highlighted the pertinent bits. But do you really have to make an issue out of an honest mistake when we've got all this other nasty business going on?"

"I don't plan to make anything of it at all. It's not really column material, it's news, so I'll pass it along to the city editor. It will be up to her and the news crew how to handle the story. You do see that it has to be reported? People are asking questions about the gravel, which is how I got onto it. These things only get worse if you try to sweep them under the rug. Best to 'fess up and move on."

The engineer sighed and shrugged, though her voice was amused. "It's not such a bad idea to let the bureaucrats know they're being watched. Even I know that. I'm a taxpayer, too, don't forget."

Encouraged by Alexandrova's tone, Neva said, "Now I need to mention something that may sound ludicrous, but I want your reaction. It has more than crossed my mind for various reasons that the three recent murders are related in some way to the riverfront project."

"Related? How related? This is a construction—wait, did you say *three* murders?"

"Yes, three. Angel, Lyle McRae, and the woman who supposedly died of alcohol poisoning. I have no proof but there are suggestive bits and pieces that she was killed too, in some way that didn't show, or that looked like alcohol poisoning."

"You are dabbling in deep waters." The engineer studied Neva, cleared her throat, cleared it again, and said, "I don't know what kind of weird information you're turning over, but I can assure you that nothing—nothing!—that has ever been said or done in my presence regarding the riverfront has any relationship to that post office wino or any of them."

"Post office wino? You mean, you aren't one of Angel de Silva's adoring fans?"

"I never did care for idle men. Life is too short to spend on a bench."

Neva would have laughed under other circumstances, but she merely smiled and pressed on. "I heard a strange story involving a gravel truck. The driver ran over Angel's cart, squashing everything in it. Lyle was there and he screamed at the driver, something about not being as dumb as some people think and having eyes and ears to see what's going on. This wouldn't seem particularly significant except that a city employee, a man, saw what happened, heard what Lyle said, and gave Angel a hundred dollars. Then Angel was killed and so was Lyle. You see why I'm wondering about it. Did you hear about the incident? The extra gravel doesn't seem like the sort of thing to trigger such a comment. What do you think?"

The engineer was slow to reply. Her general air of discomfort had deepened, and she shook her head as she said, "I don't like that, to be honest. First off, the driver should have handled it better. And that hundred bucks sure sounds like some sort of payoff or hush money or whatever it's called. Any idea who that was, the city employee?"

"None. Angel and Lyle aren't here to tell us, and the person who told me knew the man was from the city only because she saw him get out of an official truck."

"Could be any one of dozens of guys, though I'm guessing a supervisor at least. Nobody else has a hundred dollars to throw around. I really don't like the sound of this, Neva, I don't at all. I'll see what I can sniff out, for you and me both. And as for the other thing, I won't even ask you to try to get the paper to go easy on us. As they say, make your bed and lie on it, even if it's a bunch of rocks."

The city editor's eyes grew bright as Neva handed over the generous bundle of papers while relating the details of her conversation with Alexandrova. After a single question about how she had got onto the error, J.D. strode away toward Ambrose's office thumbing through the neat stack, her excitement leaving Neva feeling wistful again, wondering about the road not taken. What a business to be in, where trouble is greeted with beaming smiles. *Journalists are nothing but a pack of poltroons—murder sends them laughing and cheering to the saloons . . .* Who had said this? W.C. Fields? H.L. Mencken? This was one place where Marcum had it right. The mystery was why officials so often forget that a mistake swept under the rug doubles in size, while a mistake offered up voluntarily is apt to pass over like a spring rain shower. The possibility that the gravel error had anything to do with the killings was highly unlikely. No one would commit three murders to cover up a hundred-thousand-dollar bungle, though this did not entirely rule out other possible links with the waterfront project. There was always the possibility that a news story would knock loose more information, and meanwhile, Alexandrova was poking around behind the scenes.

The meeting with Alexandrova had changed her view of the engineer. She now liked and even trusted her. The thought was comforting, especially after the disturbing meetings with the potter and the police chief. Sensible and confident, the engineer would make a good sounding board for testing her confused thoughts. She really needed a fresh perspective, from someone older and wiser than Frankie, less hasty than Ambrose, and more cooperative than Fiori.

Back in her own office again, she imagined inviting Anya for a drink.

The telephone rang. She picked up the receiver hoping to hear the engineer.

"Neva? Is this an okay time to talk?" It was Carter Grey's smooth voice. "I want to thank you for the column. It was not only a fine tribute to the restaurant but it was entertaining and funny. Just one question. That bit at the end about Reba. Did she come to your house?

"She came on Saturday, quite early."

"Good. I was afraid she might change her mind."

"Excuse me?"

"I saw your message and went out early to see if I could catch her feeding the cats. She was upset, to put it mildly, and I have to say I was surprised that you'd do such a thing. Considering what she's been through and how important her privacy is. And I can't help wondering what all the urgency was about."

She had known it wasn't right, known this when she submitted the column, known it when a wet and furious Reba turned up at her door. She had let the self-serving business of journalism blind her to decency, and what's more, her bad behavior had been recognized by others. This was a new and deeply uncomfortable kind of blunder.

"Neva? I didn't mean to scold, but it did seem out of character. You're usually so considerate."

"No need to try to soften it, Carter. You're right, and what's worse, I knew it was a bad idea. I was just so frustrated, and I thought she could clarify some things."

"And did she?"

"She confirmed a few things I suspected but didn't add anything new. I did apologize, extensively, but it didn't do much good."

"Well, don't worry too much. She'll get over it, probably already has. She's a very interesting person. I see why you like her."

Why you like her . . . she had never told Carter about her tenuous friendship with the homeless woman, even after they'd met her on the riverfront. She had never said word one about liking or disliking Reba Winner, she was certain. Carter could not have got this from watching them together given that she had not exchanged a word with Reba that evening. The two of them must have become cozy enough over a shared interest in the feral cats to talk things over, including her. Or maybe her initial impression that they were already acquainted had been correct and for some reason they didn't want her to know it and had put on that act of meeting for the first time.

"I'm surprised you didn't know her from Clarendon." Neva's voice was hard and sounded strange in her own ears, but she didn't care. She was tired of Grey's games, and he had not hesitated to call her on the carpet about Reba. "Or maybe you did know her, and maybe it's one more thing you've neglected to mention."

"I did not know her at Clarendon. That's the truth."

"The truth? Really?"

Now the silence was at the other end of the line, and she did not step into the gap.

At last he said quietly, "Clarendon was a giant place, many buildings, hundreds of people, both residents and employees. You'd never know them all, even if you lived there. Which I did not. Reba was familiar from seeing her around town but I didn't know her name or anything else until that night on the bike path. Why should I try to falsify such a thing? My own private affairs, my business and property and so on, is different. I'm just not in the habit of volunteering personal information and I don't necessarily realize that something might seem significant to you."

"All right, then, a different subject. You told me you were drawn to Willamette because of news stories about the gay marriage thing, how the county commissioners handled it. But if you taught at Clarendon you obviously lived in Oregon before."

"True and true. I lived in Oregon fifteen years ago, for two years.

That's why I was interested in news about it. I was already thinking about coming back and possibly settling here, but I didn't know where exactly. I'd never been to Willamette but clearly the valley was where I had to be. Eugene, Portland, Salem, I didn't really see myself in any of them. Is this sufficient or should I keep going? Maybe call witnesses?"

"Did you know Win Niagra at Clarendon?"

"Negative."

"Lisette LaBruce?"

"No."

"How about Vance Fowler?"

"Also no. I would have remarked on that one, at least."

"So the only one of all these people you actually met at Clarendon was Lyle McRae?"

"That's correct. They could have been in there any time over the past twenty years. I taught part-time, in one building, for two years. Easy to give just about everyone a miss."

"All right then, just one more question. Does Reba always feed Half Tom and the others at around the same time?"

"She told me she likes to feed in the early morning or late evening, when there's no one around. I'd guess it's about a fifty-fifty chance to catch her at either end of the day."

"Thank you. And thanks for the call. I'm glad you liked the column."

"Wait, hold on a minute. Please. We haven't got to my main reason for calling. Are you free for dinner one night this week? The sooner the better. I'm thinking you could bring along a list of everything that interests you or might possibly interest you in future, and I could use it as a conversation guide. Then you could stop accusing me of keeping secrets and I could stop feeling guilty over nothing."

Chapter Twenty

Neva sat without taking her hand off the receiver. Why had she said yes? What was it about this odd man that made his company appealing despite the game playing? Were the games the attraction? Or merely his persistence? No other man had tried so hard in years. Despite all, there was something solid and comforting about his presence, even on the telephone while sparring. True, he owned the lovely greenhouse and it would be better for her park idea if they remained at least cordial, but this didn't require meeting for dinner. She had said yes because she enjoyed his company and had seen no sensible reason to say no, though she had, at least, put the dinner off until tomorrow.

Shaking her head, half inclined to call back and decline the date—for this was, now, a date and not an interview—instead she dialed Oleander's extension at the police department. Up to the moment when he said, "Oleander speaking," she intended to say something about his son, but the words did not come. There was no good way to bring up so terrible a subject so long after the fact, especially on the telephone. "Captain," she said warmly, "how are you?"

"Well enough. And you?"

"Just fine, thanks. It's my favorite season of the year, and if only the sun would stay out for a week straight I'd be even happier. I have a few questions for you, but I suspect you're going to tell me to mind my own business again—"

"I don't believe I said that."

"It's what you meant, though, and you're right, this isn't my usual territory. I've been dragged into it, really quite unwillingly, and for a number of reasons I now have to see it through. And you're not the only one who says I should keep my nose out, by the way."

"That's interesting," came the steady reply.

He didn't ask who else wanted her to stop nosing around, and the restraint was more effective than argument or anger. He was the grownup—the dignified, suffering grownup—she the pestering child.

What was it Fiori had said? *There are peculiar circumstances here that require extra care . . .* Oleander and the chief made a powerful wall—but was it the wall that made her wish she hadn't called, or sympathy for this man who had lost his only son to an invisible microbe that defied the most reliable medical tool of the twentieth century? The pure, random unfairness of it made her want to stand with Oleander in some fundamental way, not try to pry information out of him, information he was not really free to give.

"Well, Captain, I find I don't really have a lot of questions after all. I mean, I have questions but not for now. Just one thing, though, if you wouldn't mind. Something you said during our first conversation keeps coming back. You said Angel had some bad habits of his own?"

"Are you wanting confirmation or a list?"

"A list would be good."

"He was a drunk, a doper, a manipulator, a phony, and a pervert, who pulled the wool over everyone's eyes, including mine for a time. Will that do?"

"Phony how? And what sort of pervert?"

"Take your pick."

"I'm not sure what you mean. Some people consider gay sex perverted—"

"What's the point of all this now? Have you received any more anonymous letters? Is that what's driving this?"

"No, nothing more." The sudden pit that opened at her feet struck her silent. She could not tell the captain that she now knew the authors of the letters were Ernold Quick and Lisette LaBruce, not without telling him far, far more, and even revealing that she had talked with the wanted man. But she must tell someone, must spell it out in spoken words. A listener with a fresh perspective might see what she was missing, and simply speaking the facts as she thought she knew them might clear her own mind—and it would certainly be a relief.

"Is that all?" Oleander said quietly.

"For now, yes."

"Well, then," he said and hung up without saying goodbye.

It was late afternoon and breakfast had long worn off. She hadn't taken time to pack lunch and didn't want to buy it, so she drove home, poured oranges juice and drank it while assembling sliced tomatoes, cottage cheese, parsley and chives freely covered in olive oil, pepper, and chunky salt. The combination was nowhere near as good as it would be in a few months when local tomatoes started showing up and basil was abundant, but still it was deeply satisfying.

By four-thirty she was back in the car heading for Twelfth Place. Lost in speculation about her morning conversations, she was halfway down the cul-de-sac before she saw that Arva Beatrice Jacoby Fowler was not alone on her porch. A sharp crank of the steering wheel took the car to the curb. A laurel hedge that grew along the sidewalk hid her from Wygelia's house, and a blue pickup truck also parked at the curb was now between her and the two on the porch. Surely, it was the truck that had been in the craft center parking lot that morning?

She eased open the door, closed it with care, and walked up alongside the pickup until she could see the porch clearly without being too easily seen. Arva was in her usual spot in the rocking chair. Facing her, sitting on what Neva had come to think of as her chair, was Win Niagra.

To find the sculptor here was more intriguing than perplexing. Could she have triggered the visit by showing Niagra the notebook? But why seek out Arva rather than the woman who had raised Vance?

Leaning forward with his hands on his knees, Niagra talked with the intensity of a preacher working on a possible convert, then raised both hands in the air in exhortation, let them fall, and sat back in the rickety chair with an exhausted air. Neither figure moved for a moment, and then Arva must have spoken because Niagra straightened and nodded several times. Then, incredibly, the old woman's thin hand came up and was enfolded in the sculptor's two powerful brown hands.

Neva retreated down the length of the pickup and got into her car as quietly as she had left it. This meeting was not meant to be seen—and she most certainly did not want to be discovered by Win Niagra, not until she'd had time to consider a new and stunning idea.

Her search for Hogan and Tomasino had become a habit, and without conscious decision to cruise the riverfront, Neva found herself turning down First Street. And, like a mirage, there they were, sprawled asleep on the grass next to the bike path. Hogan lay on his back with his arms flung out, one hand just touching Tomasino, who lay curled on his side like a huge child.

She pulled over and parked with two wheels on the grass. The afternoon was hot. The two men slept under the open sky with no protection, no watching friend, not even a loyal dog and not a scrap of shade. Hogan's fly was down. Tomasino's pale shins stuck out below his pant legs, his bare feet huge and white but still strangely fragile looking.

The riverfront was busy today, the bike path carrying a steady current of joggers, cyclists and strollers who paid no attention to the sleeping men, though two women on bikes recognized Neva and called out greetings. Only the police were likely to pay attention to these two. To leave them alone for even five minutes was risky, but they were no use asleep or groggy. Moving briskly, she went around the corner to the bakery and soon returned with two white bags.

Hogan was sitting up, though Tomasino did not appear to have moved.

"Good afternoon," she said. "I was just going to try to wake you up."

Hogan accepted a cup and a carrot muffin with a nod but set the coffee on the grass. "Stomach," he said, and leaned to shake his friend's shoulder with one hand. "Hey, hey, you got food here."

Tomasino whimpered and curled up tighter, exposing further inches of white shins, which were as hairless as a girl's.

"That's okay," she said, sitting down cross-legged in a spot where she did not look directly at the bony legs. He needed long socks, very long socks. "The coffee will keep. Have you been here a while?"

Hogan nodded his shaggy head and bit into the muffin, showering crumbs as he talked. "We came in from camp to go canning but didn't make it. He isn't feeling too good. Joint problems, you know. He always had them since he got too tall. He gets real bad pain."

"I'd heard about that and when he wakes up I have a suggestion for him. Sleeping on the ground like that must make it even worse."

"We have a bed in camp. Sometimes he goes to the shelter, but mostly he's high and doesn't feel it. It's his medicine."

"I visited your camp a few days ago, with a photographer from the paper. It looks pretty well set up. Do you think the riverfront construction is going to have any effect on your lives down here?"

"Could bring in a lot of riffraff. Ruin the neighborhood."

Neva's laughter, spontaneous and delighted, made Hogan sit up straighter as he combed crumbs from his beard with splayed fingers. "You're that lady from the paper, Reba's friend. I have a question for you. How come you don't have it in there about racing?"

"In the *Current*?"

"My kid brother's one of those jockeys. In big races, too. Did you know they don't call it the Derby, they call it the Darby? That's how they talk in England. I wanted to read about him but I couldn't find nothing in the paper."

"The *Current* may be too small to report on horse racing. They do mostly local sports, but I'll try to remember to ask the sports editor about it and let you know. Now I have a question for you."

"Okay, shoot."

"Do you know what Angel was going to do with the money he had the night he died?"

Hogan closed his eyes, put one finger to each temple, and said, "Easy. He got it for Tomasino here. For an operation."

"Ah, that had occurred to me."

"He always told Tomasino he would pay to get his knee operation. They're the worst joints, his knees. That was real sad that the money got stole, but you know, I was talking to this nurse and she said it wasn't enough anyway. Ask me another one."

"All right, how about this. Was Lisette LaBruce a heavy drinker?"

"Dope, dope and more dope. Her and Tomasino, only she didn't have any pain." A sudden look of illumination was followed by, "Not that kind of pain anyways. Ask me another one."

"You know Win Niagra, the sculptor with the ponytail?"

He nodded.

"Were he and Angel friends?"

"That's a tough one. Sometimes I saw them both together, mostly walking down here, but I don't guess they were exactly friends. I saw them fight one time. Well, push and shove. You know."

"Who was the aggressor? I mean, who started it?"

"That artist started it. He almost pushed Angel in the river that time, but after, I saw them walking along."

"Were Angel and Vance Fowler friends?"

"Sure. But nothing special. Just like everybody down here. If you look out for the next guy, he looks out for you."

"What about Ernold Quick? Did he get along with Angel?"

"Sometimes yes, sometimes no. They're two really different cats but as long as they stayed off each other's territory, it wasn't any problem."

"Territory?"

"You know. Quickie is his own man and Angel, well, he had his tribe. He didn't like anybody messing with his kids. One time Quickie tried to mess with one of Angel's girls and that wasn't good, but they made it up."

"I'm not sure what you mean by Angel's kids. Do you mean a gang, like a youth gang?"

"Not that kind. I mean, not like a criminal gang or something. He liked kids and they liked him. It was like family." Hogan pulled the lid from the cup he had set in the grass and took a long swallow. "That's the first coffee I've drank since I forget when. How'd you know I like cream and sugar?"

"Just a guess. Now I'm afraid I have to ask this straight out just to make sure I understand. When you say Angel liked kids, do you mean for sex?"

"No way, Jose. He smoked them out and so on and so forth, whatever he had, whatever you could roll or put in a pipe. He was a pretty good dad, I mean, like as if he was their dad. They had a problem, they came to Angel. He never hurt nobody. I mean, they were street kids and a lot worse could have happened, you get what I'm saying?" He drank again, swallowing multiple times without lowering the cup. He put it down, considered Tomasino, shook his head, and opened the remaining cup.

"Was Quick a good street dad too?"

Hogan whistled, looked around as though scanning for spies, then gave a slow wink with his left eye.

Neva waited but Hogan added no explanation and his manner suggested it would be a wasted effort to press the question. "Do you know the girl they call Pet?"

"Skater girl."

"That's right. Was she one of Angel's kids?"

"Could be. I never kept track." Hogan tipped back his head to chug the second coffee though it must still have been very hot. Again he drank without stopping until it was gone, like an athlete satisfying his thirst at the end of a race, then wadded up the cup and tossed it at a nearby trash container. It overshot the can and landed on the bike path. He made a face, shrugged, and again began shaking Tomasino, but with no more success than before. "With all the shit that's been coming down, I don't want to leave him here, but I have to get going."

"Could you please give him a message from me? It's important, about his joint pain."

"Sure, no problem."

Neva explained about the anti-inflammatory drugs that were available for free if Tomasino would call or drop in at the county health department, and copied the telephone number and address from her notebook. "I'd be glad to take him over there, any time. He can find me at the newspaper office."

Hogan nodded, folded the paper into quarters and put it in his shirt pocket. She tried a few more questions, but he appeared to have lost interest in everything apart from his brother the jockey, and now and again giving Tomasino another prod or shake. She gathered his first cup, the lids, and the muffin wrapper for recycling and got to her feet, leaving the white bag with the remaining muffins. "Maybe he'll be hungry when he wakes up. Could you tell him I'd like to talk? He can come by the *Current* any time and just tell them at the front desk that he's there to see me. We could go out for a meal somewhere. You too, of course."

"Sure thing. Thanks for the coffee. Don't forget about that racing." Hogan eased his burly form back down onto the grass and closed his eyes.

She drove only two blocks before parking in front of Peak Sports on Second Street. The men's socks were at the back next to a wall of hiking and running shoes. She chose extra-large Smartwool high tops for Tomasino and large regular hiking socks for Hogan. The temptation to buy more was strong, but they would only get lost. She compromised by buying another pair each to keep in the car for the next time they met.

No more than ten minutes had passed but when she returned, the men were gone. There was only the empty white paper sack lying on its side. She picked it up, started to put it in the garbage can, then put it on the front seat with the other bits of trash for recycling at home. Driving on up First Street, she turned right, away from the river, and pulled up to the curb in front of the skateboard park. The park was busier than she'd seen it yet, the rack full of bicycles, skaters sitting on the two picnic tables, others standing around the edge of the pit singly or in small groups, figures suddenly popping up as though from the ground itself, then disappearing again.

Watching the skaters was dizzying until she began picking out one speeding figure to follow at a time through spins, jumps, and even handstands on the hurtling boards. Today, as before, there was only one girl, but this one was tall and a blond braid hung down her back below the helmet.

As Neva turned away another car pulled in beside her little Honda. A woman got out and walked rapidly to the pit and followed the rim around to the opposite side, pausing to study the pool of skaters just as Neva had done, and then walking on toward the bicycle path along the river. It was the woman she had met on the post office steps, though today her stride was hard and her posture ramrod rather than hunched with grief. She disappeared behind a clump of Himalaya vines and though Neva continued to watch for several more minutes, she did not reappear. Her son must be a skater, and most likely into other things as well, scary things, judging by what she'd said at the post office. If she did succeed in finding him down here, what could she possibly think she could do about it?

Still, though, you have to try. As a parent, you just have to keep trying.

Nearly an hour had passed since she'd discovered Arva and Win Niagra together. Neva pulled into the cul-de-sac prepared to see them still poised like figures in a dramatic tableau, but the pickup was gone and the old woman was not on the porch. She knocked hard on the door, and while waiting for an answer she studied Vance's sculpture. It had been moved from behind the pile of boxes and placed between the two chairs. The sculpture looked different today, familiar and obvious in its inspiration—of course, it was a first cousin to Niagra's deer with a woman's head. Both sculptures combined parts of figures that did not go together, creating a new, disturbing sort of figure. But why not? Niagra was the young man's teacher, after all . . . Neva shook her head slowly and then nodded. Niagra was more than his teacher, far more.

Yes, yes it must be so.

And now Arva had gone away with Niagra.

Settled on the chair with her legs out and her arms crossed, she considered the Buddha-Christ.

The porch was quiet. No vacuum cleaner roared next door today. There was only the small hum of bees on the forget-me-nots. A few wisteria buds had opened and before long the vine would make a green curtain around Arva's rocker. Maybe Vance's grandmother had planted the wisteria years ago. Maybe she had planted the original forget-me-nots in what would have been a proper flower bed in front of the house.

Maybe this house had shone with loving care once upon a time when a girl child ran through the rooms. Maybe it had rivaled the perfection next door.

For years now Arva Beatrice Jacoby Fowler had lived here as though in a shell. What would have been neglect in the beginning now seemed like settled purpose, like a choice, like an expression of personality. There was peace in it now despite the anger at the core. Neva had not been inside but she knew how it would be, every room solid with the inert detritus of living—newspapers, jars, boxes, mail, flowerpots, shoes, bags, dead appliances—so that only a narrow bit of floor remained open for passage. Some rooms would be impassable but no matter, Arva never went in them and neither did anyone else.

Next door was a different story. Next door, every room was ready to go.

Was it the child that made all the difference? A small boy racing about, creating currents, keeping the household machinery wound up and in pace with him, while the machinery of his dead mother's house sagged to a halt under the defeated hand of his grandmother.

Wygelia was not happy in her shining house. France, she had said. If only she could go to France.

Arva did not pretend to anything. She was like the Buddha-Christ figure, passive and watching . . . and now maybe her long wait was over.

Neva did not need confirmation of her new view of the relationship between Win Niagra and Vance Fowler but she drove to the jail anyway. The blue pickup was parked nose in to the curb a block west of the courthouse. She slowed down to study the dusty windows, the scarred toolbox in back, and the bumper sticker, *I brake for the Venus de Milo.*

An empty space beside the truck was tempting. It would be a treat to see Niagra's expression on finding her waiting when they came out but her own amusement was not a good enough reason to intrude on such an extraordinary family moment.

Chapter Twenty-One

Tuesday's front page was dominated by the gravel story, including a striking color photo of the quarry southwest of town where the rock was being mined. The hillside had been blasted and dug away, leaving a gray amphitheater of rock rising from a clear pool that must be fed by a spring. Above the pool plants tufted from rock ledges, suggesting a Japanese garden. The story was crisp and entertaining, with much earnest protestation of blamelessness on the part of officialdom.

Frankie's follow-up story about Lisette said her only living relative so far discovered was a brother in prison in Florida who claimed not to have communicated with his sister in twenty-two years. "Did she leave me anything?" he'd said on hearing of her death.

Neva set aside the paper. She could understand the temptation to include such a line, especially in an otherwise humdrum story, but she wished Frankie had left it out. The aftermath of Lisette's life was pitiable enough without this exposure of her sorry roots. The only tangible thing Lisette had left behind in this world, it appeared, was a page in a sketchbook, a scrawled note that summed up a sad existence.

Had she known Niagra would keep the notebook, she would have photocopied that page.

The sun had gone away again behind thin spring clouds but enough light got through to make the morning bright. And the flagstones stacked in the driveway were a warm yellow though cold to the touch before she pulled on gloves. Moving them two slabs at a time in the wheelbarrow, she transferred ten stones to the backyard and set them randomly on the sand. She walked around them, studied them, picked up a particularly nice piece with one evenly rounded edge, and placed it against the single line of upright gray stones with which she had defined the flowerbeds years ago. The curves did not quite fit. She hoisted the heavy stone again, set it aside, and tried another. It was worse. The next one was pretty close but still she was not satisfied.

When she left for work an hour later, the stones were still scattered on the sand along with others she had brought around and tested for fit.

None had worked quite well enough to satisfy her imagined picture. The web instructions had said a flagstone patio could be built in a weekend. At this rate, a lifetime would be more likely, but she could not be discouraged. The stone was everything she had imagined and more: it shone in the morning sun, the crystalline bits sparkled, the yellows, ochres and peach tones were as warm as a Mexican wall.

No matter how she arranged the rocks they would be beautiful in themselves.

Again Niagra's pickup was the only vehicle in the church parking lot. Neva ran lightly down the steps to the pottery studio, knocked twice and opened the door. The sculptor saw her before she saw him.

"Ask me if I'm surprised," he said, stepping out from behind a set of shelves. Despite the sarcastic words, his tone was not unfriendly, and he appeared calm.

"I assume I'm the surprised one here," she said. "You already knew your son."

"Ah, you sorted it out, did you?" He wiped his hands on a red cotton rag, dropped it in a box, and went to the same stool she had found him on before. "Sit down. We may as well be comfortable during the cross-examination. I have to say I could hardly believe my eyes when I saw you parked over by Wygelia's place yesterday. When I called you a tickseed, I was way off. You're a badger. You don't let go of a thing, do you? You really pissed me off at first, but now I'm actually grateful."

Niagra picked up the same hand-thrown cup that had held the cold coffee on her previous visit, and Neva saw now that it had a maple leaf design on one side. "First a hot drink, then explanations," he said. "Coffee or tea?"

Using hot water from an electric kettle, he made a pot of French press. When two cups were poured, he sat again on the stool, folded his strong hands on the table, and said, "Let me just spare you the clever questioning and tell it straight out. I'm expecting a class in twenty minutes, and, really, I'm happy to tell it now. You already figured out that Vance is my son. I don't see any reason to go all the way back to my own rotten childhood, but let's just say I was a fucked-up kid and I managed to drag Vance's mother down with me. She was Arva's daughter, and what happened is all the worse because the doctors had told Arva she'd never have any kids. But somehow, long after she'd given up, she had Sheila."

Niagra stopped, closed his eyes, and repeated the name with a puzzled, pained air. "Sheila. . . . I must have loved her. I think I did. But it was another life. No, it was a living death. I left when she got pregnant, I couldn't handle it any more than I could handle anything else. If I hadn't come back when Vance was three, everything would be different, but I did. I came back no better than when I'd gone away. We took acid, or what I thought was acid. I bought it off a guy I didn't know, but as I said it was a different reality then. It turned out it wasn't acid. I'll never know what it really was, but we both went kind of crazy. Sheila jumped off the bridge and I jumped in after her."

Neva waited and when he didn't continue, she said, "Sheila died and you ended up somehow wandering around town without any memory. Is that right?"

"That's it. I didn't remember anything about it. I still don't remember anything up to a certain day, when I looked out a window and saw a maple leaf. Just one leaf, shining red-gold."

"You were in Clarendon?"

"I was in there for another two years. I didn't know anything about Sheila then, of course, about what had happened, and I didn't find out for a long time. I started sculpting in there, and throwing pots. I married the pottery teacher, as it happened. She died of ovarian cancer three years after our daughter was born. That's when I came back here. By then I knew about Sheila, and I suppose the second loss made the other one more real, if you wanted to analyze it, and having a daughter I loved made me think about the son I'd never known. I came back to Willamette with the idea of getting to know him but I couldn't face him right away. I'd assumed that Arva raised him but I kept putting off going to see her. I used to drive past Twelfth Place thinking maybe I'd see a kid on a bike or something. When I finally met him it was nothing like that."

Niagra paused, wiped his large hands across his face, and shook his head slowly. "Sorry, but this is still pretty raw. I'd taken this job running the craft center and was down here one night when I heard a thump. That was all, just a thump, then silence again. I opened the door and here was this kid curled up in the stairwell under a big wool coat. I brought him in and we got to talking, but even then I didn't know. He called himself Blaze, no last name. I liked him right off and encouraged him to drop in. After a while he started messing around with clay and I could see he had a feeling for it. Then he told me about his life. That's when I realized he was my son. I was stunned, just stunned. Don't ask—I didn't tell him because I was ashamed. I was afraid he'd hate me if he knew. He was raised thinking his dad was a drug addict who abandoned him. I treated him like a son, made sure he had money, clothes, a place to stay. I planned to tell the truth when the time was right, even about what happened to his mother, but I hadn't managed it yet when this all blew up. I got him the best lawyer around but until you brought that notebook in yesterday, I couldn't face him, not with the truth still hanging out there untold. I'm not a particularly brave man. I never was brave. I just told him yesterday, when we went to the jail. I had no idea how he'd react. You know what he did? He hugged me. We just hugged. That's all. We just held on to each other."

Neva waited, not only for Win to recover but for her own emotions to settle. If only she could leave things on this happy note, but too much remained unknown and disturbing. She sipped coffee and watched the sculptor, and at last said gently, "You know by now that I'm after the whole story here, not just the pieces involving Vance. I wish I didn't have to press you at such a time in your life, but I do."

"Fine, fine, no problem. I'm so relieved and happy that nothing could really bother me right now. After talking to him, I know Vance will come through this okay. The truth is going to come out."

"Did you talk about what happened that night?"

"Of course. It was just as I'd thought. They stole the money but they didn't hurt him." After they left the convenience store, Vance had said, he and Quickie headed for a house over on Fifth Street where there was generally something to eat. They hung around there for an hour or so, and then Quick had suggested they find Angel to see whether he had finished the beer or passed out first. Vance had assumed that Quick wanted the beer, but when they'd found him stretched out cold, Quick had gone through his pockets. The $500 was easy to find. Why he had shoved the money into Vance's pocket he didn't really know, only that Quick had said they'd split it later.

"That's when they saw a police car and Quick said to run for the railroad tracks," Win recounted. Quick was a faster runner and Vance couldn't find him when he reached the railroad yard, and spent the night alone in a boxcar. He started looking for Quick again in the morning and saw the headlines about the murder in a newspaper vending machine. He needed change to get a paper to read the whole story and was about to hand over a twenty dollar bill from Angel's money when it hit him that he and Quick would be the first suspects. He panicked and went back to the boxcar for the rest of the day, and that night tried again to find Quick.

"It seems he was almost as scared of Quick as he was of the cops. He thought Quick might think he was trying to keep the money for himself, and then there'd be hell to pay or worse, but there was no sign of him. Quick must have seen the story too, or heard about it, and cleared out of town faster than Vance did. Vance spent another night in the boxcar, then took the bus to Portland and hung around there for a few days. But he doesn't belong up there. He missed Willamette. He missed me. I do believe him!" the sculptor concluded fiercely. "I believe him absolutely."

Neva believed him too. She was less certain about Quickie's part in the drama. Several details of the story troubled her as she walked slowly back to the *Current*. Why had Quickie told her that Vance had taken the money from Angel? Why had he not waited for the slower man to catch up? And why had he vanished without finding his partner in robbery, for surely he could have located Vance given that Vance was looking for him and the territory was small and he'd want his share of the money before it was spent.

Could he have set Vance up? If he'd gone back and killed Angel and left Vance holding the money it would get rid of his enemy while leaving someone else to be convicted of the murder. But then why stick around town and proclaim his innocence? He could easily have left town and stayed gone while his scheme played out.

Neva was still mulling over the questions when she heaved open the staff door, took two steps inside, and stopped at the sounds coming from the newsroom. The hubbub was more typical of 4 p.m., the deadline hour, than of this time in the morning. There was no way she could reach her office unnoticed this morning, but it could not be helped. As soon as she turned into the newsroom from the cloakroom doorway, J.D. hailed her with remarkably good cheer, "Hey, Neva, the phones are ringing nicely. Who would ever think gravel could be so much fun."

"How's it running?"

"About four to one outrage at the city. The others are mad at us for muckraking trivia. Thanks again for the tip. We're meeting in the conference room in five to talk about follow-up. Could you join us? I know, I know, you hate meetings and you don't have anything more to add, you turned the whole works over to us, but I'd really like you to be there. Half hour max. Promise."

The meeting, naturally, lasted the better part of an hour but it turned out to be time well spent, if for no other reason than that she managed to talk them out of going after Anya Alexandrova. The city engineer was the wrong culprit, she insisted, and she had come clean with everything she had when put on the spot. The gravel booboo wasn't the engineer's doing, and the issue was not really about money since the over-budget amounted to small change in a fat contract. The interesting question was whether the link to the jail project was more than coincidental. Her main suggestion was to look for where Assistant Police Chief Gale Marcum's path intersected the riverfront project.

Back in her office by one, starved for lunch and needing fresh air, she considered the blinking message light for an uncertain moment before reaching for the handset. She would listen but return no calls until she'd eaten. There was only one message, the voice husky, male, and unmistakable. "Jeneva Leopold? I've got something you need to hear. I'll be down behind that Pearl gallery after 5 o'clock, in the alley, close by there where you had that little car trouble I helped you out with. Come alone and don't tell nobody. I'll wait, but not too long."

Where you had that little car trouble I helped you out with . . . Whatever else he might be, Quickie did not lack wit.

Ernold Quick stood in a doorway out of sight of anyone who might happen to look up or down the alley. As she approached, he spoke softly, stopping her before she could see him and directing her to stand in a different doorway that was on the other side of the alley and offset from his. Though they were close enough for normal speaking voices, Neva could see only cigarette smoke that trailed out with his words. "I hope you know there's some really weird shit going down in this town. If you knew the whole story, you wouldn't believe it."

"After three murders, I'm ready to believe anything."

"You don't need to know it all."

"I'd like to know it all."

"No, you wouldn't."

"Excuse me?"

"You think it's a nice town, all pretty pretty. I read your stuff sometimes. It's not the same town."

"The same town as what?"

"Mine. Where me and the rest of them live. The funny thing is, everybody believes your version."

A rasping laugh led to a coughing fit and a slapping sound, more as though Quickie were hitting the wall than his own chest. She waited in silence and at last he gasped, "Hey, it's cool, never mind. I like it here myself, or used to anyway. So, here's the deal. There was a witness. What do you think of that?"

"A witness to what?"

"When Angel got killed!"

"Are you saying someone saw it happen?"

"Not exactly happen. But he saw who did it."

"Who was it?"

"A kid I know."

"A kid killed Angel?"

"A kid saw it. I'm talking about a witness here, okay?"

"Right. Sorry, this is a little confusing. Could you tell me the story, please?"

"No story, just the facts. A kid I know has a room in that big house there on the corner down the street from where he was killed at. He was on his way home when he saw the dude standing there next to Angel."

"Who was standing there?"

"Some dude. Holding a hammer."

"Did your friend see him hit Angel with the hammer?"

"He's not my friend, okay? Just a guy. He didn't actually see the dude hit him. He didn't think nothing of it at the time. He was kind of wasted himself, okay. He didn't know anything about it until he heard people talking at the Beanery, about the bloody sidewalk and everything."

"Why didn't he tell the police what he'd seen?"

"Dudes that don't get up for a job every day live different from you, okay? He got scared and ran."

"Why should he be scared?"

"Because the cat with the hammer saw him walk by and he figured maybe he'd go after him, too. You know, get rid of the witness. He only came back yesterday."

"Why?"

"Shit if I know. You can't hide forever."

"Then couldn't he talk to the police now?"

"He doesn't want to stick his head up and get blamed. And he's right, too. It wouldn't be so bad if he hadn't of ran."

"How did you find out about him?"

"I keep my eyes and ears open. You don't seem too excited about this information. I thought you wanted to know who really did it."

"I do. Of course, I do. But it's difficult to take this in, to picture a witness who actually saw the murderer standing there with a hammer when, when—"

"When everybody thought it was me and Vance. So what are you going to do about it?"

"That's difficult to say without some thought, but one thing is clear. This witness has to come forward. He really has to talk to the police."

"You don't have to convince me, but I thought you could do the cop bit. You're a big shot."

"I'm well known, sure. That goes with being a journalist, but it wouldn't count for much in this situation. Coming through me, the information would be third hand. Would he talk to me?"

"I doubt it. Like I said, the dude's scared."

"Could you tell me his name?"

"No way. I promised. And don't go trying to find him. He moved out of that place."

"Quickie, I'm sure you know that information like this should go straight to the police."

"So tell them. That's why I'm telling you, to get me off the hook."

"I'll have to tell them where I got the information."

"Why's that?"

"It's just the way it works. It's bad enough that it's third hand, and if I say I can't even tell where I heard it, that weakens the story even more. In fact, they could legally require me to tell. It doesn't mean I would tell, but that can get quite nasty. In any case, it isn't really enough information, 'some dude with a hammer.' Could you please ask him to talk to me? I might be able to get more information out of him, a description or something. We could do it just like this, if he wants, so I don't even see him, and then I could at least tell the police I got it straight from him and leave you out of it. And I might be able to persuade him to go to the police himself."

"Sure, I'll ask, but don't count on nothing. The dude's freaked out, as who wouldn't be."

"And another thing." She was taking a risk but she needed to know. "A person close to Vance told me he said you took the money from Angel and gave it to him."

"So?"

"So why did you tell me Vance took it from Angel, even that it was his idea to rob Angel."

"Because it's true. Vance is a turkey, but you can believe who you want. Now I have to split. You leave first, back the way you came. I'll be in touch."

Neva walked only a half block to the river path to look for a bench. The sky had been overcast all day, but now, as she turned to look west before sitting down, a clear stripe opened along the horizon. It was a familiar reprieve at the end of a gray day, a bit of atmospheric theatricality that Willamette specialized in. The final half hour of even the worst days often turned like this, with the sky opening to let light wash over the town and fields.

Neva faced the light, soaking it in along with the touch of warmth it brought despite the late hour. The conversation with Quick had left a taint despite the promise of a possible witness. Whether Quick was telling the truth or not, he was a dodgy character, a very dodgy character.

A skateboard clattered close by. Turning just her head to look up the bike path, she saw Pet speeding toward her. For days she had searched for the girl, and now here she was arriving as though by appointment. Turning full around and stepping onto the path, Neva smiled as she held up her hand. Pet hopped off the board, kicked the back so it flipped, and caught it neatly.

"You're graceful on that thing. I wonder why more girls don't skate?"

"Not cool." Pet shrugged and looked away, though with no suggestion of discomfort. "I don't really care. About being cool, I mean."

"Do you remember me? We talked the other day at the skate park."

The girl nodded and stuck her free hand in her hip pocket.

"I've got some questions for you. It's rather important. Would you sit with me for a minute?" Neva sat down on one end of the bench and waved toward the other end.

Pet let the skateboard drop and settled on it with her legs loosely crossed as though lounging in a comfy chair.

"You know, I think you could take a nap on that board going full speed." She really did like this girl, particularly the striking combination of athleticism and street-kid slovenliness. She must tread carefully and not drive her away like Reba. "Well, here we go with the serious bit. You're out on the streets a lot. You were at Angel's memorial service, and I noticed you put an offering on his memorial bench outside the post office. It seems you knew him pretty well."

Pet looked down and picked at the fringe around a hole in her jeans.

"There are lots of different stories going around concerning what happened to him, and a lot hinges on figuring out what's true and what's not. I want to ask you about some of what I've heard. I have the feeling you'll tell me the truth or say you don't know."

For a moment Pet regarded her without expression. Then she giggled. "You should be on T.V. One of those crime shows."

"Oh, dear. Sorry if I sound pompous but I'm afraid of saying the wrong thing and having you run away."

"I won't run away. You could just say what you want. We always say what we want."

"We?"

"Skaters. But mostly we don't talk much. It gets kind of boring actually. I like to talk."

"Great. So do I. Here goes then. You said last time that Angel didn't tell people what to do, and I've been wondering why that would be important since he wasn't anybody's parent or teacher. What did you mean by that?"

"He didn't treat you like a kid is all. And he always gave us food."

"Food?"

"Bagels and stuff. People always bought him sandwiches and whatever, mostly from the bakery, and he saved it in his shopping cart. And he told good stories."

"What sort of stories?"

"Any kind. He said they were true but they were mostly made up. He was funny. If you were feeling bad he cheered you up."

"Do you often feel bad?"

A shrug. "Anybody can feel bad."

"True enough. It sounds like he was a pretty nice guy overall."

Another shrug.

"Not completely nice?"

A surprising mischievous look came into the girl's eyes. "You should ask my dad. He said Angel corrupted kids, which I guess means he gave us drugs or something."

"Were you corrupted?"

"Totally."

Neva raised an eyebrow and waited.

"Just kidding. He smoked us out a couple of times. Some of the girls went with him but I never did. He smelled like pee. I've got a good nose."

"Something else we have in common. Were you told not to hang around Angel?"

"Well, yeah. Especially after my brother died. I mean, I'm the only one left and they want to keep me in a box, if you know what I mean. Anyway, is that all you wanted to know?" There was a distinct note of disappointment in the girl's voice.

"I'm very sorry to hear about your brother. Was it an accident?"

"You could call it that." The girl looked away. "It's getting late."

"I'd be glad to give you a ride home. But first, if you don't mind, did you know Lisette LaBruce?"

"Nope."

"How about Lyle McRae?"

"The yelling guy. If you skated too close to his precious flowers he went crazy. He was weird."

Again the girl appeared uncomfortable and again studied the hole in her jeans.

"Weird how?"

"He was always after me, if you know what I mean. That night Angel died he tried to catch me. I was skating back to my friend's place to sleep and he was standing there talking to Angel."

"When was that? Are you saying you saw Lyle McRae with Angel the night he died? Or earlier in the day?"

"Night. Pretty late. I stopped to see if Angel was okay because he was flat on the sidewalk. That guy, Lyle, tried to grab me. Angel told him to quit it but he wasn't really any help because he couldn't stand up, so I took off."

"What did Lyle do?"

"Just stood there. I was skating."

For a long moment, Neva could only look at the girl. The gardener had said nothing about being on the scene the night Angel died. Was Lyle the "dude with a hammer" that Quickie's friend had seen?

"Was Lyle carrying anything, say a shovel or hammer or some other tool?"

"I don't know. I didn't see any. No, I don't think so. I mean he tried to get hold of me."

"Right. Did you see anyone else there? With Angel and McRae? Or in the area?"

"I didn't look."

"Have you told anyone else you were there the night Angel died?"

Pet shook her head.

"Not even your parents or a close friend?"

Another head shake. "I think I'd better get going," she said, and stood up.

"How about a ride home?"

"I don't live at home. Not now. If I did, I'd be in trouble for being late."

"Where do you stay? In case I need to talk with you again."

"With a friend."

The statement was flat and final, a closed door, and Neva let it go. Pet had been incredibly forthcoming and she saw no reason to push the girl further. "Thank you for talking with me. You've been very helpful, and if you think of anything more that might be important, you can find me at the *Current* and in the phone book."

"I see you around. But I told you everything, so I guess that's it. And, you know, if you're thinking I should have told somebody, you don't know my dad." This last was tossed over her shoulder as she sped away.

Watching her go, Neva drew out her notebook but did not write in it. She had meant to sit here while jotting down Quick's comments before she forgot the details, but it was late, the sun was well down, and the conversation with Pet had elbowed Quick out of the way for the moment. Better to type up her notes, to let her fingers fly over the keyboard rather than scrawling in the narrow notebook. Slipping it back into her bag, she glanced up First Street in the direction Pet had gone. A lighted sign caught her eye, *Au Courant, Fine French/Northwest/Asian Cuisine*—oh, lord!

The dinner with Carter. She had forgotten the dinner date with Carter.

Chapter Twenty-Two

The restaurant was crowded but it was easy to see that Grey was not there. Their usual table was occupied by a merry group that had pulled up extra chairs, and no lone figure waited at a different table. In fact, every table was taken, most by groups of more than two. Her column had done Grey a favor, whether intended or not.

It was twenty past the hour, not unforgivably late, but still he must have given up. Hoping to avoid random chats, she circled toward the kitchen with her eyes firmly on the swinging door, but a glance through as a waiter hurried out was enough to warn her away. Disappointed—she hadn't yet heard Lucy's reaction to the column that had featured her so amusingly—she turned to ask the bartender about Carter, but he, too, was swamped.

The shift from twilight to full darkness was nearly done. Walking briskly, she first headed back toward the newspaper building but at Second Street she turned right rather than crossing. Grey might well have gone back to his shop. It might not even be too late to stroll back to *Au Courant* together, a possibility that struck her suddenly as highly desirable. It was time to confide in someone, to talk out the morass of detail cluttering and clouding her mind. In many ways, Carter Grey was an ideal sounding-board, a bright and thoughtful man with a detached view of life around him. He might well see a pattern she had failed to discover.

Though it had seemed only a slim chance, she was disappointed to find the shop dark apart from a mild nightlight, the closed sign turned face out inside a glass panel on the front door. The hidden light was just bright enough to reveal a striking tableau. Years ago, this had been a bicycle repair shop called Jim the Fixer, as dusty and crowded as Jim was ancient. Now the bicycles and dust were gone without a trace, along with old Jim himself. Handsome armchairs and tables stood on fine rugs in deep reds and blues. Archaic maps in gilt frames covered the walls nearly to the ceiling. The traditional old-world elegance of the room was unlike anything else in Willamette, its beauty museum-like.

A sudden longing to be in the room sitting deep in one of the chairs made her grasp the massive old door handle and press the latch. Nothing happened, naturally. Grey may have failed to ensure that his warehouse was locked but he would never be so cavalier with his treasures.

The room was not deep. At the back stood an ornate wood counter that gleamed even in the mild light, and beyond it a closed door led to what she guessed would be a workroom or storeroom. Had Grey ever said whether he did his own framing? She could not recall. The workroom must open onto the alley—which, of course, is where Reba had been feeding the cats.

Hurrying now despite knowing the errand would be futile, Neva went around the corner of the block and was pleased to see that a streetlamp positioned midway along the cross street shone full down the alley. Carter's back door was easy to find, for like the front it stood out from the slightly scrubby businesses to either side. The door was of solid dark wood and beside it stood an old tool cupboard that opened easily. The can of Iams was on the bottom shelf along with three empty aluminum pie tins. The only other items in the cupboard were a plastic container of water with a spigot, also clearly for cats, and a whisk broom and dustpan. Very tidy, indeed.

Back on the street again, Neva hesitated, tempted to stroll around to the greenhouse but not sure why. She wouldn't go in, it would be dark and dismal, but it would be interesting to see whether the door was locked again now that the police and Grey knew that the place had been trashed.

The door was locked. Though this seemed right, and she'd had no intention of going inside the warehouse, she felt mildly thwarted. To continue her campaign for an indoor park, she would need a key, but this should be no problem. As she turned away from the door, a vehicle rounded the nearest corner and pulled up to the curb. It was a patrol car. The window slid down and Gale Marcum demanded, "Since when did the *Current* get a night beat? I'm beginning to think you live down here."

"Since when did you do night patrol duty?" Neva countered, looking with surprise at the blue uniform.

"I like to keep my hand in. No officer is above street duty in a well-run department."

"Ah, I see." Neva had never known Kitty Fiori to dress up in regulation blues and take to the streets. The uniform did not suit the assistant chief of police, and in fact, didn't appear to fit well in the shoulders. She would not want to be Reba or Hogan on Marcum's watch.

"What are you doing down here?" he pressed.

"Nothing to do with work, as it happens. I was late meeting a friend for dinner and missed him. I thought I might catch him at his shop and then strolled around here."

"Ah, yes, Mr. Grey, of course. Interesting fellow. Have a good evening then." And up went the window.

Looking after the car, Neva felt a current of pure exasperation wash through her. Why had she answered his nosy question? It was none of his business what she was doing here or anywhere—and how had he known it was Grey she was to have met for dinner?

That Grey would have tried to call her and left a message was so obvious she could not at first believe it wasn't the antique dealer's smooth voice on her answering system. It was Quick's throaty rasp. "He says he'll talk to you, okay, but same deal as before. Same place. Eight o'clock. That's tonight."

This was the entire message but still she listened to it a second time, and was struck by the strange way things sometimes work out—had she been on time to meet Grey for dinner she would have missed this second appointment with Quick. You just never knew when a seeming disappointment or failure would turn out to be fortuitous. She could patch things up with Grey but had she missed the meeting with Quick and his sidekick she was unlikely to have got a second chance.

It was a quarter to eight when she left the building. Though the meeting spot was just six blocks away she drove this time, parked half a block from the alley, and got her heavy jacket out of the trunk. There was only a mild chill in the air but she'd be standing in one spot for at least half an hour and the night would only grow colder.

Here no friendly streetlamp shone down the alley, and she hesitated on the sidewalk, peering into darkness. The smell of the river hung heavy, but still it was not enough to hide the smell of oil and dumpsters. She had noticed the smell only vaguely that afternoon, but now it flowed out of the blackness between the buildings in a palpable current. Keeping her breath shallow, she felt for the penlight in her bag.

"Hey!" Came a hissing call.

"Hello?"

"Don't stand there!"

"Sorry. It's just that I can't see where I'm going and I didn't know if you were here. I'd like to use my little flashlight, if you don't mind. It's tiny. No one will see it." She flicked the light on without waiting for an answer and went toward the doorway where she'd stood mere hours ago.

"Shut it off!"

She stepped into the small recess in the wall and turned off the light.

"You didn't tell nobody?"
"Of course not. Are you both there?"
"We're here."
"Great. Just let me get settled. It's a little tricky in the dark. I'll have to use the light for notes but I'll keep it down." As Neva propped her left foot against the wall behind her so her thigh could serve for a table, she noted with surprise that she felt shaky, as though from a sudden scare. She was not afraid of Quick, certainly—for one thing, he needed her to help prove his innocence. Maybe it was simply the adrenalin thrill of secrecy, not so different from her excitement playing hide-and-seek as a kid. Waiting to be found, her pulse would pound as though what pursued her was a hungry tiger rather than one of the neighborhood kids.

"You ready?"
"Okay, ready. It would be nice to have a name, even just a first name."
A young male voice said, "Derek. That's my middle name."
"Fine. Derek. First of all, thank you for agreeing to talk to me. I know it's not easy. There are a couple of ways we can do this. I could ask questions, or you could describe what you saw and then I could ask for clarification on the uncertain bits."
"Just tell it," Quick commanded.
"Angel was in the wrong place," said Derek. "I mean, he usually slept in that same doorway, that place down the block with the green glass windows. I was on the other side of the street but I could see he was laying in some bushes with his feet sticking out. I guess I was kind of tired."
"Wasted, you mean," put in Quick.
"My place is a few houses over from where he was laying so I crossed the street. I'd forgot that the porch light quit working a while back and I couldn't find the keyhole and my lighter wouldn't work, so I went up the sidewalk to the street light to try to get the lighter going. That was the other direction from Angel. When I was coming back I think the dude was already there standing by him but I didn't really look, you know what I mean. I just went in and fell on the bed. Like I said, I was tired."
"Wasted," repeated Quick.
"And you went to sleep?"
"If only. I forgot I left a bunch of crap on the bed, a music stand and some other shit. Cut my head. You can still see, right over my eye. I had to take a shower."
"Wrong," said Quick. "Only makes it bleed. You need pressure, man, don't you know anything?"

"Not much, I guess. I only had one towel. I got it around my head and went back to bed, but first I went over to the window to close the curtain. That's when I saw the mailman dude had a hammer."

"*Mailman*? Are you saying there was a mailman standing over Angel?"

"That's right. He was standing there with the hammer, just kind of looking down."

"The mailman had a hammer?"

"That's what I said."

"Right. Just to be sure. This is rather confusing. I hadn't heard about the mailman, just that a man was standing there. Could you see Angel very clearly? I guess the real question is, was he still alive?"

"I couldn't see, only his legs sticking out."

"You didn't see any blood?"

"Yeah, I saw blood. It was in my eyes. I wasn't looking for anybody else's."

"Right, of course, but did Angel look okay to you, what you could see of him?"

"He wasn't moving, but then he wasn't moving before, when I looked over."

"And the mailman was just standing there. You're sure it was a mailman? Did he have a mailbag?"

Derek didn't answer for a moment, then said firmly, "No mailbag. Just the blue duds. Not shorts, long pants. My dad was a mailman."

"What did he do? The mailman. Did he do anything besides just stand there while you watched?"

"It was only a few seconds. I had to lay down or die."

"And you could see for sure that he was holding a hammer? Was the hammer, uh, wet or anything?"

"You mean bloody, well, I don't know. I didn't look and it was too far anyway. Then I shut the curtain."

"Did you see anyone else? How about a girl on a skateboard?"

"No girl, no skateboard."

"What about the gardener who works in Azalea Park, Lyle McRae? Someone else said he was seen talking with Angel that night."

"Didn't see him, not unless he wears blue mailman duds. Is that it then?"

"Do you remember anything else about the man? Hair color? Size?"

"Just average, or maybe a little on the big side. Not much to notice, and I couldn't see good anyway."

"What happened in the morning?"

"Not morning. Well, in the morning I guess I heard sirens but I put the pillow over my head. It was dark when I got up. I didn't go out. I called for pizza, played some video games, went back to sleep. I didn't even know about it for two days. And then, you know, I was scared. I've learned to stay away from the law, as far away as I can get. I mean, I was almost a witness, wasn't I?"

"Looks like it. But a man has been arrested, a man who apparently didn't do it. And they're looking for your friend there."

"They're looking for me, the stupid bastards." There was the strike of a match, an in-sucking of breath, and then the match flying from the doorway. It burned briefly on the gravel and went out.

"Derek, this is very important information. I appreciate it and appreciate your courage in talking to me, but I think you know that it has to go to the police. And it should come from you directly, not secondhand through me. Does that make sense?"

"Couldn't I just write it down and sign the paper and you could give it to the cops?"

"Not nearly as effective as telling them in person, and they wouldn't leave it at that. They'd have questions. They'd keep after me to find out your identity, which I wouldn't give away, don't worry about that. I promised. And I don't really know who you are anyway. But it's time to get the information to the right people. I'd be happy to set up a meeting and go with you, if that would help. With the chief of police, Kitty Fiori. She's pretty reasonable. And you did nothing wrong. You didn't even fail to call in a report of suspicious activity because there was no reason to think anything was wrong at the time. You'd seen Angel lying out drunk on the sidewalk before. The only thing they might make a fuss about is how long it took you to speak up once you knew he'd been killed."

"Maybe," Derek said after another silence. "I've been thinking about it but I need to think some more. How about we let you know tomorrow?"

"It won't get any easier tomorrow. Why not arrange a time and place to meet? The afternoon would be best. That would leave the morning to set up something with the police chief."

The men conferred in whispers, Quickie forceful, Derek murmuring, but at length he said, "Okay. I don't like it but I'll do it. Is there a reward or anything?"

Chapter Twenty-Three

Again, Quick directed her to leave first. For about fifteen minutes she sat in the car without starting the engine, hoping they would come out her end of the alley, though she would have been surprised at such carelessness. It didn't happen, and there was no sign of them when she circled the block to check the other end of the alley. They would have had to cross open space on leaving this end because the entire block of buildings had been cleared to make way for the parking lot next to the skateboard pit. They must have headed straight over to the dark bike path, or maybe Quick had a hidey-hole somewhere close by.

Scanning the cars and bicycles on the far side of the parking lot, she could not help thinking of Pet. If she could persuade the girl to meet with Fiori, either at the same time or back to back with Derek, it might result in real progress.

But Pet was not among the skaters whizzing around in the pit. Before heading back to the car, Neva circled the skate area to be sure the girl wasn't resting on one of the benches around the perimeter, some in heavy shadow. East of the pit a weedy lawn stretched to the bike path. As she rounded the far side of the pit and headed back she saw a hunched figure crossing the lawn, and as it came within the glow from the flood lamps she recognized the familiar yellow jacket.

Curiosity and pity got the upper hand this time. Changing course and walking faster to get as far from the skaters as possible before their paths met, she cast about for what to say, how to put the woman at ease and give her an opening to spill the sorrow that was written so plainly in her face and bearing. When they were only about ten feet apart and the woman showed no sign of seeing her, she said, "Hello again. Sorry to startle you. We talked the other day. I'm Neva Leopold."

"Yes. Of course." A moment of silence passed before she said flatly, "How are you?"

"Pretty well, thank you. You're the only other adult I ever see here."

A slight nod was the only response.

Leave her alone, Leopold. She doesn't want to talk. But the words would not stay down. "I wanted to thank you again for your comments the other day at the post office. What you said about Ethan reminded me that I no longer write much about kids. I tend to write about what's happening around me and now that I live alone I have to be careful not to turn inward too much, that is, to be too self-centered in my choice of subjects."

"You don't expect them to go," the woman said, speaking with low intensity. "You can't know. You're never ready."

"That is very true. You think they'll be kids forever."

"You think they're happy. And healthy. And then they're gone."

"And here we are."

"Here we are."

Crickets started up around them despite the clatter of skateboards. They stood close enough for Neva to detect a faint smell of onions on the woman's clothing, as though she had come straight from cooking dinner to pursue her errand on the river. The impulse to touch her, to take her arm in womanly understanding for the losses that time brings was so powerful that when a hand closed on her own arm it felt natural.

"I must find my daughter," came an urgent whisper as the hand gripped with almost painful force. "Lindsey. Do you know Lindsey?"

"I don't believe so." Neva laid her free hand gently on the hand that enclosed her forearm. The grip eased but did not release her.

"She's small for her age. She needs to come home. That's all. She can skate. I want her to know that before it's too late. We won't mind if she skates. She's here somewhere, I know she's here!" The last words came out in a low wail and the grip tightened again.

Neva's hand closed more firmly around the hand on her arm, lifted it free, and held it. "Is your daughter sometimes called Pet?"

"Where is she?"

"I don't know. I'm sorry. I believe she's staying with a friend but she didn't say who it is or where they live." This was Pet's mother. Pet had said her brother was killed in an accident—this woman was not looking for her son down here. She had lost her son and now her daughter had taken to the streets. No wonder she was a wraith of despair.

"I've talked to her friends. They don't know anything." With a sudden twist the hand was wrenched from Neva's. "She wanted to play drums. It wouldn't have hurt."

The woman shifted on her feet and looked toward the skate pit. Neva waited, hoping for an opening that would allow her to say what should be said, but the woman only pulled the yellow jacket closer and thrust her hands hard into the pockets.

"I'm so sorry about your son," Neva said at length, taking the risk. "Words don't mean anything, I know, but I can't help speaking. It's the worst thing that could happen to anyone, to lose a child."

"You don't know." The words were low but hard. "You don't know what can happen. You think you have a family, you think everything is fine, you think it will go on and on and then it's gone. It's gone!"

That night Neva lay awake far too late, unable to stop thinking about Pet's mother. *Jeanette, but I'm called Jean,* she had said when Neva asked her name. Then she had walked away, not toward her car but in the opposite direction, into the night, searching for her remaining child. Neva would have done the same in her shoes, she would have walked the town day and night until she found her daughter and brought her home by whatever means necessary.

When she slept at last, her dreams were vivid, but they were not the usual jumbled and seemingly meaningless sagas about people known and unknown. She dreamed about flagstones. Not *about* flagstones, no, she dreamed *flagstones,* she dreamed she had become a flagstone and was setting herself into the pattern around her. Moving left, moving right, pivoting a little to sink in deeper, adjusting for the correct distance to the edges on all sides, setting herself into place, a flagstone amid curves and corners, just so, a perfect fit with a push here and pull there, so important that everything fit right, the edges running parallel but not quite touching, the curves matching, the straights matching . . . she woke up staring into darkness.

Pieces were all around her, pieces that must fit though she could not see how.

In the morning, drinking coffee made with beans that were burned just enough to be unsatisfactory but not enough to throw out and start over, she sat at the kitchen table and started her list for the day. *Find Pet, arrange meeting Derek/Fiori, apologize Carter.*

The prospect of visiting the lovely shop in daylight and settling into one of the vintage chairs with the antiquities dealer in another, listening to her complex tale with alert attention, made a bright spot in the day ahead. Though the lack of a message certainly was puzzling and even a bit worrisome. True, she had failed to contact him as well but it was not for lack of trying. She had failed to find a home number. Returning his calls, she had always used the business number, but the shop did not open until noon. She, on the other hand, was the easiest person in town to find.

Her first call of the day, made from home after breakfast, was a bust.

Chief Fiori was away at a conference for two days. It was not a good start, and after pacing the hall, she decided to meet Derek on her own. Then she called the *Current* switchboard and said she would not be in until afternoon and please to route calls to her home number.

It couldn't hurt to take the morning off, to give herself a few hours to clear her thoughts. Soon on her knees scooping sand and moving rocks, she let her mind go empty of everything apart from this moment. The slabs went together naturally, just as they'd done in her dream. A glance and she knew which one to place next along the undulating edge of the last row.

Working with dreamlike ease, she was barely aware of the clamoring jays, the warm spring sun, her growing hunger for lunch. She could not have said later how it happened, only that a moment came when she sat back on her heels and stared at the rock in her hands without seeing it. She set it down and deliberately drew off her gloves. She didn't dash to the house or snatch up the telephone book when she reached the front hall. Every movement was methodical, the turning of pages until she reached the O's, the running of her finger down the columns, the halting of the finger on Oleander, the careful reading of the names there: Lars and Jean.

Jean was Oleander's wife.

Pet was Captain Oleander's daughter. Her brother who had died was the son who died of MRSA. The boy had been a drug user and street dealer, and must have known Angel. Lars Oleander hated Angel with passion that had seemed out of proportion to the panhandler's importance, but it made sense if he blamed Angel even indirectly for his son's seedy habits, habits that could have weakened him and made him vulnerable to the worst that MRSA could do.

Quickie and Vance had been scared away from Angel by the approach of a patrol car. Derek had looked out the window and seen a man in a blue uniform standing over Angel's prostrate figure.

But it was not a postman he'd seen; it was a policeman.

Lars Oleander had killed Angel.

The policeman had killed the man he believed to be responsible for his son's death, and what's more, his wife knew or suspected it. *Tell Lindsey to come home*, she had pleaded as they were parting last night. *We just want her home before it's too late. Tell her we love her. Her father loves her. He will always be there for her no matter what happens.*

Jean Oleander knew it was just a matter of time before her husband was arrested.

Could it be that Pet also suspected her father had killed Angel? That she had observed more than she admitted and this is why she had told no one about seeing Angel that night so close to the time of his death? And why she had left home? *I don't live at home. Not now . . .* No, this did not ring true. The girl was far too emotionally well-knit to be struggling with any such knowledge. She was suffering from teenage anger at her parents and from the loss of her brother. She also, no doubt, had suffered shock on finding out that Angel was killed almost under her eyes. But she was essentially cheerful, healthy, and wholesome. She was not a child hiding from the knowledge that her father was a murderer, though she might well have picked up on new tensions in the household that helped drive her away.

Neva had no real evidence for this scenario but she was certain about one thing: the girl must be found and made to see her mother.

Chapter Twenty-Four

Lunch was bread and cheese eaten in the car on her way downtown. Though it was not yet noon, she meant to check on Carter first, but thoughts of the Oleander family so engrossed her that she found herself at the foot of First Street and getting out of the car without having passed the shop.

Just one head could be seen whizzing around in the pit and it was definitely not Pet's. Still, she stood for some time watching the young man's solitary swooping up and down, and when he looked her way, she beckoned. He streaked toward her, shot up out of the pit, and landed with a clatter of wheels.

"Dunno," he said. "Don't know any girl skaters. Would like to, though."

The girl was not sleeping out, as far as she knew, but just to be thorough, she left her car at the skate park and followed the bike path to the mouth of Coffee Creek and along the creek to the homeless camp under the railroad overpass. A figure lay curled in a torn sleeping bag, but a glance was enough to determine that it was a medium-size man and not a slender girl.

Before returning to the car she walked back along the entire length of the bike path to where it ended north of the boat landing, watching for Hogan and Tomasino—and Reba—as well as the girl but not a single skater clattered within earshot and no lumpy figures shuffled or sprawled anywhere in sight. Next, cruising by car, she checked the Beanery, Azalea Park, the bakery, the comic shop, the two skateboard shops—they knew Pet but thought she was living at home—the youth drop-in center, even the boys and girls club because a recent article in the *Current* had mentioned a skateboarding safety class and it was easy to imagine Pet teaching such a course. The girl was not there, though the manager said he thought she had helped with the class the previous year.

The block where Angel had been killed was without visible life. The apartment building where Derek had lived was starkly bedraggled in the morning light, the rain gutters sagging, steps missing from an outside stairway, scraps of tarpaper roofing shingle embedded in the weedy grass. It was rare to see such a rundown building in Willamette, and, in this case, the gentrification creeping west from the riverfront would be welcome when it arrived.

Despite Quick's claim that Derek had moved, she pulled over to check the names on a row of rusting mail slots. The labels were rain-smeared and illegible.

Sitting in the idling car she cast about for ideas, any ideas, for where to search next. Reba might be able to steer her to the girl but Reba was as elusive as Pet. Thinking of Reba took her thoughts to the warehouse, and this in turn reminded her of Carter. A U-turn sent her back through downtown to the antiquities shop. It should have been open for half an hour by now, according to the discreet sign on the door, but the windows were dark and she did not need to get out of the car to know the store had not been opened yet today. Perplexed, she sat for some time thinking, then circled around to First Street and pulled up in front of the warehouse.

The front door was locked, as before. She had never tried the alley door, and found it a narrow, flimsy thing that appeared to be locked on the inside. Irritated, she rattled the handle and leaned hard into the weathered wood. The door popped open. Staggering inward, she grabbed for support, seized a broom that toppled behind her, caught herself against a pillar with her right forearm, and stood rubbing her smacked elbow.

The broom had come from an open storage area next to the door. As she set it back in its spot between a battered metal dustpan and a shovel, she felt a sudden powerful awareness of the gardener. These had been his—his broom, shovel, rake, loppers, turning fork . . . The tools were clean, the handles smooth and dark with use. He had not been the innocent recluse of her initial impression but he had been a passionate gardener and the community was the better for it. If the greenhouse did not become a park, she would urge Grey to find good homes for the tools as well as the plants.

With the back door open, she didn't need her pen light to circle around to the stairs. Today she did not linger among the plants, but went right to the apartment. The white geraniums that flanked the doorway had wilted. Making a mental note to water them and to remind Grey that they were not on the automatic system, she knocked, got no reply, and turned the large brass knob.

Pet Oleander was sitting in one of the white armchairs facing the door, her hands folded in her lap, the skateboard parked on the floor by her feet. With an uncertain smile, she said, "I needed a place to sleep."

"Good choice," Neva observed, but her attention was not on the girl. Someone had restored the room to immaculate beauty. Not a single item appeared out of place and the coffee table gleamed with fresh polish. Two open windows had carried away the smell of grease and cheap drink.

"Did you clean it up?" At the girl's look of confusion, she added, "The apartment. It was a wreck the last time I saw it. Were you the one who put it back in order?"

"I didn't do anything. I only stayed here last night. I can't stay with my friend every night."

"So it was like this when you arrived last night?"

The girl nodded, then turned to look toward the high bunk and its uneven edge of blanket. "I'm not very good at making beds. Anyway, I hate everything tucked in."

"You came in the back door?"

"I saw him go in one time. You have to kick it."

"Right, so I discovered. I almost fell on my face." A pause, and then, "I met your mom at the skate park yesterday, in the evening. She was looking for you."

Pet shrugged and dropped her gaze to her hands, but lifted her head almost immediately and regarded Neva with sudden resentment. "I don't know why I talked to you yesterday, I just did. What did you tell Mom?"

"Only that I'd seen you and you appeared fine and said you were staying with a friend. But things have got more complicated."

Pet had been sitting up straight but now slid down into the chair, crossed her ankles, and pushed her hands into her jeans pockets.

"I don't know quite where to start with this." It simply wouldn't do to tell the girl what her real suspicions were, but Neva wanted to convey sufficient urgency to get her to go home. "There's a lot going on right now that I don't understand, and I don't really know what's connected to what. None of it may have anything to do with you or your family, but I'm, it's just that I'm uncertain and concerned. Among other things, I'm wondering whether you might have seen more that night Angel was killed than you like to admit."

"I told you I didn't see anything. Anybody, I mean. Just Angel lying there. And the gardener guy talking to him. I was stupid to tell you about it. What did my mom say?"

"She talked about you, and about families falling apart."

Shifting on the chair, Pet pulled her hands out of her pockets, laced her fingers and inverted her hands so that her knuckles popped like a pitchy fire. "My mom hates that."

"So do I, frankly. My son used to do the same thing. He said it felt good."

"Guess so. What else did she say?"

"She was feeling sad about your brother and had gone out to look for you. She's extremely worried and I can well understand it. She gave me a message. She said please to come home, that they love you, your father loves you and will always be there for you. Also that they won't mind your skating."

"That was it? The whole thing?"

"You sound disappointed."

"Oh, well, I don't know. They don't owe me anything. Some people would say I owe them but I didn't ask to be born, did I?"

"None of us do."

"Don't you ever get mad?"

"Sure, well, actually not very often. I was born without a temper."

"Lucky you." A pause. "I didn't mean that how it sounded. I mean, you're lucky. I have a temper. I got it from my dad."

"Ah, yes, your dad. He blows up sometimes, does he?"

"No way. I wish he would. He just gets all puffed up like he's going to blow and then leaves. Sometimes I feel sorry for the criminals."

"You think he takes it out on the people he arrests?"

"Oh, I guess not. He just shoots his gun out at that shooting place."

"He seems like such a calm man."

"That's what everyone says. Just goes to show."

"Do you think he would be capable of real violence, even killing someone?"

Pet's face went through so many changes in a matter of seconds that the only real message to come through was distress.

"I'm sorry if that upset you—"

"I'm just hungry, is all. I can't think."

"It's past lunch time. Why don't we go over to the bakery. Or anywhere you'd like."

"I guess not. Thanks anyway but I like to lay low during the day, just kind of keep out of sight except when I need to skate or go crazy."

"I'd be glad to bring you some food. First, though, I'm wondering about something. If you heard that one of your parents was really sick or dying would you go home?"

"Who's dying! Why are you saying these things!"

"No, no, sorry, that was clumsy. They're fine, I mean no one's sick or dying. I'm just trying to make a difficult point. I suspect there's some serious trouble in your family and your mother really needs you. Soon. Right away."

"Okay then. I'll go home. So what's the trouble? I mean besides me and a dead brother and so on."

Her flip manner seemed out of character but it was also relieving. Surely she could never talk like this if she knew her father had killed Angel. No child could put on this sort of act. Once Pet was safely with her mother, Neva would have to start the ugly ball rolling toward Oleander's arrest and then the roof would collapse on Pet's world. For now, however, she was just an angry kid who had to be managed with care.

"I'm not sure of the details." Neva spoke slowly, watching Pet's face. "And I could be wrong, but I have good instincts. I think it would be better for you just to go home and stay around for a bit and see what's up than for me to say any more. Try to have an open talk with your mother."

Pet stood up as though to head for the door, but instead looked toward the wall of windows and did not turn back toward Neva as she said, "If I was your kid would you always tell me the truth?"

"Yes and no. My son and I have an agreement, have had since he was old enough to understand such things. We always tell each other the truth but there are also certain areas we don't ask about. For instance, I've never asked him about his girl friends or how much he drinks at parties. If he wants to tell me, that's fine. Now, if I thought he had a serious problem and needed help I wouldn't hesitate to cross those lines. Is that ok for an answer?"

"OK. Pretty good, I mean. Most parents won't leave you alone."

"It's because they love you and they're worried, and it's not easy to know when it's none of your business as a parent."

"You know."

"No, I don't. That's why we have a rule. If I gave in to my real curiosity and concern I'd drive him crazy. Maybe drive him away. On the other hand, don't forget all those parents who never talk to their kids about anything. It wouldn't feel good to be let alone in that way."

"Well. I don't know." Pet picked up her skateboard and studied patterns on it that she must know by heart. "Anyway, I could use some food. My mom's a pretty good cook." She moved toward the door but stopped to look back. "I know what this is about, you know. I was going home today anyway. I just had to get my head around it."

Then she was gone and her energetic young feet were pounding down the stairs. Listening with an expression of weary sorrow, Neva was sure the girl did not know as much as she thought she did. She could only hope her own conclusions were wrong.

Derek was not at the Beanery at the appointed hour, which wasn't a great surprise. Neva didn't really expect him to show up, but she stood patiently outside the café door and looked closely at any young man who walked in alone, hoping Derek would recognize her even if she failed to know him. At last, disappointed despite her low expectations, she went inside, ordered a toasted bagel, and was pouring half-and-half into her coffee when a voice at her side said, "Are you treating?"

"Of course," she replied, and laughed as a tall young man pulled the empty lining out of his front pockets.

"Broke, as usual."

Soon settled with a Panini sandwich, potato salad, chocolate-peanut butter pie and a large milk, Derek talked and chewed at the same time. "This sure hits the spot. I almost didn't come but I figured it wouldn't hurt and anyway I was hungry. Where's your cop friend anyway?"

Though clearly disappointed at missing the chief of police, he refused to try again in a few days. "Nope. Can't handle more than one of these things. I'm going to San Diego. Have some serious surfing to do."

"I thought you wanted to give evidence to help Quick."

"Help Quick! I wouldn't walk across the road to help that dude. It was just bothering me and he came around asking."

"He was asking. . . what did he ask you?"

"If I saw anything that night."

"You hadn't mentioned it to him?"

"Nope, or anybody else either."

"Why would he ask you specifically? You live right there, it's true, but did he think you'd just happened to look out the window? Did he ask other people in the building?"

"Beats me. I was moving out when he showed up. Said did I notice anybody in particular hanging around Angel that night. So I told him."

"He was there earlier that night, when they took the money. Could he have seen you then?"

"No way. I was at Squirrel's playing pool until I went home, if you know what I mean. I was sick that night. Quickie kept saying I was wasted but I was sick. I had a fever and took some cold medicine to help me sleep and I guess I overdid it. I felt great when I woke up. Until I found out about Angel." He stuffed the last quarter of the sandwich into his mouth and followed it closely with a long swallow of milk.

"I have one very important question for you," Neva said, looking away. He was healthy and even attractive—not the seedy pothead she had expected, but a strapping young man with clear skin and lively eyes—but he was not nice to watch eating. "Could you please describe the mailman again. Specifically, is there any possibility you could have mistaken a blue police uniform for a blue postal uniform?"

"No way. I told you my dad—" he paused, cocked his head with a bite of pie suspended on the fork. "Maybe. I suppose so. It was just a blue uniform, shirt, long pants, belt. There was something on his belt. Could have been a holster, a gun, I don't know. My dad never had anything on his belt. No, wait, he had a dog whistle, the kind that drives them crazy. I've still got that whistle."

"Was there a car, maybe a mail truck or patrol car?"

"Didn't see any."

"You said the man was holding a hammer. Can you remember anything more about that?"

"Just a hammer."

"A builder's hammer you mean?"

"Is there any other kind?"

"Oh, sledgehammer, rock hammer."

Derek shrugged, drained his glass, wiped his mouth with his hand, and looked around restlessly. "Any more questions? I've got some packing to do."

"Is there some way I can reach you once you leave town?"

"I don't—well." He considered her for a long, silent moment before speaking. "Okay, my brother's phone number. But don't pass it along. I don't want to be hauled back here to testify when I don't know anything more than what I told you. I wouldn't even recognize the guy again, you know?"

Chapter Twenty-Five

Standing in front of the Beanery watching Derek saunter around the corner to the parking lot, Neva knew she was way out of line from an official standpoint. He was a significant witness and she was letting him walk away, walk out of the town and the state, without properly reporting to the police what he'd seen. But officialdom had slid far into the background over the past week or so. Her attempts to persuade law enforcement that they were headed down the wrong track had got nowhere—and now she could not help wondering whether Fiori had suspicions of her own about Lars Oleander. What had she said? *There are peculiar circumstances here that require extra care...* Maybe not her precise words but close enough, and in the light of recent information, extremely suggestive.

Frankie, too, had sensed something strange in the way the investigation was being handled, and had said he believed the police knew they had the wrong man and were holding him for reasons of their own. Oleander would cave once he was accused, she felt certain of this. He had killed out of passionate grief and this would spill in a different way once he was faced with public knowledge.

But not yet, she was not ready yet. A few more details had to be corralled—enough that when she took the story to Fiori there would be no more official stonewalling. As for the question of who had killed Lyle and Lisette, it was simply more than she could think about at the moment. One murder at a time.

The windows of Winton & Grey's Fine Antique Prints were still dark. Peering through a glass pane in the door at the elegantly appointed shop, she was struck by a vague sense of oppressiveness. So silent in the middle of a business day, so dim and dusty, for surely that was dust on the table nearest the window? Tables don't turn dusty overnight.

The store front to the north of Carter's also showed dark windows but that shop had been vacant for at least a year. The shop on the south side sold women's footwear. No, said the slim girl who was stacking shoeboxes in an artful tower at the back of the store, she had no idea where Carter might be. In fact, she didn't even know what his "product" was.

"Old postcards?"

Across the street an elderly man in a furniture resale store said he'd noticed the shop hadn't opened at its usual time but he wasn't surprised. "That Grey fellow, he's deep. Never know what he's up to. You know what he told me? He said his store used to be called Jim the Fixer and some famous writer that used to live in town called his book *Jim the Fixer* after it." The man thought for a moment, opened his cash register drawer, lifted the money tray, took out a small card and shook his head. "Nope. Sorry. The book was called *The Fixer*. Written by, hmm, looks like Barnard Malamute. What do you think of that?"

Briefly cheered up by the incident—it was well known in town that Malamud had named the novel after the bicycle repair store; where had this old gent been?—Neva went around the corner to the alley intending to try the back door but with no real expectation that a man like Grey would leave anything about his business unsecured. The sight of a sturdy figure in front of the cat food cupboard made her hurry forward even as she braced for a scowl. She had not seen the homeless woman since the unfortunate, rainy Saturday morning visit.

"Well, it's that Jeneva Leopold person." Reba regarded her with the old look of calm interest.

"Tidy cupboard you have there," Neva said, relieved, though she was careful not to show it, and deliberately matched the other woman's flat though not unfriendly tone. "Where do the cats hide out?"

"In secret cat places. Like, right behind you."

Neva turned to discover two large cats stalking toward them. Apart from a couple of recessed doorways, there was nowhere they could have been hiding, no dumpster or wood pallets or collapsed cardboard cartons waiting for recycling. She said, "They must take lessons from you."

"Ha. It's the other way around," Reba said, scooping cat food briskly. The cats went to their separate pie pans as though trained and ate with decorum. The third pan, full of water, sat between them. Reba stroked one scruffy feline back, then the other.

"I don't leave till they're done. That's why it takes so long," she said. "What are you up to?"

"Way too much, as it happens. Have you seen Carter today?"

"He's gone."

"Gone? Where? For how long?"

Reba shrugged. "I was out here the other day with the cats when he came through the door there. He was taking out the trash. He said he wouldn't see me for a few days and did I have enough Iams to last. I said sure as long as I didn't get too hungry and eat some myself."

"Why don't we get some lunch—or early dinner might make more sense—after you're done here? All I've had since breakfast was a bagel."

"That was a joke, Jeneva Leopold."

"I know it was a joke, Reba Winner. I'd just like to talk to you and it's pleasant to talk over a meal."

It was nice of her to ask, Reba conceded, but she wasn't hungry at the moment, and anyway she didn't like eating with other people around. Couldn't they talk right here?

"All right then." Neva leaned a shoulder into the dusty brick wall and crossed her arms. "First, you really have no idea where Carter went?"

"Not a clue. Is it important?"

"I'm just wondering because we were supposed to meet for dinner last night and I was late. He wasn't there and he didn't leave a message. And he didn't put a sign in the window saying he would be closed for a few days. It just seems odd, out of character, and no way to run a business."

"He's a big boy. What else?"

"A young man who lived on the block where Angel was killed looked out the window that night and saw a man in a uniform standing over him. He assumed it was a mailman but I'm thinking it could have been a policeman."

"Yeah, I heard that."

"You heard it! Where? I mean who told you? Was it Quick?"

"That's right."

"I thought it was a big secret." Thinking of the cloak-and-dagger bit she'd been put through by Ernold Quick to get this information she felt suddenly ridiculous. She was being played with, or at least used, though the information appeared to be solid. Derek was as believable as Quick was dodgy. "Any idea who it might be? Which policeman?"

Reba nodded thoughtfully but didn't reply.

"Who, for instance?" Neva pressed.

"I never knew his name but I heard he's a big cheese in the cop shop. I heard he's not really a patrolman but likes to dress up and drive around at night. He's the one that likes to drive down the bike path. A jerk in other words."

Gale Marcum? Surely not. . . "What does he look like?"

"A cop."

"What about his eyes?"

"That I can tell you. Weird blue. Hey, you all done there?" Reba stooped and retrieved the empty pie pans. The larger of the two cats twined around her legs, the other sat and twisted to lick its back. "Is that it for the big talk? I've got a lot of hungry little guys waiting."

"There are a number of patrolmen on the night shift. Why do you think it would be that one in particular who was seen with Angel?"

"Good question, Jeneva Leopold."

Neva waited while Reba stacked the three pie pans and closed the cupboard. Her patience had nearly run its course when Reba said, "I've seen him down there before. Like I said, he drives the bike path."

"Do you know any reason why that officer or any of them would want to kill Angel?"

"They'd like to kill us all. No, just kidding. Without us their lives would be too boring."

"What about Lyle and Lisette? Any reason why a policeman would specifically want them dead?"

"Can't you think about anything except dead people, Jeneva Leopold?"

"Sorry, Reba. I'm sick of it myself but I don't seem to have a choice, the way it's going. What about Lyle and Lisette?"

"Well, I did think about that. Let's say Lyle saw Angel get killed and tried to do his blackmail thing so they had to get rid of him too, and his girlfriend knew who did it so she had to go too. One, two, three. So all you really need is a reason for the first one. I'd say that's pretty neat."

"His blackmail thing? I'd heard that Lyle was blackmailing Win Niagra but are you saying he made a habit of it?"

"I heard things. But I can't say for sure. I stayed clear of him myself."

Afternoon was turning to evening by the time they finished the cat rounds. Neva had not meant to do the whole route, only to follow along in the hope of picking up more tidbits from the canny and watchful Reba, but as they made their way into stairwells, sheds, fenced lots, and unfamiliar alleys, she was drawn in to yet another of the many worlds in this little town she knew so well and yet didn't know. The slow pace, the conversations with multitudinous cats, the varied settings where they lingered until each pie pan was empty. . . She had assumed that Reba's life must be difficult and dull but wandering in the twilight it seemed quaintly domestic, the out-of-the-way spots as familiar as homey nooks in a big old house.

They didn't talk much and Neva found this helpful, the homeless woman's quiet serving as a stimulant to her own thoughts, which were unquiet enough. Topping the tumult was the guilty fact that she had not turned up at the newsroom all day. She'd told the switchboard to route her calls to the house but this was not the same as letting Ambrose and

NO ANGEL

J.D. know she would not be in. She had not intended to stay away through the afternoon—there was a column to write by tomorrow—but the day had gone as it had gone, one thing leading to another, leaving no time to check in at the office. . . *Face it, Leopold, you were steering clear of Ambrose's keen eye.*

True enough, and a lucky thing, too. This morning she had been sure of herself and sure about Captain Oleander being the man in the blue uniform, and she would have said so, would have told Ambrose and possibly started an appalling chain of events. Now she was not so sure. Marcum seemed a far likelier type to commit murder, though with no motive that she could see for killing Angel. The joshing with Frankie about the timeliness of the murders just when the new jail was being pushed had been only joshing.

And what about Ernold Quick? What complex game was he up to?

"They're all neutered," Reba was saying as she led the way through high weeds to an ancient tear-drop trailer. "I trap them, have them fixed and take them back home."

"Home?"

"Where I found them."

"And who pays for the operations?"

"Some of the vets donate time. I pay if I have to."

Neva's protest died unspoken. If Reba chose to spend her monthly $523 disability check on feral cats that was her business. The cats certainly appreciated it, and most came running as she approached. Two with a Siamese look slid out from under the trailer as Reba swung open the rusty door and hauled out a sack.

"Have to hide it from the squirrels," she said. "I wouldn't mind feeding them but they just bury it."

The last stop was the path under the railroad bridge that crossed Coffee Creek. Here a mother and six kittens occupied a hollow in the bank.

"You'd better have one," Reba said as she knelt to scoop food into a hub cab. "I could hear mice in your walls. They're just about ready to leave home."

They separated at the skate park, with the homeless woman again refusing a ride, a meal, anything at all. "Have things to see to, Jeneva Leopold," she said, turning to head back down the bike path.

Neva watched her out of sight and then walked briskly over to Second Street and turned right toward Carter's shop to retrieve the car. The possibility that she had sent Pet off on a track that might turn out to be wrong—terribly wrong—lent urgency to her step. To knock on the Oleander's door was not possible without a defined reason, but maybe she could learn something simply by driving past the house. Maybe luck would be with her, and the girl would be out skating in the street or the driveway.

The Oleanders lived in the southwest part of town, in an area she hadn't visited in years. The houses, built mainly in the Fifties, were widely set along streets that wound steeply among oak trees. Gentian Drive, on the south side of the neighborhood, was especially curvy and steep, and the houses were few and far between, as were the streetlights. It was difficult to see the numbers and cruising through dense tree shadows with the window down, she slowed almost to a stop in front of each house to listen and peer toward the front door. It really was baffling that so many homeowners failed to make their addresses visible at night, though come to think of it, her house number had been buried for years under a Lady Banks rose.

The Oleander place was nearly the last on the street, which ended at a cemetery where she turned and went back. The porch light was on but otherwise the house was dark, and no car sat in the driveway. She pulled up close to the triple bay garage doors and turned off the engine. . .

Where was the Oleander family? She had expected to find something quite different, something active and intense—if, that is, Pet really had come home. For some time she studied the dark and silent house, then she got out of the car, walked resolutely to the front door, and rang the bell. Chimes sounded within, followed by a low thud that could have been the slamming of a distant door.

She rang again. Silence.

The curtain had not been drawn over the front picture window but only a shadowy suggestion of chairs and lamps could be seen inside. It was full dark now, the night air cool and damp. The grass, uncut for some time, brushed against her pant legs as she circled to the right around the house. For a moment she thought she would not be able to get through but the high fence turned out to enclose only a small garden patch and not the entire yard.

A light was on at the back, dimly revealing a shaggy sloping lawn dotted with flower beds and shrubs, the whole bordered by dark trees. There was no reason to be inspecting the Oleander backyard, none whatever, and yet she lingered for some time listening and watching before returning to the front porch.

Someone was home, she felt certain. Someone had slammed a door inside, someone had not answered her ring—had Pet come home to an empty house? Was the girl here on her own, waiting for whatever disastrous developments her imagination had conjured in response to Neva's hints?

Twice more she rang the bell but with no response and no more sounds of life inside. The thud could have been made by a dog or heavy cat jumping to the floor. But she didn't think so. She really did not think so.

Her hand was on the knob before she knew she was going to try it. The knob turned, she took a breath, pushed gently. The door opened but only to the length of a burglar chain.

"Hello?" she said softly through the crack, and breathed in the smell of neglect. Stale, dusty, faintly greasy, with a hint of Willamette Valley mold, not what anyone would expect in a house of this solidity and value. "Pet? Hello? Jean? It's Jeneva Leopold, from the *Current*."

For several minutes she waited without calling out again, then eased the door shut and returned to her car.

The newsroom was empty apart from a cluster of sports reporters watching a basketball game in the corner. Naturally, her phone message light was blinking and the in-basket was full. Voicemail consisted of three tips for columns, none of particular interest, and a brief message from Anya Alexandrova that she listened to twice: "Neva, thanks for going easy with us on the gravel situation. On that other business, that squashed shopping cart, I think I sorted it out for you. Here's the deal. One of our planners, a young guy, saw what happened and was embarrassed, he says. He apologized to Angel and gave him ten bucks. Not a hundred. Nothing to ring alarm bells there anyway. I don't know about the other bit, what Angel said about having eyes and ears or whatever it was. Just noise, I'd guess. Call me if you want to but this is all I've got. Hope it isn't disappointing—just kidding, ha ha."

Scratching *gravel* off her mental list, Neva reached for the in-basket. A quick sort yielded two letters that had been hand-delivered. The first was a rant about the city wasting money on useless gravel. The other, from Win Niagra, was to the point.

Neva,

I just remembered something Vance told me that I meant to pass along. It didn't happen exactly as I'd thought he said the first time we talked. He said they both ran off together when Quick saw the cop car but then he got ahead and looked around. Quick wasn't running anymore. He was standing there looking where they'd left Angel. Then he turned around and saw Vance and waved at him to keep going so that's what he did. Makes me wonder if maybe Quick didn't go back and do the dreadful deed, but then I never did like that guy and tried to get Vance to keep away from him. Anyway, thought you'd be interested. Win

Neva's thoughts churned so wildly as she left the newspaper building that she was barely aware of starting the car, rolling through the night streets, parking yet again at the warehouse, and feeling for her pen light. The narrow beam was bright in the black alley but she hesitated before following it, acutely aware of the solid dark mass of the old brick building close enough to touch on her left. Surely, Pet would not have returned here even if she hadn't gone home. But this was the only place she knew of that Pet had stayed and it had to be checked.

The narrow back door jammed, as before, but gave way with a kick. Moving with a quick, firm step, she climbed the stairs and strode down the path to the apartment door. But here her nerve weakened and she paused, listening and working up the will to enter. This sort of pursuit was way outside her usual writer's realm, but she had set certain things in motion and now must see them through. What she would say if she found the girl she didn't know precisely, only that she must try to backpedal on the frightful hints about her father that she'd dropped earlier in the day.

The door opened on candlelight. The chair where Pet had sat was occupied, but it was not the girl who returned her steady look. It was Ernold Quick.

"I didn't care for the dude but he made a cool place here," he said with a languid wave of the hand. He lay sprawled in the chair, legs outstretched, arms crossed over his chest, all trace of his previous intensity gone. The single fat candle stuck directly onto the coffee table surface lighted his face from a low angle with the usual goblin-like effect, though rather than the scowl she remembered from the library he was now almost grinning. "I figured you'd come looking for me one of these days."

"And why is that?" Neva said, and took a small step backwards to lean against the door frame with her arms crossed. Was he stoned? Drunk?

"Why? Why? Why? You think there's an answer for everything, don't you?"

"Mostly, yes, I guess I do."

Again the wave of the hand, dismissive this time. "So what did old Derek have to say? He was going to chicken out but I made him go. Was your cop lady impressed?"

"She was out of town, as it happened. But we had a good talk."

Wiggling backward into the chair to sit up straighter, Quick also crossed his arms and fixed her with a more focused look. "What about? What do you mean a good talk?"

"About other things he remembered seeing."

"Like what, for instance?"

Rather than reply, Neva scanned the deeply shadowed room. Nothing appeared to be out of place apart from the candle, and there was no skateboard or other sign of the girl. This now seemed a very good thing. "And then I got a note from someone who's close to Vance," she said, half musing. "He said when the two of you were running away after robbing Angel you fell behind, and when Vance looked back to see what had happened you waved him on and turned like you might be going back, going to see Angel again."

"And?"

"Did you go back?"

"What if I did?"

"It would explain why Vance couldn't find you where you were supposed to meet." She allowed a moment of silence before adding, "It could also make you the last person to have seen Angel alive."

"Meaning what, exactly?"

"Did you go back?" *He tore the head off a kitten because it spit up some milk. You have to see his temper.* Who had told her this? Lyle? Yes, it had been Lyle, right here in the greenhouse not fifty feet behind where she now stood. A sudden awareness of the open space at her back made her straighten away from the doorjamb and listen hard. The silence of the greenhouse did not seem benign or reassuring at the moment. Easing farther backward so that she was more out of the room than in it, she spoke in a carefully speculative tone. "I'm thinking it was a policeman Derek saw and not a mailman, and he pretty much agrees. What do you think?"

"What the hell does it matter anyways," Quick growled with abrupt fury. "The whole fuckin' town was down there."

"Who, exactly? I mean who else besides you and Vance and Derek and the policeman, or whoever it was that Derek saw?"

"I told you already, that crazy woman."

"What crazy woman? You didn't mention any woman at all."

"She was acting crazy, screaming."

"Screaming how?"

"Jesus, just screaming. You know, like screaming? You never heard of screaming?" Quickie was sitting forward now, gripping the tops of his thighs, his face hanging above the candle like an angry mask.

"There's no reason to be sarcastic. I'm just trying to understand. Do you mean screaming in fear, or screaming in anger? Screaming words?"

"Just screaming, that's all. Standing over Angel and screaming. I didn't know her, okay? Never saw her before."

"Do you think she could have killed him?"

Quick's shrug was barely visible in the candlelight.

"What did she look like?"

Another shrug.

"Was she old? Young? What was she wearing?"

"How would I know? I don't care what anybody wears. Well, it was something yellow. I thought she was some emergency dude. But they're supposed to help people, not yell at them."

Jean Oleander in her yellow parka? Had all three of the Oleanders been there that night? Could it be a family crime, a family conspiracy, revenge for the son and brother's death? No, no, not Pet. The girl showed no signs of concealing such a dreadful secret. Then it was the parents, maybe, killing Angel before he became a serious threat to the girl, who had taken to the streets like her brother. No, no, still not right. Jean, then, acting alone. Mothers will do anything if driven to it. She understood this all too well. Jean had killed Angel and then Lars Oleander had come along and discovered what had happened—but it was the policeman who had stood over Angel with the hammer in hand. Derek had seen him. He had not seen a woman. And if Reba's offhand theory was correct, that Lyle had tried to blackmail the killer, it was far easier to imagine Oleander strangling the gardener with twine than Jean killing him and then Lisette as well. Or had Oleander arrived after Angel was killed and realized that Jean had done it—yes, yes, this she truly could imagine, the captain silencing McRae and LaBruce to protect his emotionally crazed and suffering wife.

In which case, Quick was not guilty, not of murder at least.

"*Did* you go back?"

"You know I did," he said with a sudden air of amusement that was more jarring than his anger. "That's how I saw her do it, that lady in yellow. She had the hammer."

"Are you saying you saw her kill Angel? You told me you had no idea who did it."

"Did I? Sorry about that." He did not quite laugh.

"So now you say you saw a woman kill Angel. What about the policeman?"

"I didn't see any policeman, okay? That was Derek. We saw a police car up the street, a police *car*, not a—what the hell was that?"

She had heard it too, a distant slam like a door blowing shut. Surely, she had closed the alley door securely behind her?

"Shut the door," Quick commanded.

"Excuse me?"

"I said shut it!"

"That was just the alley door blowing—Quickie, don't! Don't touch that candle."

He hesitated, his fingers poised to snuff the flame, his black eyes on hers. There was a faint hiss and the room went dark.

Neva's reaction was immediate and instinctive. She retreated back and sideways to get clear of the doorway, smashed into the column holding the geranium pot, and fell hard.

Chapter Twenty-Six

Lying half curled on the cold planks, one arm buried in soil and dry stalks, a leg pinned against the floor, Neva did not try to move. She couldn't see much but she could hear. What was Quick doing? Who was downstairs?

A surreptitious scraping sound came from the apartment. In the empty room below several soft thumps were followed by creaking.

And then there was silence in the warehouse.

Listening, waiting for adrenalin to settle down, she tried to make sense of the situation. Quick had not dashed past her and down the stairs so he must still be in the apartment or he knew some other way out. He would have no reason to hide or flee from her, so he must be afraid of whoever had followed her into the warehouse—but who could he fear besides the police? It surely was no officer of the law creeping around down there.

As for her own situation, she had just two choices: try to follow Quick out, if he did go out, or face whoever might still be waiting below. Though she did not want to meet Quick again, he was at least a known quantity, and the look of alarm on his face before he doused the candle remained vivid. Anyone who scared him like that was no one for her to face alone in the dark.

Stealthily, she worked her arm free of the potting soil, used both hands to lift the column off her right knee, stood up, and took a tentative step. It hurt but she kept going in slow motion to the open apartment door. A single flick of the light switch was enough to show that Ernold Quick was gone. There was no Quickie and nowhere to hide. And apart from dropping twenty feet from a window into the alley, there was no visible way out—not even a chimney.

The candle remained stuck to the table in its hard wax puddle. Rather than risk the bright electric light again, she broke the candle free, lit it with matches from the kitchen counter, and circled the room. Nothing appeared out of place until she reached Lyle's raised bed. The covers were pulled halfway off and a long pole with a hook on the end rested slantwise against the built-in stepladder at the foot. The pole and hook were as good as a sign saying *Look up*, which she did.

High above the bed a long trapdoor was set flush into the ceiling, with a small brass handle at the near end.

Neat. Very neat.

More excited now than fearful, she raised the pole overhead, fitted the hook through the handle, and tugged. The trapdoor came down with perfect, well-oiled ease, unfolding to become a flight of steps. The bottom step touched down on the bed without a sound.

The candle flickered in the draft. She blew it out and stood looking up, waiting for a signal or internal impulse to tell her what to do next. The open rectangle showed black night dimly spangled with stars. That Quick might still be up there was a real possibility, though he might just as possibly have left via a fire escape or by stepping onto the building next door and going back indoors through another roof entry.

If he had got out this way then so could she. The roof also would allow her to watch any comings and goings, and once it was clear she was alone in the warehouse she could leave by the front door if the other routes looked risky . . . already she was climbing, easing her weight onto each step, quietly feeling her way up the ladder and then up the stairs. Her head drew level with the opening. The night air was brisk and Quick had been wearing only a light shirt. He must be long gone.

He was not gone.

Looking straight across the roof with her eyes just above the trapdoor frame, she could see him on the far side silhouetted against the glow of downtown. Pale smoke drifted around his head. His arm swept outward, a red spark arced through the darkness, and he turned back toward the trapdoor.

Neva ducked, froze in a half-squat, then backed down fast, first the steps and then the ladder. At the bottom, she slipped off her shoes. Gliding across the apartment and through the pale light of the greenhouse, she reached the top of the stairs and stopped to listen. Not a sound came from the rooftop or the darkness below. She had to get out of the warehouse, had to get out of here . . . the back of the stairway was open. Her legs could be seen—or grabbed—from behind.

Barely breathing, gripping the shoes to her chest, she stood in rigid indecision. She would not go back to the roof and she could not make herself go forward.

The sudden clang of metal overhead made her stiffen and step away from the stairwell. In the same instant, a light flashed on below.

"Who's there?" boomed a voice. The light beam stabbed upward through the stairwell opening.

Neva was already on her way to the closest row of plants. She squeezed in between two small trees. There was no room to move, no room to crouch. Letting herself fall, she dropped down sideways through leaves and branches and struck the gritty floor. Light flickered overhead and heavy boots thudded on the stairs.

The fall had left her scratched and breathless, but she had landed on her side facing outward with a view between pots.

A dark head appeared above the steps.

"Who's up here?"

The voice was quieter now—and familiar. It was Captain Oleander.

Relief swept through her with the force of nausea, but still she did not move or cry out. Though she no longer believed the captain had killed Angel, the Oleander family was deeply involved somehow, and his behavior did not make sense. He must know she was here. Her car was parked in front of the warehouse and he would instantly have run a license check. Knowing she must be in the warehouse, why had he waited down there in the dark without making himself known? Why did he not call for her by name?

"Where are you?" Oleander stepped away from the stairwell, let the light beam play back and forth on the row of potted trees, then trained it on the foliage above her head. "What are you doing in there?"

Without answering, she shoved at the nearest pot to make a gap. Branches snagged her hair and loose shirt as she stood up and stepped out to face him. *I didn't know it was you. . . I was just looking for your daughter and you startled me . . .* No explanation sounded right in her head so she said nothing.

Oleander, too, was silent. He stood with heavy arms, breathing audibly, the flashlight now aimed at the floor. He was wearing wool. And he was sweating. She could smell the sharp mustiness of it, ranker than wool that is wet from rain.

Watching him, she squatted to pick up the dropped shoe that had given away her hiding place. It seemed a very long time ago that she'd driven past this man's house, hoping for a miracle and finding only desertion.

"Did Pet go home?" she said at last.

"What is . . . What . . . What are you doing here?" He took a step closer.

She backed into prickly shrubbery. "I don't know what's going on with you, but Ernold Quick is on the roof. This roof."

"Ernold Quick?" Oleander looked around, puzzled, as though he'd never heard the name before..

"Ernold Quick. Quickie. The man who's wanted for killing Angel. I just saw him on the roof of the warehouse. He may be able to hear us through the air vents."

"Quick is here?"

"I just talked to him. He said he saw Jean there that night. He saw your wife with Angel."

The flashlight dropped from Oleander's hand and rolled, flinging shadows until it struck a pot and went dark. "It's nothing to do with her—nothing!"

"But she was there."

"She didn't kill him."

"I'm not saying—"

"She was going to. I thought she did. But he wouldn't wake up. He wouldn't wake up and she couldn't do it. She left the hammer. Do you understand that? She left the hammer and went home. She's innocent, completely innocent. If only—"

He broke off as a dark figure dashed past them and plunged into the stairwell. Like a cat conditioned to chase, Oleander spun in the same direction, bellowed "Stop!" and rushed for the stairs.

Neva followed and was halfway down the steps when shouts broke out and lights blazed. Below her, Reba Winner stood with her arms clamped around Ernold Quick. Carter Grey was beside her, a chunk of wood in hand.

"That'll be enough now," he said.

Lars Oleander stood frozen at the foot of the stairs.

"Captain?" Carter said.

"Sir," came the husky reply. Oleander blew out a heavy breath, pulled a set of handcuffs from his belt and stepped forward. He snapped one side onto Quickie's right wrist, snapped the other onto his own left wrist, and turned to address Neva.

"Do what you can for Jean and Lindsey. Please. I've failed them, failed them both.

Chapter Twenty-Seven

Carter Grey sat at the completed end of the patio, feet on a stool, hand around an empty cup. The morning paper lay folded in his lap. "I'm inclined to fire that damned bartender, Neva, really I am," he said with rare heat. "It's just plain idiotic."

"Oh, don't do that." Neva sat back on her heels in the sand and considered the stone she had just placed. It was good, very good, the edges not only lined up but nearly flush with the neighboring stones. "No harm done. I was late, remember. I almost asked him but the bar was full, with people waiting."

"He should have been watching for you. I left detailed instructions. They were supposed to wine and dine you, and instead, they didn't even deliver the message. The whole crew failed me."

"Failed you? They had a full house, Carter. A happy full house. Which is what you want in a restaurant. The message just got lost in the shuffle."

"Well, but really, a simple note! I can't understand it."

You could have left me a phone message about your father's fall or sent email from somewhere . . . But Carter had left town too suddenly even to place a notice in his own business window, so his taking time to leave word for her at the restaurant was something to appreciate. And its failure to reach her truly did not matter, not today. Today she had far more important matters on her mind. Today she needed to face her colossal gullibility and the misjudgments she had been committing for weeks. She had been fooled by Ernold Quick. She had trusted Reba's faith in him. She had failed to protect Lyle McRae—no matter that his own game was dirty. By taking his story to Oleander she had put a second murder in motion. She had missed Lisette's calls and had been barking up the wrong tree about her death.

What had she done right in all this? Yes, she had precipitated Quick's arrest, though purely through bumbling. She had caused Win Niagra to be honest with his son at last, but that would have happened soon anyway. She had collected information that would help convict Quick of killing Angel with Jean Oleander's hammer, but again, the police would have sorted that out eventually. So much was sad and perplexing. Even the lovely warehouse garden was tainted. Who could have believed that a creator of such wholesome beauty could also be wicked indeed? At least she had been right in doubting McRae from the beginning, though he'd at least been right about Quick being the killer.

"Neva? You still there?" Carter observed her with quizzical concern. "Maybe you should take it easy for a few days."

"I am taking it easy."

"Then why am I the only one sitting in a chair? You appear to be doing hard labor. And if you'd stop thinking about rocks for a bit you could clear up a few puzzles for me. The hammer, I understand, was Mrs. Oleander's, from the trunk of her car, though why she carried a hammer—"

"Habitat for Humanity. She was quite big in it."

"Okay, right. So Oleander found it next to Angel's body. But didn't he *ask* her if she killed Angel? Surely, any rational person would do that."

"I don't know about the rational part. Pet said her father was always bottled up, and both the Oleanders blamed Angel for what happened to their son."

"But to kill a man because you suspect your wife killed another man?"

"McRae claimed he saw her do it, he saw her there with the hammer. That was the point of the blackmail. It might be easier to understand if you had children."

"Are you saying you do understand it?"

"I can understand the agony and the need to do something. Angel was killed for far less reason, for the sake of petty revenge."

"But not by a policeman."

"True, not by a policeman. Is it okay with you if we stop talking about all this, just for today? I need to let it sort out and settle somehow, and I'm not proud of the part I played—no, please, let's leave that for the moment as well."

"Just one more little question that's bugging me?"

"Let's have it."

"Okay, why did Quick go to such lengths to convince you he didn't do it? He should have bolted for Canada."

"I don't know for sure, but I'd guess it was for the same reason a lot of people talk to me. They think if I believe something I can make other people believe it. That's what Vance's aunt said. And McRae said he wanted me to know the story so if something happened to him, at least someone would know the truth. Of course, he turned out to be mostly lying. Though he was right about the murder. And I think Quick was captivated by the whole situation in a weird way. He had some exaggerated idea of being able to manage everyone. He certainly thought he had me on a string, and he did, up to a point."

"I wonder if he'd have got away if Reba hadn't seen you go in there. I'd just got back and was checking the shop. Another thirty seconds and I'd have been gone. She said she waited and you didn't come out and she had a bad feeling about it."

"You two made an amazing rescue party."

"Except that you didn't need rescuing."

"I'm not sure about that. Do you have any idea what's taking her so long? I'm getting hungry."

"She'll get here when she gets here. She probably doesn't know what 'lunchtime' means. Why don't you go ahead and eat. Asparagus pie is best at room temperature so no need to warm it."

"I'd rather wait. How about you?"

"I'll wait too, but I'd definitely go for more coffee. If we could mass produce it like this at the restaurant we'd get a Michelin rating."

Neva smiled as she took the cup, but in the kitchen waiting for the water to boil she leaned wearily against the counter. It had seemed a fine idea when Carter called but now she wished she'd said no to the celebratory lunch. She needed time to herself. The only really good thing about the day so far had been a call from Fiori—Oleander was not a double murderer. He had not killed Lisette LaBruce. He had said this in his statement and the autopsy confirmed it. He had meant to, he certainly had meant to get rid of the only witness to Lyle's death. But he had found her already unconscious, lying near the empty vodka bottle, and he had stood over her with a pillow just as his wife had stood over Angel with the hammer. *But I couldn't do it. I tried to wake her up but she didn't respond.* Could he have saved her by calling an ambulance? The question would never be answered. And how her body came to be on the bike path would also remain a puzzle, though she'd have bet that Quick had dragged the dead woman out of the apartment so he could stay there.

One small thought made her nod with satisfaction as she poured water through the grounds. Gale Marcum's campaign for the new jail would have to stop blaming the murders on a justice system with a revolving door. Even the assistant police chief could not say this with a straight face when Lyle's killer had been one of their own.

Neva removed the filter cone, tipped a little coffee into the sink from the over-full mug, stepped out the back door, and discovered Reba

Winner and the antiquities dealer looking down into a small cardboard box cradled in Reba's arms. Her puzzlement lasted mere seconds. Only one thing would get such care from Reba.

"I've named her already." Reba reached into the box and lifted out a striped kitten. "Bridger."

"Bridger?" Carter stroked the kitten with one hand while accepting coffee with the other.

"Born under the bridge."

"Sounds like a boy's name."

"Cats don't care."

It was impossible for Neva not to take the ball of fluff into her hands or to enjoy the featherweight vitality and shiny black eyes. Even so . . . she had vowed after the death of Ethan's last pet—a nameless purple fish which seemed destined to live forever—that it was to mark the end of an era. No more animal house guests. How could she say this to Reba Winner?

"What's the matter?" Reba said. "Don't you like her?"

"She's darling, and if I wanted a cat this would be the one. But I've sworn off pets, cats in particular. For one thing, they kill birds. I have three feeders."

"So train her. Put a bell on her."

The distant ring of the telephone allowed Neva to hand the kitten to Carter without replying. She returned some minutes later to find Carter sitting with Bridger on his lap, nodding as Reba explained the proper age for spaying and the best vet for the job. They didn't notice Neva until she dropped a rock into place with a thud, at which they merely glanced over before resuming the tutorial for what clearly had become his cat. Their absorption was just as well. Yet again she needed to examine her actions. If only she'd had time to prepare for the call, to have an answer ready for Frankie's elated crowing at the other end of the line. *Neva, you aren't going to believe this—Vance is Win Niagra's son! They're letting him out on bail this afternoon and he agreed to an interview. I mean, it's like a soap opera around here. Sorry you're missing it.*

Should she have confessed that the news was not news to her? It would have been so deflating to the young reporter . . . and yet, if he found out later when talking with Win and the boy, it might well be worse. Either she had to call Frankie back and tell the truth or let Win know the situation and ask for his cooperation, which would just compound the deception. Oh, lord, nothing is simple.

Except for rocks. Lovely yellow-streaked rocks that are warm to the touch and glint with mica on a sunny spring afternoon. Gripping the rough edges of a slab of Lone Pine Gold quartzite, she muscled it up on edge, steadied it with one hand while she used the other to scoop a hollow in the sand, and lowered the slab into place. She stepped onto the rock and jumped up and down to tamp it into the sand. Shifting her weight from foot to foot, she could detect no rocking movement.

A solid piece of work, no question about it.

AFTERWORD

Coroner confident
LaBruce died of drink

By Charles Frank of the *Willamette Current*

The April 22 death of Lisette LaBruce resulted from alcohol consumption complicated by hepatitis, according to the coroner's report released Friday.

The immediate cause of death was "esophageal varises," which are "caused when scar tissue in the liver interferes with normal blood flow, stressing the veins in other organs and causing internal bleeding." Records show that doctors told LaBruce a year ago that her condition was severe and she should stop drinking.

The dead woman lived mainly on the streets, but during the final days of her life she apparently stayed in the warehouse apartment that belonged to Lyle McRae, the gardener who had been murdered a week earlier. The two were known to have been friends. Lars Oleander, a long-time Willamette police officer, has been charged with McRae's murder.

LaBruce's body, smelling strongly of alcohol, was discovered next to the riverfront path two hundred yards from the warehouse. An empty vodka bottle was found in the apartment, and DNA analysis confirmed that LaBruce had handled the bottle and a nearby glass.

"There is no way to know whether she drank the vodka all at once," Police Chief Katharine "Kitty" Fiori said following the release of the report. "But Lisette LaBruce was a long-time abuser of alcohol and this, plus recurrent bouts of hepatitis B, caused severe and irreversible liver damage."

LaBruce's friends insist she was not a heavy drinker, but according to information from the Centers for Disease Control and Prevention, a liver already damaged by hepatitis could easily be over-stressed by even small amounts of alcohol.

LaBruce's remains were cremated on Tuesday and buried at St. Mary's Cemetery in the area reserved for indigents. The three community members who attended the burial asked not to be named, though one agreed to be quoted: "Lisette never hurt anybody but herself, and she was real gentle with cats."

ABOUT THE AUTHOR

Ashna Graves is the author of three mysteries featuring journalist Jeneva Leopold: *Death Pans Out* (Poisoned Pen Press, 2007); *No Angel* (Lychgate Press, 2012); *Gripper* (Lychgate Press, 2013). Graves has lived in Oregon for more than 30 years.

Made in the USA
Coppell, TX
20 January 2025